CRITICAL 1

DEATH IN THE ASHES

"Engaging characters... Bell continues to make ancient Rome live and breathe."
— *Publishers Weekly*

"Best of all, in Gaius Plinius, a warm, engaging character is created, someone one would like to know and hang out with in real life."
— *The Detective and the Toga*

"This is a fine, well crafted, and entertaining read. What excels is the way in which Bell handles the task of educating us about first century Rome. Such a process could easily bog down in endless sidebar commentary about small details of Roman life, or just as easily leave the reader clueless as to specific phrases or terms that hold the story together. Happily, neither has occurred. Bell navigates skillfully between the Scylla and Charybdis of these extremes, and brings readers safely through the straits. Fans of historical fiction, particularly of the Roman era, will thoroughly enjoy this novel."
— *Over My Dead Body*

"Pliny is an engaging, if conflicted protagonist.... The good-versus-evil, love-versus-duty plot points make *Death in the Ashes* an unusually engaging mystery."
— *Mystery Scene*

"The smart, witty Pliny is a likable detective, the bantering friendship between Pliny and Tacitus adds humor to the suspenseful tale, and there are ample details of Roman life in A.D. 84. Bell admirably juggles his multiple storylines and characters. A helpful glossary and list of characters is included. Although part of a series, I found it enjoyable as a stand-alone mystery, and I'd recommend it to anyone who enjoys the novels of Steven Saylor, Lindsey Davis, and Ruth Downie."
— *Historical Novels Review*

THE EYES
OF
AURORA

MYSTERY FICTION
BY ALBERT A. BELL, JR.

CASES FROM THE NOTEBOOKS OF PLINY THE YOUNGER

All Roads Lead to Murder

The Blood of Caesar

The Corpus Conundrum

Death in the Ashes

The Eyes of Aurora

CONTEMPORARY MYSTERIES

Death Goes Dutch

FOR YOUNGER READERS

The Secret of the Bradford House

The Secret of the Lonely Grave

THE EYES
OF
AURORA

A FIFTH CASE FROM THE
NOTEBOOKS OF
PLINY THE YOUNGER

ALBERT A. BELL, JR.

MMXIV
PERSEVERANCE PRESS · JOHN DANIEL & COMPANY
PALO ALTO / MCKINLEYVILLE, CALIFORNIA

A Perseverance Press Book
Published by John Daniel & Company
A division of Daniel & Daniel, Publishers, Inc.
Post Office Box 2790
McKinleyville, California 95519
www.danielpublishing.com/perseverance

Distributed by SCB Distributors (800) 729-6423

Book design by Eric Larson, Studio E Books, Santa Barbara, www.studio-e-books.com

Cover painting: "Aurora" © by Chi Meredith
Egg tempera on panel

10 9 8 7 6 5 4 3 2 1

LIBRARY OF CONGRESS CATALOGING-IN-PUBLICATION DATA
Bell, Albert A.,(date)
The eyes of Aurora : a fifth case from the notebooks of Pliny, the younger / by Albert A. Bell, Jr.
pages cm.
ISBN 978-1-56474-549-1 (pbk. : alk. paper)
1. Pliny, the Younger—Fiction. 2. Tacitus, Cornelius—Fiction.
3 . Women household employees—Fiction. 4. Rome—Fiction. I. Title.
PS3552.E485E94 2014
813'.54—dc23
2014008705

For Jacob E. Nyenhuis

"Jack"

Longtime friend and mentor, and the only person

who ever offered me a job in academia

AUTHOR'S NOTE

It goes without saying that I am extremely grateful to Perseverance Press and my editor, Meredith Phillips, for the confidence they've placed in me. I also need to thank, as I have in all my books, my writers' group, the West Michigan Writers' Workshop, for their feedback, encouragement, and morale boosts during the writing of this book and over the decade and more that I've been part of the group. And I need to thank my wife, not just as a formality but because of how much she means to me.

.　　　.　　　.

An aspect of this book that may make some readers uneasy is one character's attraction to young girls. I intend nothing salacious and I don't dwell on it; it is simply a plot point. We need to recognize that, in the ancient world, girls became women when they reached puberty. It was quite common for a girl of thirteen or fourteen to be married. There was no such thing as adolescence as we know it for girls. Pliny writes about a friend's daughter who died shortly before her wedding, when she "was not yet fourteen" (*Ep.* 5.16). His own beloved Calpurnia was about that age when Pliny, about forty years old, married her. Numerous inscriptions mention girls in their late teens who have died, most likely in childbirth.

This book introduces one new feature, which I feel I need to comment on. The character Aurora first appeared briefly in *The Blood of Caesar*, the second book in this series. She played a larger role in *The Corpus Conundrum* and figured significantly in *Death in the Ashes*. I decided that it was finally time to let her speak in her own voice, not just have Pliny reporting what she said. After all, the book is titled *The Eyes of Aurora*, and not just because I needed an *E* word to maintain the alphabetic sequence of titles in the series. Throughout this book, then, the reader will hear what Aurora is thinking, in separate sections set off in italics.

Readers, and my students, sometimes tell me that the Roman names are hard to keep track of. If I could name them all John and Bob, I would. The Cast List at the end of the book should help, and the Glossary will explain unfamiliar terms.

THE EYES
OF
AURORA

I

VOCONIUS ROMANUS, a longime friend, raised his cup in a toast to the bust of my uncle. We were standing next to the pedestal on which the bust sits in my favorite corner of the garden in my house on the Esquiline Hill on the east side of Rome. "The old man would have been proud of you, Gaius Pliny."

I allowed myself a modest smile. "I would like to think so. For winning the case, but even more, for beating Regulus."

"You didn't just beat him, my friend." Voconius, a thin, wiry man, clapped me on the shoulder. "You utterly humiliated him. If it had been a gladiatorial combat, they would have jabbed hooks into his heels and dragged his bloated corpse out of the arena."

Though I detest the games, I liked that image. "I have to admit I was surprised by the margin of victory, even though I was confident that my speech was good."

"Good? No. It was superb. How could you have doubted yourself?"

"You don't have to flatter me to get your dinner." Although I didn't mind hearing a bit of praise. Who does? "When I was working on it these last two days I felt something I might even call inspiration."

Voconius gave his throaty laugh. "Watch out. If you don't believe in gods, you can't believe in Muses who are the daughters of a god."

"You're right. That's a logical impossibility."

"And I've never known you to be guilty of such a thing. Will you send me a copy of the speech?" Originally from Spain, Voconius had settled near my home town of Comum. We exchange our writings for criticism and revision.

"I certainly will. My scribe will make a fresh copy."

"I noticed him scribbling furiously."

"Yes, with the Tironian notation he can capture any changes I make while speaking."

"Tironian notation can be deadly."

I looked at him in bewilderment.

"Remember that Augustus had a fellow stabbed to death on the spot for transcribing one of his speeches."

And Augustus was one of the good emperors. "I didn't say anything politically provocative. There were a few spontaneous moments. Although I won't call them inspired, I do like to have them preserved."

Voconius threw his head back and laughed. "I just wish there was some way we could preserve the image of the veins swelling in Regulus' temples and neck, his face getting redder and redder. And he just kept getting louder."

"As Cicero says, 'Orators are most vehement when their cause is weak.'"

I closed my eyes and called up the vision of the end of the trial this morning in the Centumviral Court, a scene I hope I will still be able to see if I live to be an old man. Marcus Aquilius Regulus was acting on behalf of Quintus Vibius, whom I was prosecuting for embezzling 200,000 *sesterces* from the widow Pompeia Celerina, cousin of my uncle and mother and the mother of my bride-to-be.

Other trials had ground to a halt as participants and spectators turned their attention to Regulus and me. The prosecution is often at a disadvantage because the defense speaks last, but when the *iudex* called for the vote, thirty-five of the jurors stepped to my side and only ten to Regulus'. The crowd erupted in applause.

"So now your future mother-in-law adores you," Voconius said.

Back to harsh reality. I stepped away from my uncle's bust and sat on the bench beside it, under a trellis that supported an ornamental vine. Voconius joined me.

"Yes," I said dispiritedly. "She sent a message an hour ago that the money Vibius embezzled has been returned to her house, along with the fine imposed by the court."

"So quickly? Didn't the fellow spend it?"

"Oh, I'm sure Regulus paid it and I pity Vibius. Regulus will extract a painful repayment, with heavy interest, probably in the form of bits of his flesh."

"I suspect he's not done with you either."

I nodded slowly. "How he'll get his revenge on me, I can only guess. You know he's been waging a war against my family for over twenty years. It drags on like Rome and Carthage. Losing one battle will just make him more determined to win the next one."

"Well, enjoy this victory as long as you can." Voconius drained his cup. "Nothing lasts forever. This wine, for instance, isn't staying with me for long, so I'm going to stop in the *latrina* before we have dinner."

When Voconius left I had the moment of repose for which I had come into the garden. The last two days had passed in a blur that was only now beginning to clear, like a fog lifting off a bay.

Yesterday morning Julius Agricola, the father-in-law of my dear friend Cornelius Tacitus, had appeared at my door with a hundred of his veterans. Agricola and his men live on estates and farms of various sizes to the north and east of Rome. Tacitus' wife, without his knowledge, had sent a message asking her father to come and support me in court. His men camped out in my atrium and garden and whatever empty rooms we could find in the house. This morning I was accompanied to the Forum by my own clients and Agricola's century. Even without their weapons, it was an impressive procession. No one even tried to stay on the sidewalks in front of us. Regulus went pale when we walked up to the steps of the Basilica Julia, where the trial was held.

The whole crowd in the Forum buzzed when they realized Agricola was there. I could hear his name flitting from one person to the next, like a rumor buzzing through the marketplace. No one had seen him in several months. His popularity has only risen since Domitian recalled him from Britain and sent him into a sort of genteel exile. Everyone knows Agricola could be *princeps* if he chose to. Agricola knows it, and so does Domitian. What makes me nervous is that Domitian also knows that Agricola's son-in-law is my closest friend.

I took a sip of wine and shivered slightly. The weather's changing, that's all, I assured myself. It is the middle of October, and the linen dinner robe I'm wearing is lighter than a tunic or a toga. It's made for indoor wear, not for musing in a garden on a fall evening.

I believe my speech was good enough in its own right to win, but it certainly helped that Regulus' supporters were far outnumbered and shouted down every time they tried to express their approval of their patron. Agricola's men had even brought small pieces of wood which they clapped together. Most importantly, he did a good job of keeping his men under control, ignoring provocations from Regulus' clients. An outbreak of violence would have been a disaster for him as well as for me. Agricola and his men departed immediately after the case was settled. I hadn't asked him to do that, but he knew his continued presence in the city would provoke some reaction from Domitian.

"I thought I would find you here." Tacitus, whose friendship I've come to cherish over the last two years, emerged from the shadows and sat down on the bench beside me. He is almost a head taller than I am. Most men of that size intimidate me, but an air of friendliness and good humor emanates from Tacitus as soon as you meet him. And yet I've learned that his perception of people is keen and deep.

I slid over to make room for him. "Since I was a child this has been the place I've retreated to when I needed to be quiet for a while, to renew my strength." I put my head back against the wall and looked up. The reddening sky was clear. It would be a chilly evening. "This day has been exhausting."

"It won't get any more peaceful, I'm afraid. The rest of your guests have arrived."

I let out a long sigh as my shoulders sagged.

"Be prepared," Tacitus said. "Pompeia is kissing and embracing everyone. She may be all over you like a cheap whore this evening. All she can talk about is how brilliant her son-in-law is."

"Future son-in-law," I snapped. "How many times do I have to remind people? *Future* son-in-law."

Tacitus shook his head like a man delivering bad news. "That's not how your mother and Pompeia see it. Livilla, your blushing bride-to-be, is going to be reclining on the couch next to you tonight, with her mother on the other side of her." He used the diminutive form of Livia's name, as is common for the younger sister in a family.

"Livilla? Next to me? That's not…not proper. She and her mother belong on the middle couch."

"Your mother says Livilla is family now—even closer than just a cousin—not a guest, so she should recline next to you."

"Damn that woman!"

"She could have done worse by you, you know. She could have gotten you engaged to the older daughter. At least you get the pretty one."

"I don't think I've ever seen the older girl."

"You would remember her, if you had. She's a year older than you and, the last time I saw her, well on her way to becoming the image of her stumpy, heavyset mother. And a nagging shrew into the bargain."

"Where does she live?"

"She's been in Spain for the last two years. Her husband, Liburnius, is serving on the staff of the current governor. He and I were quaestors together a few years ago, right after the eruption of Vesuvius. I was at his wedding."

"Well, I guess 'my' Livilla is going to be reclining beside me for some time to come, so let's go face the inevitable."

Tacitus wagged a finger at me. "You know, if we had kept up the traditions of the old Republic, the women would be sitting in chairs behind our couches. That would solve this problem—and many others."

"For once I'm inclined to approve of your devotion to the ideals of the Republic." I raised my cup to my uncle's bust again. "We who are about to die salute you."

.   .   .

Tacitus and I were crossing the darkening garden toward the front part of the house when I heard a woman crying behind the shrubbery. It had to be a servant, since my mother is the only woman in the house who's not a servant, either slave or freedwoman, and she would not vent her tears behind a bush. Normally I don't concern myself when my female servants become upset—a problem better left to my mother or my steward to deal with—but I was eager for any excuse to stay out of the *triclinium* for even a few more moments. I put my cup on a bench.

"Who is that?" I asked, taking a step toward a form huddled between the shrubbery and the garden wall. "Show yourself."

Like Venus rising out of the ocean foam, Aurora emerged from the bushes, her eyes red from weeping. Her mother, Monica, had been my uncle's slave and mistress. Aurora and I have known one another since she arrived in this house when we were both seven. She has always enjoyed a privileged status in my *familia* and has gone from being my playmate to being my personal attendant—and has become the woman I love but cannot have. My mother deeply resented her brother's relationship with Aurora's mother and, since Monica's death, has turned that animosity toward her daughter.

I put a hand on Aurora's shoulder. "What's the matter? Why aren't you in the *triclinium*?" Aurora always waits on me at dinners of this sort, sitting on a stool behind my couch. The touch of her hand on my foot—just my awareness that she's nearby—can help me endure the most tense or most tedious evenings. From the way she was dressed, in a green gown with yellow trim and a necklace that had belonged to her mother, I knew she was planning on waiting on me.

"Your mother sent me away. She said Pylades would wait on you."

"Damn that woman again! How far does she think she can go in arranging my life?" I took Aurora's hand and started toward the *triclinium*.

"Gaius, wait." She pulled back. We have an understanding that she may address me by my *praenomen* when no one else is around, as she did when we were children. This was the first time she'd done so in Tacitus' presence. I heard his quick intake of breath, but he didn't say anything.

"What is it?" I asked impatiently.

"Maybe it would be better if I were not there tonight. Your mother is so upset she even called me Monica. With Livilla next to you and your mother so...determined to be rid of me, it will make everyone uncomfortable."

"I don't care about everyone. The fact that Livilla's going to be next to me is all the more reason I need you there. *I'll* be uncomfortable."

"Yes, my lord. As you wish." Aurora lowered her eyes, her soft brown eyes. She and her mother came from the area around Carthage, so there is something Punic in her—the thick brown hair and long slender face, but especially the eyes. Sometimes I wonder if those eyes were what Aeneas saw when he gazed on Dido's face. It took a direct command from Jupiter to drag him away from them. What would it take—

"Gaius Pliny, your guests are waiting," Tacitus reminded me.

.   .   .

Tacitus and I entered the *triclinium* side by side, with Aurora following us, her hands demurely folded in front of her and her head down. All conversation stopped, as abruptly as though someone had slammed a door. The room, the smaller of two indoor dining rooms in my house, has a mosaic floor with sea creatures worked in it and frescoes of several mythological banqueting scenes, standard fare for a *triclinium*, but nicely done by my uncle. I've seen no reason to redo it, as I did the atrium. Tonight it was set up with only three couches, with a table for each couch and a central table where the servants would present the dishes and cut up those that needed it.

I already knew who was going to be on the high couch with me. From the way everyone was standing, I deduced that my mother was to have the middle couch between Voconius Romanus and another friend of our family, Calestrius Tiro. Tacitus and his wife Julia were relegated to the lower couch.

Voconius and Tiro happened to be in Rome on business and I had invited them to dinner before I even knew this would be a celebration. They had also been in court this morning. Despite my mother's objections, I had insisted that Tacitus and Julia be invited because of Agricola's role in our victory. My mother's recent antipathy toward Tacitus, demonstrated to all by his placement in the least prestigious place at the table, was one more stone in a wall that she seems to be raising between herself and me.

"Ladies and gentlemen, friends," I said, spreading my hands in a gesture of greeting, "it is my pleasure to welcome you to my house and my table. Please, take your places and let's begin."

I walked around to the position reserved for the host and was met by Pompeia, who grabbed my shoulders and kissed me on both cheeks. "Thank you so much, Gaius Pliny. You were brilliant."

"I'm glad things turned out so well," I said, prying her off me and guiding her to her place on the couch.

Once she was settled, I snapped my fingers at Pylades and sent him out, daring him with the set of my jaw to look at my mother for a counter-order. Then I reclined in my own place as the host, and Aurora took her accustomed place, removing my sandals, wiping my feet with a wet cloth, and letting her hand rest on my foot a moment longer than necessary before she withdrew it. I didn't need to look at my mother to feel the waves of anger rolling off her.

"Good evening, Livilla," I said. Her black hair was piled on top of her head and toward the front in what I assumed was the latest fashion. A strand of pearls ran through it. Her gown was lilac with a silver border. Her perfume, I had to admit, was enticing.

"It's nice to see you, Gaius," she responded, glancing unhappily over her shoulder at Aurora, who kept her eyes down. She was reclining on both elbows, so she could talk with me more easily.

Livilla will make a charming wife for some man. She is small, delicate, with a high forehead, blue eyes, and smooth, alabaster-like skin that needs little cosmetic enhancement, and she is wise enough to know that. She must resemble her deceased father, whom I never knew. Her mother is a stout woman with eyebrows that would grow together over her nose like a hedge if she didn't pluck them assiduously. She seems to apply her cosmetics with a mason's trowel. If her older daughter does truly resemble her, I had to wonder how she had found a husband.

My mother had assigned servants to wait on Voconius and Tiro. Tacitus and Julia had brought a handful of their own, as had Pompeia and Livilla. Mother's closest companion, the slave Naomi, sat behind her, with another, younger girl to assist her.

A hired *auloi* player seated in one corner of the room took up her instrument, accompanied by a woman softly plucking a lyre. I have musicians in my household, but Mother said she especially wanted these two, who were gaining renown all over Rome.

The music was the signal for the servants to bring in the *gustatio*—lentils from Egypt, kale cooked in vinegar and salt, pickled broccoli and carrots, and snails, stewed and salted. The snails were served with our silver *cochlearia*. Guests could use the spoon end to scoop up the snails or the thin sharp handle to spear them.

I've often thought the handle of a *cochlearia* would make a fine murder weapon. Being so sharp and as long as a man's hand, it would penetrate deeply—straight into the heart, for instance—with very little effort. Even if the person was as thick and heavy as Pompeia.

Before my musing could turn any darker, a final dish was placed on the tables—dormice, fattened in clay pots and roasted. Mother had outdone herself.

"There was a conversation going on when I came in," I said, in an effort to break the tension that made the room feel as tightly wound as one of the lyre player's strings. "What was the topic?"

"We were talking about the October Horse," Voconius said. "I've never been in Rome at this time of year before, so it was my first chance to see it."

"Wasn't it every bit as barbaric as I told you it would be?" Tiro asked. Like most of my compatriots from the north of Italy, he has dark hair and frank, open features. One of the most jovial men I know, he's a few years older than Voconius and I, already thickening a bit in his waist and chest.

"Oh, it was all that and more," Voconius said, popping a piece of broccoli in his mouth. "We see animals sacrificed all the time, but I've never seen one fight like that horse did."

"Sheep and oxen are docile by comparison," Tacitus said. "Oxen have their horns to fight with, but nothing is quite as deadly as a horse's hooves. Oxen can't rear like a horse. A blow to the head drops them."

"I suppose any male animal would resist," Voconius said, hiding a smile behind his cup, "if he had any suspicion about what was going to be cut off."

Amid the laughter that went around the table, Livilla said, "They cut off the head and the tail, don't they?"

We men all looked at one another, waiting for someone to explain a delicate subject to the child. Tacitus, being the only married man in the group, finally said, "The word 'tail' is a euphemism, my dear Livilla, for the part that's cut off. Cicero says, 'Our ancestors called the penis a tail.'"

Livilla blinked as though thinking for a moment. "But if…that's what they cut off, why…why do they say they cut off the tail?"

Voconius chuckled. "It might be because of the way men react anytime there's a reference to cutting off…that particular part." He squeezed his thighs together and bent over. The older women lowered their eyes and tried to hide their smiles.

Because the topic of conversation was becoming repellent to me, I cast my gaze around the room, stopping at the door as my steward, Demetrius, entered the *triclinium*. A stalwart fellow anyway, at that moment he looked like a man with a purpose. He came to stand behind me, leaning down.

"Excuse me, my lord," he said softly, as I looked over my shoulder at him, "but there's someone to see you. He says it's urgent."

II

NORMALLY I WOULD have been annoyed with Demetrius for intruding into dinner, but I welcomed any break in this strain of conversation. My mother, though, had heard him and did not share my enthusiasm.

"Business? At this hour?" she snapped. "Can't it wait until morning?"

Demetrius leaned closer to me and this time whispered, "It's Nestor, my lord. He's in the Ovid room."

"Tell him I'll be right there." I raised myself up and sat on the edge of the couch. "Ladies and gentlemen, will you please excuse me?"

Livilla had heard the name. "Nestor? Isn't he—"

"This doesn't concern you…dear. I'll be back shortly."

From across the room Tacitus looked up with a question on his face.

"Would you come with me?" I said. Aurora slipped my sandals on and the servant behind Tacitus assisted him.

Nestor is Regulus' steward. His real name is Jacob. He was among the prisoners taken after the fall of Jerusalem and fell to my uncle's lot, along with Naomi and her son Phineas, now my scribe. My uncle sold a number of those slaves, including Jacob, to a dealer who, unbeknownst to him, was working for Regulus. He would never have sold any slave to Regulus, he told me with deep regret.

Because Jacob is such a good steward, Regulus has refused to sell or emancipate him, even though he is getting on in years. Behind Regulus' back, I have had some dealings with Jacob over the past few years. I have never asked him to spy for me, and he would refuse if I did ask him, but we talk whenever we have a chance. Since Regulus and I live within sight of one another on the Esquiline Hill, it's easy for Jacob to stop by when he's out on an errand.

One thing I don't understand is Naomi's disdain for Jacob. I would think that, being of the same race and religion, taken captive at the same time and place, they would feel some camaraderie. They did not know one another in Jerusalem and Naomi, when she will speak of him at all, calls Jacob a traitor. I once asked her if he attended her synagogue or if there was another one in Rome. She said he does not attend any synagogue, but she would not elaborate. I concluded that Jacob's experience in the war taught him that his god was of little use and Naomi feels he has betrayed their religion, to which she adheres fervently. As one who does not believe in any god, I can respect Jacob for knowing when he has outgrown childhood myths.

I wish my mother weren't so attracted to Judaism, due to Naomi's influence. Phineas says my mother even offers prayers for me when she goes with them to their synagogue. I can't try to break the friendship because it obviously means so much to my mother. Both she and Naomi lost children at birth years ago and have never quite recovered. Both have lost husbands and, a few years ago, both lost a brother. They support one another in their grief. No bond is stronger among women than shared sorrow over the men and children they've nurtured and lost.

We found Jacob in the room decorated with frescos based on Ovid's *Metamorphoses*—Pygmalion fashioning the statue that became his beloved; Pyramus and Thisbe, the lovers who could be together only in death; and Baucis and Philemon, who asked the gods that they might die at the same time so neither would have to live without the other. I had chosen those stories because they appeal to me for several reasons, one being that they are told only by Ovid, another being my attraction to any story about a man who gets to be with the woman he loves, no matter what it costs him.

I felt a bit silly receiving a guest in my dinner garb, but he was another man's slave, not one of my peers, and the late hour excused the need for formality. Demetrius had lit some lamps and Jacob stood as Tacitus and I entered the room and closed the door. Like all of Regulus' slaves he was dressed better than most free men in Rome, in a light brown tunic with a dark green edging around the sleeves, neck, and hem. On a strap around his neck he carried a pouch, the sort of thing in which one sends messages. The flap was closed with a seal, no doubt Regulus'.

"My lord, thank you for seeing me," he said. "I'm sorry to disturb you at this hour."

"It was a relief to get away from that table. Is something wrong?"

Tacitus took a seat and I gestured for Jacob to take the remaining chair, partly in deference to his gray hair and partly out of respect for a man whose nobility of character raises him above any man he might have to call his "master."

Jacob's wrinkled face betrayed his agitation. "I thought I should warn you, my lord. Regulus is in an absolute rage because you won that case so handily today. He's blaming everyone but himself. He's threatening to withhold the donative from *all* his clients for the rest of the month because the ones who were in court didn't make enough noise to sway the jury."

"Well, they were up against some strong opposition," Tacitus said.

Smiling, Jacob turned to Tacitus. "They certainly were. Thank you, my lord, and please convey my thanks—and the thanks of many in our household—to Julius Agricola."

His face became somber as he directed his attention back to me. "But I'm afraid that Regulus is devising some plan to get revenge on you, my lord. In all the years I've known him, I have never seen him so consumed by anger. He's sending word through his whole network of spies. You will be watched wherever you go and attacked whenever they perceive an opening. In addition, he has sent me out tonight with a message for Domitian." He patted the leather pouch.

My breathing quickened. "Do you have any idea what's in it?"

"No, my lord. He sealed both the message and the pouch."

"Why is he sending you to deliver it?" Tacitus asked. "Meaning no offense, but he must have younger and faster slaves."

"He certainly does, my lord, and I take no offense. But I am the only servant in his house whom he does not suspect of being a spy for someone else."

"The only one he can trust not to break the seals," I said.

Jacob put a hand on the pouch. "But I am willing to do so, my lord, if it means saving your life."

I shook my head. "No. It would cost you yours, and I can't have that on my conscience."

Jacob sat back in his chair. "I would expect no other answer from you, my lord." Relief washed over his face. Until that moment I guess he wasn't entirely sure whether I valued my life more than his.

"Perhaps it's just as well I'm planning to be out of town for a few days."

"Will you be far away, my lord?"

"No, just down the Ostian Way. While Tacitus and I were on the Bay of Naples, Aurora befriended a woman who was trying to find her lost husband. She put the woman and her son up at an inn and has asked us to go down there and see what we can do for her. It shouldn't take more than a couple of days."

"A true good Samaritan," Jacob said with the smile of a man who has a deeper understanding than you do of something you've just said.

"A what?" I knew Samaritans lived north of Judaea, but they had no particular reputation for goodness, as far as I knew.

"Nothing, my lord. I was just reminded of a story I once heard, about a man who befriends someone who is bereft, puts him up at an inn, and pays for his expenses. It's of no consequence. I'm glad you'll be away, but I doubt that mere distance will prevent Regulus from striking. And he will hit at your family and your friends—anyone connected with you. Even without knowing what's in this message, I fear for your safety just walking on the streets of Rome. For the safety of anyone in your *familia*, for that matter. I could not rest tonight until I warned you."

"I appreciate the risk you've taken," I said.

"I'm happy to do what little I can, my lord, for someone who has been so kind to those I love." He stood with some difficulty and touched the pouch. "Now I must finish my errand and get back before I'm missed."

"Let me see you out," I said. "Cornelius Tacitus, please tell the others that I'll be back in the *triclinium* in just a moment."

When we reached the door and I was sure no one was in earshot, I leaned in close to Jacob. "What do you hear from Nomentum?" I had given a piece of property in that area, northeast of Rome, to Valerius Martial and a woman named Lorcis, a former slave of Regulus' who had helped me save my mother during the eruption of Vesuvius. I'd given the farm to Lorcis, really, but I needed a man's name to put on the deed. Martial just happened to be the father of her child and her husband, more or less.

"I was out there at the beginning of the month, my lord. Everyone is doing well."

"Erotion is about three now, isn't she?"

"Yes, my lord. And the prettiest, most charming child one can imagine. A little love, indeed."

I laid my hand on his shoulder. "Let me know if there's anything else I can do for them."

Closing the door behind Jacob, I turned to look for Demetrius. I found him in the atrium, keeping a respectful distance but obviously curious about my whispered conversation with another man's slave, at this late hour, and my gesture of friendship. I motioned for him to join me in a quiet corner.

"Is something wrong, my lord?"

"I'm not sure. Do you have any idea why my mother is acting the way she is right now? You see her and deal with her as much as I do, perhaps more. Why is she so set on me getting married?"

I can't remember a time when I did not know Demetrius. We are usually as comfortable in one another's presence as an older and a younger brother, but tonight he seemed not to know what to do with his hands.

"She does seem anxious lately, my lord. And I've noticed that she sometimes forgets things. Naomi might be able to help you understand what's happening. If I may say so, I think she has chosen an ideal wife for you. Livilla is a lovely girl, quite demure. And her family is a good match for ours."

"But I don't understand why it has suddenly become so important to her that I get married. My uncle never married. You didn't marry until you were thirty." Demetrius had married another of my uncle's slaves, an Egyptian, and they have two darling little girls who call me "Uncle Gaius."

Demetrius took a deep breath. "My lord, if I may be so bold, I think you do understand. You just don't want to admit the reason to yourself, like a man who's blinded by the sun rising at dawn but says he can't see it. At dawn, my lord."

In all the years that Demetrius has served me and my family I had never felt so strong an urge to strike him. I clutched my robe to keep my hands at my sides. "You are going beyond bold. You are downright impudent."

He lowered his head. "Forgive me, my lord. You know how much I love you and your family and how grateful I am to be able to raise my own family here. But there comes a time when some things must be said. Is that all?"

"No." I took a deep breath to throttle my anger. "There is one more matter I need to discuss with you."

I'm sorry Gaius didn't ask me to come with him and Tacitus. I feel like everybody in this room is staring at me. His mother could more accurately be said to be glaring *at me. I know she despised my mother, but why do I have to inherit that hatred?*

When I was younger I wrote about some adventures that Gaius and I had, watching what people were doing in the streets of Rome and around his uncle's estates. Several times we helped his uncle investigate people's misdoings because no one ever suspects a child of being a spy. No one will ever read those accounts, of course, and I've stopped doing such a childish thing. Those scrolls are locked away in a box my mother left me.

I wish I could write about how I feel about Gaius now. I can't tell anyone, but the simple act of putting the words on a piece of papyrus would be almost as good as sharing them with another person. I have to keep my feelings a secret, and there are no secrets in a house like this. You'd think in a house so large and with so many nooks and crannies that you could hide something, but it's not possible. Someone would find anything I wrote, and then his mother would probably insist that he sell me to a brothel. That's where she thought my mother belonged. She never did understand how much my mother and the old man—as Gaius and I called him—loved one another. I never quite understood it, either. Gaius' uncle was fat and snored awfully. But, like Gaius, he was a gentle man who always treated my mother with respect and love.

My feelings for Gaius have always been there, but they have been brought into sharp focus in recent days by the announcement of his engagement to Livilla. There she lies on the couch right now, her hand on the spot still warm from Gaius' body. I can't hate her. I have no right to hate her. I'm only a servant.

I could get up and leave—excuse myself and go to the latrina *perhaps—but I won't give his mother the satisfaction and I want to be here when Gaius returns.*

"Well, at last," my mother said when I returned to the *triclinium.* "What sort of 'business' kept you so long at this hour?"

I reclined on the couch next to Livilla. Spearing a snail with the handle of her *cochlearia,* she offered it to me with a smile and I let her slip it into my mouth. Swallowing it and wiping my lips, I said, "I was making some plans."

"Plans for the wedding, I hope," Mother said with a smile. "I was just asking Lavinia whom we should invite."

From the end of the couch Pompeia said, "Plinia, dear, my daughter's name is Livilla, not Lavinia."

Mother looked confused, even a bit frightened. "What did I say?"

"You called her Lavinia."

"I did?"

"Yes, you did." Pompeia's voice rose in irritation. "And that's the second time this evening you've done it. What's the matter, dear?"

"I'm sorry. I know her name. Of course I do.... I don't know—"

"The wine may be too strong," I said. "With older women in attendance, I should have been more careful about that. I hope no one else is bothered."

The arrival of the main course relieved me from saying anything else. Roasted capons, newborn rabbits, and bread were brought to the table and cut up by a servant. Dishes of *garum* sauce were placed where they could be reached from each couch. I saw sadness in my mother's eyes as she picked at her food, a look of fear and confusion I had never seen before.

.   .   .

I was never more relieved to see a dinner come to an end. Even with two longtime friends and my newest friend for company, with an ex-

cellent selection of dishes, and with delightful, soothing music, the
evening was an ordeal. When I had bid good night to Tacitus and Julia
and cautioned Tacitus to be especially watchful on his way home, I
returned to the *triclinium*, where Mother and Naomi were supervising
the cleaning up. Aurora hung behind me in the doorway.

I waved the other servants out. "Mother, I need to talk with you.
In private."

Naomi made no movement to leave. Mother nodded toward Aurora. "Does 'in private' mean that she's going to be here?"

"If Naomi stays, then Aurora stays."

Mother set her jaw. "That's the way it will be then."

When the others were gone, I said, "I'm going to be away for a few
days, along with Aurora and Tacitus."

Mother crossed her arms. "Humph! Of course with those two.
Where are you going this time?"

"We have some unfinished business on the road to Ostia. It's no
concern of yours. By the time I return I expect you to be in Misenum,
at least until the new year. Demetrius has been instructed to oversee
your packing."

The dismay on her face pained me. If it had not been for the spec-
ter of Regulus, I would have sent her to Laurentum, a place closer to
Rome and one I know she loves. Now, if I owned any more distant
property, I would be sending her there. There had to be some outer
limit to Regulus' web of spies.

"I hate Misenum," she said. "The volcano. I won't go."

"If you refuse, I've instructed Demetrius to tie you up and throw
you in the back of a wagon."

She looked like she wanted to laugh.

"I'm not joking, Mother. Those were my direct orders to him."

She clutched the front of my robe. "Why are you doing this, Gaius?
If you want to throw me out, why can't I go to Laurentum?"

"I'm not throwing you out, Mother. I need for you to be someplace
safe for a while."

"Why do I need to be safe? Has your meddling into other people's
affairs endangered us?"

For once I found the courage to shake my finger in her face. "No,
Mother. The assistance I rendered Pompeia—at *your* request—has
infuriated Regulus. I'm not sure how he's going to retaliate, and I need

time to sort through some things. You've put me in an…awkward position by arranging this marriage."

"But you need to get married before it's too late." It was as though she hadn't even heard the first part of what I'd said.

"Too late for what?"

"For you to have children." Her voice rose with an edge of desperation.

"There's plenty of time for me to have children, Mother. Most men my age are just beginning to think about getting married. Tacitus was the only man at dinner who's married."

"Oh, and a fine example *he* is." She turned her head and spat. "You need to be getting married. Having a child can be difficult. You know I lost my first one, and Tacitus' wife lost hers. Even when the child is healthy, the birth can be taxing on the mother, sometimes even fatal."

"Mother, I fully expect to get married and produce an heir, just not yet and, preferably, not with Livilla."

"You need to be married before you become…distracted." She looked straight at Aurora. "Lavinia is an excellent choice."

"Mother, her name is Livilla. Why do you keep calling her Lavinia?"

She rubbed her hand over her forehead. "Did I say that? You must be mistaken."

"We all heard you."

Mother looked for confirmation to Naomi, who nodded slowly, reluctantly. "I don't know, dear. I guess I'm worried that you won't go through with this marriage."

"You've made the promise. I'll fulfill it." I knew that I could simply refuse, but, since the eruption and the death of her brother, my mother has been frail. I didn't want to cause her any more anguish. "I just wish you had let me have some choice in the matter."

"Why don't you want to marry…her?" She waved her hand at the door where Livilla had departed.

"She's your choice, Mother, not mine."

She locked her eyes on mine. "And who would your choice be?"

I managed to hold her gaze without flinching. "The 'who' is not the issue. I simply don't want anyone forcing me to choose right now."

"Do you hate me because of this, Gaius? Is that why you're sending me away?"

"No, Mother, of course not. How could I hate the woman who

bore me and loves me? I just need time to think. You do too. I'll come down to Misenum for the Saturnalia. Perhaps by then we'll both see things more clearly."

Mother threw her hands up in surrender. "I'm going to the *latrina*. Naomi, are you coming?" She started for the door.

"I'll join you at your room in a moment, my lady."

Naomi stepped close to me and I knew she wanted to say something I would not be happy to hear. "My lord, your mother—"

"*Now*, Naomi!" Mother snapped from the doorway.

Naomi looked from my mother to me and back, her loyalty split between her legal owner—whom she was bound to obey—and her closest friend. "We need to talk, my lord."

"I will not discuss it any further. She's going to Misenum, and I guess that means you'll be going as well."

"I will not leave her side, my lord. You know that."

"Yes, I do, and I thank you for it."

I wish I were not the cause of so much dissension between Gaius and his mother. She is as kind and forbearing to the other servants as any Roman matron could be. She and Naomi are as close as sisters, but she has disliked me since the day my mother and I were brought into this house as slaves when I was seven.

She has never liked the close relationship that Gaius and I have shared. When I came here, I did not speak enough Latin or Greek to understand her, but I knew she didn't like me. Through my friendship with Gaius I learned the languages. He insisted that I have lessons from his tutor along with him. Sometimes I forget that he lost his father when he was even younger than I was. Even though his uncle and several other men have raised him well, I believe he missed that bond with his father, just as I did.

But his father merely died. He didn't sell his wife and child into slavery, as my father did.

For as long as I've been in this house I have tried to be a loyal servant, to return the kind treatment I have—for the most part—received. I know I have special privileges. Gaius allows me the liberty of a free person. Our steward, Demetrius, is not permitted to inspect my belongings, as he does with the other servants, nor is Gaius' mother. I do not have to share a room with anyone, as most of the other servants do.

By the time I started my monthlies I assumed Gaius and I would eventually have the kind of relationship his uncle had with my mother. The old man never married. He and my mother were content to live as man and wife, in spite of snide comments from his friends and especially from his sister, Gaius' mother. Her dislike of my mother has been shifted onto me. Lately she sometimes even calls me Monica. I can endure that, as long as I have the assurance that I will be with Gaius.

But now plans are in progress for a wedding, possibly soon after the Saturnalia. Gaius has told me he doesn't want to marry the girl, but his mother is insisting, more adamantly than seems necessary. He's a good son, so he'll do what she wants. I don't know what that means for me. It has made me think about being a slave in ways that I never have before. I didn't have to because I never felt like a slave the whole time I was growing up here.

And then, five years ago, Vesuvius erupted and Gaius' uncle died. In a single day Gaius became a man and my master, no longer my childhood friend and the nephew of my master. He inherited me along with the rest of his uncle's property. Most of the time I don't think of myself in those terms, but I am his property, in the same way as his lyre or the scrolls in the library.

III

AT DAWN the next morning Saturius, owner of the stable where I frequently rent horses, had mounts waiting at my door. I ignored my clients, waving them into Demetrius' care. Walking the horses, as the law requires us to do within the city walls, Aurora and I, accompanied by four armed freedmen—four of my burliest—set out for the *taberna* where Aurora had left the woman and child she was trying to help several days earlier. When we stopped by Tacitus' house on the Aventine Hill, he raised his eyebrows at the guard.

"Do you really think they're necessary?" he said

"Under ordinary circumstances, no, but…" I raised my eyebrows and gestured slightly with my head toward my servants to remind Tacitus that we had to be careful about what we said. He isn't always. "The Ostian Way is heavily traveled, so there's little likelihood of being attacked. But you heard Jacob last night, and you know where he was going to deliver that message from Regulus. I felt we ought to be prepared for trouble."

We came to the Porta Raudusculana, close to his house, which opens onto the Ostian Way. At that point we could mount. Tacitus guided his horse so that Aurora was riding between us.

"Do you really think Dom…a certain person might assist Regulus?" he said. "That certain person was warned by Agricola, over a year ago, that there would be fierce retribution if he ever harmed you or me or any member of our families. I recall explicit threats about heads on pikes and bodies thrown into the Tiber."

Aurora's eyes widened.

I nodded as the memory of that terrifying confrontation crowded

into my mind. "But when has fear of punishment ever deterred a man
from doing something he considers to be in his interest? If a...certain
person sees a way to help Regulus carry out his vendetta against me,
Agricola's threat isn't likely to protect me or my family. Or yours, for
that matter, since you are in position to sire an heir for Agricola."

"But he hasn't bothered us."

"I think he's just biding his time until we relax our guard."

Tacitus glanced back at my freedmen. "Maybe you're right." He
touched the knife he now regularly carries under his tunic and I nodded. I carry a short legionary sword myself. I had even given Aurora
a knife, one embossed on the handle with a dolphin, my personal
symbol. A slave caught carrying a weapon could be severely punished,
but the advantage of having one more armed person in our company
seemed to me to outweigh that risk, especially since she was the last
person an attacker would expect to be armed.

She had strapped the knife to her thigh before I could turn my
back. Of course, I had been deliberately slow to turn away. I glanced
over at her now. Her green tunic, even though it was longer than a
man's, rode up, exposing the lower part of her shapely legs. Sometimes
I wonder if she's aware of how much she makes me want her.

We joined the flow of traffic toward the coast. Vehicles dominated
the throng—wagons transporting goods to Ostia for shipment, others carrying passengers. Some people were walking, but most were
riding. I scanned the crowd, looking for anyone who had the look of
a henchman of Regulus', even though I wasn't entirely sure what that
look would be. The only people who stood out were two men riding
donkeys. They looked poor and had an air of discouragement about
them, a good disguise for a couple of spies.

On a day like this it was hard to contemplate the possibility of
trouble. As one travels from Rome to Ostia the land flattens and in July
and August the heat can be oppressive along this road. But not today.
Today the air felt cool, yet still comfortable, the sun bright enough to
be slightly painful to my sensitive eyes. The trees along the road were
showing what passed for their fall colors in this part of Italy. This far
south and along the coast, the season is little more than a slightly cooler
version of summer.

Autumn, more than any other time of year, makes me miss my

home town of Comum. The brilliance of the colors in the foothills of
the Alps against the blue of the lake inspired me to write my first poem
when I was thirteen. How did it start? Something about "*O, time of
year most glorious…*" Did I still have a copy of it? When I got home I'd
have to ask Phineas to unearth it.

I touched the Tyche ring that I wear on a leather strap around my
neck and under my tunic. Aurora saw the gesture and smiled. She and
I found the ring in a cave near my uncle's house at Laurentum when
we were children. Since then we have passed it back and forth between
us, depending on who we think most needs the luck it's supposed to
bring. Neither of us really believes in luck, but things have had an odd
way of turning out well for whoever was wearing the ring.

This time I didn't think we would need luck. We weren't going far
and no one had been killed. Any time I set out to travel, though, I'm
reminded of the metaphor of life as a journey that many philosophers
have developed. If one doesn't have in mind a goal—a place at which
one wishes to arrive—then the journey is nothing more than aimless
rambling. But, even if one does have a goal in mind, there is no guarantee one will reach it. There are so many twists and turns along the
way, which no one can foresee.

Today, though, the road was straight and our destination lay halfway between Rome and Ostia, so we would arrive in about an hour
without pushing Saturius' horses. I tried to make myself take a breath
and enjoy the scenery and the company, but I kept glancing at the
travelers around us. The Ostian Way is one of the busiest roads in
Italy. With so many people on it today, there was no way to know
which ones might be Regulus' henchmen, or even some of Domitian's
Praetorian Guards in disguise.

Tacitus broke my contemplative mood. "What do you think you'll
be able to do for this woman?"

"Probably not much. If a man wants to abandon his family—and I
suspect that's the case here—the Roman Empire offers a vast territory
in which to hide."

"But, my lord," Aurora said, "he told her he was going to Rome."

"Just because he said it, there's no guarantee that was his destination. By now he could be in Gaul or on a ship to Spain or Africa. I'll
do what I can, but please don't expect too much."

I couldn't tell her that my motive for making this trip was to try to smooth over my difficulties with her. She was angry at me, with good reason, and hurt, also with good reason.

I'd been to this *taberna* before. Anyone who's traveled between the capital and the port knows the place. There's no town, just two *tabernae*, a few small houses, a livery stable, and a small public bath—hardly enough to deserve the title "village." The distance between Rome and Ostia is short enough that there's no need to stay overnight, but it is convenient to have a place to get a drink and relieve oneself along the journey. The little settlement grew up at that point because the Ostian Way is joined there by a road from the south, not a regular paved road but a small local road of hard-packed dirt that follows a stream and connects with the main road from Rome to Laurentum. I sometimes take that route when traveling to Laurentum, and I know several people in Rome who have estates on that road.

For myself, when I get away from Rome, I want to get *away* from Rome. Even Laurentum, only seventeen miles from the city, feels a bit too close, especially if Regulus and Domitian are conspiring against me with a renewed energy. I hoped Misenum—a two-day journey, even three at a leisurely pace—would keep my mother out of harm's way. I had written a letter to my steward there to put my *familia* in Misenum on the alert for anything or anyone out of the ordinary.

As we left the outskirts of the city behind, Tacitus leaned slightly toward Aurora. "Gaius Pliny has told me why we're making this trip, but I'd like to hear your account of how you found this woman."

"Certainly, my lord."

I was relieved to hear her address us properly in the presence of other servants. And I was glad to get another chance to hear her tell the whole story. People don't always tell a story the same way twice, even when they're telling the truth, and the differences can be revealing. I decided not to intervene in the conversation so I could appraise it more objectively, like a juror in a trial instead of one of the advocates.

"I was on my way back to Rome," Aurora began, "after my lord Gaius Pliny and I…had a disagreement in Ostia, just before you and he sailed to Naples to help the lady Aurelia. It wasn't long after dark and I was thinking about stopping for the night when I heard a woman calling for help in some trees beside the road."

"Do you know just where you were?" Tacitus asked.

"I was only a short distance, my lord, to the west of the point where the side road joins the Ostian Way. I could see the lights from the *taberna*."

Tacitus nodded.

"When I stopped I found a woman and her son. The boy was ill, leaning against a tree. The woman said no one else would stop to help them. I put the two of them on my horse and walked beside them to the *taberna*."

I couldn't help but recall the story Jacob had told us briefly about the Samaritan. When we had time, I'd have to ask him to give the full account.

"You're certain the boy was her son?" Tacitus asked.

"She said he was, my lord. I had no reason to doubt her."

"What were their names?"

"She said her name was Crispina, my lord, and the boy's name was Clodius."

Tacitus snorted. "Common enough names. But go on."

"Well, my lord, I stayed with them for a couple of days and bought food for them. My lord Gaius Pliny gives me money occasionally to meet unexpected expenses."

I was glad Tacitus didn't press that issue in front of my other servants. I give them all small sums now and then, to encourage good service and to *dis*courage them from stealing from me, but none of them get as much as Aurora.

"Did she explain why they were out there like that?" Tacitus asked.

"She said she was looking for her husband, my lord."

"What's his name and why was she looking for him?"

"His name is Publius Clodius Popilius, my lord. She said he went to Rome on business and she hadn't heard from him in over a month."

A tradesman's cart passed us, with his tools and pans rattling. Aurora's horse whinnied and shook his head, fighting the reins, but she brought him back under control, tightening the muscles in her legs to keep her on the animal.

What would it be like to have those legs…? No, I couldn't allow myself such thoughts.

"He's a bit high-strung," she said, patting his neck and cooing to him. "That's the kind I like to ride."

I have always envied her mastery of horses. She told me she started riding ponies in North Africa when she was five, before she and her mother became slaves.

When she had stilled the animal, Tacitus resumed his interrogation. "Did she say what kind of business her husband was on?"

"Not specifically, my lord. Just that he was looking for someone to invest in a plan that he was sure would make them rich. There was no one around them who had enough money."

"Where did they live?"

"Somewhere along the coast, between Ostia and Laurentum, was the best I could gather, my lord."

"Why were she and the boy on foot?"

"She said she had set out with the boy and some supplies on a mule, my lord, but the animal went lame a few miles outside of Ostia, so they left it."

"And all of this happened while Gaius Pliny and I were in Naples?"

"Yes, my lord. Once the boy seemed to be getting better and the woman was calmer, I told her to wait to hear from me and I returned to Rome. I didn't want my lord Gaius Pliny to think I had run away. I hoped he would be willing to help the woman find her husband."

"And, being the magnanimous fellow he is, he of course agreed." Tacitus gave me a mock salute.

"Yes, my lord, except for the delay to assist his mother-in-law in court." She shot me a glance that I had no trouble reading.

"*Future* mother-in-law," I said. "What else could I do?" I suddenly wondered if Clodius Popilius had found himself in such an intolerable situation that he could see no solution except to run away. Perhaps he didn't want to be married to this woman any more than I wanted to be married to Livilla. I wondered how long I could endure it and how far away I could get—how far Aurora and I could get.

"There's the place." Tacitus pointed ahead of us as the settlement came into view, to my enormous relief.

"Yes, my lord. It's the one on the right," Aurora said. "The innkeeper's name is Marinthus."

"I wish we knew the names of the men who are following us," I said. "And don't turn around."

Tacitus and Aurora both forced themselves to look straight ahead.

"Do you have eyes in the back of your head?" Tacitus asked.

"I noticed them out of the corner of my eye while I had my head turned, listening to you two talk. They're the ones on donkeys."

"What makes you think they're following us, my lord?" Aurora asked.

"We're moving at a leisurely pace. People keep going past us, but these two have kept the same distance behind us since I first noticed them."

"Gaius Pliny," Tacitus said in exasperation, "donkeys aren't the swiftest beasts on four legs."

"Several have passed us, my lord," Aurora pointed out.

"Well, then, perhaps those fellows are just waiting to fall on us," Tacitus said. "Out here in the open, two of them against us with four guards. Next you'll be telling me that Regulus sent them."

The way he put it, it did sound ridiculous. "They won't attack us, but they may send word to someone who *will* attack at some more opportune time." I took one more glance over my shoulder, and I couldn't shake the idea that everyone else on the road when we started had passed us or turned off.

When I traveled this road a few days ago, I wasn't sure I would even return to Rome. Gaius was so angry at me and wouldn't say what I needed to hear. If he marries Livilla, I will have to ask him to send me away, to another of his estates. My only alternative would be to run away.

I was so upset with him that I almost did that on my trip back from Ostia. As I rode along this very road, I could see the Tiber on my left. Once across it, I knew, I could make my way north, over the Alps, across the Danube, and into Germany. North is the only direction in which one can find freedom from Rome. Even Spartacus knew that. The poor man almost made it, but Pompey got in his way, just like Pompeia's daughter—well, that's what I was thinking as I rode. Did I really want to go back to Rome? All I had to do was cross the Tiber.

But the current was too strong for my horse to swim. At one point I spotted a man with a boat tied up. I offered him money to ferry me across the river. When he said he would take me for free, I saw the look in his eye, even though it was already dark, and heard the threat in his voice, so I turned and rode away. Shortly after that I ran into Crispina and her son. I hope I did the right thing by helping them. Our meeting seemed so

fortuitous. Gaius had every right to be angry at me, but I did come home.
I'm counting on him, now that he has calmed down, to be willing to assist
them. Crispina seems desperate—almost frantic—to find her husband.

We pulled our horses to a stop in front of a two-story building that
appeared to be in better repair than most *tabernae*, with a fresh coat of
whitewash and a minimum of graffiti. The shutters on the windows on
the second floor were painted red. By contrast, the other *taberna* across
the road did not appear to have been painted in years. First, though,
the owner would have to cover the cracks in the plaster.

Several of the other people on the road also stopped, some at the
taberna where we were going, others across the road. A few, including
the two men I thought were following us, merely went down to the
banks of a stream that flowed into the Tiber just beyond the *taberna*.
Refreshment could be found there at no cost, as well as a place to re-
live oneself. We dismounted and handed the reins to my freedmen. I
moved to help Aurora down, but before I could get to her she slid off
her horse gracefully—I don't think she could do it any other way—
and straightened her tunic.

Marinthus' establishment sat only ten or so paces from the Tiber,
with a terrace behind it where customers could sit and look over the
river. Marinthus had built a small dock to try to pick up business from
the traffic on the river as well as on the road. With the sailing season
almost at its end, the river was thick with barges and small boats. The
track worn by animals pulling barges up the river cut across the path
leading from the *taberna* to the shore.

I walked around the building, pretending to be stretching my legs,
and taking in my surroundings. Of the people who stopped when we
did, the two men I thought were following us seemed to be especially
interested in our activities. Both looked to be about forty. One was a
dark-haired man about my height with a scar over his right eye, the
other a bit taller and heavier but with no distinguishing marks. While
they drank and relieved themselves, at least one of them always had
us in view.

The interior of the *taberna* was painted a creamy almost-white,
with a motif of vines and animal life, brightening an otherwise dark
room. Like any such establishment, its walls bore the scribbling of

its patrons and the records of their debts and boasts of victories in various board games. One, prominently displayed to catch the eye as customers came in, announced DRUSILLA FELLAT, accompanied by an illustration of a woman on her knees in front of a man performing the act and the going rate for it.

"I'm surprised he hasn't painted over that," I said.

"He told me that she paid him to let her put it up," Aurora said.

As we entered, Marinthus called a greeting to us from behind the counter he was wiping. He was a man about my mother's age and as tall as Tacitus. He still had a full head of hair, although it was going gray. Some childhood disease had pockmarked the pale skin on his face. His build was that of a gladiator going to seed.

"Well, there she is," he said brightly. "And she's brought company. My son will be quite glad to see you again, young lady."

I do not mark my slaves, nor do I require them to wear a bracelet or collar that would identify them as slaves. This man had obviously taken Aurora for a free woman and she had not corrected his error. I would have to caution her. The penalty for a slave who pretends to be free is severe, but I decided to let it stand for now. Aurora and I approached the counter while Tacitus wandered around the room, examining the graffiti. He claims he can learn more about the true nature of a place from this gibberish than from official inscriptions.

"Yes, indeed," Marinthus went on, stirring something in one of the pots that was heating on the counter. "Theodorus has talked about nothing else the last few days."

Blushing, Aurora drew me aside and put her head close to mine. "I assure you, Gaius, nothing happened between us. The bathhouse was closed, so on my first night here I was washing off in that stream that feeds into the Tiber. The son chanced on me, but that was all. It was dark. He didn't see…much."

Whatever he saw, I thought, *he's a lucky bastard*. As children, Aurora and I used to swim together, until my mother demanded that my uncle put a stop to the practice when we were nine. I had not seen her unclothed since then.

I turned back to Marinthus. "We've come to see about the woman and child that my…this lady left here a few days ago."

"I hoped you would be back," he said. "But the woman and the boy are gone."

"Gone?" Aurora said. "When?" She glanced at the door, as though she could still stop them.

"They left yesterday, just about this time."

"How? Did they go with someone?"

"They got into a *raeda*." He paused and put a hand to his chin. "At least, the woman did. Come to think on it, I didn't see the boy get in. He must have already been in it before I looked out the door."

"Was there anyone with her?" I asked.

"Yes, sir. A man."

"Did you know him?"

"No, sir. He was a pretty ordinary-looking fellow, but I don't believe I've ever seen him before. We do get a constant stream of people through here, you know. Not what you might call regular customers, people I would recognize."

"Did the woman appear to be getting in of her own will?" I asked.

"Why, yes, sir. The man with her looked like he was assisting her, not forcing her."

"If they had her son already in the *raeda*," Aurora said, "she would have to get in. Did you see anyone else?"

"Only the driver."

"Did you know him?" I asked.

"Why, I guess I did. It was my brother-in-law, Justus. He owns the *taberna* and the livery place across the road. Somebody must have hired him to drive them."

"Did the *raeda* come back?"

"Yes, not long after midday."

"But the woman and the child weren't in it?" I asked.

"No, sir. Haven't seen 'em since." Marinthus finished wiping the counter and moved to a table. I noticed he walked with a limp and a grimace, as though his left hip caused him pain.

Aurora stepped closer to him, like a client pressing her case. "Weren't you concerned about them?"

"Didn't see reason to be concerned. Their room was paid up for several more days, thanks to your generosity, lady, and they'd left their belongings. I figured they'd be back."

"Did your brother-in-law tell you where he took them?" I asked.

"Him and me don't have much to say to one another. You'll have to ask him yourself."

"Where are their things?"

Marinthus drew himself up, offended. "Right where they left them, sir. Since their room is paid up for several more days, I've not bothered anything. If they're not back by tomorrow, I have every right to take whatever they left."

"I paid for the room," Aurora said. "I believe I have the right to whatever's been left in it." That brought a snort from Tacitus, loud enough to be heard across the room—his wordless commentary on how much freedom I allowed her.

"Yes, you did," Marinthus said. "And you said you would pay for any other expenses. I've kept a record right here." He pointed to a tally on the wall behind the counter, under the name Crispina. "Help yourself to whatever's in the room, as soon as you pay up. Not that those scraps and rags will bring you any profit."

If he hadn't been through their belongings, I wondered, how did he know they were just scraps and rags? Aurora looked at me with a question in her eyes and I paid the sum.

"Thank you, sir," Marinthus said, taking up a brush to scrub off the writing.

"Excuse me," Tacitus called from the other side of the room. "What is this?" He pointed to a spot on the wall behind a table. Marinthus threw his cleaning cloth over his shoulder as he and I joined Tacitus.

"I'm going to look at their room," Aurora said. "I'll be back shortly." Her face showed how upset she was by what she'd heard from Marinthus. She started up a set of stairs to the right of the main entrance.

The innkeeper and I looked at what Tacitus had found. It was five lines in a square, scratched into the plaster:

$$
\begin{array}{ccccc}
R & O & T & A & S \\
O & P & E & R & A \\
T & E & N & E & T \\
A & R & E & P & O \\
S & A & T & O & R
\end{array}
$$

"Oh, yes, sir," Marinthus said. "Somebody marked that on the wall a couple of months ago. I decided to leave it because I was so puzzled by it. And it amuses my customers. I've known many of them to buy an extra round so they can think about it a bit longer."

"Do you have any idea what it means?" Tacitus asked.

"None, sir. I offer twenty *sesterces* to anyone who can decipher it."

"A tidy sum."

"I offer that much because I'll never have to pay it."

"All the words are Latin," Tacitus said, "except AREPO. I've never seen that word before. Is it supposed to be someone's name? The plowman Arepo holds the wheels diligently?"

"That's been suggested, sir, but no one's ever known a fellow named Arepo. At least he's never stopped by here."

"Gaius Pliny, you've used codes and ciphers, haven't you?" Tacitus said. "What do you make of it?"

As children, Aurora and I devised a simple code that we still use if we need to communicate in writing. My uncle encouraged our interest in ciphers, but this was unlike anything I'd ever seen. "Well, there are twenty-five letters in all," I said, "but only eight *different* letters are used. *R, O, A, E,* and *T* are each used four times. *S* and *P* are each used twice. *N* is used only once. That strikes me as curious."

"Yes, sir, people have noticed that," Marinthus said. "And you can read it across in either direction as well as up and down. It reads the same, no matter which direction. You can even read one line right to left and the next left to right and so on, like an ox plowing a field. Or one line down and the next up and so on. Doesn't matter. It still reads the same."

"If you read the lines diagonally," I said, drawing my finger over the figure, "you have all consonants or all vowels. But that just creates gibberish."

"As if the whole thing isn't gibberish," Tacitus said.

I could understand why someone might want to linger over a drink and delve into the puzzle. I was determined to unearth something about it that no one had seen before. "The word TENET is embedded in the center," I observed, "no matter how you read it. 'He holds' or 'it holds' and it seems to hold the puzzle together, to be the framework on which it's built. If you draw a line connecting the *T*'s, it makes a square within the square." I traced the diamond with my finger.

Marinthus raised his eyebrows. "Now *that*, sir, no one has mentioned before. I'll have to think on it."

"Is that worth twenty *sesterces*?" Smiling inwardly with my little triumph, I heard Aurora descending the stairs before I saw her. We all turned as she stormed across the room, stopping in front of Marinthus.

"What have you done with the bag?" she demanded.

Putting up a hand in defense, Marinthus leaned back away from her. "What bag, my lady?"

"Crispina had a leather bag. About as large as a rolled-up sheet of papyrus." Aurora held up her hands to show the size. "It's not there."

"I know nothing about any bag," Marinthus said, convincingly enough. "What was in it?"

"She said it contained her only hope."

"So you don't know what was in it?" I asked her.

Aurora shook her head. "But I know she considered it important. Vitally important."

"Did you talk to this woman?" I asked Marinthus, feeling in my stomach that what had started as a simple act of kindness was about to take on a different complexion. "Did you find out anything about why she was here or where she was going?"

He straightened the chairs around a table, leaning on each one to take the weight off his hip. "We talked a bit. She told me she was trying to hide from her husband."

"That's not right," Aurora said, perplexity clouding her face. "She told me she was trying to *find* her husband. You must have misunderstood."

"No, my lady, I understood her quite clearly. When you run a place like this, you learn when to listen and when not to. With her, I listened." Marinthus' voice took on an edge. "She asked me not to tell anybody she'd been here if someone came looking for her."

"Did she say why she was hiding from him?" I asked.

"She was afraid the man would kill her."

Everything is going wrong! Where are Crispina and her son? Why would she tell me one thing and Marinthus another? I was a fool! What is Gaius going to think? He came out here because of me.

And Theodorus. I did not want to see him again. I couldn't be entirely honest with Gaius about what happened that night. I was desperate to get off the dark makeup I was wearing as part of my disguise when I met

*Crispina. Even though the bath was closed, I found that the stream beside
the taberna makes a pool before it flows into the Tiber. I was bathing there
when Theodorus came upon me. I had noticed him watching me earlier.*

*"Do you need someone to wash your back?" he asked, his teeth flashing
white in the dim light.*

"No, I'm just taking a quick bath," I told him.

*But he took off his tunic and stepped into the water with me. I didn't
want to scream or draw anyone's attention. I covered myself as best I could
and got out of the water before I had washed off my makeup. I really couldn't
scream because Theodorus is so handsome! A young Apollo or Dionysus.
Between his looks and the cold water, I was having trouble breathing. I love
Gaius, I truly do, but not because of his looks. His face is a bit too round
and his ears larger than they need to be. But he is such a dear man.*

*Nothing happened between Theodorus and me. I couldn't...I
wouldn't...but I almost did. He aroused such a longing—an ache—in
me. Every woman knows one way to satisfy that feeling, of course, but
sometimes even that isn't enough. If Gaius doesn't acknowledge his feelings
for me soon—and in a very real way—I don't know what I'm going to do.
If this marriage to Livilla actually happens...I may have to leave.*

IV

W E HUDDLED OUTSIDE Marinthus' establishment, using our horses to screen us from prying eyes and ears. I even sent my freedmen to get a drink and relieve themselves.

"He must be mistaken," Aurora insisted. "I know what Crispina told me."

I put a hand on her arm. I'd never seen her so agitated about something that did not seem that important. Why did these people matter so much to her? "I'm sure that's what she told you," I said. "I don't know what reason Marinthus might have to say otherwise."

"But why would she say such different things to different people?"

"She's the only one who can clear that up," I said in my calmest tone, "so we'd better find her. To do that, we need to know where she went in that *raeda*."

One of my servants returned, so we left the horses with him and walked across the road to the livery stable, where three *raedas* stood in the yard. A man of about forty was fastening iron *hipposandals* on a team of horses. The awkward, noisy devices are normally used only when a horse is going to pull a heavy load for some distance or in a place where the animal needs solid traction.

"Are you Justus?" I asked.

Barely looking up from his work, he took in the equestrian stripe on my tunic and Tacitus'. I suspected he would have ignored us entirely if not for those stripes.

"So my father named me, sir. But I'm full up for today." He tied a knot in the leather strap used to secure the *hipposandal* and tested it with a jerk.

"I don't want to hire anything," I said. "I'd like to ask you about someone who hired one of your *raedas* yesterday."

He dropped the horse's hoof with a clank and stood up. "Sir, I'm a busy man. My time is worth a lot to me."

I dug into the money pouch sewn inside my tunic and dropped two *denarii* into his filthy palm. He touched his hand to his forehead.

"What would you like to know, sir?"

"You were hired to drive a woman and a man somewhere yesterday morning."

"Yes, sir. I was."

"Who hired you?"

Justus moved around the horse, checking the harness. "Didn't know him. He came in, told me what he wanted, and paid me. That was all the introduction I needed."

"Where did you take them?"

"I dropped them at a villa about two miles down this side road up here. The fifth house on the right. Run-down–looking place."

"Was there a child with them?" Aurora asked.

Justus seemed surprised to have her enter the conversation. "Oh, yes, my lady. A boy, about seven or eight years old."

"Did the woman seem frightened?" I asked.

"No. Not happy, maybe, but not frightened neither."

"What about the boy?" Aurora asked.

Justus' horse stomped and Aurora patted his neck to calm him. Justus seemed impressed. "He clung to the woman. His mum?"

"We think so."

"I did too. He was a little scared, but not crying or carrying on. About what you'd expect from a child, when he's not sure what's going on."

The horse stomped again and threw his head back. Aurora patted him on the neck and talked to him in a sing-song voice. The animal stood quietly, and Justus studied Aurora through slitted eyes.

"Did the man ask you to wait for him or come back for him?" I asked.

"No, sir." Justus turned his attention back to me. "I dropped them and left, as I was told to do. They said somebody was meeting them."

"Did they tell you why they were going out there?"

"The woman said they were thinking about buying the place."

"Did you see anyone else at the villa?" Aurora asked.

"No, my lady. Place looked deserted." Justus picked up another *hipposandal*, leaving no doubt that, as far as he was concerned, the time I'd paid for had run out. "Is there anything else you'd like to know?"

"No," I said. "This has been helpful."

"Any time, sir." He bent over to grasp a hoof.

When we returned to our horses I saw an unfamiliar young man talking with my freedmen. Beside me Aurora whispered, "Oh, no."

"What's the matter?"

"That's Marinthus' son. I was hoping we could get out of here without seeing him."

The young man's face brightened as soon as he saw Aurora approaching. He lifted his hand to her.

"That's the son?" I asked her. *He was big and handsome, damn him.*

"He's Marinthus the Younger, but his mother calls him Theodorus."

"'The gods' gift'? Why?"

Aurora waved and smiled weakly. "His mother, who's Greek, told me she had almost given up hope of ever having a child, but her prayers were answered. Unfortunately he thinks he's the gods' gift to humanity, especially the female portion."

Theodorus took a few steps and met us in the road. In his early twenties, he was as tall as Tacitus, with the chiseled profile of a statue of Adonis. And he had seen Aurora bathing. I had two good reasons to dislike him instantly.

"My lady," he said with a slight bow of his head, "what a pleasure to see you again. Are you going to stay with us for a while?"

"Hello, Theodorus. No, we're just passing through this time."

"I am sorry to hear that. I was hoping to see more—"

"Do you know anything about the woman and the boy whom Aurora brought here?" I asked, stepping between him and Aurora.

His smile faded as he seemed to notice me for the first time. "Why, no, sir. I spoke to her at dinner the evening before last, but that's the last time I saw her."

"Did she say anything about leaving?"

"No, sir. We didn't have a lengthy conversation."

"And we don't have time for one now. Please excuse us." I took Aurora by the arm, just to show Adonis that I could but he couldn't.

Without saying any more but glaring at me as much as he dared, Theodorus turned and went back into the *taberna*.

"Let's go," I said.

Two mounting stones were set in front of the *taberna*, so we were soon back on our horses and heading west.

"You didn't exactly make a friend of that fellow," Tacitus said.

"I have other things to worry about," I said. "To begin with, why would a man have himself and at least two other people driven out into the country and strand themselves like that?"

"He said he was meeting someone. Presumably they would have horses, a wagon."

"Then why hire Justus' *raeda*? Why wouldn't his associates just meet him at Marinthus' *taberna* and pick up him and the woman here? The woman seems to have gone with them of her own volition. They weren't kidnapping her or doing something they needed to conceal."

"Why puzzle yourself so much about it?"

"It's an anomaly," I said, setting my face toward Ostia, "and anomalies bother me as much as coincidences."

What had begun as an opportunity to take a pleasant ride and mollify Aurora was showing every sign of turning into a knotty problem. We'd heard two versions of why the woman was on the road. She had left the *taberna* under odd, if not threatening, circumstances. And something valuable—at least important to her—seemed to be missing. Without thinking, I touched the Tyche ring.

·   ·   ·

When we mounted our horses and set out on the Ostian Way again, the two men who seemed to be following us also mounted their animals, but so did several other travelers. Some passed us, while others continued at a leisurely pace behind us. It was when we turned onto the side road that I became concerned. As everyone else continued toward Ostia, our two donkey-riding shadows turned, staying the same distance as always behind us.

"This road makes a sharp bend up ahead," I told my party. "Here's what we're going to do."

The Empire's major highways are engineered to be straight, so that troops and government couriers can move as rapidly as possible. Obstacles are demolished, rivers bridged, mountains tunneled through. A side road like this one, though, originated from animal trails and follows the terrain rather than overpowering it. A large outcropping of rock had forced the earliest travelers on this route to veer to the right.

As soon as we were around that bend, two of my freedmen, as I had instructed them, turned their horses into the woods, dismounted, and circled quietly back the way we had come. The rest of us stopped and turned, weapons drawn. Tacitus, my two remaining freedmen, and I blocked the road, with Aurora behind us.

As soon as they came around the bend in the road, the two men stopped and their jaws fell. Without a word they turned their donkeys, kicking the little beasts furiously, only to be confronted by my other freedmen, who stepped out of the woods brandishing their swords.

The man with the scar over his eye held out his hands. "Sirs, please don't hurt us."

"I told you it was a mistake to come this way," the second man said, like a frightened child. "We've rode right into a trap."

"We mean you no harm," I said. "Dismount and we'll talk. Try to run and my men will cut your animals out from under you."

"Yes, sir," they both said, sliding off their donkeys.

"Turn around and drop your weapons." I should have told Aurora to turn her head first. Both men raised their tunics up to their armpits. The man with the scar unstrapped a sword. The other man showed that he had no weapon, just a virile member that, in an emergency, might serve as a weapon.

"Who are you?" I demanded, wondering even as I said the words if I would get a truthful answer. I seemed to have ridden into a strange world where people's stories changed from one moment or situation to the next.

"We're just poor men, sir," the man with the scar said, his voice quavering.

"Even poor men have names. I want to know yours." I nodded and my freedmen poked the men in the back with their swords.

The overly endowed man fell to his knees and raised his hands in supplication. "Please, sir, don't kill us." His companion did likewise and added his voice to the cacophony. They reminded me of the buffoons in a farce, overplaying their parts, but I wasn't laughing.

"We're not going to kill anyone," I said. "But I will know who you are and why you're following us."

"My name is Segetius," the scarred man said. He jerked his head toward the other man. "He's Rufinus."

"All right, that's progress. Now, why were you following us?"

"We're poor men, sir," Segetius said.

"You've said that." And their paucity of weapons and the donkeys they were riding confirmed it—or made for a good disguise.

"We're on our way to one of the villas down this road, sir."

"We're freedmen from there," Rufinus broke in.

"We thought we could do better for ourselves in Rome," Segetius said, "so we left when we were freed eight months ago. We had a bit of work in the city, but we've lost it, so we're going home. To give us some protection, we decided to keep close to any party that looked large enough to scare off attackers."

"The Ostian Way was easy enough," Rufinus said. He seemed unclear about what he ought to say next, as though he'd forgotten his line.

"Forgive my friend, sir," Segetius said. "He's a bit simple, if you know what I mean. We were worried about this stretch—it's lonely and so wooded. When you turned onto this road, we thought the gods were with us."

I turned to Tacitus. "Do you believe them?"

Tacitus shook his head and twisted his mouth, as though considering a hard question. "I would favor tying them to a tree and leaving them at the mercy of the wolves or bears or whatever ravenous beasts roam these woods."

Tacitus has a knack for sounding utterly serious when he is saying the most ludicrous things. But Segetius and Rufinus didn't know that. They both began to weep. Segetius shuffled toward me on his knees.

"Oh, sir, please, have mercy!" he wailed.

"Stop your caterwauling!" I said, thrusting my sword down to prevent him from clasping my leg and perhaps pulling me off my horse in his desperation. "No one is going to hurt you. I give you my word."

"On the honor of your stripe, sir?" Segetius asked.

"Yes."

That seemed to reassure him. "May I get up, sir?"

"I never told you to kneel, did I?"

"Well, no, sir. I guess you didn't." He stood and brushed himself off, signaling for Rufinus to rise also. "As you can see, we are poor, ignorant men. We mean you no harm. May we go now?"

"To which house are you headed?"

Segetius pointed to the south. "The fifth one on the right, sir. That's our master's home."

How could these men be going to the very same place we are? Not just another house along the same road, but the same *house.*

As soon as I heard the man Segetius say that, I knew Gaius would be thinking about coincidence and how there is no such thing. Studying his face, it's clear that he is mulling it over, probably trying to find some connection with Regulus. I wish he could stop worrying about Regulus, although the man has displayed his enmity toward Gaius and his family many times. But what could two freedmen whom we encountered by chance on the road have to do with one of the richest, most powerful men in Rome?

Unless this wasn't chance.

Is there any such thing as chance? Is everything we do—everything that happens to us—accidental, or is it determined in advance, as the Stoics maintain?

We let Segetius and Rufinus ride along with us, still at our rear. Once we were underway I turned back and asked Segetius, in Greek, if he and Rufinus were lovers. Nothing in either of their expressions indicated that they understood what I'd said. Tacitus and two of my freedmen chuckled. Aurora, still riding between Tacitus and me, blushed. Segetius seemed the more loquacious of our two shadows, but all he could say was, "Sorry, sir, Rufinus and me don't speak anything but Latin, and he doesn't do that very well."

I wasn't entirely convinced, but I figured the two of them were far enough behind us, working to keep their donkeys trotting hard and with my freedmen between them and us, so they couldn't hear what we said. Still, I switched to Greek and lowered my voice when I said to Tacitus, "You know I don't believe in coincidence. It cannot be mere chance that they're going to the same house we're looking for."

"Gaius Pliny," Tacitus said patiently, "can't you admit that, once in the entire history of humanity, something could happen by pure chance?"

"At some point, yes." Aurora's arrival in my house, perhaps. "But not here. It's too convenient. I can't help but think—"

Tacitus held up a hand to stop me. "Consider your words carefully. I swear, if you tell me Regulus is behind it, I'm going to turn around and ride straight back to Rome."

"These men have been in Rome for the past eight months," I reminded him sharply. "At least that's their story. They're down on their luck, no patron—just the sort of men who would jump at any offer someone like Regulus—I said someone *like* Regulus—might make them."

Tacitus shook his head like a man who isn't convinced by an argument but is tired of hearing it. "My friend, Regulus doesn't have to plot against you. You keep imagining that you see a plot every time a shadow falls across your path. You know Terence's play, *The Man Who Tortures Himself*? It could have been written about you."

"Do I have to remind you of what Jacob said?" I decided I would, mostly for the sake of Aurora, who hadn't been present at our conversation with Regulus' steward. "Regulus was furious about losing Pompeia's case. He's planning something to even the score. And he sent a sealed message to Domitian."

"Yes, a *sealed* message," Tacitus said. "Which means you have no idea what was in it. It could have been a recipe Domitian asked for at their last dinner party, or the name of a particularly lively whore."

Before I could reply, Segetius shouted out, "It's the next house, sir."

"We'll talk more about this later," I said.

"Oh, I'm sure we will."

                            .   .   .

"By the gods," Segetius said when we drew to a stop in front of the fifth house on the right. "What has happened?"

The house was abandoned and clearly had been abandoned long enough for vandals and animals to begin the process of reducing it to rubble. It sat back from the road, with a semi-circular lane of hard-packed earth giving access for horses and vehicles.

I turned to Segetius and Rufinus. "When did you say you left here?"

"Right on eight months ago, sir," Segetius said. "Everything was fine then. I mean, the place was never a palace, but it was a nice enough house."

"You men wait here," I said to my freedmen as I dismounted. "Keep an eye on those two."

Tacitus and Aurora got down from their horses as well and stayed slightly behind me. "There are the tracks of a *raeda*," I said. "They're still sharp and clear, so I think they're recent. And the horses were wearing *hipposandals*."

We walked slowly up the lane, examining the tracks.

Aurora knelt and peered closely at the ground. "There's another set of hoofprints. Several sets, I think. They're bare. And some of them are on top of the *hipposandal* prints."

I knelt beside her, forcing myself to ignore her perfume and concentrate on the prints. "Those horses don't seem to have been pulling anything. There aren't any other wheel tracks."

By the time we reached the door of the house the prints had become such a jumble—mixed in with the footprints of the people who had dismounted or gotten out of the *raeda*—that I couldn't make any more sense of them.

"So Justus dropped off Crispina, the boy, and a man," I said. "And at least a couple of riders arrived and seem to have dismounted."

"But why would anyone come *here?*" Tacitus asked, shaking his head in disbelief. "The place is a wreck."

He was right. The barns and stables on my estates are in better condition than this, which was supposed to be a living space for humans. The front door stood open, not inviting us to enter so much as daring us.

I motioned for Segetius and Rufinus and my freedmen to join us. "What was the state of affairs in this house when you left?" I asked them. "Was there any illness or dissension within the family?"

"Why, no, sir," Segetius said. "The master was elderly, but everything was in order."

"Have you heard anything from others in the house since you left?"

"No, sir. We were happy to get away from the place. We've not looked back."

We heard people coming through the woods and put our hands on our weapons. A small, elderly man emerged, followed by a retinue of half a dozen servants, all showing swords.

"Who are you?" the man asked. "What do you want?"

"I am Gaius Pliny. This is Cornelius Tacitus. We're looking for someone who came to this house yesterday. Are you the owner?"

"No. I live in the next house. My name is Titus Lentulus." He ran his eyes over the rest of my party until they rested on Segetius and Rufinus. "So, you two scoundrels have returned."

"Good day, master Lentulus," Segetius said. Rufinus bowed his head.

"You know these two?" I asked.

"They were servants here until they were emancipated eight months ago. And they must have emancipated those donkeys from somewhere. They didn't leave here with them."

"We worked for them," Segetius said, drawing himself to his full height, "in the house of Quintus Vibius."

I gasped and turned on Segetius. The hand holding my sword went up involuntarily to Segetius' throat. "Did you say Quintus Vibius?"

Segetius tilted his head back and spoke like someone was strangling him. "Yes, sir. Rufinus' cousin is a freedman in that house. He said he could get us work there. Vibius was doing well, planning to add on to his house. And everything was fine until yesterday. Then Vibius lost some kind of big case in court. It must have cost him a lot of money. He told all of us who weren't slaves or his own freedmen that we had to leave. He wouldn't be able to support us."

"Do you know anything about the case?"

"Well, sir," Segetius said, swallowing carefully, "I believe I did hear your name mentioned."

With my sword still at Segetius' throat, I glared at Tacitus. "Tell me this is a coincidence. Go ahead, tell me."

"My lord," Aurora said, putting her hand on my arm. "These men have done nothing. Why are you acting like this?"

"Quintus Vibius?"

"Oh," Aurora said as recognition struck. "Oh! He was the client—"

"Yes, the client for whom Regulus was acting when I defeated him in court yesterday morning."

.   .   .

I pulled Tacitus and Aurora aside into the trees in front of the house. I was so angry I could barely form words. "We should have left those two tied to a tree back there, like you suggested."

Tacitus sighed like a father trying his best to be patient with a stubborn child but losing the battle. "Gaius Pliny, what do you think they're going to do? They're two ignorant men on donkeys—which they probably stole from somebody."

"They came directly from a house with a close connection to Regulus."

"Which proves nothing, except how easily you can work yourself into a panic. They're freedmen from this house. Lentulus has corroborated that. They have a perfectly good reason to be coming here."

"Gaius," Aurora said in her most soothing voice, "I have to agree with Cornelius Tacitus. These men just happened to leave Rome at the same time we did. If we had been half an hour earlier, as you wanted, they would never have seen us."

I wasn't ready to give up. "Unless they were waiting for us outside the gate and had been told to look for us."

"But how would they know when you were leaving, or even *that* you were leaving? You didn't post a notice in the Forum, did you?" The note of sarcasm in her voice suggested that I might indeed be giving her too much liberty.

"Everyone in our house knew. Someone could easily have informed Regulus. Someone *did* inform Regulus, you can be sure of it."

"And Regulus," Tacitus said, "dug down to the very bottom of his barrel of spies and scraped up these two idiots to follow you. On donkeys, no less, just to make sure they would stand out."

It did sound ridiculous when he put it like that. I leaned against a tree and closed my eyes, trying to reason with myself. Was I being so insistent on the impossibility of coincidence that I couldn't recognize one when it stood up and jeered at me? "All right," I finally said, "for now I'll accept what you're saying. But I'll believe nothing those two say until someone corroborates it."

"All right." Tacitus put a hand on my shoulder. "Now, let's find out what happened to Crispina and the child, and get home. We might still make it before dark."

I very much wanted to get back home. We walked over to where Lentulus and his men were standing.

"Thank you for waiting for us," I said. "Do you have time for us to ask you a few questions?"

"Certainly."

"Who is the owner of this place?"

"His name was Sextus Tabellius."

"Was?"

"He died six months ago." Out of the corner of my eye I saw Segetius and Rufinus look at one another in surprise.

"Does he have heirs?"

"Yes, sir, two sons, Marcus and Lucius. They can't agree on what to do with the place. Lucius wants to sell, but Marcus refuses. I've offered to buy it to increase my holdings, but they can't come to a decision."

"There isn't much left to sell," Tacitus said.

Lentulus waved his hand. "I don't care about the house. I would tear it down anyway. I want the land, to enlarge my vineyards."

"The sons don't want to live here?"

"No, sir. They have much grander houses in Rome and to the north. They're leaving this place to crumble into dust while they argue over it. Not that it was ever much to begin with."

"Did you see a *raeda* stop here yesterday?"

"No, sir, I did not. As you can see, the woods are thick here. There's quite a bit of traffic on this road. People have come and gone."

"What sort of people?"

"Strange people. I've heard music, loud noises, seen lights."

"But you don't know who was here?"

"I've been leery about inquiring, especially at night. I happened to be out this morning and saw you people, so I thought I would see what was going on."

I hesitated, wondering how much to tell Lentulus. He seemed trustworthy and disinterested, but I'm always careful—

"We're looking for a woman and child," Aurora blurted. "We were told that they were brought here yesterday."

"A woman and child?" Lentulus seemed to be thinking about something. "Well, as I said, I didn't see anyone yesterday."

"Would you object if we went in and looked around?" I asked.

"It's not my property, sir. Do whatever you like. Just lock up as you leave." He chuckled at his own joke.

Leaving two of my men and Segetius and Rufinus on guard with the horses, we pushed aside what remained of the front door and entered the atrium of the house. Instead of holding water, the *impluvium* was dry, filled with half-burned wood. There was no furniture or statuary left, only the unoccupied *lararium*, its walls decorated with a fresco of a man—presumably Sextus Tabellius—making an offering.

"As though the household gods did much good," I said. "They couldn't even protect themselves. Let's spread out and search the place. Call for help before you go into a room where the door is closed."

Aurora and my two freedmen started for the back of the house while Tacitus and I examined the atrium and the rooms off it.

My warning about closed doors proved unnecessary. None of the rooms had doors left on the hinges. Some of them had been splintered and used to make what must have been a large fire in the atrium. Others lay next to the openings they had once protected. The rooms were empty or contained only smashed-up furniture.

"This looks like the work of an enemy army," Tacitus said. "Who would—"

A long scream rang out from the back of the house.

"That's Aurora," I said as the scream was repeated.

We ran to the back of the garden, but the scream was coming from beyond there. A door opened off the rear wall of the garden. When I stepped through it, I saw Aurora, her hands to her mouth, looking at something off to one side which I couldn't see at first because of the way the wall jutted out. She couldn't stop screaming.

Not until I stood beside her and looked in the direction she was looking did I see what was causing her terror. Tied to a large wheel, propped up against the wall, was the nude body of a woman.

Minus her head.

V

I TOOK AURORA by her shoulders and tried to turn her around. She was rigid, her eyes fixed on the horrible sight of that bloody, splayed body.

"Come on," I said. "You've got to get away from here." I finally got her turned and wrapped my arms around her, pulling her head onto my shoulder, shielding her from the awful sight. She still would not move more than a couple of steps but at least she had stopped screaming. I could feel her entire body shaking now.

Tacitus started into the garden, but I stopped him. "Don't let anyone in here until I've had a chance to look the place over. I don't want this area disturbed."

As I held Aurora I could look beyond her and survey the scene. That was the first step in any investigation like this—to have a comprehensive view of the site where the crime was committed. Where were things in relation to the victim and to one another? Was there anything here that seemed not to belong? Was something— other than the head—missing that I might expect to find in such a situation?

What I saw over Aurora's shoulder was that, although a modest house, this one did boast this second garden. Not a formal peristyle garden with a fishpond, but a working garden. With the owner dying in the spring, no one had planted anything this year, but the trampled remains of crops from the previous summer were evident, along with a few hardy plants that had come up on their own from seeds dropped last autumn. From the way the vegetation was flattened, I suspected that a good number of people had been walking around in here. Were they the audience or participants? There were two sheds, which I hoped contained tools and not a severed head.

"Let's get you into the other garden," I said, "where you won't have to look at this."

She clung to me, gripping my arm so tightly she was hurting me. "No. Don't leave me, Gaius."

"I have to examine her." Aurora wasn't going to let me get far away from her, so I had to find some place for her in this second garden. I saw a bench in one corner and turned it so it faced the wall. "Sit here. I won't go anywhere."

Releasing me reluctantly, she sat on the bench and put her hands over her stomach. I stayed beside her longer than I otherwise would have because I really had no enthusiasm for the examination I knew I had to make.

"Are you all right?"

"How could I be?"

My two freedmen were standing in the doorway of the garden, their jaws dropping. The horror of the scene at least kept them from noticing how informally Aurora addressed me, I hoped. Tacitus stood beside them as though waiting my permission to go any further. Rats—at least a dozen of them—frightened away by our presence at first, were crawling back onto the body.

"Get those beasts off her," I told the freedmen. "And don't touch the body." I didn't really have to add that last admonition.

They began waving their swords, killing and scattering the rats, which ran squealing and scurrying in every direction.

By the gods! I think I'm going to be sick. I've never seen anything so horrible, not even that time when I went to the games in the arena. I've seen a few people lying dead in the streets of Rome—everyone has—but nothing like this.

How could anyone do such a thing? I've got to…I've got to throw up.

I was about to approach the body when I heard Aurora make a gagging sound. I turned to see her on her knees, beginning to retch. She was wearing her hair loose today. I pulled it back out of her face and held it until she stopped vomiting. She collapsed onto the bench and I sat down beside her. When she threw her arms around my neck, I hoped my freedmen would take it as a sign of a master comforting a servant and nothing more.

"Oh, Gai—my lord, how can you stand to look at that? That poor woman!"

I rubbed her shoulder. "You know how I work. If I'm going to learn what happened to her and get any clue to who might have done it, I have to make an examination. You've been very concerned about this woman. Don't you want to know what happened?"

"But I don't know if it's the same woman."

"What?" I let go of her and she sat back on the bench.

"The only thing I had to recognize her by was a scar on her left cheek. If I can't see that, I have no sure way to identify her."

From behind us, Tacitus said, "All right, men. Look for her head. I'm sure you'll recognize it. There can't be that many lying around." He went to one of the tool sheds. "I'll look over here."

Aurora began to cry again. If there was one thing I would change about Tacitus, it would be his sardonic—often inappropriate—humorous remarks.

I hugged Aurora one more time, then stood up. "I'm going to examine the body. You can go back to the front of the house or you can sit right here. You don't have to look at her again."

"I'll stay here." She turned on the bench so her back was to the ghastly scene, drew her knees up and clasped her arms around them. "I'm sorry to be so childish, Gaius. You know I can stomach a lot more than most women, but this… I've never seen anything so horrible."

I couldn't admit to her that the main reason I hadn't retched was my determination to act the man in her presence. I hoped I could keep my stomach under control when I began a close examination.

Tacitus emerged from the shed, wiping his mouth on his arm.

"Any sign of the head in there?"

"What?" He lowered his voice. "Oh, I just needed someplace to throw up, where Aurora wouldn't see me."

"After all the slaughter you've seen in the arena, *this* nauseates you?"

"This is entirely different, my friend." He shuddered.

"How can it be?"

"To begin with, in the arena you're not this close to it. At least we equestrians aren't. Our seats, behind the senatorial section, put us at some distance from the floor, as you would know if you ever went to the games. It's like seeing a trireme out at sea. You have no idea how big the thing really is until you're standing beside it on the dock. Or, in this case, how revolting death is and how bad it smells. The perfume that's sprayed in the arena masks that."

"Well, let's see if we can learn anything from what the rats have left us." We had to kick a few of the bolder beasts out of our way again.

"The cause of her death is not in question, is it?" Tacitus said.

"No. From the way the blood sprayed on the wall behind her, I'm sure she was still alive when she was decapitated."

Tacitus shook his head mournfully. "By the gods! Poor thing. I hope the blade was sharp and it took only one blow."

"That's the best we could hope for her."

Without touching the woman, I knelt and slowly examined her body from her feet to what was left of her neck. The wheel to which she was tied was unusually large, about three cubits in diameter, with five spokes. Its size was emphasized by how small the woman was.

"She's young, isn't she?" Tacitus said.

"Yes. Hardly more than a child. I'd say she was seventeen or eighteen, if that."

The girl was tied with her back toward the wheel, exposing the front of her body to a whip before she had been decapitated and to three stab wounds in her belly. One of the stab wounds had something barely protruding from it. I didn't touch it because I didn't want to upset Aurora any more than she already was. I could look at it later.

"I've never seen that large a wheel on a vehicle," Tacitus said, and I turned my attention to him.

"Nor have I." I twisted the wheel slightly and found it wobbly. "It's very weak. It would never hold the weight of a wagon. I suspect it was made especially for this purpose."

"From the stains on it," Tacitus said, "I don't think this was the first time it was used like this."

The woman's wrists, ankles, and neck were tied where the spokes attached to the rim, so that her hands, feet, and—at one time—her head had hung over the rim. I had never had the opportunity to gaze down into a body like this. I could see tubes, flesh, and the spine.

"I believe these are what lead from our mouths to our stomachs," I said.

Tacitus stood several paces away, not interested in any closer examination. "How long do you think she's been dead?"

I tried to move one of her arms. "The death stiffness is still on her. I would say she's been dead barely a day. From the way the bones of her spine are crushed, I'm afraid it took more than one blow to sever her head."

"I hope she was dead after the first blow."

"Yes. I can't imagine the agony, the horror, of dying this way." I ran my eyes down her body and peered more closely between her slender legs, offering the poor woman an unspoken apology for the indignity. Her pubic hair was shaved, adding to her childlike appearance. Roman woman typically remove other body hair, but not in that area. I did not touch her. "It's even worse. She was violated, brutally violated."

I stood back and fought to keep my stomach under control. Nothing about this made any sense, any more than the wanton destruction of the house. I walked back over to Aurora and put a hand on her shoulder. "See if you can find a large piece of cloth so we can take her down and wrap her up."

"What are you going to do with her?"

"Take her back to the *taberna*. I can examine her there, where I'll have more time and fewer distractions. Then I'll give her some kind of funeral."

Aurora found a blanket in one of the rooms off the peristyle garden. I took it from her so she wouldn't have to get any closer to the woman's body. She looked like she was going to be sick again as my servants untied the woman. They had to break the joints of her limbs loose from the death stiffness. The cracking unnerved me as well. Before the woman was wrapped up, I studied her belly one more time.

"Aurora," I called, "how old do you judge Crispina was?"

"Between thirty and thirty-five," she replied over her shoulder. "Why?"

"This woman was nowhere near that old. And I'm not sure she has had a child."

While my freedmen wrapped the woman's body and loaded her onto one of the donkeys, Tacitus, Aurora, and I walked around the rear garden one more time, to be sure we hadn't missed anything. I craved some place to wash my hands, but the best I could do was rub them on my tunic, which I vowed to burn when I got back to Rome. I stopped beside a sturdy post stuck in the ground in the center of the space. It had a hook inserted into it near the top and was streaked with dark stains.

"Look here," I said. "There are some bloodstains—just drops, really—that make a trail from the wheel to this post."

"The head…?" Tacitus said.

I nodded and walked from the wheel to the post. "I think someone carried the woman's head from there to here."

"But why?"

"We might understand that if we knew more about this post," I said. "Call Segetius and Rufinus in here," I told one of my freedmen.

The two men had to be pushed and prodded by my servants. When they were standing before me, I asked them what purpose the post served.

"Well, sir," Segetius said, "that…that was Sextus Tabellius' whipping post. If a slave displeased him, he would tie him to that post and give him however many lashes he thought would be enough punishment, and then a few more for good measure." He turned his back to us and lifted his tunic to show the scars of a severe beating, surely more than one. "Rufinus' back looks much the same, sir."

"So these are bloodstains," I said, pointing to the dark splotches on the post.

Both men nodded. "And the rest of the household was forced to watch," Segetius said.

"Is that why you decided not to stay here when you were emancipated?" Tacitus asked.

"Yes, sir," Rufinus said. "We've no good memories of the place." He looked around and grimaced. Aurora, standing on the edge of our circle, patted him on the shoulder sympathetically.

"Did Tabellius emancipate you outright?" I asked.

"No, sir. We paid for it."

So the man was a miser as well as a brute. Whatever their behavior might have been, I could not condone such cruelty on the part of any master. Beating a slave that badly teaches him nothing but resentment, even hatred. A horse, beaten that badly, would never be useful afterwards. And inflicting such punishment turns the master into a monster—a *dominus* into a *daemon*.

Tacitus pointed to the foot of the pole and a streak down the side of it. "Can you tell what that is?"

I nodded. "Someone was tied here with his back to the pole. Segetius, come here. And watch where you step."

Segetius trembled from bad memories as he walked up to the pole.

"I'm sorry to put you through this, but I need to verify something." I positioned him with his back to the pole and hands behind the post, as though they were tied.

"Rather like Odysseus tied to the mast of his ship so he could listen to the Sirens' song," Tacitus said.

"If he was tied that way," Aurora said, pointing to the blood-soaked wheel, "he would be forced to watch the beheading, and I'll bet his head was tied so he couldn't turn away."

"I'm sure he would have welcomed wax in his ears, as well as over his eyes," I said. "Now, what about this wheel?" I asked Segetius and Rufinus. "I've never seen anything quite like it."

They looked at one another, neither one willing to speak first.

"You're free men," I said, "and your former master is dead. No one will harm you for telling the truth."

Rufinus shook his head and turned away, like a child confronted with something that arouses fear from deep within him.

"Well, sir," Segetius began slowly, "the wheel was Tabellius' own invention. It was for punishing female slaves. You saw how that poor girl was tied...."

I looked at the disgusting thing again. It was as fiendish as Procrustes' bed. The five spokes provided places to tie a woman's legs, arms, and torso. She would be splayed, left vulnerable to whatever her master wanted to do to her.

"Tabellius usually tied them facing the wheel," Segetius said. "That allowed him—"

I raised my hand to stop him. I didn't need to hear anything else and I didn't want Aurora to hear any more. My fondest wish at the moment was that Tabellius had died a painful death, preferably at the hands of his servants.

Dismissing the two freedmen, Tacitus, Aurora, and I moved into the peristyle garden to stand around the *piscina*, which had no fish in it nor even water for them to swim in, if there had been any fish. It was sad to think any Roman house could fall into such a state of decay.

"What do we make of it?" I asked. "We have no way to determine if this really is Crispina, although she seems too young anyway. If it is, where is the boy? If it's not, did Crispina have anything to do with this woman's murder?"

"She couldn't have, my lord," Aurora protested. "If you'd seen what good care she took of her son, you wouldn't be able to think such a thing."

"All I can see is what's right before me—a woman, whom we cannot identify, brutally abused and murdered in a horrifying fashion. We have no idea why she was here or who was here with her. Lentulus says he did not see or hear anything. We'll have to talk to Justus again. He's the only one who might give us a clue."

"There's another house to the south of this one," Tacitus said. "Perhaps they know something."

"All right. We'll talk with them before we leave. Now let's search this place thoroughly one more time."

"Do you think we'll find her head?" Tacitus asked.

"I doubt it. I think someone cut it off to take it with them."

"Like Perseus with Medusa's head?"

"We should also be looking for Crispina's bag," Aurora said. "It wasn't in her room, so she must have taken it with her."

"Was it large enough to hold a head?" Tacitus asked.

·   ·   ·

An hour of searching did turn up a bloody axe in one of the tool sheds, but no head and no other clothing that looked like it might have been worn recently by a young woman, and no small bag. I checked to make sure that the body was securely tied across one of the donkeys. Even though her feet protruded from the blanket, we made sure her headless state was concealed.

"Segetius, you can lead that donkey behind yours," I said. "Rufinus, you'll ride with one of my men."

Lentulus must have had someone watching us because he returned as we were preparing to leave. "What did you find?" he asked.

"Not what we were looking for," I said. "A young woman was murdered here in the last day or so—"

"By the gods! Who was she?"

"We don't know." I decided not to give any details. There was no point in spreading lurid stories up and down the road. "We're taking the body so we can give her a proper burial. If you see anything going on over here, please send someone to tell me. My house is on the Esquiline Hill."

"Yes, by all means." He rubbed his chin. The servant who shaves him, I thought, must have trouble with that mole. "Do you think we're in any danger here?"

"I doubt it. It looks like someone seized on the opportunity of the empty house. I'm going to talk to Sextus Tabellius' sons in Rome. Do you know where I can find them?"

"The older one lives in an insula on the Aventine Hill, on the side away from the Circus Maximus."

"He's practically a neighbor of mine," Tacitus said. "We'll find him."

"I'll urge them to reach some decision about the place before it does become a menace to those of you around it," I assured Lentulus.

"Thank you. Remind them that I'm eager to purchase it."

We spent the next couple of hours talking with the owners of the two closest villas but learned nothing more than what Lentulus had told us. Sextus Tabellius kept to himself, rarely having any visitors. His *familia* was small. The servants who weren't freed in his will went to live with one or the other of his sons. I encouraged everyone we talked with to keep an eye on the house and report any unusual activity to me.

·   ·   ·

It was midafternoon by the time we returned to Marinthus' *taberna*. While Aurora went to the *latrina*, Tacitus and I took Marinthus aside and explained what was wrapped in the blanket. His jaw dropped.

"Do you have someplace where we can keep her for the night?" I asked him.

"There's a shed out behind, sir." He pointed toward the river. "Lay her in there. I'd rather my customers didn't know."

"I certainly understand. My people have been ordered to keep quiet. Can you send someone to Ostia for a magistrate to take charge of her? Someone reliable—your son perhaps?" That would get him away from Aurora.

"I'm afraid he's not all that reliable, sir, much to my shame. His mother's filled his head with notions of how handsome he is—all of that 'gods' gift' nonsense. I'll find a better man."

Thwarted on that front, I focused again on the problem at hand. "I want to examine the body one more time. I'll leave money for the funeral."

"So you're staying the night?"

I looked at Tacitus. "I'm staying. Are you?"

"Yes. I'll need some place to sleep after I get as drunk as I possibly can. It's the only way I'm going to get that horrible scene out of my mind."

"I've got just the thing, sir," Marinthus said. He went behind the counter and found an unopened amphora. "It's the strongest wine I've got."

"I'll take it, and I'm going to sit with those fellows at the ROTAS-square table. Perhaps they've had some insight into the puzzle. Maybe it'll take my mind off this business." He made his way to the table, where the amphora appeared to be well received.

"All right," I said. "Do you have room for us?"

"You've already paid for two more nights in the room that Crispina was using, and I have one other empty room next to it."

"I suppose those will do for Tacitus and me."

"You might try Justus' place for the rest of your people. It's not as nice as this, quite frankly, but it's decent. My sister sees to that. Now, excuse me, sir. Customers are calling."

I sent two of my freedmen to Rome to let my household and Tacitus' know that we would not return until tomorrow. The other two I sent to secure rooms in Justus' *taberna*, including a room for Segetius and Rufinus. I wasn't quite sure yet what I was going to do with them, but I wanted to keep them close in case they were more than the bumbling fools and maltreated servants they appeared to be.

Aurora returned from the *latrina*. "What is your plan?" she asked, her tone carrying a hint of a challenge.

"We'll stay the night, take care of the woman's body tomorrow and inform the magistrates in Ostia, then return to Rome by the afternoon."

"Isn't there anything else we can do, Gaius?" Disappointment filled her eyes.

"I don't see what it would be."

"But she was murdered in such a horrible fashion."

"Murder is, by its nature, horrible, no matter how it's done. Smothering someone in rose petals has the same result as stabbing or beating them to death. People get killed every day. Somebody will probably be killed in Rome by the time we finish this conversation. I regret that I cannot do anything in those cases or in this particular one, but I can't. In so many cases, the killer is never found. It frustrates me as much as it does you."

"What about the boy?" Aurora asked.

"What about him? How do you expect me to find someone when the only clue I have is that he was taken to a particular villa on a certain day? But there's no one at that villa now and no one has seen the boy since then."

"Couldn't you find the farm Crispina and the boy came from?"

My voice betrayed my growing impatience. "Oh, certainly. It's somewhere south of Ostia." I waved my arm in that direction, the rest of Italy. "That is, if she was telling the truth, and the odds in favor of that are not any I would bet on. Remember, she told you one story and told Marinthus an entirely different one and then another one to Justus. Logically, all of them can't be true."

"All three could be false," Aurora said.

"Exactly. For all we know, she could have come from Milan or Brindisium or anywhere in between."

"Gaius, I've never known you to give up before. You always seem to know one more avenue to pursue."

"I am truly sorry, Aurora, but there comes a point when I must stop wasting my time and resources and simply admit that I can't solve a problem. There are other things I need to attend to, such as—"

"Such as the problems of your rich friends."

"I was going to say, such as protecting myself and my household from Regulus and trying to understand whatever is affecting my mother."

Aurora turned her back on me and folded her arms across her chest.

Without touching her, I made one last effort. "When we get back to Rome, I'll talk to Tabellius' sons. They might know who's using the house. That's the only other thing I can do right now."

"I guess I'll have to accept that," Aurora said over her shoulder as she started up the stairs.

I opened my mouth to call her back. No servant should ever speak to her master like that and then flounce off without being dismissed. But then I thought, *What if she didn't come back? Would she defy me that blatantly?* I wasn't sure of the answer to those questions. What had begun as an effort to improve my relationship with my own slave—admittedly my favorite slave—had driven an even thicker wedge between us. At this rate, I might as well sell her, marry Livilla, and be done with it.

Tacitus left the people he was drinking with and walked over to where I stood. "It's going to take a sizeable gift to make things right with her, my friend."

"What are you talking about?"

"When a wife or lover leaves the room with her head tilted at *that* angle"—he jutted his chin up and out, exaggerating the position of Aurora's chin, but not by much—"the man has to pay the price. The higher the tilt, the higher the price."

"Aurora is neither my wife nor my lover. She's my slave."

"Oh, Gaius Pliny, Gaius Pliny." He shook his head and chuckled.

"Just leave me alone," I snapped. "The woman is being entirely unreasonable. She wants me to look for some farm that Crispina might have come from."

"That would take some searching, wouldn't it?" Tacitus walked uncertainly back to his newfound friends.

I went out to the shed to make sure the woman's body had been properly stored, if that was the word for what one does to a decapitated corpse. I'd told Segetius and Rufinus to put it on a table or board, up off the ground or floor. It was too dark in the shed for me to do much more than satisfy myself that they had followed my instructions, except that they had taken the blanket off her. Just as well. I wanted to examine whatever was protruding from the stab wound. By the door I found a small lamp and a flint to light it.

I laid a hand on the woman's belly. When I was a child and had an upset stomach, my mother used to rub my belly. I wished I could do something to allay the terror and the agony this woman must have suffered. No human being should have to endure such things. In the dim light my hand found the stab wound with the protrusion. I managed to pull it out a bit farther.

Because I have seen animals give birth and because of what I had experienced recently in Naples, I recognized what I held between my fingers—the cord that connects a baby to its mother's womb. It must have gotten hooked on the knife when the woman was stabbed and been pulled partway out. This woman had been pregnant, for not more than a couple of months, because there was no outward sign, but she was carrying a child.

Whose child was it? If this was Crispina, I could assume the child was her husband's. If this wasn't Crispina, then I had no way of knowing who was the father of the child. What was supposed to have been a quick trip down the Ostian Way to help someone Aurora had tried to rescue was becoming far too complex a piece of business. I felt like Theseus entering the labyrinth but without Ariadne's thread to guide him back out.

How could I be such a fool? Why did I talk like that and storm up the stairs like a spoiled child? It must be because I'm so upset. I can't get that horrible sight out of my mind, that poor woman. Was she Crispina? If she wasn't, then what have I gotten Gaius into?

I hoped that this trip, this opportunity to work together again like we did when we were children, might bring us closer together. Yes, I'm that desperate as I see his marriage drawing closer. I believe Gaius has feelings for me—as more than just a playmate and childhood friend—but I don't know if he will ever admit them or bring himself to express them. He is so respectful toward me—toward all women, really—and yet I see the way he looks at me. He doesn't look at his other servant women that way and certainly has never looked at Livilla like that.

I wonder if I should be bold enough to tell him how I feel. I would be content—happy, even—to have the kind of relationship with him that my mother had with his uncle. I have to be realistic. The possibility that I could ever become the wife of a man with any prospects in life ended the day I became a slave. If Gaius were to free me—which I would never ask him to do—I might become the wife of a freedman. We could keep a small shop, I suppose, or live on a little farm, and work ourselves into an early grave.

I've heard Lorcis, Martial's "wife," argue that, no matter how hard she has to work, she is better off now than she was as Regulus' slave.

But she didn't love Regulus.

As much as I dislike being on boats, I find it soothing to sit beside a body of water. That's why my villa at Laurentum is my favorite. It practically hangs over an inlet off the sea. The breaking of the waves below the house provides a kind of rhythm to my thinking. The flow of a river offers a different kind of tranquility. That's what I was seeking as I walked down to the Tiber behind Marinthus' *taberna*.

A river makes me think of the passage of time, of my own passage through life. I was there, now I'm here, and I'm going to be somewhere else. I can't know what's ahead of me—downstream—only what's be-hind me—upstream. Past, present, and future—grammatical tenses as a metaphor for life. And yet it's all connected. But the woman in the shed and her child had no future. What it was in their past that led them to the awful present, I would have to find out.

I don't know how long I stood beside the river. I was jolted when Tacitus ambled up behind me.

"There you are, Gaius Pliny. It looks like we've done whatever we can here and those nice people I've been talking to are on their way to Rome, so I'm going to ride with them."

He hadn't been drinking long, but the wine must have been strong and he must have drunk a lot of it. I was just as glad to hear that he was leaving. Tacitus is not a pleasant companion when he's in his cups.

"A parting thought," he said, wagging a finger at me. "My friends and I were exchanging ideas about that ROTAS square on the wall. Amazing how a *little* wine clears the mind before a *lot* befuddles it.

Anyway, it occurred to me that *rotas* appears in the square. And it means 'wheel.' You know, a *wheel?*" He jerked his head in the direction of the villa.

"That's probably just a…a coincidence." I couldn't find any other word.

"But all of the words in the square can be written in a circle, starting with ROTAS and coming around so the *R* at the end of SATOR overlaps that first *R* in ROTAS." He handed me a piece of papyrus he was holding in one hand and pointed to the letters of the puzzle written in a crude circle. "See, a *wheel.* Also, the puzzle has five lines in it, and the wheel in that damnable garden had five spokes. Do you think that means anything?"

"I'll have to give it some thought."

"You do that." He patted me clumsily on the shoulder. "And, while you're at it, think about this. The word SATOR means a plowman. Right?"

"Yes. We all know that."

"Well, I know it's crude to say this, and I'm slightly drunk and I apologize in advance to you and to that poor girl in the shed over there, but think about sex and plowing. You know, there's a long tradition of plowing as a metaphor for coupling." He belched loudly and thrust his pelvis forward a couple of times. "For example, in his *Antigone*, Sophocles has Creon say, 'There are other furry meadows for him to plow.'"

As much as this strain of conversation disgusted me, I couldn't dismiss him summarily. "Are you saying there might be some connection between that square and what happened to that girl—even the way she was violated?"

"Maybe. Or maybe it's all just coincidence." He waved an unsteady hand. "I know how much you love a good coincidence."

VI

SINCE TACITUS would not be using it, I let Aurora stay in the room Crispina had been in and I took the other vacant room in the *taberna*. Those were the only two rooms at the top of that staircase. They'd originally been intended for the owner of the place, Marinthus said, but because of his aching knee joints he had had rooms added on the back of the building for himself and his family. I felt Aurora would be safer close to me, even if we weren't speaking to one another, than across the road in Justus' *taberna*. I had hoped Tacitus would agree to take Segetius and Rufinus—"the two asses on their asses," as he called them—back with him, but he was too inebriated to consent. I stuck them in a room in Justus' *taberna*. It was a relief to have everyone, even Tacitus, situated somewhere else for the time being. I needed to reflect, think, ponder.

But all of those proved difficult in Marinthus' dining room. A young couple celebrating their marriage came in with friends and took over the place. From the look of them and from their speech, I gathered they were from some of the neighboring farms. This was probably the most festive night they would enjoy in their entire lives. To find some peace and quiet, I took my meal on the terrace, even though it was a bit cool for eating outdoors. But the stew was hot and the bread still warm from Marinthus' oven. The heat that the tufa paving stones had absorbed during the day kept my feet comfortable.

As I sat in the gathering dark, thoughts of two women whirled in my mind. One was the poor girl whose decapitated body lay in the shed behind the *taberna*, out of my sight now, thankfully. How could one human being do such a thing to another? How could men rape a defenseless girl like that? How could other human beings stand by and watch it being done? Was it part of some bizarre ritual, like Dionysus' Maenads tearing an innocent animal apart? Did they take perverse pleasure in it?

Those were questions I'd often asked myself about the games in the arena. This situation, though, was different in a significant way. The games had originated as *munera*, a blood sacrifice to the gods and the spirits of the dead—another good reason not to believe in such things. The people executed were being punished for crimes committed—at least in theory—and their deaths were supposed to gain the favor of the gods and the spirits for the rest of us.

But what had happened in Tabellius' villa was murder, pure and simple. In spite of what I had told Aurora, I resolved to continue to try to find out who had done it. That poor girl and her never-to-be-born child had to have an advocate—no, an avenger. A person savage enough to do such a thing must be punished. And what if he had another victim in mind? He had to be stopped. But, without the first clue, how could I find him? It had to be a "he." Of that I was sure. I couldn't imagine a woman who could devise such a horror—especially inflicted on another woman—or have the physical strength to commit it. And it had to be a man (or men) to rape her so violently.

Tomorrow I would examine the girl's body more closely, and when I got back to Rome I would question the two sons of Sextus Tabellius to see if they had any idea who might have been using their father's house for such a nefarious purpose, if it was not one of them. Beyond that I did not know what else I could do.

The other woman in my mind was, of course, Aurora. What if something happened to her? I didn't expect her to be murdered—though that was not impossible on the streets of Rome—but she could get sick or have an accident befall her. How would I live if she were no longer part of my life? And what part *could* she have after my marriage to Livilla?

With the raucous wedding celebration going on behind me, and absorbed in my thoughts, I paid no attention when someone came out of the *taberna* and onto the terrace. Only when she sat down in the chair next to mine did I realize Aurora had joined me. She had cleaned herself up, put on a different gown—a dark red one—and applied perfume. The gown and the perfume, which was not her usual scent, must have belonged to Crispina. I knew Aurora hadn't brought any with her on what we thought was going to be a short jaunt out here and back, overnight at worst. The fact that Crispina hadn't taken any of her possessions except her bag with her when she left meant, to me, that she had intended to come back. What had prevented her?

Neither of us spoke at first as we gazed out over the river. A torch in a bracket on the wall behind me let me see Aurora's face while leaving mine mostly in the dark.

"I must apologize, my lord," she said at last, looking at the river, at the shed—anywhere but at me—"for being angry at you earlier. I know there is only so much you can do, only so much anyone can do. You have no obligation to Crispina. I appreciate the effort you've made and your care for that poor woman who was murdered, whether she was Crispina or not."

I let her apology linger in the air between us for a moment. It doesn't hurt to let a servant—even one you love—experience a moment of anxiety now and then. "I'm sorry I was so abrupt with you," I finally said. "When we get back to Rome I'm going to continue to search for the person who did this. If necessary, I will come back out here."

She closed her eyes and lowered her head. "Thank you, Gaius. That means so much to me."

We couldn't talk for a few moments as the revelers poured out of the *taberna* and made their way down the path to two boats tied up at Marinthus' small dock. Aurora had to shift her chair closer to mine to make room for them. They lit lamps, hung them from poles at the front and rear of their boats, and embarked, full of good spirits and lewd jokes, most of them about the copulatory practices of farm animals.

"Are you getting ideas for your wedding celebration?" Aurora asked.

I let the question sink of its own weight.

After they had passed, Aurora did not shift her chair back to where it had been. "I'm sorry. That isn't a joking matter, is it?"

"No."

"When you marry Livilla," she said, still watching the wedding party cast off, "please send me away. To Misenum would be best, I think."

My head jerked toward her. "What? Why would you say something like that?"

"Because I couldn't stand to watch you making another woman happy." Her voice had a catch in it.

"Do you think I'm going to make her happy?" I didn't see how I could when marrying that sweet little girl was the most dismal prospect I had ever contemplated.

Aurora turned in her chair toward me. Her face glowed in the light of the torch. "Yes, I do, Gaius, because that's the sort of man you are—so tender and loving, so thoughtful. You always have been, as long as I've known you. Do you remember the first day my mother and I came into your uncle's house in Comum?"

"Yes. You looked so lost, so frightened, clinging to her."

"I was. I had no idea what was going to happen to me. I couldn't understand most of what was being said around me." Her voice faltered at the memory of that fear. "You were on the other side of the atrium, playing with a pair of clay horses. You came over and gave me one and we sat down by the *impluvium* and played together. I felt that, as long as I was with you, I would be safe. For the last fifteen years I've never lost that feeling."

"But we've grown up, Aurora. Our lives are bound to change. Just like the Tiber, we move on to different places. You have the skills to make a life for yourself. I could…emancipate you. I will, if you want me to." I'd never said that before because I was so afraid of her answer.

"No," she said quickly. "Please don't."

My heart began beating again.

"I want to belong to you, Gaius, and this is the only way I can."

That I was surprised to hear. "But if you were free, we might—"

She held up her hand to stop me. "Don't start imagining what can never be. Your friends—even Tacitus—would laugh behind your back. Your mother would never let us be together. If you defied her, it would make you miserable and eventually you would hate me."

We watched a few boats sailing down the river, their lights flickering like stars come down to earth. "I can't deny that most of what you said was true." How could I, when I myself had snickered at men of my class who had had affairs with slaves or freedwomen? "Except the part about hating you. I could never do that."

A large piece of wood floated by, probably the last thing we would be able to make out before darkness became complete.

"What's to become of us, Gaius?" Aurora said softly. "Are we just going to drift, like that wood, carried wherever the current of our lives takes us?"

"By the gods, you have a gift for asking the most vexing questions."

"And you have a gift for evasive answers."

"That's how one survives in Rome." I turned to face her, almost in despair. "How *can* I answer that question? Do you think I haven't been searching for an answer? You know I love you."

"But you've never told me you do."

"Didn't I just say it?"

"No, you said that *I* know you love me. That's not the same thing as you simply saying it. Like this." She blinked back tears. "Gaius Pliny, I love you."

Thankful that, in the dark, she couldn't see how wet my eyes were, I said, "Aurora, I love you." Then, from somewhere deep in my heart, other words gushed up, words that I could not suppress, any more than I could have stopped Vesuvius from erupting. "I know now that I have loved you since the first time I laid eyes on you, and I will love you as long as I live."

She reached over and took my hand, sending a warm, aching sensation coursing through my whole body. The urge to take her up to my room was overwhelming.

"I know what you're feeling," she said, her voice growing husky. "I feel the same way. I want the same thing."

"But we can't. We both know we can't." I tried to pull my hand away, but she wouldn't let me. Instead she kissed it and drew it to her breast.

"Why can't we, Gaius?"

"There's another one of your vexing questions."

She moved my hand so that it cupped her breast. "But we both know we can't evade the answer to this one."

·   ·   ·

Marinthus and his servants were too busy cleaning up the dining room to notice us as we hurried through. I didn't see Theodorus. He was probably off being the gods' gift to some woman. When we got up to my room I embraced and kissed her with the eagerness of a man who hasn't eaten for days. She seemed equally hungry. Our garments dropped to the floor. Even with just a single lamp lit, her beauty took my breath away. Forget Praxiteles and his *Venus*. The most beautiful woman on earth was standing right in front of me—from the rise and fall of her perfect breasts as her passion deepened, to her slender waist, to the curve of her hips, and those long, graceful legs.

As she lay down on the bed and I was poised over her, our eyes met. We both knew that, in an instant, we could pass the point that would change our lives forever. This was our last chance to stop. Breathing hard—almost gasping—she arched her back, put her arms around me, and pulled me into her with a moan.

Perhaps it was the years of unacknowledged yearning finally finding an outlet. Or perhaps we knew we weren't likely ever to have another opportunity like this. It was well into the early hours of the morning when we finally lay quietly, breathing deeply, with my arm around her, her head on my shoulder and her hand on my chest, playing with the Tyche ring. I knew she had never been with a man, but she had clearly learned some things from talking with other women in my house.

"Are you sorry we did this?" Aurora asked.

"How can you ask that? I'm just glad Tacitus went back to Rome ahead of us. He would recognize what happened in an instant when he saw us, as clearly as if we were slaves for sale, with placards around our necks listing our virtues and faults."

Aurora propped herself up on one elbow. "And what *are* my faults?"

I kissed her breasts. "That side of your placard would be blank."

"Very good answer. Not at all evasive." She laughed and snuggled closer, if that was possible. "Do you think, by the time we get back to Rome, we can resume some pretense of being master and servant?"

I caressed her hair and kissed her forehead. "We both know we haven't been master and servant for a long time, perhaps never. I just thank the gods that my mother is on her way to Misenum. As keenly as she watches everything—"

"I thought you didn't believe in gods," Aurora said.

I touched the Tyche ring and smiled like the besotted fool I was at that moment. "After tonight I may have to take a different position on that."

She slid her hand slowly down my chest. "Speaking of a different position—"

But before she could finish the gesture or the thought, someone outside shouted, "Fire! Fire!"

·   ·   ·

The yelling grew louder, and we heard someone ringing a bell. We both jumped out of bed. I slipped on my tunic and looked out the window to see a sizeable fire blazing behind the *taberna*.

"It's the shed."

Holding her gown in front of her, Aurora stood beside me and craned her neck out the window. "The shed where the woman's body is?"

"Yes. I need to go down there. You wait here."

"But I want to see—"

"We can't be seen together in the middle of the night. Count to a hundred, then come down. There should be a crowd by then."

By the time I got downstairs people were coming from all directions, including my freedmen, Segetius and Rufinus, and other lodgers at the *taberna* across the road. Marinthus formed them into a line to pass buckets, hauling water from the Tiber. He stuck a bucket in my hand before I could even volunteer.

"Buckets!" he yelled. "Anybody who's got a bucket or anything that will hold water, please bring it."

As soon as Aurora arrived—and she must have counted rapidly—she took a position in the line close to the Tiber. Marinthus' son, Theodorus, stationed himself beside her. A few hours ago that would have bothered me.

The shed was built of stone, with wooden beams supporting the tile roof, and a floor of packed dirt. It was slightly taller than the height of a typical man. The fire we were trying to douse was coming through the roof, sending tiles crashing into the interior. The buckets had to be lifted and the water thrown over the walls.

Our biggest handicap was the small number of buckets, pots, and other containers we had. I heard a crash and a shout from Aurora's end of the line. While waiting for the next bucket to reach me, I looked in that direction, with the flickering light of the fire providing barely enough illumination for that distance. There was some sort of altercation taking place. Theodorus pushed a man out of the line. I heard him say something about a clumsy oaf, but then another bucket found its way into my hands.

We managed to put out the blaze before it could spread to any other buildings and before my hands were rubbed raw. I was relieved that Aurora kept herself modestly in the background. That's our technique when we're investigating: one comes to the fore, draws attention, while the other observes from the background.

Shaking his head slowly, Marinthus surveyed the smoldering remains. "I don't understand how it burned so fast, sir. A fire needs air. There aren't any windows in this shed. I've seen a fire in a closed room smother from the very smoke it produces."

Since it wasn't safe to go into the little building yet, Marinthus and I walked around it. On the back wall I noticed that one stone had been knocked out from the inside. It lay at the foot of the wall.

"That's never been there before, sir," Marinthus said when I called it to his attention.

"Then the fire was no accident."

When we returned to the front, I pointed to the bottom of the door. "There's a worn space under the door, almost a hand deep."

"Yes, sir. We go in and out of here quite a bit, often dragging things."

"That, along with the new hole in the back wall, would create a draft that would give the fire enough air for it to burn."

"Yes, sir. I can see how it would."

The sturdy door was too hot to touch. "Do you have an axe or something we could use to knock the door down?"

In response to his father's call Theodorus brought us a mallet.

"What was all that noise about?" I asked him. "When you pushed that man out of the line."

"The idiot dropped a pot and broke it," Theodorus said, "and he had already dropped one bucket."

"Who was he?"

"I don't know. Never seen him before. A guest at Justus' place, I suppose. He was doing more harm than good. Kept babbling to himself and just getting in the way."

Marinthus, grunting with the effort, pushed the door of the shed in enough to allow us to put our heads through and look inside. In addition to the smoke I smelled burned cheese and flour. The stone walls had suffered little damage. Everything inside, though, was reduced to ashes. In the middle of the shed, partly covered by tiles that had fallen in from the roof, lay a smoldering mass. Only its shape and the odor of charred flesh enabled me to identify it as human remains. The woman's body was so badly burned that I knew immediately I could not hope to recover any more information from examining her.

"As effective as a funeral pyre," I said.

"Yes, sir, and you didn't have to pay for it." Marinthus gave me a congratulatory pat on the back.

I ignored the inappropriate humor and the over-familiar gesture. "It's clear the fire was set inside the shed. Someone must have poured oil over everything."

"I store my extra oil for cooking and lamps out here. It looks like there's several amphoras smashed."

I nodded. "It must have burned for quite a while before it broke through the roof."

"At least the place can be repaired, after it's cleaned out." Marinthus stepped back and surveyed the damage in its entirety. "But who set the fire, sir? And why?"

"With dozens of people trampling around here, there's no hope of finding a clue about *who*. As for the *why*… Have you had anything like this happen before?"

"No, sir. This is a peaceful place, except for the occasional drunk or a dispute over a bill." He lowered his voice. "I suspect this has more to do with…what you were storing in here."

I moved closer to him and spoke softly. "I hate to admit it, but I agree with you. Because of that I'll give you some money to cover the cost of the rebuilding."

"That's very kind of you, sir. So, what are you going to do now?"

I stepped away from Marinthus and brought my voice back to its normal volume, shaking my head as I looked at the burned-out shed. "I don't think there's anything more I can do. I'll post my two men as guards for the rest of the night. If a magistrate arrives from Ostia tomorrow, I'll hand the remains over to him and tell him what I know, which is actually nothing. Then I'm going back to Rome."

"Without finding out who did this?"

"More crimes go unsolved than are solved, I'm afraid." I held my hands up as though surrendering. "I just don't think there's anything else I can do about this one."

"Well, I hope you can sleep for the bit of the night that's left, sir. Thank you—and your lady—for your help."

By the time I got back upstairs Aurora was already in the room. It was sweet to think of it as *our* room, even though we had only a couple of more hours to spend together in it.

"Gaius, I'm so disappointed," she said as soon as I closed the door.

"That wasn't what you said an hour ago."

"No, not about that." She blushed and waved her hand toward the bed. "I heard you say you weren't going to try to find that girl's killer. But you told me you were going to."

I took her by the shoulders and sat her down on the bed. "You know I would not go back on my word to you. The person who set the fire must have some connection to whoever killed her. Someone doesn't want me to be able to examine the body and possibly identify her, which might lead me to the killer."

"Do you think he could still be around?"

"I believe so. I told Marinthus I was giving up in hopes that the person who set the fire would hear me and think he'd gotten away with his crime."

"So you're not giving up?"

"No, I most definitely am not. Beyond talking to the sons of Sextus Tabellius, I'm not sure what I can do, but I'm going to do that much and then—"

I couldn't finish the sentence because Aurora's lips were planted firmly over mine.

·   ·   ·

"Gaius, wake up. Wake up."

Aurora's voice was soft in my ear but insistent. When I reached for her, though, she wasn't lying in the bed next to me. I opened my eyes to find her standing over me, already dressed, much to my disappointment. The earliest glimmer of dawn was coming through the window.

"What—"

"Wake up. I need for you to come to the shed with me."

"The…shed?" What did she want to do in the shed? Something erotic—Oh, yes, the shed. The memory and the smell of smoke hanging in the air jarred my groggy head. "What about the shed?"

"I want to show you something. Something important."

"All right. Give me a minute." Rubbing my eyes, I sat on the edge of the bed and reached under it for the chamber pot. Aurora stepped outside the door. Funny, we had sat side by side in a *latrina* on more than one occasion, covered by our clothing of course, but this must be some new level of intimacy that she wasn't ready for. I didn't understand, especially after last night. She had seen—and touched—anything she would see now.

When I was dressed and had thrown some water on my face from the bowl on the small table—the only other piece of furniture in the room—I joined her on the stairs and followed her out to the shed.

"What's this all about?" I asked.

"I saw something in the shed that you need to see."

I stopped in surprise. "How did you get in there? I posted guards."

She snorted in derision. "Guards who were sound asleep as of a few moments ago." Her face showed her dismay at betraying a fellow servant. "But don't punish them, please."

By the time we got to the shed the first rays of the day's sunlight were visible and both of my freedmen were on their feet. "Good morning, my lord," the man at the door said, unable to stifle a yawn. "Good morning, Aurora."

"Has anyone tried to get in here?" I asked.

"No, my lord. It's been very quiet."

I knew they should be punished, but the only way I could reveal that I knew they'd been asleep was to implicate Aurora, and that I could not do. "You're dismissed," I said. "Get something to eat and… rest a bit. We'll leave as soon as we can."

As they ambled away Aurora said, "It wasn't quiet when I came down here. That man was snoring as loudly as your uncle used to."

I chuckled. When we were children we once sat in the garden outside my uncle's room and laughed at his snoring. We wondered how Aurora's mother could stand to sleep with him.

When Aurora pushed the door of the shed open, a cloud of smoke drifted out. The moisture in the cool morning air kept it close to the ground. As it settled, we fanned it away and stepped into the ruins. "The ashes are still warm," she said. "Be careful."

No sooner had she said the words than I began to feel heat through my sandals, like walking on the floor of a bath.

The wooden shelves on two walls of the shed had collapsed, dumping their contents. The table on which the woman's body was placed had burned more at one end than the other, leaving her lying at an angle, about to slip off the table entirely.

"Why did you come out here?" I asked Aurora.

"I wanted to say good-bye to…to her—whoever she is—in private, and I knew this would be our last chance to examine the site before we disturb things. I moved some of the tiles off her body and then I saw this."

She pointed to a knife protruding from the chest of the charred body.

"Why would someone stab a person who's already dead?" I wondered.

"It's not only that. Look more closely."

Then, in the dim light and through the haze, I saw it—my dolphin insignia embossed on the handle of the knife. "By the gods. That's *my* knife, the one I gave you before we left Rome. How did it get here?"

"I have no idea," Aurora said. "I unstrapped it from my leg when I cleaned up and changed last night, before I came to sit with you on the terrace. That's the last time I saw it."

"That means someone got into your room while we were talking or while we were…"

"Otherwise engaged?"

"Yes, that will do."

Aurora blushed. I could see her face redden even in the gloom. "Oh, no! I hope it was while we were talking on the terrace. I hate to think someone was outside the door while… What would they have heard?"

"What *wouldn't* they have heard?"

"Gaius, now you're embarrassing me."

I kissed her cheek. "Sorry. You were wonderful. It was all wonderful." I felt so free, being able to speak to her at last in such an intimate way, and so odd because I was doing it in such a macabre setting, a place Ovid never would recommend in his *Art of Love*. "But, more to the point, why would somebody take the knife? They must have found it while they were looking for something else. They couldn't have known you had it."

"No. I didn't show it to anyone. I mean, I couldn't dare to."

"Did anyone brush up against you, so they might have felt it?"

She shook her head. "I'm sure of it."

"So what could they have been looking for in that room?"

"If someone knew you had given the room to me, they could have been looking for something of mine or of Crispina's."

I pulled the knife out of the corpse. "All right, let's say they happened upon the knife while they were searching that room. Pure chance. Then why do this?"

"It feels like some kind of message, or warning."

"A message of what? A warning against what?" I looked around at the ruins of the shed. What had someone hoped to accomplish by stabbing and incinerating the body of a headless dead woman? How many times do you need to kill someone? "If they thought this would scare me off, they were badly mistaken. It makes me more determined than ever to find the person responsible."

The sun was fully up now, and light filtered into the shed through what used to be the roof. I looked at the body and the area surrounding it one last time, but in the lingering haze I saw nothing that gave me any hope of unraveling this knot, in spite of my braggadocio.

"I guess that's all we can do here," Aurora said, taking a few steps toward the rear of the shed. "With the fire destroying any clues that—" She gasped.

"What's the matter?"

All she could do was point to the ground. Following her finger, I saw a head.

"Is it hers?" Aurora whispered.

"I don't see how it could be anyone else's."

"How did it get here?"

"I'd wager that the person who started the fire left it here." I stooped and looked as closely as I dared at the charred lump, poking it lightly with my knife. "It must have been on the table with the body but fell off when the table collapsed."

"But that means someone who was at the villa brought it here."

"Perhaps the person who killed her."

.   .   .

I wiped my knife as clean as I could on the grass outside the shed. We made it back upstairs without being noticed and I put the knife in my bag. Aurora filled her bag with her things and all of Crispina's belongings. By the time we had eaten a little something, Marinthus' servant was back from Ostia with a magistrate, who took possession of the woman's blackened remains as reluctantly as if I were asking him to take charge of an overflowing slop jar.

"Why is the head separate from the body?" he asked. Hearing my explanation, he twisted his lip. "That makes this a more complicated matter."

He allowed me to give him a report of what had happened, which his wide-eyed scribe took down as I dictated it. When we were done, I pressed my seal into some wax at the bottom. The magistrate promised to visit the villa where the murder had taken place.

"I'm not sure my jurisdiction extends that far," he said in conclusion, "but I'll look into it." His attitude and his tone were already turned back toward Ostia, where he clearly hoped to be in time for his afternoon bath, followed by a leisurely dinner, where he would regale his companions with the gruesome details of his morning. I hoped he didn't dump the body into the Tiber along the way to lighten his load or invite his friends to gaze at it to gain himself a few moments of celebrity.

Theodorus made certain he was there when Aurora was ready to mount her horse for the trip back to Rome. She accepted his help with a smile. Looking down at his eager face, with admiration smeared over it like oil on a wrestler, I thought, *If only you knew what a lucky bastard I am now. If only you knew....* Happiness—no, utter bliss—does lose a bit of its glow when you can't tell anyone why you're so ecstatic. For the first time, I understood how the initiates of a mystery cult must feel, and yet they can't tell anyone what they've experienced. Aurora wasn't the first woman I'd coupled with. That wasn't the mystery. I was in love with her, and that made all the difference.

When we were far enough away from the *taberna*, Aurora said, "That *mentula* of a magistrate's not going to do anything, is he?"

I looked down to cover my smile at hearing a rare vulgarity from her lips. "No. Not that it really matters at this point. We've gotten all the information we're likely to get from the villa and the woman's body and the neighbors."

"What we need to find is a witness," Aurora said.

"That would be a big help. But Crispina is the only person we know for certain was there, and that may have been her body."

"If it wasn't, then we need to find her. That's the simplest, most obvious solution."

"It's certainly the most obvious," I said, "but the simplest? The woman has disappeared. We don't know if she's still alive, or if Crispina was actually her name. We don't even know if she wanted to disappear. Perhaps whoever took her out to the villa carried her away from there after…whatever happened."

·   ·   ·

During the ride back to Rome Aurora was the model of a servant's decorum toward her master. If anything, she overdid the "my lord" when she spoke to me. I wondered if we would be able to conceal this new development in our relationship from others in the household. Even more, I wondered if I would ever get to spend another entire night with her.

I did not want to be sneaking around, hiding from my mother and, eventually, from my wife. At least we didn't have to encounter either of them for a while. We would have time to settle in to this new development in our relationship. My mother we wouldn't see until the Saturnalia, two months from now. Livilla would expect to see me much sooner than that. I would delay that meeting as long as possible, and I'd make sure Aurora wasn't there whenever it happened.

We dismounted when we entered the city gate and walked the horses to my door. I sent my freedmen to return the horses we had hired for the trip. Aurora and I stood unseen in the recess created by the covered *vestibulum*, not yet knocking on the door. We both knew that, as soon as that door opened, the special moment we'd shared would come to an end. Since no one could see us from the street or from inside the house, we kissed one more time, long and deep.

Demetrius answered my knock and welcomed me back home. Aurora stayed the proper distance behind me as we entered the atrium. No sooner had Demetrius closed the door than I heard a woman ask, "Is that Gaius?"

I gasped. My mother was here! Coming toward me across the atrium!

VII

UNSMILING, MY MOTHER stopped in front of me but did not give me the kiss on the cheek I would normally expect.

"Mother. What…what are you doing here?"

"I live here. At least I hope I still do."

"But you're supposed to be in Misenum. Why aren't you in Misenum?" I addressed her but turned to glare at Demetrius, who could only shrug.

"Because I don't want to go there." She looked from me to Aurora and back again, exhaling a sharp breath. "Humph! Well, I know what you two have been up to."

I heard Aurora take a quick breath behind me.

"Mother, how—"

"Don't think I can't see it on your faces. It's more of that…scary business, isn't it?" She fluttered one hand toward us. "Since you were children, you've sneaked around and pried into people's affairs. And you have this smirk on your faces, like a couple of conspirators who think they've got everyone else fooled."

"Mother—" That seemed to be the only thing I could think to say.

"My lady," Aurora cut in, "forgive me. Your son has done nothing to cause you any concern. He is the model of a Roman gentleman. Always."

Mother looked her up and down. "More's the pity that you're not the model of a Roman slave. But then your mother never was, so why should I expect any more of you?"

"I'm sorry to be such a disappointment to you, my lady." Aurora lowered her head and clasped her hands in front of her. "And I thank you for your patience with me."

All I could give thanks for was that, at that moment, Mother knew she was talking to Aurora, not Monica.

"Just go on to your room," Mother said to Aurora, who looked at me for a nod of approval and made her way to the stairs. Mother watched until she was out of sight, then turned toward the back of the house with the satisfied air of someone who has taken care of a bit of trouble.

Demetrius edged up to me. "I'm sorry, my lord, that I wasn't able to carry out your orders. The only way I could have sent your mother to Misenum would have been to tie her up and throw her into a wagon, as you suggested."

"Well, you know I didn't mean that literally."

"Yes, my lord. But she seemed so anxious about the prospect of the trip that I decided to wait until you returned to see if it really was your wish to upset her that badly."

Of course it wasn't, but if she found out what had happened at Marinthus' *taberna*, she would be ready to banish *me* to Misenum and sell Aurora to a brothel.

⁓

I can't believe it happened. I guess I was brazen, but it seemed the time had come. We were away from here, in a place where we could be alone and where we will never be again. I didn't think through or plan what I might do. I wouldn't have approached him if he was already married.

He knew some things, from other women he's been with, that I hadn't expected, but he seemed satisfied, to put it mildly. I wonder how I compare to other women he has coupled with. I have no basis for comparison with other men, just what I've heard other servant women talk about and what I've read in poets like Ovid. I thought the experience was wonderful—from the first time he kissed my breasts to that moment of ultimate satisfaction!—but I don't know if it was as wonderful as it should have been or could have been.

My mother always said I thought too much and asked too many questions. But I have no one to ask about this. I can't go to other women in the house and say, I've slept with our master and it felt like this. Is that what it should have felt like? He did this and that. Should he have done something else? Something more? Did he do something he shouldn't have? Could I have done something more?

I need to read Ovid again, especially the third book of the Ars Amatoria, *but I'll have to get the copy out of our library without anyone noticing.*

"We're so pleased you could join us tonight, Gaius," Pompeia Celerina said for at least the third time since we began eating. "I wish we could have eaten outside, but with the rain and as chilly as it is…"

"Well, this is the next best thing," I said. "These frescoes make me feel like we're outside." The walls of their *triclinium* were covered with trees, birds, and fruit in vivid colors—some of the most garish artwork I'd ever seen, as overdone as Pompeia's makeup. "I'm going to take a chance and say that you suggested the design."

"Why, yes, I did," Pompeia said, nodding her head with satisfaction. "Thank you. This was all painted shortly before my husband died. I'm sorry you never met him."

"As am I. And I'm sorry it's been so difficult to find an evening that was convenient for both of us."

"We know your days and evenings are filled," Pompeia purred, "what with all your clients and the demands on your time. If you help them as much as you helped us, I wonder that you ever have any free time."

"Will I have this much trouble arranging a dinner—or anything else—with you after we're married?" Livilla said, trying for a suggestive lift of an eyebrow which her youth and innocence only made ludicrous.

"We'll be able to manage a couple of evenings a month, I'm sure." I hoped my smile gave both women the impression that I was joking. They did laugh, but not much.

"Oh, you're terrible sometimes," Pompeia said with a wave of her jewel-laden hand.

For the last three days, since my return from Marinthus' *taberna*, it had taken some of my most resolute evading and cleverest lying to delay this dinner. I had extended invitations to each of the sons of Sextus Tabellius but learned nothing that would help me identify the murdered woman or find her killer. I did encourage them to move forward on selling their father's villa. Once they heard what had happened there, they became eager to get the place off their hands before someone accused them of being involved. But a place with a reputation like that would be hard to sell. They were glad to hear of Lentulus' interest.

On another evening Tacitus invited me to dinner. I took Aurora to attend me. It was our first evening out from under my mother's nose since the night at Marinthus' *taberna* and all the more frustrating because we could do nothing but look at one another, and even that we had to do with the utmost caution.

Eventually, though, I had to give in to the inevitable. Pompeia wanted just the three of us to dine, so we could get better acquainted and discuss plans for the wedding. After the experience Aurora and I had in the *taberna*, I was more determined than ever that there would be no wedding, but, like a deer being driven toward the nets, I could see no way to escape the trap that was closing around me. And I felt the same panic rising in me that I had seen in the eyes of deer when I was hunting.

We were halfway through the main course—a particularly tasty roast pork—when Pompeia's steward entered the *triclinium*. "My lady, forgive me. There is a message for Gaius Pliny. I was told that it's urgent."

I looked at Pompeia apologetically. "I made it clear to my household I was not to be disturbed this evening." I was truly puzzled and worried, but I hesitated to take the note that the steward thrust toward me.

"Certainly you must see what it is," Pompeia said. Meaning, I knew, that *she* couldn't find out what it was until I opened it.

The man handed me a folded piece of papyrus, sealed only with a thumbprint in the wax—Aurora's device. I tried to keep my face impassive, but my eagerness showed in the speed with which I broke the seal.

"What is it?" Livilla asked as I opened the note. "I hope your mother's not ill."

"No, she's not." The message was short: *Crispina is here. Please come at once.* Aurora had written in Latin instead of taking the time to write in the simple code that we typically use and had signed the first three letters of her name.

"I'm sorry, but an emergency has come up at home. I have to leave. I promise you that we will get together again in the next few days. The meal was superb." I sat up to put on my sandals. When I did, Livilla picked up the note.

"*Aur.* That's Aurora, isn't it?"

"Well…yes."

Her soft, childlike face hardened into a dark scowl. "So *I* have to beg and plead for days to get you to come to dinner, but *she* writes one line and you drop everything to rush to her."

I tried to take her hand, but she pulled away. "My dear Livilla, you don't understand. This woman, Crispina, may know something about a murder that I'm investigating, a brutal murder. I know this is rude, but—"

"Rude? It's absolutely insulting." Livilla gathered her gown around her and ran out of the *triclinium* without another word. Her mother, however, more than made up for that dearth.

"Gaius Pliny, you are exhausting my patience," Pompeia said, heaving her bulk off the couch and gathering momentum toward me, like a boulder rolling downhill. Several servants hovered around her, like pebbles being drawn along in the landslide. "Your mother warned me about this girl. She's afraid she might seduce you away from my daughter. I told her I believed you were a man of higher character than that, but now I'm not so sure."

As she drew another breath, like a storm god preparing to continue the onslaught, I bowed and said, "My lady, with all due respect, I don't have time to listen to this blather."

.   .   .

Since it was raining, I had come to Pompeia's house on the Caelian Hill in my litter. The bearers were being fed in the kitchen and weren't ready for my departure. I knew I could make better time on foot anyway, so I told the slave who was guarding the litter to come along when they finished eating. Pulling my sword from its hiding place in the litter, I ran most of the way home, not even thinking that I was alone in the streets of Rome—dressed for dinner, no less. Fortunately, the weather was too foul even for the cutthroats who usually control the city at night.

When I turned the last corner before arriving at my house, I ran into a small group of men. We all brandished weapons before someone said, "Wait! It's Gaius Pliny."

"Tacitus?" I peered into the rain. "What are you doing here?"

"The same thing as you, I imagine. Answering a summons from Aurora."

I caught my breath. "I'm glad you're here. It will save having to repeat what we hear from Crispina."

"And, who knows, I might ask a helpful question or two."

"You have been known to do that. I won't deny it."

As the door of my house came into sight, Tacitus drew back and looked at me. "Are you all right, Gaius Pliny?"

"Of course. I'm soaked to the skin and winded and have just insulted my bride-to-be and my future mother-in-law, but otherwise I'm quite fine. Why do you ask?"

"Since our trip out to Marinthus' *taberna* you seem…different somehow."

Because I knew he would eventually say something, I had rehearsed a response. "It's the murder of that girl. I can't get it off my mind. I still see her whenever I close my eyes."

"Hmm." He sounded like a man considering whether to call someone's bet. "After you were at dinner last night, Julia said she noticed something different about the way you and Aurora looked at each other."

Damn! Were we *that* obvious? "Well, you know Aurora's taken a deep interest in Crispina, too. We share that concern."

Tacitus still looked dubious. In the past he'd told me that he could see Aurora's affection for me and urged me to…couple with her. I'd told him that I would never force myself on a servant woman. While there had been no force involved, I couldn't bring myself to tell Tacitus what had happened. Not yet. When, or if, I might tell him, I didn't know.

"I'm certain I'll feel better when we talk to Crispina. She's the witness we've been waiting for." I pounded on my door.

Aurora was waiting in the atrium, holding a cloth for me to dry off, but I would have to get past my mother, with the ever-present Naomi beside her. Everyone was huddled around the edges of the atrium, to get out of the rain that was blowing through the *compluvium*.

"What is the meaning of this, Gaius?" my mother demanded. "You're not due home for another couple of hours. And why has Monica let some strange, haggard woman and her filthy child come into the house?"

The mention of the child surprised—and relieved—me. At least the boy was still alive. "Aurora did exactly what I wanted her to do, Mother. I need to talk to this woman right away." I walked around her and asked Aurora, "Where is she?"

"I put her in the library, my lord. Clodius is with Hashep and Dakla. I wanted to give them something to eat, but your mother wouldn't let me." Her expression said what her words could not.

"We don't feed every beggar who comes to our door with a child in tow," Mother said, raising her chin and trying to get back in front of me. "As it is, you give far too much to your clients."

"Naomi, get something for this woman to eat at once," I ordered. "Some of whatever you had for dinner will be fine. Bring it to the library. Make sure the boy is fed, too." I turned to Aurora and Tacitus. "Now, let's see what she can tell us." We left my mother working her jaw, like a fish gasping on the shore.

"What is Crispina doing here?" I asked Aurora as we crossed the atrium. Instead of handing me the cloth, she dried my arms and hair as we walked. I realized it was too intimate a gesture, especially in my mother's sight, but I didn't stop her. The touch of her hand sent a warmth coursing through me that knocked off the October chill.

"She is hiding from her husband, my lord, contrary to what she first told me. When I was with her, she heard me mention your name, so she came to Rome and found your house. She didn't know where else she might go and be safe, she said."

"Is her son all right?"

"He seems to be, my lord. The girls are entertaining him."

Hashep and Dakla are the daughters of my steward Demetrius and his Egyptian wife, Siwa. They have perfectly good Greek names, but we have always called them by their Egyptian ones. They are nine and seven.

"I guess he's in good hands," I said. "We should talk to him at some point, though. He's been through a horrible experience."

Crispina was sitting on a scribe's bench in the library, with her head lying on her arms on the table. One hand clutched a small bag, the valuable one Aurora had been looking for in the *taberna*, I assumed. Her clothes were dirty and tattered. When she looked up at me, I saw an attractive woman with a scar on her left cheek and a hint of madness in her eyes, or possibly just extreme hunger. We would soon find out. And I hoped we would find out who the murdered girl was.

"This is my master, Gaius Pliny," Aurora told her.

"He's the one you talked about," Crispina said. "The one who's going to marry the skinny little girl?"

Aurora turned an alluring shade of red. "Yes, he is. And this is his friend, Cornelius Tacitus. They can help you."

Crispina shook her head. "I don't think anybody can help me, sirs, but thank you for tryin'." Her speech was that of a woman with little, if any, education.

"We need to hear your story," I said. "Then we'll see what we can do. We know something awful happened at Sextus Tabellius' villa."

"He kilt my daughter. That's what happened." She put her hands over her face, as though trying to blot out something she would never be able to forget, like me trying to forget the eruption of Vesuvius.

"Who killed her?" I knew she didn't mean Tabellius. He was long-since dead.

"My husband, Popilius. Clodius Popilius. He tied her to that wheel and…"

I put a hand on her arm. "He did that to his own daughter?"

"No. She was my daughter by my first husband."

"Please start at the beginning," I said, sitting down across the table from her. Tacitus pulled up a chair at the end of the table and Aurora sat on the bench beside Crispina, putting an arm around her. Under the table her foot touched mine.

Crispina ran her fingers through her disheveled hair and wiped away tears. "I'm not sure where the beginnin' is. You see, Popilius wanted to marry me almost twenty years ago, but my father and me chose another man, Fabius Albinus. He died ten years ago, and I discovered that he'd gambled away ever'thin' we had, even the pittance I inherited when my father died. We were never rich, but when he died I had nothin'. I had to marry somebody if my daughter and me was goin' to survive."

After a soft knock on the door, Naomi entered with a bowl of stew, some bread, and a jug of wine on a tray. Placing them on the table, with

Crispina's thanks, she stood back by the door until I said, "Have you fed the boy?"

"Yes, my lord."

"Then that will be all. And close the door behind you." I wondered if she had seen where Aurora's foot was.

Once Naomi was out of the room, Crispina dipped a piece of bread into the stew and bit into it, closing her eyes with a sigh of relief. "I've not ate for two days. Anything I could find I give to my son."

"How did your first husband die?" Tacitus asked.

Crispina wiped her mouth with the back of her hand, then wiped that on her tunic. "Our farm is near the coast. He fell off some rocks into the sea and drowned."

Or killed himself in despair, I thought. *Or was pushed by people to whom he owed money…or by someone who wanted his wife.* The arch of Tacitus' eyebrow told me those possibilities, or similar ones, had occurred to him as well. Though she was neither elegant nor young any more, the woman across the table from me was attractive, still slender, with a square face with well-defined features, and must have been quite lovely ten or more years ago. I had no difficulty believing that a man could become obsessed with the idea of having her.

"When Fabius' body was recovered," Crispina continued after another bite of bread and stew, "I started to make arrangements for the funeral. That's when I discovered I didn't have no money. But Popilius stepped in and paid for ever'thin', like he was a member of the family."

"Is Popilius wealthy?" I asked. In some rural villages, a man could be reckoned as well-off with only a fraction of my resources or Tacitus'.

"I never knew him to be, but he had 'nough to give Fabius a nice funeral, with some hired mourners, even."

"Is that why you married him?" Tacitus asked. "Out of gratitude?"

"Like I said, sir, I had to marry somebody or turn to whorin' to keep me and my daughter from starvin' to death. And Popilius still wanted to marry me, even though I rejected him the first time."

"Why did you chose Fabius over him?" I felt myself beginning to shiver beneath my wet clothes.

"My father and me thought Fabius'd be a better provider. And Popilius has always been given to strange moods and whims. Ever'body in our village knew he was… Well, you never knew what to expect of him."

"So, unpredictable? Unstable?" Tacitus asked. I sat back and let him take charge, just to see what he had learned from me.

"Yes, sir. Them's the right words. Only, maybe a little more so. He claimed he was destined for bigger things than just bein' a farmer in some little pigsty of a village."

"That must have made him popular with his neighbors," Tacitus said.

"Actually, sir, there was a small group of men—mostly lazy louts—who looked to him as a leader of some sort."

Doctors would say Popilius' humors were out of balance. Others might say a god had inflicted madness on him, like Hera did to Heracles. Whatever the cause, I could imagine how he might have nursed his disappointment when Crispina married Fabius Albinus and plotted—perhaps for years—to get rid of her husband. Maybe he encouraged Fabius' gambling so that Crispina would have to look to someone for support when her husband was gone. He might even have been the one to whom Fabius had lost his money. And he seemed to have some delusions that he was a leader of men.

"You called him a farmer. He did the plowing?" Tacitus asked.

"Yes, sir. We have a couple of servants on the place, but Popilius did a lot of the work hisself."

My eyes met Tacitus'. SATOR—the plowman.

"That's the beginning of the story," I said. "Let's move on to the middle part now."

She looked puzzled—not well-versed in Aristotle's literary theory, I suppose.

"I mean, in general, what happened after you married Popilius and what led him to kill your daughter?"

"Well, in gen'ral we was all right. He loves me, I know, but in a way that scares me sometimes. And I come to realize he hated Fabia 'cause she was the reminder of me bein' with Fabius."

"Did he harm her?" Tacitus asked.

"Not in the way you prob'ly mean. He was cold and harsh to her, though. She always knew she wasn't his."

There are so many stories of the sufferings of stepchildren. It's usually the step*mother*, though, who is the guilty party.

"Things got better when I give him a son. When Fabia was ready to be married, I thought we could get her out of the house and we'd be happier after that. But he refused to find her a husband."

"Why?" I asked. That was one of the most basic duties of a father, even a stepfather.

"He said he didn't want Fabius' line—his seed—to survive into another generation. And if Fabia had a child, he knew I would look on it as mine and Fabius' grandchild. He told me he'd kill her before he'd let her marry."

And what if he found out she was pregnant without being married? I thought. *Carrying the hated Fabius' seed into the next generation.*

"How old was Fabia when you married Popilius?" Aurora asked.

"She was seven."

"So that would make her seventeen when…"

Crispina nodded and began to rock and keen shrilly. Aurora hugged her more tightly.

When she seemed to be in control of herself again I said, "You saw Popilius kill your daughter. Is that your testimony?"

"Yes, sir."

"Was your son there?" Aurora asked.

Crispina shook her head quickly. "He spared the boy that. He was in another part of the house."

"Why did Popilius…kill the girl in…such a bizarre fashion?" I asked.

"'Cause of that riddle that was scratched on the wall."

"I don't understand," I said, but what else could she be talking about?

"In Marinthus' *taberna* there's some letters in a square—"

"The ROTAS square?" I reached over to the next table where I had left a copy of the puzzle for my scribe Phineas to ponder. "This?"

"Yes, sir. That looks like it. I know a few letters, but I can't read."

"This is an exact copy. What does it have to do with Popilius killing your daughter?"

"Well, a month or so past we went to Rome—the four of us—to see the games. On the way back we stopped at Marinthus' place for a drink. Popilius saw that thing and heard some men talkin' about what it might mean. One of 'em—some sorta wild-eyed man the others called a prophet—said the only way to understand it was to figure out what *that* line means." She pointed to the AREPO line. "He said it would only be understood by the one it was intended for. Popilius made a copy of it and worried over it for days after we got home. A few days ago he said he'd solved it."

"Solved it?"

"Yes, sir. He knew what that line meant and what he had to do. He wrote it down. He didn't know I took this." She pushed the bag across the table to me.

Tacitus leaned toward me as I opened the bag and pulled out and unrolled a piece of papyrus with the square written at the top. Beside it were the letters SPQR and the words SENATUS POPULUSQUE ROMANUS, then DM and DIS MANIBUS. Below that were various interpretations of the AREPO line, assuming the letters stood for words, as was the case in SPQR, DM, and any number of other phrases. The last one read AD REG EXCID POPIL OPT.

"By the gods," Tacitus said. "Does that mean what it seems to?"

I nodded. "*Ad Regis Excidium Popilius Optatus.* 'Popilius has been chosen to destroy a king.'"

"What on earth does that mean?" Tacitus said. "What king?"

"Domitian," Crispina said in a whisper. "He believes he's bein' sent by the gods to kill Domitian."

VIII

NO ONE in the room except Crispina dared to breathe. She broke into tears again.

"You can't mean what you just said," I told her.

"But I do, sir. He's plannin' to kill—"

Aurora clapped her hand over the woman's mouth. "Please, don't say another word. We heard you. You don't have to repeat it. We don't want you to repeat it."

"How does he intend to…accomplish this plan?" I asked.

"He says he don't know yet. He just knows he has to do it. 'It's my destiny and the gods will show me a way.' Them's his very words. That's why he sacrificed Fabia that way, to get the gods' help, like…like…that story with them long names and the long war."

"Like Agamemnon sacrificing Iphigenia," Tacitus said.

"Yes, sir. That's the one."

"A goddess substituted a deer for Iphigenia at the last moment."

"There warn't no such interference in this case."

"And why does he think he's been called by the gods to do this?" I asked.

"He's actin' for the people, he says. His name—Popilius—he says it comes from *populus*, the people. He's goin' to cut off the head of Rome, just like he cut off that poor child's head."

"Would you say your husband is a madman?" Tacitus asked, folding his hands on the table in front of him. His voice was the same as if he were asking about the color of the man's hair.

Crispina hesitated at first, then nodded. "I think that's fair to say."

"And yet he has followers?"

"Yes, sir. At the villa there was six men with him. I don't know if there's any others."

"How did Popilius get you and your son out there?" I asked.

"He left our farm one day while I was at the market. When I got home my son told me he had took Fabia and said I wasn't to try to find him. But I couldn't let him take my daughter, could I? I knew how much he'd been thinkin' on that square and what he'd written about it, so I figured he was goin' back to Marinthus' place. All I could do was go there. This girl was so kind to help me." She patted Aurora's arm. "I'm sorry I couldn't tell you the truth, dear. I thought it would scare you off, and I needed help."

"It's all right," Aurora said. "You did what you had to."

I had to admire the woman's courage. In spite of a warning from a man she knew to be unbalanced and having only limited resources herself, she was determined to save her child.

Crispina took a deep breath and continued. "Two of Popilius' men saw me at the *taberna*. They come to see the square for themselves—like it was some kinda holy place—and they reco'nized me. The next day a man drivin' a *raeda* come to fetch me and showed me my daughter's necklace. I had to go with him."

"I won't ask you to describe what happened," I said. "I'm sure that horrible sight will always be with you. You were tied to a post, weren't you, and forced to watch?"

Crispina nodded, giving way to another flood of tears. A shelf behind us held cloths that my scribes use to wipe the ink off their hands. Aurora found a clean one and gave it to Crispina, then held her again.

"Did he tell you why he did it, other than his hatred of your first husband?"

"He said he was goin' to cut off the head of Rome. He told his men he wanted them to see that he would stop at nothin', once he set his mind to somethin'. And he said by helpin' him do this, they were all guilty, but they would all share in the glory."

"How did they help him?"

"They tied her up and gagged her. And they… Oh, gods! They raped her." She collapsed into more tears. Aurora pulled her to her shoulder and let the poor woman sob.

As I watched her shoulders heave, I felt dissatisfied. Somehow the woman's story seemed incomplete. And yet she was in such obvious distress that I didn't want to push her too far.

"I have just a couple of more questions," I said, "then we'll let you clean up and get some sleep."

Aurora frowned at me. "My lord—"

I held up a hand to stop her. "How did you get free from the post?"

"I rubbed my hands up and down 'til the ropes come loose." She held out her hands to show me the redness on her wrists. "Then I found my son and we just started runnin'."

"Do you know what happened to Fabia's head?"

"Gaius Pliny!" Tacitus interjected. "Don't keep dragging the poor woman back into that horror."

"All right. That's enough for now," I said. "Aurora, help her clean herself up and get her another tunic. Put her in a room near yours. After she's had some sleep, we can talk again." I laid a hand on Crispina's arm. "You must not tell anyone else what you've told us. Not *anyone*. Do you understand?"

She nodded and Aurora helped her up and out of the room.

.   .   .

As soon as the door was closed Tacitus said, "I'm glad I was here. I never would have believed you if you'd told me what she said."

I got up and started to pace around the library. "But something's not right. She said nothing about Fabia being with child and stabbed in the belly. That doesn't seem to have anything to do with killing a king."

"Perhaps Popilius wanted to symbolize that there would be no successor in the line."

"But what about the head? It wasn't there when we arrived and yet it reappeared in the shed when the girl's body was burned."

Tacitus nodded. "That means somebody removed it from the villa."

"But Crispina says she freed herself, got her son, and ran. Did she pick up the head?"

"That seems highly unlikely."

I sat back down at the table. "That's why I want to question her again. Some things just don't make sense."

Tacitus picked up the papyrus Crispina had given us and looked over it again. "And this is one of them."

I nodded. "This most of all. She can't be serious about this plot, can she? How does some raving lunatic with a handful of followers plan to kill…a certain person?"

"He hatched a rather elaborate plan to kill poor Fabia. And I suspect he killed Crispina's first husband, don't you?"

"Oh, I'm sure of it. It's clear he's patient and clever."

"Madmen often are. He might be able to—"

"How could he? He was attacking people who had no one to defend them. Dom—that is, his next intended victim has guards on all sides."

"But Popilius now believes he's the messenger of some god. He's convinced a few others it's true. Some men have that ability. Remember the fellow in the province of Asia who convinced hundreds of people that he was Nero returned from the dead. And there was even a false Germanicus after he died. A man with that kind of persuasive power can be hard to stop." Tacitus leaned back in his chair with a trace of a smile on his lips.

I sat down again and leaned toward him. "And you wouldn't mind if he *wasn't* stopped, would you?"

Tacitus slid the papyrus across the table. "I'm not saying anything. But I think it's inevitable that someone will kill Domitian—and I'm not afraid to say his name."

"What would happen then?" A thought flashed into my mind like a lightning bolt striking a roof. "Would Agricola seize power? Is that what you're hoping for?"

Tacitus waved me away. "Having my father-in-law as *princeps* would be no improvement over what we have now. As good a man as he is, though, I think Agricola would use his influence to guide us to a restoration of the Republic if Domitian were…out of the way."

"Are *you* mad? The Republic has been dead for over a hundred years. No one alive today would know how to make it work."

"We figured it out the first time. We could do it again. It might be hard, I grant you, as hard as a woman giving birth—"

"Women sometimes die giving birth. Choose your analogies more carefully. There's no guarantee Rome would survive if…Domitian were…assassinated." It was hard to say the words, even in a place that was as safe as any I was likely to find.

"We survived after Caligula was killed," Tacitus said. "And after Nero."

"But we didn't restore the Republic."

"No, and that was where we made the mistake." Tacitus picked up Popilius' scribbling again. "Are you going to try to stop him?"

"I think we have to, whatever we think of Domitian. If he succeeds, it will mean chaos. If he gets anywhere near Domitian but doesn't succeed in killing him, it will just make Domitian more suspicious of everyone. He'll lash out, you know he will."

Tacitus stood and sighed heavily. "I can't say I wish you luck, but I can't say I don't."

"Aren't you going to help me?"

"I'm going to have to think about that."

"Are you going to tell Agricola? Put him on alert?"

"I'll have to think about that, too."

A profound silence rose between us, like a curtain going up at the end of a scene in a play to allow the actors a chance to get off the stage. But neither of us moved.

"I'm sorry I can't share your dedication to an ideal," I finally said. "I do admire it, no matter how old-fashioned and ill-fated it may be."

"And I admire your pragmatism—your realism might be a better word. Perhaps we can't restore the Republic, but I see no reason why we shouldn't try." He put a hand on my shoulder. "I promise you one thing, Gaius Pliny. This is not the end of our friendship."

I covered Tacitus' hand with mine. "I certainly hope not." But I was deeply hurt that a man I'd come to trust and, yes, love would abandon me at this moment.

"When we got back from Naples, I had word that my brother is not doing well," Tacitus said as he drew away from me and reached for the door. "I haven't seen him in almost a year, so I'm going to make that trip. Because of our friendship I postponed it to support you in your prosecution against Regulus and for our ride out to Marinthus' *taberna*. I don't think I should wait any longer. And southern Gaul is lovely at this time of year. I might be there for a month or so."

Tacitus' younger brother was born with some abnormalities which make it necessary for someone to care for him at all times. My uncle mentioned his condition in a section on human oddities in his *Natural History*, so I had heard of Tacitus before I met him. His brother, who has the mind of a child, lives on Tacitus' estate in the south of Gaul, not far from the coast. Everyone is surprised he's lived as long as he has.

"Julia's going to visit her mother," he continued, "so I'm going to send those clowns Segetius and Rufinus over here. I don't want them in my house if I'm not there to supervise them."

"That's fine. I'll put them to work cleaning the *latrina*. Have a safe journey."

With his hand on the latch, Tacitus turned back to me. "Before you wade too far into what could be a treacherous stream with all sorts of slippery rocks under the water, remember that this interpretation of AREPO has been put forward by a murderous madman under the influence of some self-deluded 'prophet.' The letters—if they stand for anything at all, which I doubt—could have dozens of meanings. The *R* could be for Roma. The *P* could be for Publius or Poppaeus.... Or how about this?"

He stepped to the table, picked up a pen, dipped it into an inkwell, and wrote on a scrap of papyrus: AD REGIS EXCIDIUM PLINIUS OPTATUS. Then he crossed out REGIS and under it wrote ROMAE. "You could destroy Rome, Gaius Pliny."

⋅   ⋅   ⋅

I was still sitting in the library, cutting up the papyrus Tacitus had written on—I dared not leave something that incriminating lying around—when Aurora came in with one of my tunics over her arm. "Crispina is saying good night to Clodius," she said, "and I showed her where her room will be." She glanced around. "Oh, has Tacitus left?"

"Yes. He's going to see his brother in Gaul."

She let that sink in. "So…he's not going to help you in…this matter?"

"No. As you know, he wouldn't shed a tear if something happened to Domitian. He would sound more like Cicero exulting in the death of Caesar."

"Well, we can work on it then," she said brightly, "like we did when we were children."

"My darling, if we pursue this, we could be risking our lives, maybe even more. I can't ask you to do that."

She handed me the tunic. "You're going to risk getting sick if you don't get on some dry clothes."

As absorbed as I'd been in Crispina's story, I'd almost forgotten how damp and uncomfortable I was. I thought the chill came from what I was hearing, not what I was wearing. "Yes. Thank you." I stood and took the tunic from her. "There's no one outside the door, is there?"

"I didn't see anyone on my way in."

I peeled off my wet dinner garb and slipped on the dry garment. Aurora did not turn her back. Instead she smoothed the wrinkles so the tunic would hang properly and gave me a quick peck on the cheek.

"We probably shouldn't do things like that," I said. "You know my mother can sneak up on you without any warning. And Naomi's as silent as a shadow."

"As you wish, my lord," she said, teasing me with a smile and a deep bow. When she was standing up straight again, I took her face in my hands and kissed her. Outside in the atrium someone dropped something. Aurora stepped back and took a breath.

"I guess that's how it has to be for us from now on," I said, "frightened at every sound."

"We can't go back, and I wouldn't if we could." She turned Popilius' papyrus so she could read it. "Gaius, you know I'm not going to let you get any more deeply involved in this…whatever it is…without my help. I got you into it to begin with. Please don't use your authority over me to make me step back."

I smiled. "Do I still have any authority over you?"

"You certainly do…legally."

"I guess I'll have to be content with that."

We sat down on opposite sides of the table and Aurora began to play with the pieces of papyrus I had cut up.

"You don't usually waste scraps like this. What was written on it?"

"Something no one needs to see." I swept the pieces away from her and gathered them on my side of the table. Fetching a lamp, I began to burn them. "If we're going to work on this puzzle together, what do you make of Crispina's story?"

Before she could say anything there was a knock on the door. Without waiting for an invitation, Naomi stuck her head in. "Your mother sent me to see if you need anything, my lord." She didn't have to add, *And to see what you're doing.*

"No. We're almost finished here."

"Yes, my lord." She withdrew, leaving the door partly open. I walked over and closed it. By the time I'd done that, I was sure, my mother knew that Aurora and I had been seen sitting together.

"What do *you* think of Crispina's story, Gaius?" Aurora asked as I returned to the table.

I sat down next to her, with my shoulder touching hers. "It may be the most bizarre thing I've ever heard. But, if it's true, it could rock Rome to its foundations. I don't see how Popilius can succeed, though."

Aurora leaned against me and picked up Popilius' papyrus. "It might succeed *because* it's so outlandish. Agricola, or someone like him, wouldn't be able to kill Domitian because Domitian's forces would resist him, but Popilius might be able to slip into the palace like a little mouse that nobody notices. Or he could get close to him in the Amphitheatre or the Circus Maximus, just one more face in a crowd. A few of his henchmen could create a diversion and he could be within arm's reach of Domitian before anyone sees him. Doesn't Livy say that's what happened when the king Lucius Tarquinius was killed?"

"Livy admits that most of those stories from the early days of Rome are more suited to poetry than to history. Orators use them as *exempla*, but I wouldn't want to base a course of action on them." I sat back down at the table and looked at the piece of papyrus that Popilius had scribbled on. "I need to talk to someone who has Domitian's ear."

"One of his secretaries? The captain of the Praetorians?"

I drew back in horror. "By the gods, no! If I even hinted to one of them that I knew about a possible assassination plot, I'd be tortured until they squeezed everything I know out of me."

"But you don't know anything."

"That wouldn't matter. I would be arrested and never seen again. No, I need to talk to someone who has Domitian's ear but who has no power to arrest me—a conniving scoundrel whose only interest is his own advancement."

Aurora's shoulders slumped. "You mean Regulus, don't you?"

"Who else?"

"You want to talk to *Regulus*? After you humiliated him in court like that? I doubt he'll even let you in his house. He's more likely to set his Molossian hounds after you. And he certainly won't come here for a nice convivial dinner."

"That's why I need to meet him somewhere else, on neutral ground. And I know just where that will be. And now, my dear, I need a little time to myself. I've got a lot to sort out."

"Of course. I'll go see if Clodius is all right. He wanted to sleep in the same room with Hashep and Dakla. Is that all right with you?"

"I have no objection. He didn't want to sleep with his mother?"

"No, and she didn't ask to have him with her."

"That's strange, considering what they've been through these last few days."

"There's something odd about this whole family. I hope we don't come to regret that I brought them into our lives."

"You were trying to help someone in need. Whatever happens, I can't blame you for that. We can never foresee all the consequences of even the best of our deeds."

.   .   .

Aurora had barely left the library, leaving the door partly open, when I heard her say in surprise, "Oh, good evening, my lady." I thought she had run into my mother, but I couldn't hear the other voice distinctly.

"Yes, he's in the library," Aurora said. "Shall I—"

She didn't say any more. I braced myself for another intrusion, another tirade from my mother. Nothing could have surprised me more than to see Livilla step into the room. She had changed from her dinner gown into a light blue *stola* and a dark blue cloak, drawn up over her head to protect her from the rain.

"Good evening, Gaius. I hope I'm not disturbing you." Her voice, always soft, was barely a whisper. The redness in her eyes told me that she had been crying.

"Not at all." I jumped to my feet and held out my hand to her, but she drew back. "Livilla, what's the matter?"

"I have something to say, Gaius, and I can't wait until a more opportune time."

"Please, sit down. Do you want something to drink?"

She remained standing and dabbed at her eyes with the edge of her cloak. "No. I just want to say this and be on my way." She took a deep breath. "I do not want to marry you, Gaius."

"What? Why—"

"The reason is quite simple. I've seen the affection—no, the devotion—you have for Aurora. It was auspicious, I suppose, that I met her coming out of this room a moment ago."

"She's…she's a servant. We've known each other for fifteen years." *As long as you've been alive*, I thought. It didn't take an oracle to see that this conversation wasn't likely to end well.

"Don't take me for a fool, Gaius." Her voice betrayed more sadness than anger. "There's a great deal more to it than that. Your face lit up like a beacon when you got that message from her at dinner tonight."

"We're working on a puzzling case." I picked up the piece of papyrus Crispina had shown us. "It looked like she had some important information."

"I appreciate your trying to spare my feelings." Livilla drew up her small, slender frame as much as she could. "You don't have to love me in order to marry me. I didn't expect you to. My father never loved my mother, and their marriage lasted twenty years. Like him, you are a kind and thoughtful man. I know you would never do anything to hurt me—not intentionally—but you have no idea how much you hurt me tonight."

"I'm truly sorry. You must hate me."

"No. I envy her. I don't love you, although I'm sure I could learn to. No matter how we feel about one another, I could live happily with you, but I won't live in the same house with the woman you *do* love."

"Livilla, please—" I took a step toward her, but she moved toward the door.

"I've thought about what I should do. I could marry you and demand that you sell her or send her to another of your estates, but that would only make you miserable, and I would be miserable in turn because you would hate me. I don't want to punish you or antagonize you, just release you."

I started to protest, but she reached out, put a finger on my lips, and shook her head.

"I don't know how you will ever work things out so you can be with Aurora, but I hope you will find that happiness." She stretched up to kiss me lightly on the cheek and flashed a tearful smile. "I won't tell my mother the real reason why I'm doing this. You may tell your mother whatever you like. Now, I know you're enough of a gentleman that you won't heave a great sigh of relief until I'm out of sight."

She turned and ran out of the room.

I know Gaius hates it when servants try to overhear conversations that aren't any of their business, but after our experience at Marinthus' taberna, I feel I have a right to know certain things. I thought, once Livilla left, that I might go back in and continue my conversation with Gaius about Crispina and the ROTAS *square.*

But Livilla was in tears when she ran out of the library and Gaius closed the door. I can't believe he would have told her he wanted to end the engagement. What did they talk about? I don't want her to be hurt.

Livilla and I have more in common than she probably realizes. Like all women in Rome, it is our fate to be controlled by some man. Our fathers rule over us until we're married or—in my case—sold into slavery. Just as Medea says in Euripides' play, if we are fortunate, we find a husband, or a master, we can tolerate. Many husbands think they are our masters. In either case, a man has control of our bodies.

What they cannot control is our feelings. Even if we have to keep them bottled up, they are ours.

IX

BY MIDDAY the next day, accompanied by half a dozen servants, I was outside the Baths of Titus, one of Martial's regular haunts. Hastily built at the bottom of the Esquiline Hill to celebrate the opening of the nearby Flavian Amphitheatre a few years ago, it already shows its need for repair. In addition to its physical decrepitude, it has gained a reputation as the most disreputable bath in all of Rome, becoming little more than the largest brothel in the city. Assaults and murders are almost daily occurrences here. Domitian—in spite of a string of moralizing decrees forbidding castration of slaves, excessive spending on dinners, and so on—had made no effort to clean it up. Some say he wants its unsavoriness to be associated in the public mind with his deceased brother's name.

Although this is the public bath closest to my house, I have been inside it only once, and then only out of dire necessity, because I needed to get into the ruins of Nero's Golden House, which lie beneath the bath. But the depravity of those who frequent the place makes them a natural audience for the most risqué of Martial's poems. He tells me that he garners dinner invitations and other, less desirable, overtures every time he reads his work here.

The day was proving warm and humid after last night's rain. Crowds of men played games on the "boards" scratched into the steps of the bath. Keeping one eye on a hotly contested game of *latrunculus*, I hoped to catch Martial on his way into the building, and I was fortunate. He came along only a short time after I arrived.

"Why, Gaius Pliny, this is most unexpected," he said as he responded to my signal to join me. "And most welcome."

"Good day, Valerius Martial. I hope you're well." He is a robust man, whose physique and straight dark hair make him stand out from the foppish, well-oiled habitués of Titus' baths.

"I am well," he said. "I am, though I'm still smarting from the insult you offered me at the beginning of the month."

"How did I insult you?" I hoped I hadn't, because Martial can repay an affront by spearing a person on his epigrams, like a fisherman with his trident, and holding him up to flop and gasp, for display and ridicule.

"One morning, on your way to court, just before you were doused by a chamber pot, I gave you a copy of my newest book, and you invited me to dinner. Then you left town. I was told you went to Naples." He stuck out his lip, as though pouting. "I've had people go to some lengths to avoid hearing me read, but never quite that far."

"It was urgent business, I assure you."

"Have you had a chance to read my poems?"

I was afraid he would ask. At the moment I didn't even know where the damn book was. "I enjoyed them very much."

He cocked his head. "Any particular one a favorite?"

"I would be hard-pressed to choose." I wanted to get off this subject. "But I do apologize for not being there to greet you at dinner. You did attend, didn't you?"

"Yes, I did."

"I hope you were treated well."

He shook his head. "Your mother put me on a couch so far toward the back of the room that my feet were hanging out the door."

"I am truly sorry." That was even closer than I would have placed him to my table. The man amuses me, and—for the sake of his relationship to Lorcis—I have helped him on occasion, but I would rather not have him around. I hold him on the fringe of my *clientela*, not someone to whom I would grant friendship, my formal *amicitia*, just someone who can be useful and entertaining now and then, if I'm in a salacious mood. "I promise I'll invite you over another time and try to atone for the insult. But right now I need to ask a favor of you."

"And what would that be?"

I put an arm around his shoulder and drew him closer to me so I could lower my voice. "I need for you to arrange a meeting for me with Regulus."

He drew back, his face looking like he had bitten into something that didn't taste at all like he'd expected. "Why don't you knock on his door, or send a servant to ask him?"

"It has to be a meeting no one can know about or possibly eavesdrop on."

He arched an eyebrow. "And you want me to play host at my farm."

"You're well ahead of me."

"My livelihood, Gaius Pliny, depends on my being able to anticipate what people of your class are thinking." Though not a poor man, Martial had no stripe on his tunic.

"Can you arrange it?"

"Since you didn't rub my nose in the fact that you gave me the place—or rather gave it to Lorcis—yes, I'll see what I can do. When would you like for this meeting to take place?"

"Tomorrow, if at all possible, by midday."

"Hmm. Sounds urgent. What shall I say is the purpose of this meeting?"

"I can't tell you what it's about. All I can say is that it is indeed urgent."

"Are there any special conditions you want to impose?"

I hadn't thought that far ahead, but I knew the most important one. "Ask him to keep his retinue as small as possible. Tell him he should bring one other person to be in the room with him, and I will bring one. They should be people that we trust absolutely."

I already knew that, for me, that person would be Aurora. I would have chosen her even if Tacitus were available.

"And Lorcis and I should arrange to be elsewhere?"

"She doesn't want to see her former master again, does she?"

"I doubt it. She named our largest hog Regulus. I know she's looking forward to slaughtering him, though she may castrate him first."

I flinched at the word, as most men do. Lorcis had been mistreated by Regulus, even worse than slave women are often mistreated by heartless masters. I hoped she could be satisfied with a symbolic revenge.

"Very well, then," I said. "Come to dinner tonight and let me know what you've been able to arrange."

·   ·   ·

When I returned to the house the women were finishing their baths. In my house, as in most homes with their own baths, the women take their turn in the late morning, allowing them time to prepare lunch and leaving the room free for the men in the afternoon. In the houses of Domitian's most devoted sycophants men and women now bathe together, a practice which the *princeps* recently introduced in the public baths.

My *topiarius*, appropriately named Melanchthon, was pruning shrubbery in the garden, a job his father did for my uncle for years. Aurora and Crispina were sitting by the fishpond in the middle of the garden. Crispina, wearing a clean gown, with her hair combed and arranged, did not look like the madwoman she had seemed to be last night. Aurora stood when I approached them.

This was the first time I'd seen Aurora today. I had stayed in my room for the morning, writing and wondering when my mother's and Pompeia's wrath would fall on me because I had driven Livilla away. The relief I felt was largely offset by the knowledge that I would be facing serious consequences for a long time to come. I wished I knew whom she had told about her decision. What reason had she given?

What did this mean for Aurora and me? From the look she gave me, I could see that she wanted to ask me about Livilla's visit the previous night but knew she had no right to bring up the subject.

For now I had to focus on the problem I might be able to do something about. "How are you feeling today?" I asked Crispina.

"I'm better, sir. Thank you for yer kindness." Although she looked refreshed, her voice was flat and lifeless, her gaze fixed somewhere beyond me. "I'll ne'er be right ag'in, but you've helped me a great deal a'ready."

Aurora patted the woman's shoulder. "I told her that you had made arrangements for a funeral for Fabia, my lord."

I trusted that Aurora would not have told her about the fire in the shed and the knife—my knife—in her dead daughter's chest. We should spare the poor woman as much heartache as possible. Her glance reassured me.

"That was most gen'rous of you, sir," Crispina said. "I won't be imposin' on your hospitality much longer. We'd best be leavin'. I think by tomorrow at the latest."

"You don't need to be in a hurry," I said. "Stay and rest for a few days. You and your son need some time to recover from what you've been through."

She took my hand and kissed it. "Oh, sir, you've been so kind. I just didn't know where I might go and be safe."

"Do you think your husband would harm the boy?"

"I didn't think so, sir. But I ne'er would've thought he'd do what he done to Fabia, no matter how he felt about her." She raised her hands, then dropped them helplessly back in her lap. "I just don't know what he's capable of."

I took her chin and raised it. That seemed to be the only way to get her to look at me. "Don't despair. I'm going to protect you and your son. And I'm going to do everything I can to find your husband and stop his mad plan. Now, get something to eat and don't worry about staying here a while longer. You're quite welcome."

I actually wanted her to stay because I needed to talk to her again about Popilius. Whatever she could tell me about him might help me devise a strategy against him. Someone who knows the working of your opponent's mind can be as helpful to you as an extra cohort of troops. But can one ever fathom the mind of a madman? Success in a venture of this sort depended on being able to predict, to some degree, what my opponent might do. An unbalanced mind like Popilius' was likely to be entirely *un*predictable.

Before I could turn away, Crispina said, "Forgive my boldness, sir, but last night, as I was on my way to my room after I'd said g'night to my boy, I saw a young lady comin' out of your lib'ry. Pretty little slip of a thing. Was that your bride-to-be?"

"Yes, it was." I bristled at the intrusion. *In a double sense,* I thought. *It was Livilla and she* was *my bride-to-be.*

"She looked right upset. I hope there's no hard feelin's between you."

"We had some matters to talk about."

"Don't let nobody come between the two of you, sir, if I may offer my advice." She looked askance at Aurora.

"I'm always eager to hear unsolicited advice," I said, uncertain if she knew the meaning of the adjective.

"Yes, it's a terrible thing when somebody interferes between a man and a woman. A terrible thing."

"I'm sure we all agree on that," I said. "Now, if you're up to it, I need to ask you about one more thing."

"Certainly, sir."

"Did you know that your stepdaughter was carrying a child?"

"A child? Fabia? Sir, she was hardly more than a child herself. What makes you think—"

"I noticed her condition when I was examining her body."

"But, sir, that couldn't be."

"It certainly was."

Crispina pulled away from Aurora, got up, and walked—almost ran—out of the garden.

.   .   .

As I turned toward the bath I heard the voices of children coming from the rear of the garden—the familiar voices of two young girls and another, unfamiliar voice. It had to be Hashep and Dakla and, most likely, young Clodius. I assumed the girls were doing their lessons and keeping poor Clodius occupied. Two years ago I assigned Phineas the task of teaching the girls to read and write. Hashep has caught on quickly, while Dakla struggles.

Hashep's musical voice rose over her sister's, reciting a piece of poetry and feeling her way toward a song in the process. They were sitting so that their backs were to me and all I could see was their heads over the shrubbery. Drawing closer to them, I tried to decipher what Hashep was saying. A few of the words seemed familiar. Then recognition struck, and I hurried around a bend in the path to where they sat.

Phineas jumped to his feet and motioned for the girls to do likewise. Hashep has her Egyptian mother's dark features and straight, inky-black hair. Dakla resembles her Roman father, Demetrius, in her thick body and curly brown hair. The boy with them had sandy-colored hair and big brown eyes, sad eyes. Uncertain of himself, he stood with the girls.

I've always been casual in my treatment of these girls. Until recently they called me "Uncle Gaius," but now Hashep has taken to calling me "my lord."

"Uncle Gaius," Dakla said, "this is our friend Clodius."

"Welcome, Clodius," I said.

"Thank you, my lord, Uncle Gaius. Do you know where my papa is?"

"Not right now, but I intend to find him."

"Thank you, sir. I hope you do."

I turned to Phineas. "But first I have to deal with this rascal. Is that what I think it is?"

"It's your poem, my lord, the one about autumn that you asked me to find." He seemed pleased with himself.

"Find it, yes, not share it with everyone, including a visitor in my house." I could feel my face reddening. "Did you tack it up in the Forum?"

"I'm sorry, my lord. I…I thought the girls would enjoy reading it, since it is autumn. You've let them hear other poetry of yours." That was his plea of "not guilty."

"Not anything this juvenile." I took the piece of papyrus from his hand.

"It's pretty, Uncle Gaius," Dakla said.

"Did you compose a tune to go with it, my lord?" Hashep asked. "Could you play it for us?"

When I was much younger, one of our servants taught me to play the lyre. I don't play like a professional musician—no Roman man of my class would want to—and I don't dance. As Cicero said, "No man who's sober will dance." But I do take pleasure in my lyre from time to time. When these girls were younger, I used to sing to them quite a bit. Hashep has been receiving musical training from one of my servants. I think she can become an entertainer, escaping a life of working in the kitchen, the fate toward which Dakla seems headed.

"I don't have time to get my lyre and tune it, but I believe I remember the melody. Give me a moment to think." I began to hum.

When I looked up from the piece of papyrus, Hashep asked, "What mode will you use, my lord?"

"The Dorian. It seems to fit the time of the year."

By the time I was halfway through the poem, Hashep had joined me, perfectly in tune and meeting my eyes in anticipation of where the melody was going. Toward the end her jealous little sister tried to make it a trio. Phineas winced as we sounded like two skylarks singing along with a crow. Clodius cast his eyes from one to the other of us as though we were all quite mad.

"That was beautiful," Dakla said. "Can we sing it again?"

I kissed her on the forehead and handed the papyrus back to Phineas. "I have a lot to do, sweetheart, and you girls need to get back to your lessons. You have more important things to read than one of my poems."

"But that stuff's all so dull, Uncle Gaius," Dakla said.

Oh, to have nothing more onerous to worry about than reading dull poetry!

.   .   .

Since Martial was coming for dinner, I would have to change into different clothes. Before I did so I sat alone in my room, trying to make some sense of what I had learned over the last two days, and trying to understand why Tacitus had done what he did. His brother might very well be ill, but the timing was certainly opportune for a man looking for an escape, and I felt abandoned, though not in the sense of relief that Livilla's decision offered me.

Had Tacitus just been looking for an excuse to disconnect himself from me? My friendship with him has made me appreciate a melancholy passage from one of Cicero's letters to Atticus. "My house is crammed of a morning," the great orator wrote. "I go down to the Forum surrounded by droves of 'friends,' but in all the crowds I cannot find one person with whom I can exchange an unguarded joke or let out a private sigh."

With Tacitus I had found that one person. And yet we disagreed profoundly on one important matter. Tacitus would welcome Domitian's death, whatever happened afterwards. I suspected that, in the long run, Rome would be better off if we did not have a king—which is what we have, although no one will use the word. But I could not bring myself to will it. It's too uncertain a chance.

Getting rid of a king would be difficult, for two reasons. First, we have no system ready to replace him. The Republic would not just reappear, like a magician pulling a lost coin from behind someone's ear. Other men would try to seize power. Few men of my class were devoted to the notion of a Republic or had the strength of character to forge a new form of government. Most just wanted to grab whatever they could for themselves. If Domitian were killed, there would be a period of turmoil. Only a fool would deny that possibility. The provinces might revolt, as they did when Nero died. During those months of civil war—less than twenty years ago—part of Rome itself was burned.

In the second place, no one could predict who might be harmed in the chaos following the murder of the *princeps*. When Julius Caesar was assassinated, mobs ran through the streets, looting and burning indiscriminately. My first responsibility was to protect my family. In order to do that, did I have to accept the presence of a *princeps* who, whatever his faults, keeps order? Is the problem with the system or with the man at the top of the system? Could we prosper under a philosopher-king? Plato thought so, but there has never been a true philosopher-king, at least not that I know of. Sometimes I hate myself for being so cautious, but—

"My lord." Demetrius' voice sounded through my closed door.

"Yes. Come in."

He opened the door. "My lord, Valerius Martial is waiting to see you."

"Now? He's too early for dinner. Did he say what he wants?"

"Just that it's in regard to a favor you asked of him, my lord. And he's not wearing dinner clothes."

As I crossed the garden my mother intercepted me. "That dreadful man is standing at the door. You didn't invite him to dinner again, did you?"

She didn't know about Livilla! I wished the girl would just tell everyone so I could endure the storm, repair the damage as best I could, and get on to the next problem in my life.

"In fact, I did invite him, Mother, to make up for the way you treated him last time, but I don't know why he's arrived so early. Please wait here while I talk to him."

"Gladly. I don't want to be under the same roof with him. If he's eating here tonight, I'll have dinner in my room." She gathered up her stola like a woman about to cross a mucky street. "Come, Naomi."

Having dinner without my mother and Naomi present would actually be a relief. If what Pompeia had said was true, my mother was growing even more resentful of Aurora. I could not bear the thought of having to choose between them.

"Good afternoon, Gaius Pliny," Martial said as I passed the *impluvium*, which was full almost to the top from the recent rains.

"Thank you for coming by," I said. "Do you have a message for me?"

Martial looked around the atrium, where several servants were going about their tasks. "Let's step outside."

We closed the door behind us and huddled in the *vestibulum*. Ironically, this outdoor, public part of a *domus* can be the most private space in the house. There's no place for anyone to hide, no opening for them to look through. Noise from the street covers your conversation.

Martial took one look around, just to be sure we were alone. "The meeting you asked for has been arranged, at midday tomorrow. The other party, who is extremely curious, asks that you bring no more than six in your retinue, and he will bring the same number. He agrees to your condition that each of you will have only one attendant in the room during the meeting."

"That's acceptable. Thank you."

"I'm glad to be of service to someone who has been so kind to me and my family." He turned to leave.

"Aren't you staying for dinner?"

"I need to get out to the farm and make Lorcis aware of who's going to be there tomorrow. It's a long walk."

"Of course." I hadn't really thought of the inconvenience this might cause for Martial. But a man who accepts a gift as substantial as a farm must expect to find himself obliged to the donor. Some clients complain of a "hook" in the gifts given to them. They could, I suppose, refuse to accept them. No gift, no hook. When I give a gift, I don't think of myself baiting a hook, but in this case I needed Martial's help, so he would just have to wriggle on the end of my line. "If you have no objection, I'll try to arrive early and say hello to her and Erotion."

"I'm sure they'll be pleased to see you." He bowed his head and took a step toward the street.

"Wait just a moment. Let me give you money to rent a horse."

His face brightened. "I would be grateful for that."

I went inside and got a few *denarii* from Demetrius, more than enough to hire a horse. Scribbling a note and affixing my seal, I gave everything to Martial. "Go to Saturius' stable, outside the Viminal Gate. That's where I hire my horses. Show him this note and he'll give you a decent one at a reasonable price."

He made a slight bow, not as much as a servant would bow to

a master, but enough to acknowledge a kindness. "Again, thank you, Gaius Pliny."

Watching him start down the Esquiline, I wondered why he had chosen the life he had. A Spaniard by birth, he had received as good an education as mine. With his wit and his impressive speaking style, he could have enjoyed some success in the courts. His parents, both dead now, had left him enough money, according to his own account, to launch a career, if not to sustain it. But he had chosen—or fallen into—the hand-to-mouth existence of a poet, dependent on gifts from patrons like Regulus and me. When he was in Rome, he lived in a run-down *insula* on the edge of the Subura. As he disappeared around a corner, I reminded myself how fortunate I was not to live a life like his, beholden to people who barely tolerated me.

But then, unlike me, he could live openly with a woman he loved— a former slave—and have a child by her.

It will be good to see Lorcis again. Our first meeting, in the Forum a few years ago, was purely by chance. Even though Gaius denies coincidences, I can see some in my own life. They're either that or whimsical decisions of the gods or the Fates, and I'd rather not believe in such things. I don't like the idea of being tossed around by some power I can't see or understand.

We met and talked a few times before she escaped slavery. We found some similarities in our lives. Neither of us is Greek or Roman. The people who settled around Carthage—my ancestors—originally came from the same part of the world where Lorcis was born. Both of us were sold into slavery to settle our fathers' debts—actually a stepfather in her case. Her mother died before she was sold. My mother and I were sold together.

Having my mother with me made it easier for me to bear being a slave, I guess. That and the fact that I have always been in the house of a kind master, unlike Lorcis. I never forget that I'm a slave, but it isn't always the foremost thought in my mind. My kind master gave Lorcis and Martial the farm where they now live on the road to Nomentum. I've never been there before.

X

AT THE SECOND hour the next morning, Saturius fell all over himself as he apologized. "Sir, I have only six horses at the moment. I gave your friend Martial one yesterday afternoon, as your note instructed me to do." He didn't point the blame at me with his finger; his voice did the job. "If you can wait an hour, I'm sure I can procure another one for your party."

"No, we need to leave right now," I said. "We'll have to make do." I looked at Aurora with an eyebrow raised. She nodded.

As my other servants moved toward their horses, I reached for the reins of one.

"Not that one, my lord," Aurora said. She patted another beast. "This one has a stronger back."

Saturius helped me mount. Once settled, I extended my hand to Aurora and pulled her up behind me. She worked her tunic down as far as she could and wrapped her arms around me. Let my other servants think what they would. I felt I was being rewarded for my act of kindness to Martial and regretted that his farm on the Via Nomentana was only six miles away.

We took the road alongside the wall of Servius Tullius until we came to the Via Nomentana. Turning there, we headed northeast. On my instructions, my other servants stayed far enough behind Aurora and me that we could converse quietly. She was tall enough—and I was short enough—that her chin could rest on my shoulder. Her hands came to rest farther down.

"Your sword's not the only long, hard thing under your tunic," she said when we were less than a mile from the city.

I was relieved of the necessity of a reply because her attention was drawn to the estate we were passing.

"That's an impressive property. Whose is it?"

"That was the estate of Antonia Caenis," I said.

"Oh, this is where it is," Aurora said. "My mother knew her. She was Vespasian's…mistress, wasn't she?"

"More like his wife in all but name. My uncle used to talk about how much influence she had on him, for the good, fortunately."

"Did you ever come out here?"

"No, but my uncle did."

Caenis was a former slave of Antonia, mother of the *princeps* Claudius. Vespasian had been a favorite of Antonia's and had met Caenis while at Antonia's house. Their relationship had lasted for years, even when Vespasian was married. In his capacity as an advisor to Vespasian, my uncle had been invited out here, a place where Vespasian could escape the pressures of life on the Palatine Hill.

"He brought my mother with him, didn't he?" Aurora said. "She told me about meeting Vespasian, but I didn't realize this was where it happened."

"Yes. Since my uncle's relationship with Monica was similar to Vespasian's with Caenis, the two men formed a close bond. I think your mother and Caenis even became friends."

"They did. My mother grieved when Caenis died." Aurora fell silent until we had passed the estate. Then she said, "Gaius, am I going to be your—"

"You will always be the woman I love." She squeezed me tightly. "That's what Livilla came to talk with me about night before last. I'm sorry I haven't found a chance to tell you before this."

I could feel her body tense against mine.

"What did she have to say?"

"That she will not marry me."

"Because of me?"

"Yes."

"Oh, Gaius. I'm so sorry—"

"Why? It's the best news I've had in a long time. I don't know what it ultimately means for us, but it means I don't have to marry right now. We have time to think about how things might work out."

"Your mother will hate me more than ever now."

"I'll take care of my mother."

"You can't send her far enough away to take care of this."

I knew she was right, but at the moment—on a beautiful day, with her arms around me and her body pressed against mine—it didn't seem to matter at all.

.   .   .

The sun was well up over the mountains now, bright enough to bother my eyes but also knocking the night's chill off the countryside.

"What's this farm like?" Aurora asked.

I had to look straight ahead. If I turned my head even slightly, I could kiss her, and I was aching to do it. "It's nondescript. It never was one of our most important properties. My uncle took it as payment for a debt before I was born but never did anything other than rent it out to tenants. It's a working farm, with a small house, not a villa."

"Still, it's out of Rome."

"Given the rate at which Rome is growing, it won't be long before you'll be able to see the city from there, and that will spoil whatever charm the place might have."

We rode in silence for a while, at a slow pace to make it easier on the horse carrying the two of us. Aurora's closeness, her warmth, her scent, her breasts pressing against my back—it all made me want to goad my horse, outdistance the men riding with us, and just keep going.

"We've seen no sign of Regulus," Aurora said. "Do you think he might have gotten there before us?"

"I'm more worried that he might have an ambush waiting for us. He knows where we're going and when. It would be easy to set up."

She cocked her head toward me. "Do you think he's capable of that kind of treachery?"

"He's capable of anything when it comes to his hatred of me."

"Gaius, sometimes I think Tacitus was right when he said you over-estimate how much Regulus dislikes you. The streets of Rome are thronged with people he hates, and who hate him in return. Do you really hold so high a place in his...disregard?"

"My uncle turned Vespasian and Titus against him. For over ten years Regulus had no access to the *princeps*. He has never forgiven me for that. I've beaten him twice in court now—humiliated him a few days ago. That just stokes the fire."

She gave me an extra squeeze. "But today you've piqued his curiosity. That may outweigh his desire for vengeance."

"Only temporarily, I assure you."

"I just hope the whole business doesn't take long."

"Are you still thinking about what happened at Misenum, shortly after the eruption?"

"Yes."

"I'm sorry you had to massage him after his bath, but he was a guest and I had just taken on my uncle's inheritance. Regulus was a powerful man—"

"You did what you had to, and so did I."

"He probably won't even remember you. It was five years ago. Who knows how many hundreds of girls have massaged him since then?"

.   .   .

We arrived at about the fourth hour. Regulus and his party hadn't arrived yet.

"It's a pretty little place, my lord," one of the men said as we dismounted and tied our horses to the fence that surrounded the front of the house and served to keep animals out of a vegetable garden during the spring and summer.

"Someone's been fixing it up," Aurora said. "It's quite lovely." She looked at the man who had spoken first, so I hoped everyone assumed she was addressing him, not me, since she had omitted the honorific "my lord."

"I'm sure it's all Lorcis' work," I said. "Martial's not the type to get his hands dirty with anything except his pen and ink."

Beyond the gate, a path led to the front door, where Lorcis and her daughter waited to greet us. I waved and smiled.

The first time I saw Lorcis was the day before the eruption of Vesuvius. Her owner at that time was a friend of my uncle's who had come out from Naples to Misenum to visit us, a decision that probably saved his life. Lorcis was entertaining us with her *auloi* on the terrace of the villa that afternoon when my mother spotted the cloud rising from the volcano. The next day, as ash and darkness descended on us, Lorcis helped me guide my mother to safety. I didn't see her again until a year later, after her owner had sold her to Regulus in an effort to recoup some of his losses caused by the eruption.

A dark-haired woman with a Syrian background, Lorcis has always struck me as beautiful, her only flaw a slightly pointed chin. A slave with a talent like hers lives a pampered life, compared to those who toil in the kitchen or do other kinds of drudge work. Two years on a farm had hardened Lorcis' body, trimmed her down, but her face glowed with contentment. Part of that no doubt came from the little girl clinging to her tunic—her nicest, I assumed, though it was shabbier than the one Aurora was wearing.

"Good morning, sir," she said, "and welcome. It's wonderful to see you. And Aurora! I never imagined you would come out here."

Aurora stepped forward and hugged Lorcis. "I'm so glad to see you again, and to see you here."

"Wait," I said. "How do you two know each other?"

"Our paths crossed one day in the Forum," Lorcis said, still holding Aurora's hand. "It was about four years ago, wasn't it? I was still Regulus' slave."

Aurora nodded. "We had a short conversation, but a memorable one."

"Yes, we talked about our masters." The two women smiled the way women do when they share a secret that no man can penetrate. "Aurora gave me a lot to think about. We met and talked a few more times before I…left Rome."

"Well, perhaps you can reminisce some other time," I said, wondering what Aurora would have said about me four years ago that might have prompted such a smile. She stepped back behind me. "Thank you for your hospitality on such short notice, Lorcis. I hope this isn't too much of an intrusion."

"Not at all, sir. You're welcome at any time. How is your mother?"

"About as well as can be expected, I suppose, at her age." I didn't want to talk about that, so I turned my head to survey the farm. "I haven't seen this place in quite a while. You've done a lot of work on it. And I'll bet you have a good helper." I knelt and extended a hand to Erotion, but she clung more tightly to her mother's tunic.

"She's a bit shy." Lorcis picked the little girl up and settled her on her hip. "We don't get many visitors." Erotion threw her arms around her mother's neck and turned her face away from me.

"She's a beautiful child."

"Thank you, sir. We just wish we knew where she got this golden hair." Lorcis ran her fingers through Erotion's long, curly hair, but the child still would not turn around.

"Is Martial here?"

Lorcis shook her head. "He left before dawn for Rome. He's going to guide…our other guest out here, to be certain he can find the place. Erotion and I are about to take a walk. Do you think this meeting will last long?"

"I'd be surprised if it takes an hour. Should we send up some sort of signal when we're done?"

"No. We'll be able to see from up there." She nodded toward a tree-lined ridge fifty paces or so behind the house. "We'll take our leave now. The house is yours. There's wine, bread, fruit and cheese in the front room on your right. Help yourselves."

As Lorcis and her daughter followed a path around to the back of the house, Aurora and I entered the front door. The house was built on a model from the early days of Rome, before everything was influenced by the Greeks. The atrium was the center of the building, and there was no peristyle garden on the rear.

"It's just half a house," Aurora said.

"But out in the country, you don't need an enclosed garden."

The two front rooms did not open to the street, as they would in a modern house in Rome itself. Because it was not jammed up against any neighbors, sharing a wall with them, this house had a few windows. Since I last saw it, it had been transformed—cracks in the walls patched, everything painted in soft colors that made the rooms seem larger, somehow restful.

We entered the room where Lorcis said she had laid out food. It contained a good-sized table and several chairs. On a chest in one corner of the room lay a pair of ivory *auloi*. Aurora bent to examine them.

"The inscription says these are a gift from Gaius Pliny. Is that you or your uncle?"

"It's me. She lost hers during the eruption. I gave her those to thank her for helping me save my mother."

"I wish I could have been there with you."

"And you know how much I wish the same. But my uncle was still grieving over your mother's death. It was difficult for him to have you around. That's why he ordered you to be left in Rome when we went to join him in Misenum. And maybe it was just as well. Don't forget, several of our servants died in that disaster."

That memory made this moment somber. Then we heard the clopping of horses' hooves and the rumbling of a *raeda* coming to the front of the house.

"We're here!" Martial called out. "Lock up your wives and daughters."

.   .   .

I left the house and stood behind the gate as Regulus' party dismounted. A quick count confirmed that he had brought a dozen men. I touched my sword. Had I set up a trap for myself?

The door of the *raeda* swung open and Regulus eased his bulk out with help from two of his servants. Behind him I could see the rich woods and gold-and-silver fittings of the interior. I also caught a glimpse of the woman who was riding with him, pulling her gown back up onto her shoulders and fastening her brooch. She spat and wiped her mouth on the hem of her garment.

"Welcome, Marcus Regulus," I said. "Thank you for coming. I trust your journey was pleasant."

Regulus' face reminds me of a man who needs to move his bowels but can't. Even when he smiles while making a speech in court, the left side of his mouth is all that turns up. He is vain about his black hair and goes to great lengths to disguise the fact that he's losing it. There is an oiliness about him that makes me want to wipe my hands whenever I'm in his presence. And yet he's considered by many to be a charming man. He has endeared himself to many childless widows who have left him huge sums of money or estates.

"Do I look like it was pleasant, Gaius Pliny?" He brushed himself off and moved his shoulders and arms like a man stretching out his discomfort. "What is the meaning of this? It had better be something of earth-shaking importance."

"I believe it is. That's why, before anything else is said, we need to go inside, as agreed, with one trusted observer each."

Regulus rolled his eyes as though acceding to the whims of a petulant child. "Very well. Nestor!"

Until then I hadn't noticed that Nestor—or Jacob, as I knew him—was in Regulus' retinue. He looked like the ride had been difficult for him. At his age, that wasn't surprising.

"Are you content," I asked Regulus, "to have Valerius Martial stand at the gate here with one man from each of our parties and make sure no one gets any closer?" I knew Regulus would trust Martial, and I—well, I would have to. "I'm afraid we don't have provisions to feed this many people. I was expecting you to bring only six."

"Then you *are* a fool." Regulus started up the path. "My people will be fine. There's food in the *raeda*. I need something to drink."

Aurora was pouring wine and arranging food on a table in the main room of the house. Regulus' head jerked when he saw her.

"*This* is your trusted observer?" He waved a hand heavy with his signet ring and several other baubles.

"Yes, she is. I'm almost as surprised at your choice, meaning no offense to…Nestor."

"I take none, my lord," Jacob said, backing into a corner.

"There is no servant—no living person—in my house whom I trust more than Nestor."

"I didn't think you trusted anyone in your house."

"I don't. That's my point. At the risk of some cumbersome negatives, it might be more accurate to say I *mis*trust him less than anyone else in my house."

"That's why you sent him with that message to Domitian a few nights ago, isn't it?" I said.

Regulus nodded and chuckled, taking a cup of wine from Aurora's hand. "I knew I could count on him to do two things: run straight to you and not break my seal. I also knew *you* were honorable enough not to break the seal. Seeing that the message was intended for Domitian, you would simply imagine the worst. That was what I wanted and Nestor was the only servant I have who wouldn't go straight to Domitian."

"You misjudge the man, Marcus Regulus. He has never informed on you to me."

"I'm not blind, Gaius Pliny. Nestor hates me, but he is a man of honor. I understand both of you perfectly."

"What if you had misjudged one of us and we had opened the message?"

"I never misjudge people, Gaius Pliny. For instance, I judged that you would be honorable enough to bring only six men today." He took a long swallow of the wine. "But if you had opened that note, you would have found a message telling Domitian that I was sending it as a joke on you."

"You mean—"

"Oh, I thought about writing *Please kill this messenger*, but Domitian might have taken me seriously, and I can't afford to lose good ol' Nestor." He slapped his servant on the shoulder like they were two friends having a drink in a *taberna*.

"So you weren't spying on me when I rode—"

"Out to Marinthus' *taberna*? No more than usual."

"And Segetius and Rufinus aren't your men?"

"Who?" The lack of recognition on his face seemed genuine.

"Never mind. Then you had nothing to do with what I found out there?"

"Nothing whatsoever. Decapitated bodies aren't my style. They lack subtlety."

How could he know so much? What did he *not* know? My mind raced through the names of the freedmen I'd taken with me. Was one of them an informant in Regulus' pay? Could it be someone at the *taberna*—Marinthus himself perhaps? No, Theodorus. It had to be Theodorus.

"I decided I didn't have to torment you," Regulus said with a smirk, "if I could get *you* to do the job for me. Do you really think you're so important to me that I have nothing to do besides looking for opportunities to attack you? You're nothing more than a minor annoyance in my life, Gaius Pliny, like a fly that I swat at once in a while, when it buzzes around my face—as you did when you prosecuted Quintus Vibius and made me look bad in front of all of Rome. The rest of the time I forget about you."

I had the sensation that I was being played for a fool, like the old man in a comedy—the *senex*—who doesn't see how his servants and his son are conniving against him. "So none of your people have been following me or watching me?"

"Of course they have. They always do, just as they follow a dozen other people at any given time. I know things about you that your own mother doesn't know. But my people have not been interfering. Not even when you and a lovely young lady went upstairs at Marinthus."

Aurora dropped the cup of wine she was about to hand me.

"So it *was* her. I wasn't given a name, but I had my suspicions. I hope she performed better that night than she's doing today." Regulus stepped aside so the spilled wine wouldn't run under his feet. Aurora grabbed a cloth off the table and wiped up the mess. "Oh, wait, I recognize her now! When I stopped over at your house at Misenum a few years ago, she gave me a massage after we bathed." He clapped his hands. "Yes, that's it. As I recall, I offered to buy her, but you—"

"I refused," I said, desperate to put an end to this part of the conversation.

"Oh, you did more than refuse, Gaius Pliny. You said you'd rather sell me an intimate portion of your anatomy. But I already have two of those—"

"Marcus Regulus, there is serious business that we need to discuss."

"About a murdered woman? I had nothing to do with that."

"It's not about that. I know who the killer is."

"And I had nothing to do with it, did I?"

"Not as far as I know." It was hard enough to say that. I could not apologize to him.

"I accept your *implied* apology. Now, don't think that I won't eventually get my revenge for that humiliation in court, but at my own time and in my own way." He tore off a piece of bread and continued to talk while he chewed it. "So, what's so damned important that you had to drag me all the way out to this hovel?"

"I believe the man who killed that girl is planning to kill again."

Regulus rolled his hand the way we do when we want someone to hurry up and get to the point. "And…"

"And he's planning to kill Domitian."

Regulus choked. Jacob pounded him on the back, harder than he really needed to, until Regulus waved him away. "Are you out of your *mind*? Do you realize how much trouble we could be in if one word of this gets back to…the Palatine?"

"Do you think either Aurora or Nestor will report what they've heard?"

Regulus glanced at the two servants. "No, I suppose not." He stepped closer to Aurora, running his eyes up and down her as though formulating another offer. "Trustworthy *and* beautiful. A rare combination indeed. Are you sure, Gaius Pliny, that you don't want to—"

I clenched my fists but kept them at my sides. I didn't care how many men he had outside. If he touched her… "Yes, I'm sure. Not now. Not ever."

"Funny. That's what your uncle said when I offered to buy his Monica. And the daughter here is much prettier, now that she's fully developed."

Aurora opened her mouth and I knew I had to say something quickly. "Marcus Regulus, I asked you out here to discuss a serious matter in the utmost privacy."

Regulus stepped away from Aurora and she let out a long breath. I relaxed my hands.

"Oh, yes, a madman wants to kill Domitian. And what, by Zeus' snot rag, do you expect me to do about that?"

"I believe we will have to work together, as distasteful as that may be to both of us, to prevent it from happening."

This is not going the way we thought it would. Regulus is keeping Gaius on the defensive, bringing up issues that he wants to settle. Gaius shouldn't have set up a meeting like this. With only two slaves as witnesses, no one will ever be able to verify what happened or what was said.

I still feel dirty when I think about that "massage" he made me give him five years ago at Gaius' house at Misenum. I washed my hands in water that was almost boiling afterwards, and I still couldn't get him off my hands. And he remembers me. Gaius was wrong about that.

Regulus sat in a chair under a window that looked out on the road. By sitting down first he had put me in the position of a client, a suppliant. "*You* want to save Domitian's life? I thought his death was the thing you desired above all else, the very first thought that came into your mind when you opened your eyes in the morning."

"I can truthfully say that is not the case." I looked at Aurora, who was the first thought that came into my mind each morning.

"What about your friend Tacitus?"

"I cannot speak for anyone else." I sat in a chair on the opposite side of the room.

"This is preposterous, Gaius Pliny. Why should I help you? The smartest thing for me to do would be to go straight to Domitian and tell him that you're aware of some plot and let him deal with you in his own inimitable way."

"And I'm sure I would break under torture. To save myself, I would be forced to tell him what I know about your involvement in the murder of Lucius Cornutus two years ago in Smyrna."

Regulus gave a short, ugly laugh. "I've never been in Smyrna."

"But one of your henchmen was there, carrying out your orders. Did you know Domitian was grooming Cornutus for some important posts? He sent Cornutus' father a personal note of condolence. I doubt he would be happy to hear how a favorite of his died and who was responsible."

Regulus took a sip of wine and pursed his puffy lips while he pondered a response. I hoped he didn't think too long. My threat was largely bluff, with nothing to back it up but a confession from a man now dead. But Regulus didn't know that, and even the faintest possibility of standing accused before a *princeps* has broken stronger men than he.

He drained the cup and handed it back to Aurora. "You don't have a shred of proof." It was almost a question.

I felt myself gaining the upper hand. "Even if I didn't have proof, as you well know, with Domitian I don't need it. All I have to do is plant a suspicion."

Regulus got up and walked to the door, then stopped and turned back to face me. "All right, damn you. We'll work together. I'm glad to learn that you're such a true patriot." He sat back down.

"I think I am, but in this case I'm merely being a pragmatist. Domitian has no heir, no successor of any kind in place. His death would mean civil war, just as happened when Nero died without an heir."

"Yes. Well, Nero kept killing off the male members of his family. Domitian's not been guilty of that."

Except for his brother, I thought but did not dare say. Even four years after Titus' seemingly natural death, the rumors of Domitian's involvement would not be quieted.

"And he does also have his cousin, Flavius Clemens," Regulus continued.

I had met Clemens on two occasions. He was a great-nephew of Vespasian and married to another cousin of his, Flavia Domitilla, a descendant of Vespasian's brother. His *cognomen*, "the mild one," fit him perfectly. He spent most of his time reading philosophy; rumor had it that he was attracted to Judaism.

"Clemens has shown no interest in matters of state," I said. "The Praetorians wouldn't be likely to support him, since he has no military record. Domitian's not given him any offices to mark him as a successor. If the Praetorians did hail him, commanders on the frontiers would probably march on Rome."

Regulus nodded. "It would be Galba, Otho, and Vitellius all over again. I supported Otho and barely escaped with my life."

"Exactly. I don't think Rome would survive another year with four emperors." That was what people were already calling that dreadful time sixteen years ago. "Keeping Domitian alive is the best thing for Rome right now. And for you."

"For me?"

"You don't know if another *princeps* would let you whisper in his ear the way Domitian does. He might shut you out like Vespasian did."

"Thanks to your uncle." A flash of dark anger crossed Regulus' face. "Your friend Agricola wouldn't try to take power?"

"Even if he did, it would require a long fight."

Regulus sighed and took another cup of wine from Aurora. "What do you want me to do, Gaius Pliny?"

"Help me find out what's going on. Your network of spies is the most extensive in Rome, after Domitian's own." Regulus nodded as though acknowledging a compliment. "I need to know what your spies know."

"It's easier if my people are looking for someone specific."

"We're looking for a man named Clodius Popilius."

"What does he look like?"

"I don't know." I upbraided myself for not asking such a basic question. "I'll ask his wife when I get back to Rome and let you know."

"My lord," Aurora said, "if I may—"

"Yes?"

"Crispina said he is about my height, with thick, light brown hair."

"And you're the same height as I am," Regulus said. "That's something to go on. Any marks to look for?"

"Crispina didn't mention any."

"He plans to assassinate Domitian," I said, "and present himself to the Praetorians. He has a son whom he could put forward as his successor."

"Is this son with him?"

"No, he's at my house, with his mother."

Regulus shook his head slowly, the way one does when confronted with something utterly unbelievable. "The man must be absolutely mad."

"He is. He was the one who beheaded that girl."

"Why?"

"She was his stepdaughter. He was jealous because his wife had been married first to someone else. By killing her in such spectacular fashion, he got his revenge and showed his accomplices what he's capable of. He beheaded her to show that he was going to cut off the head of Rome."

"You mentioned accomplices. So he has people working with him?" Regulus finished his wine and handed the cup to Aurora to refill again.

"Only a handful. His wife says he has convinced himself and a few others that he is destined to rule Rome in the name of the people. He's told them that his name comes from *populus* and means something like 'the little people,' or 'man of the people.'"

"How did he come to such a bizarre conclusion?" Regulus asked.

"It's his interpretation of an obscure line of poetry that he ran across."

"Something from the Sibylline Books? Gaius Pliny, I know you don't take such things any more seriously than I do."

"It's even more obscure than that."

Regulus' legal instincts were coming to the fore. "Did he tell you this? Have you talked to him?"

"His wife did. She showed me the papyrus he scribbled on when he figured it out." I couldn't help but think also of the piece on which Tacitus had scribbled the line with my name substituted for Popilius'.

"If you want my support, you'll have to show me this poem or prophecy, or whatever it is. I need to know as much as you know."

I had hoped to avoid spreading this bit of information around, partly because I felt it made me look foolish to give it any credence, but Regulus was right. If he knew what it was, he might be better able to direct his spies in their search. Martial had a pile of papyrus and writing implements on a table in one corner of the room. I wrote out the ROTAS square on a piece and handed it to Regulus.

"It's nonsense," he said, squinting at the document and holding it at arm's length. "Nestor, does this mean anything to you?"

As Jacob, standing behind Regulus, took the piece of papyrus his eyes widened. "No…no, my lord. As you say, it's nonsense—the sort of thing one sees scribbled on a wall."

"That's exactly where Popilius saw it," I said. "On a tavern wall."

"What does it mean? AREPO? What is that?" Regulus asked. "And why did it persuade this man to attack Domitian?"

"He apparently took the AREPO line to be an acronym for *Ad Regis Excidium Popilius Optatus.*"

"He could just as easily have taken the *R* to stand for my name," Regulus said. "'Popilius is chosen for the destruction of Regulus.' Or the *P* to stand for your name. Are you chosen for my destruction, Gaius Pliny? You'd like that, wouldn't you?"

"We're not here to rehearse old enmities."

"No, I guess not, as much as I enjoy that." He took the papyrus from Jacob, glanced over it again, and handed it back to his steward. "And you say his wife told you this was his interpretation?"

"Yes."

"Hearsay evidence like that is the weakest kind of support for a case. It's no better than bathhouse gossip."

"If you had talked to her, as Aurora and I have, you would recognize that she's telling the truth."

Regulus tented his fingers and brought them to his lips. "Why do you think this man is such a serious threat—any more than any other lunatic in Rome with a knife in his hand?"

"I don't know of any other lunatic who has butchered a young woman to insure the success of his undertaking."

"Well, not since Agamemnon's day."

XI

WE AGREED that Nestor and Aurora would serve as the messengers between our two houses. Nothing was to be written. When everything had been settled, we waited for Regulus and his entourage to leave first, then talked a bit more with Martial and Lorcis. Erotion played in Aurora's lap but never would do more than look at me. They seemed a happy enough family, although I sensed regret on Lorcis' part that Martial spent so much time in Rome. Even though I find many things to dislike about the city and enjoy my occasional escapes from it, I could understand his attraction to the place. It inspired his poetry, and its dilettantes fed his need for acclaim. Since Cicero's day, men like us have complained about how unpleasant life in Rome can be and then complained even more about every day spent away from there. For us it is the center of the world, regardless of what the fatuous Greeks claim about the Omphalos at Delphi.

Clouds were gathering to the east, in the Apennines, as we mounted our horses.

"Sir, won't you stay a bit longer until the storm passes?" Lorcis said.

I sensed Aurora's tension as she swung up onto our horse and wrapped her arms around me, but I said, "It looks like the clouds are far enough away that we can make it back to Rome before it hits."

"I hope so," Lorcis said, glancing up at the mountains again.

"My lord," Aurora said, "the horses are nervous. Don't you think we should wait?"

"I want to get back and talk to Crispina. Let's not waste time arguing about this." I also wanted to contact Jacob and see why he had reacted to the ROTAS square the way he did. He had rolled up the piece of papyrus surreptitiously and must have taken it with him. I didn't miss it until Regulus' party was out of sight.

We made it halfway back to Rome before the storm broke with a fury that I'd never experienced. With the rain coming in waves, at times I could not see more than a single pace beyond our horse's nose. The animal was becoming increasingly difficult to control.

"Gaius, we can't go on," Aurora said.

I was about to disagree—because I didn't want to admit I'd made a bad decision—when a lightning bolt struck a tree just ahead of us. Our horse reared in panic. If I'd been riding alone, I might have kept my seat, but Aurora began to slide off and tightened her grip on me. I knew if I held the reins I risked being dragged by the animal, so I let go and we both tumbled to the ground as the horse galloped away. My servants rode over to us.

"My lord, are you all right?" one of them shouted over the thunder.

"Yes. Aurora, are you injured?"

"No, my lord, I'm fine."

I took her hand and pulled her to her feet. "You men take cover wherever you can," I said. "We'll find one another when this is over."

"What about your horse, my lord? Should we go after him?"

"He's probably in Rome by now. We'll worry about that later. Find shelter. I would stay away from trees, though." I pointed to the one that had just been struck. It was smoldering.

As the men scattered in different directions, Aurora and I made our way up a slope on the south side of the road. Peering through the sheets of rain with difficulty, I saw some overhanging rocks that might offer a bit of shelter, so I pulled Aurora after me in that direction.

What we found was more than I'd hoped for—a small opening that let us into a cave. My eyes, as sensitive as they are to bright light, enable me to see better than most people in semi-darkness such as we now encountered. Peering around in the gloom, I could not detect any sign of an animal or any indication that people had used this cave recently. It went back only about five paces, but it gave us room to walk about and it was dry. One thing I've learned about myself over the past couple of years is that I don't like being in small, confined spaces. But this cave was large enough that we could stand and I could see the entrance—or exit—so I felt no more sense of being closed in than if I were in a small room in my own house.

"I think we'll be all right here," I said with more confidence than I felt. With its view of the road, this would make an ideal spot for bandits to watch for wealthy travelers, and it could not be seen from the road. My servants might have difficulty finding us after the storm if it weren't for the tree that had been struck by lightning.

"'I think we'll be all right here,'" Aurora echoed. "I wonder if that's what Aeneas told Dido."

I looked at her with a question on my face.

"How can you *not* think of that right now?" she asked.

And she was right. Everyone in Rome knows the story, from the fourth book of Virgil's *Aeneid*. Juno was determined to keep Aeneas mired in Carthage so he couldn't found Rome, the successor of the Troy that Juno hated so much. While Aeneas and Dido were out hunting, Juno—thinking she had persuaded Venus to go along with her plan—conjured up a ferocious storm that separated the royal couple from the rest of their party. They found safety in a cave where, with flashes of lightning to serve as wedding torches, they consummated what Virgil called "a kind of marriage."

"I wonder if Aeneas and Dido were as wet and cold as we are," I said.

The mid-October rain, blasting down from the Apennines, was cold, and wool doesn't shed water. It does when it's on the sheep, but once we make it into clothing, it absorbs water like a sponge. We were both starting to shiver. Aurora was the first to take off her tunic, unfastening the brooch at the shoulder and letting the garment slip to the ground. I got my tunic off quickly. Like a couple of washerwomen, we wrung them out and hung them over a rock to dry. I laid my sword on the ground next to my tunic.

The entrance to the cave was on one side. We hung our clothes there to get some drying benefit from the wind but moved ourselves to the other side to avoid it. Aurora touched the Tyche ring, the only thing she was wearing now. "This doesn't seem to be working today."

Sitting down, I pulled her down in front of me, with her back to my chest and my arms and legs embracing her. "I'm feeling very fortunate right now," I said. "That's a nasty bruise on your hip, though." I kissed the spot.

"That's better." She snuggled up against me. "I thought you took off your sword. You know, we might be even warmer if we…"

"I wonder if that's what Dido said to Aeneas."

I've never felt more like a wild animal. Naked, in a cave, with a storm roaring outside. My legs and arms wrapped around my…mate? At Marinthus' taberna we were passionate but still aware of ourselves as civilized people. Just now, all inhibitions disappeared. I wonder if Aeneas grabbed Dido's hair the way Gaius did mine or if she clawed his back the way I did Gaius'? I even forgot about the rocks we were lying on.

His breathing has slowed, warm on my neck. What if we never had to leave this place?

Some time later we were lying quietly, as close to one another as we could get, limbs entangled, listening to the storm still raging.

"You do remember, don't you," Aurora said, running a hand over my cheek, "that Aeneas left Dido?"

"Darling, will you please forget that nonsense? It's only a story. Virgil was writing propaganda for Augustus' regime. He had to explain why Carthage and Rome hated one another. I'm not going to leave you."

"But how can we be together? Even if you don't marry Livilla, you'll eventually marry someone. You'll want to marry—"

"Hush!"

She raised herself on one elbow. "Gaius, don't hush me. We *have* to talk about it."

"No, be quiet. Listen."

From outside we heard rough male voices, drawing nearer.

"See, I told ya I 'membered this place from last year."

Two men entered the cave, carrying firewood and crooked staffs that identified them as shepherds. At this time of year shepherds move their flocks from summer pastures in mountain valleys to lower elevations to spend the winter.

Aurora and I sat up and tried to move back as far from the opening as we could. I cursed myself for getting so far away from my sword.

"Well, well," the larger man said. "Looka here, Pompo. We got company. Coupla pretty ones, already nekkid."

The men dropped their loads of firewood and smiled—expressions made hideous by their missing teeth and wet, dirt-streaked faces—as Aurora and I huddled together and tried to cover ourselves. The stench of wet, filthy clothes and unwashed men quickly filled the cave, like the smell of wet horses in a stable. The brutes spoke in a rural dialect of Latin, with some Oscan or Umbrian traces that had vanished from standard Latin generations ago.

"You'd better think twice," I said, lowering the pitch of my voice as much as I could, "before you do anything." I knew how ridiculous I sounded. Clenching my fists didn't really help.

The smaller man, Pompo, chuckled and drew a knife. The larger man, pulling a flint from a bag over his shoulder, found enough dry twigs and grass to start a small fire. He looked at our clothes and gave a rumbling laugh that made me feel like Ulysses discovered by the Cyclops. "Narrow-striper, eh? Ya'd scare me more if ya wasn't scramblin' 'round tryin' to cover yer balls. Whadda ya say, Pompo? Ya done thinkin' twice?"

The other man, who had only four teeth that I could see, rubbed my garment between two of his grimy fingers. "I think this tunic'd fit me real good, Mettius. And I don't have ta think twice 'bout that."

Mettius, bearded and in his forties, leaned forward to peer at us as the fire began to blaze and provide more light. I tried to get between him and Aurora. "Wanna protect her, eh? Don't blame ya, son. Lovely piece a stuff you got there. From them scratches on yer back, looks like she's done give ya a good hard ride."

"I'll bet he don't have much fight left in 'im," Pompo said, cracking me on the foot with his staff. I let out a sharp yelp. "Won'er where they come from?"

"Don't matter," Mettius said. "We didn't see nobody else 'round. Botha ya, over on all-fours. Now!"

I stood up and planted myself between the men and Aurora, hoping I looked less ridiculous than I felt. "No, you're not going to do this."

Pompo hooked me behind one knee with the crook at the top of his staff and flipped me to the ground, provoking a laugh from both men and a scream from Aurora. Mettius whacked me in the ribs with his staff.

"We jus' wanna have a little fun," the brute said. "We don't wanna hurt ya, but we will if ya make us. Now, get on all-fours."

Aurora pulled me to her and we turned over on our stomachs. The smaller man, Pompo, whacked me on the side again with his staff to hurry me along. I doubled over as intense pain shot through my ribs, but I would not give him the satisfaction of hearing me make another sound.

"Head on the ground, *m'lord*. Git yer arse up in the air. You, too, sweetums."

Mettius asked, "Which one do ya want first?"

"I want sweetums here." Pompo tapped Aurora between her legs with his staff.

"Well, now," Mettius said, "I kinda fancy her myself, before you dirty her all up with yer stinkin' prick."

"Then why'd ya ask me which one I wanted?" Pompo said.

"Jus' bein' perlite."

Glancing back over my shoulder, I saw him shove Pompo out of the way and pull a knife from his belt. They looked like two wolves fighting over a kill.

"All right, all right," Pompo said, throwing up his hands in surrender to the larger man. "Makes no differment to me. A hole is a hole is a arsehole, be it a he, a she, or a sheep."

"Gaius," Aurora whispered plaintively in Greek, "what are we going to do?"

I was sure they couldn't understand Greek. I couldn't hope to overcome them in a face-to-face fight, especially not when every breath brought pain. Turning my head to Aurora, I answered her in a low voice. "They're going to get down on their knees behind us. When I say, 'Now,' kick back hard and aim for the face."

"Shut up, you lot," Pompo said, smacking us both on our rear ends with his staff.

"*Ba-a-a-a*," Aurora said, raising a laugh from both men. In Greek she said to me, "That should make them feel more comfortable."

When I could sense that the men were occupied lifting their garments and preparing to violate us, I said, "Now!"

In spite of the pain in my side, I braced myself on my elbows and kicked with both legs, like a mule. My feet connected solidly with Pompo's face, toppling him onto his back. I jumped up and grabbed his shepherd's staff. Before he could draw a knife from his belt, I cracked him across the face. He spat out a tooth and crumbled in a heap.

Aurora's kick, with only one foot, had not been as well-aimed. Mettius was able to catch her leg and throw her over on her back. But she managed to slip out of his grasp and scramble to her feet.

"Hands off her!" I yelled.

The brute picked up his staff and struck the one I was holding with such force that mine splintered. Aurora jumped on his back, beating him with her fists. He shook her off, grabbed her by the throat, and flung her, face-first, against the wall of the cave. That gave me time to change my grip on what remained of my staff. I thrust it into his stomach and, when he doubled over, brought my knee up into his face. He fell back, not moving. I gave him a solid crack on the head anyway.

"Aurora! Are you all right?" I grabbed my side as I called to her.

"I think so. My head…hurts." She lay on the ground, at the base of the wall.

"Just give me a minute." Panting from exertion and fear and pain, I picked up Pompo's knife and cut enough strips off his tunic to tie up both men, hands and feet. Then I turned to Aurora, who was sitting up by now.

My touch startled her. "Gaius, why has it gotten so dark in here? Did the fire go out?"

"It's all right. I'm here. Let me take a look at your head."

Her forehead had struck a protruding rock. There was a bit of blood, but it didn't look too serious.

Aurora grasped my arm tightly, glancing around her. "Gaius, it's so dark. I can't see you. I can't see anything."

.   .   .   .

I threw more wood on the fire. I thought about taking Mettius' tunic, since he was the bigger man, and putting it around Aurora and me, but it was so filthy and stained that I couldn't bear the thought of it touching my skin. But I had to keep Aurora warm. Then I found a treasure.

Pompo was carrying a cloak in his bag, cleaner and of high quality—obviously stolen. It was big enough that I could wrap it around both Aurora and me.

"Just stay close," I assured her. "We'll be warm in no time."

"What's wrong, Gaius? Why can't I see?"

"It must be the blow to your head." I kissed her eyes. "I've read in my uncle's notebooks that a blow like that can cause loss of memory or blindness, or it can cause a person to act strangely. But it doesn't last. We'll get a doctor to see you as soon as we get home. You're going to be all right."

Aurora pulled away from me and started to cry.

I tried to draw her close again, but she wouldn't budge. "What's wrong?"

"It's my guilt, Gaius. This is the punishment for what I've done."

The lightning flashing outside might as well have struck me. "Punishment? By all the gods, what are you talking about?"

"It's what Virgil said. 'Dido called it a marriage. With this name she covered her guilt.' Her *guilt*."

"Listen to me, you silly girl. You're not guilty of anything except loving me. And for that I will be grateful as long as I live."

"But I shouldn't love you…my lord. I *can't* love you. And you can't love me." She took off the Tyche ring and threw it across the cave. "If it weren't for me, you'd be planning your wedding. I've ruined everything."

I put both my hands on her shoulders and did not let her jerk away this time. "You're upset, frightened. I know that. But you don't have to panic. We will deal with this when we get home."

"But Virgil said—"

"Virgil had no idea what Aeneas and Dido said. That wasn't real. He made it up. You're reading too much into one line of poetry."

All Aurora would do was cry. I wished I had Virgil's gift with words. Perhaps then I could console her. Was her blindness going to be temporary? I had no way to know, but I couldn't tell her that. All I could do was hope.

One of the trussed-up shepherds moaned. I had gagged them as well as tying them, and I did not mind in the least pushing pieces of their filthy tunics into their mouths. Now that I had my sword in

hand, I didn't think they posed any further danger to us, but I wanted
my servants to find us and get us out of here.

· · ·

Aurora cried herself to sleep, huddled next to me for warmth, if not
out of love. The storm had passed and the fire was burning low. In my
uncle's unpublished notebooks he describes the way people react when
they've been hit in the head. They recover more quickly, he concluded,
if they are kept sitting or standing up. I had followed that advice recently when I took a blow to the head and I believe it hastened my
recovery.

Before I lost the light, I leaned Aurora against the wall of the cave
and managed to find the Tyche ring and hang it around my neck. I put
the last of the shepherds' wood on the fire, including their staffs. I was
contemplating cutting their tunics off them for a little more fuel when
I heard someone calling my name.

Trying not to disturb Aurora, I put my head out the entrance to the
cave. My heart leapt with joy to see a *raeda* stopped by the scarred tree.
Demetrius himself stood beside it, calling my name in all directions.
Several of my men were riding up and down the road, calling for me.

"Up here!" I cried.

In only a few moments Demetrius, puffing from the exertion, was
at the entrance of the cave with dry clothes over his arm. "My lord, are
you all right?"

I stopped him and took the garments, giving him our wet clothes
in return. His eyes widened as he realized that he was holding both
of our tunics. "We've been better. We'll be down shortly. Get the *raeda*
turned around."

"Yes, my lord. I brought some food."

"That's welcome news indeed."

A dry tunic—and a heavy winter one at that—had never felt so
good. I put my sword on under it, then turned to the task of getting
Aurora dressed. No matter how I tried to rouse her, she seemed to stay
half asleep. I got the tunic on her and wrapped a clean cloak around
her. I could see that I would practically have to carry her down the hill.
As wet and slippery as the ground was, I was afraid I might let her fall
and injure her even more.

Before we left the cave I drew my sword and bent over Mettius. He whined and moaned. I guess I cut a more impressive figure wearing my stripe and waving a sword.

"What are you doing, my lord?" Aurora asked groggily from where she was sitting on the other side of the cave.

"I'm going to do to these swine what they would have done to us."

Suppressing the urge to gag, I grabbed Mettius' greasy hair, jerked his head back, and held my sword against his throat with enough pressure that, if he even swallowed, he would break the skin. Behind his gag he cried more loudly. His entire body stank even more as he soiled himself. At least this time he was taking me seriously.

"My lord!" Aurora pleaded. "Please don't hurt them."

I flung Mettius' head back to the ground with a thud and turned to Aurora in disbelief. "Don't hurt them? After what they were going to do to us?"

"I know, my lord. But you're a kind and humane man. They're defenseless. If you kill them, you'll be no better than they are. Please, don't. I beg you."

My hand tightened around the handle of my sword. These men had subjected me to the threat of the ultimate humiliation a man can endure and had threatened to rape the woman I love. And now she was asking me to spare them.

I grabbed Mettius' hair again and put my sword to his throat. "You have no idea," I said, grinding the words between my teeth, "how much I want to slit your filthy throat. But I have to yield to this lady's request, even if I don't understand it. You're strong enough, I'm sure, to free yourself before a bear or a wolf finds you. I'll even leave your knife. It's by the fire. When you do get loose, sacrifice to whatever foul god you worship and give thanks that you're still alive. But I know your name and"—I increased the pressure on my blade ever so slightly—"if this woman's injury proves to be permanent, I will hunt you down and *kill* you, no matter what she says. And I promise you it won't be a quick or merciful death."

I stood up as though to leave, then turned back to Mettius, letting the point of my sword rest heavily on his crotch, eliciting one more groan from him. "Oh, if you had actually raped her, I would be feeding your genitals to you right now."

·   ·   ·

Aurora came to her senses enough to walk down the hill with my assistance. Her grip on my arm was so tight it was painful, almost as painful as the rib on the other side of my chest. "Why can't I see?" she kept asking.

"We're going home," I assured her. "Everything's going to be all right." Sometimes the easier a promise is to make, the harder it is to keep. I could only hope that her injury was no more serious than the one I had received when I was hit on the head in an accident in a boat. Her blindness, though, worried me more than I would admit to her. Because she kept trying to go to sleep, we had to prop her between Demetrius and me, to keep her sitting up. I put a cushion behind her head so it wouldn't bounce against the hard sides of the *raeda*.

"Did the servants get home with the horses?" I asked Demetrius.

"Yes, my lord. And they found your runaway along the road. All have been returned to Saturius."

"Good, that's taken care of. It was resourceful of them to go for help and come back to get us."

"They did leave two men in this vicinity, my lord, in case you emerged from your hiding place."

I was disappointed they hadn't seen Pompo and Mettius, but in the woods and with the storm raging, I couldn't really fault them.

"There is one other surprising development, my lord."

I groaned. For me lately the word "surprise" had just meant bad news—my engagement, Tacitus' departure, now Aurora's injury. "What is it?"

"The woman, Crispina, left this morning, my lord."

"Where did she go? What did she say?"

"We don't know, my lord. One of the servants saw her in the *latrina* shortly after sunrise, but no one has seen her since. About the third hour I discovered that the rear gate was unlatched. She must have gone out that way."

"That's unfortunate. I had more questions for her." And once again "surprise" meant bad news. "What about the boy?"

"She left him, my lord."

.   .   .

When we reached my home I wanted to carry Aurora in myself, but I knew that would arouse my mother's ire and make the other servants suspicious of my relationship with Aurora. Two of the servant women helped her walk into the house, with me right behind them, my arms out ready to assist, although I couldn't have done anything because of the pain I was in.

As we came into the house, one of the women encouraged Aurora. "Come on, dear. We'll get you to bed and you'll feel better in no time."

"No," I said. "Keep her sitting up. That's an order. Put her in the room next to mine." I keep that room unoccupied to guarantee that I will have the kind of quiet I need to sleep and write. The two rooms together are not as nice as the suite I've constructed for myself at my villa in Laurentum, but it's the best I can do in a house in the city.

"Why not just put her in *with* you?" a woman's voice said.

I turned to see Pompeia and my mother emerging from a room off the atrium. Seeing my thin, fragile mother next to a hefty, robust woman like her cousin made me wonder if my mother was ill, or was growing old faster than I realized.

"That's what you really want to do, isn't it?" Pompeia continued. "To have her right there with you? Do you see, Plinia? That's what my daughter was talking about. That's why she won't have him."

So Livilla had told her mother that she wasn't going to marry me. I had hoped she might leave Aurora out of it, just say that she'd decided I would be an inadequate husband.

"He takes all kind of risks," Pompeia continued. "Livilla said she's afraid he'll get himself killed and leave her a widow before she's twenty, like her sister."

Her sister a widow? What was that all about? I felt like I'd walked into the middle of a play and didn't know what was going on. Did that mean Livilla hadn't mentioned Aurora? I would have to straighten all of that out later. Struggling to keep my voice even and wincing at the pain in my chest, I clipped the words as I said, "This woman is injured. I want to be sure she has the proper care."

Pompeia must have read the anger in my voice. She fell quiet as I turned and walked away.

But my mother wasn't quiet. "We will have to talk about this, Gaius. It must be soon, and it will be a long talk."

Nodding to her, I sent a servant with a message to Jacob, telling

him that Aurora had been injured and asking him to see me as soon
as possible.

.   .   .

While I sat with Aurora, I sent another servant to fetch Democrites,
a physician of whom my uncle thought highly. He is attached to the
family of a friend of mine, Servilius Pudens, so I had no hesitation in
requesting his services. Meanwhile I set Phineas to looking through
the medical works in my library for any information about the treatment of blindness or injuries to the head beyond what my uncle said
in his notebooks.

Democrites returned with my servant. I thanked him for his
prompt response.

"I'm glad to be of service, sir. Your uncle and I had many interesting
conversations. I had the greatest respect for him."

"As he did for you. Now, the woman who was injured is in here."

He felt Aurora's head, peered into her eyes, and asked her several
questions about where she was and what had happened to her. She
told a simplified version of the story—we were waiting out the storm
in a cave when two men found us and attacked us. During the scuffle
she hit her head on the wall of the cave. She made me sound Herculean
in the way I overcame them. Democrites raised his eyebrows but didn't
ask for further details. I corroborated her story.

When he was finished I walked with him as far as the front edge
of the garden, far enough to be out of Aurora's hearing. "What can you
tell me?" I asked. "Is she going to be blind forever?"

"That I cannot say, sir. There doesn't seem to be any serious injury.
Her memory is unimpaired. I'll give some thought to a course of treatment and return tomorrow, if that suits you."

"By all means."

"You seem to have a pain in your side, sir. Were you injured in the
fight?"

I put a hand on my side. "There is a sharp pain here."

Democrites touched the spot and put pressure on it. "I think you
have a cracked rib," he said as I moaned.

"Is there anything you can do about it?"

He shook his head. "It will have to heal on its own. I can give you
an opiate to ease the pain, with the warning that it can cloud the mind."

"No. I need to be able to think clearly. I'll see you tomorrow, and thank you again."

Watching him walk through the atrium, I noticed Hashep and Dakla playing around the *impluvium* with Clodius. They had fashioned boats out of pieces of papyrus and were sailing them. They had to retrieve them from the shallow water as they floated to a halt. I was surprised at how easily Clodius was adapting to being deserted by his mother. A boy that age, it seemed to me, ought to show some distress about her leaving. I needed to talk to him, and I didn't know when I would get another chance.

The children stood when I approached them. I picked up one of their boats and refolded it. "This is the way I made them when I was a boy." I launched the boat and it floated all the way across the *impluvium*.

Clodius' eyes got big. "Show me how, please, Uncle Gaius, sir."

"Hashep, run to the library and get me the biggest piece of papyrus you can find and a pot of glue. Tell Phineas I need it but not why. He thinks this is a waste of papyrus."

While we waited I looked at the boat Clodius had made and showed him a trick or two that I had learned as a boy. When he launched it again, I asked him, "You were out at that villa with your mother, weren't you?"

"Yes, sir."

"Did you see or hear anything?"

"No, sir. I was in a room with one of our servants. He gave me a honey cake."

"Did you see your sister, Fabia, while you were there?"

The boy shook his head. "She wasn't my sister."

"Oh, I know. She was your half sister."

"No, sir. She told me she was glad she wasn't any relation to me. She was mean to me."

Hashep returned with a large piece of papyrus. I folded it into a flat-bottomed barge, gluing it in spots to hold it together. I decided not to press Clodius any more for now, but to let the children enjoy their play. Besides, Aurora had to be my first concern.

When I sat down with her again she asked, "What did he say, my lord?"

"He's going to think about what needs to be done." That much was true.

"But, my lord, what if—"

"There's nothing we can do right now. You're going to have the best care anyone can have. That's the only thing I know for certain."

Sit up, they tell me. Don't go to sleep. But all I want to do is lie down and go to sleep. I wish I could go to sleep and, when I wake up, find out that this is all just a dream. I might as well be asleep. I can't see anything.

I should never have coupled with Gaius. That I can see. And it was my doing. He would never have betrayed Livilla if I hadn't been so brazen. Now she hates me, Plinia hates me, and Gaius himself will come to hate me, no matter how much he says he won't. He'll leave me, just like Aeneas left Dido. He'll send me to another of his estates or he'll sell me.

What would I do if that happened? Would I kill myself, like Dido did?

It was close to dinner time when Demetrius informed me that Jacob was waiting to see me. "I put him in the Ovid room, my lord."

I left a servant woman to watch over Aurora. On my way to meet Jacob, I stopped in my library and wrote a clean copy of the ROTAS square on a piece of papyrus. Jacob stood when I entered the room and I gestured for him to sit.

"I'm sorry to hear about Aurora, my lord. Do you think her injury is serious?"

"I'm not sure. A doctor was here earlier and will be back tomorrow. But that's not why I asked you to come see me. This is." I handed him the papyrus. He looked at it and raised his eyes to meet mine.

"You noticed my reaction when I saw this out at Martial's farm. I was afraid you had."

"Why were you afraid? Do you know something about the meaning of this gibberish?"

"Yes, my lord, I do."

XII

ONE OF THE LAMPS on the lamp tree sputtered and went out. I trimmed the wick and relit it from one of the burning ones.

Jacob picked up the papyrus and his eyes met mine. The light falling across his face made the lines and creases stand out as though a sculptor had chiseled them. "Why are you so interested in this puzzle, my lord?"

"As you heard me tell Regulus, it has some connection with one murder that's already been committed and another one that may be committed. Understanding what it means could help me prevent that."

Jacob shook his head. "It has nothing to do with anyone being murdered, my lord."

"Then what does it mean?"

"First, may I ask how you came to possess it?"

He omitted the honorific "my lord," assuming a kind of familiarity—almost equality—but I decided I needed information more than I needed to insist on formality. "It was drawn on the wall of a *taberna* on the Ostian Road."

"Marinthus' *taberna*." He said it rather than asked.

"You know the place?"

"Yes. Regulus sent me on some business to Ostia a few months ago. I stopped at Marinthus' on my way there and I...drew this on the wall."

I was so thunderstruck that I had to sit down. "So you know what it means."

"I know what it means to me. I doubt it means the same to you."

"How can it mean one thing to you and something else to me?" I was already facing enough riddles in the case of Fabia's murder. "Speak plainly, please."

"It can mean different things to each of us because I am a Christian and you are not, are you?"

"What? That is a preposterous and impertinent question. What does it have to do with this?"

"This square is a symbol known to many Christians."

"But what does it mean?"

"I could show you more easily than I can tell you, if I had a pen and some ink."

I opened the door and called the first servant I saw in the atrium, sending her to the library and ordering her to run, both ways. When she returned, I set the material on a table in the corner of the room. Jacob dipped the pen in the ink and wrote on the back of the sheet of papyrus.

As the pen scratched across the papyrus, I pondered his question. Of course I wasn't a Christian. In the last few years, though, I had learned that several servants in my *familia* did belong to that mysterious sect. The fact that they were Christians had not, as far as I could tell, made them disloyal to me or affected their work in my household. They said their leaders taught them to be obedient to those in authority. Uncertain what to do with them, I had isolated them on my estate at Misenum to keep them from spreading their doctrine any further.

Just what that doctrine is, no one seems to know. From what my servants told me, it has something to do with their inexplicable devotion to a man who was executed as a criminal in Judaea when Tiberius was *princeps*. They even claim he awakened from death. On my return journey from Syria two years ago I met two Christians. They seemed honorable, sensible men and even helped in my investigation of a murder. One of them, a physician, gave me a book he had written, explaining the origins of the cult. Without even reading it, I allowed the group of Christian servants I sent to Misenum to take the scroll with them. They seemed to regard it as some kind of treasure.

Jacob put down the pen and handed the papyrus back to me. "This is what the square means to me."

It took me a moment to realize that I was looking at the letters of the square rearranged:

```
                    P
                    A
          A         T         O
                    E
                    R
P     A     T     E     R     N     O     S     T     E     R
                    O
                    S
          A         T         O
                    E
                    R
```

"Pater noster?"

"Those are the first two words in a prayer which our Lord—our heavenly Lord—taught us to pray, or more accurately, the Latin translation of it. The *A*s and *O*s are Alpha and Omega. Our God is the beginning and the end."

"Of what?"

"Of everything."

That bold assertion didn't leave much room for debate. I studied what Jacob had written until I realized something. Picking up the pen and dipping it in the ink, I drew some lines. "A line drawn from one *T* to another still forms a square. And the extra *A*s and *O*s can be connected with lines that form another square." I showed him what I had drawn. "That creates a square with another square inside it, tilted forty-five degrees, leaving a triangle on each corner of the figure. Is that significant?"

"The *T* is the shape of the cross," Jacob said. "Anyone who has seen a crucifixion would recognize that."

"Did you place the *A*s and *O*s where they are deliberately?"

Jacob nodded. "The Alpha and Omega next to the *T* symbolizes the death of the son of God on the cross. Notice that when the puzzle is written in the form of a square, those letters are still next to one another. The triangles you've discerned, going from Alpha to Omega through the cross, I've not noticed before." He studied my diagram, closed his eyes, then looked at me with a chuckle. "Sir, I believe you've discovered a symbol of the Trinity."

"Trinity?"

"Yes. God is Father, Son, and Holy Spirit."

"That's three gods."

"We see it as three manifestations of the one God."

"Like Hermes Trismegistus?"

Jacob shook his head. "No. There might appear to be a similarity, but this is something else entirely."

Once again I had the feeling that I was being misled, lied to. Could I not get a believable statement from anyone these days? Avoiding any further delving into mythology, I asked a direct question. "Does Regulus know you're a Christian?"

"I don't believe he does. Are you going to tell him?" He asked the question without any fear in his voice or on his face.

"I see no reason to. It's not against the law to believe something, no matter how absurd it may seem to others. Aristarchus believed the earth moves around the sun. Domitian believes he's a god. I'm not convinced by either, though I'm more inclined to believe Aristarchus."

"I can assure you that Domitian is no god," Jacob said. "More likely a demon in the flesh."

My mouth twitched. "You should be more circumspect in what you say about the *princeps*," I cautioned him, while I tried to suppress a smile. "Someone who's not concerned about your religious views might inform on you for political reasons."

"What would they gain? I've no fortune to be seized."

He had a point. Men like Regulus amass their wealth by informing on rich men and women and receiving a portion of whatever the government confiscates when they're found guilty, and they're always found guilty. Jacob was right. No one would inform on him from a financial motive.

"But the demand for victims in the arena is insatiable," I said, to keep some pressure on him.

Jacob closed his eyes for an instant. "I believe that is my destiny, and I'm not afraid of it. But that's not why you asked me to come here. You wanted to talk to me about the square. I've told you what I can."

"You haven't explained AREPO."

Jacob shrugged. "There's nothing to explain. It's a nonsense word that results when the letters of the *Pater Noster* are rearranged in this way. It means nothing, but it distracts non-Christians from the true secret of the square, which we use to identify ourselves to one another. When we see that someone who wants to talk about the square is not a Christian, we emphasize the AREPO line."

"Who created it?" As much as I enjoy codes and ciphers, I felt envious of someone who could create a puzzle that read the same backwards, forward, and up and down, even if it had the serious flaw of a meaningless word.

"I don't know. Christians first came to Rome in Claudius' time. I'm told it has been in use since then."

Over thirty years then. "My friend Tacitus and I examined this puzzle closely at Marinthus'. I find it hard to believe we were staring at a Christian symbol all that time and never realized it."

"That is its purpose." He chuckled. "I saw people at Marinthus' argue over it at length. I even told one fellow that, if he could understand the AREPO line, he would understand the entire square. He thought I was some kind of prophet or oracle."

"Wait. When was this?"

"About…a month ago."

I leaned forward in my excitement. "Did that man have a woman with him?"

"Yes, he did."

"Did the woman have a scar on her left cheek?"

He closed his eyes, as though calling a scene up from his memory. "Now that you mention it, she did."

"What else can you tell me about them? Don't leave out any detail, no matter how small."

From Jacob's description I knew he was talking about Crispina. "Did you hear any names?"

"The woman called the man Popilius. I presume he was her husband."

I nodded. "What puzzles me is that you make Crispina the more assertive and inquisitive of the pair, the one who was more interested in the puzzle, and the better educated."

"She definitely was. I'm not even sure the man could read. The woman kept pulling him back to it when he just wanted to drink."

That wasn't what Crispina had told us, but eyewitnesses almost always disagree about what they've seen. Thucydides noticed that, five hundred years ago.

"My lord," Jacob finally said. "I do need to return to Regulus' house."

"Of course." I escorted him to the door and thanked him for all the information he had given me. "Since Aurora is injured, I will have to find someone else to exchange information between my house and Regulus' in that matter we spoke of earlier. I'd like to use Phineas. I consider him most trustworthy."

"I think you'll find that Phineas, while entirely trustworthy, would rather not communicate with me."

"Why not?"

"He and his mother consider me—and all Jews who become Christians—traitors to their faith and to their nation."

"Their nation no longer exists."

"Perhaps not in a physical sense."

"If not Phineas, then whom should I send?"

"If I give you a name, my lord, you'll suspect that person is a Christian."

"I'm already aware that some of my servants are Christians. I've not punished anyone."

"You sent some of them to your estate at Misenum."

How much did this man know about the inner workings of my house? "Being sent to live on the Bay of Naples hardly qualifies as punishment."

"True, my lord. And it has allowed them to spread the seed of the Word in another field."

There seemed to be some allusion to the plowman—the SATOR of the puzzle—in that statement, but I wanted to get back to Aurora. "If you name someone you trust, I will not make any inquiries about his or her beliefs, nor will I take any action against them. You have my promise."

"Very well, my lord. Dorias, one of your kitchen maids, should be your choice."

"Dorias? I thought she was one of Regulus' spies. She's been seen making frequent trips to his house."

Jacob laughed. "You need have no fear of her, my lord. She's one of my flock. She comes to see me whenever she's troubled. One thing I urge upon her is loyalty to her master."

"Very well then. Dorias it shall be."

As I returned to Aurora, I tried to digest what Jacob had told me, but some of it sat on my stomach like a disagreeable meal. Should I be worried that these Christians were cropping up in the most unexpected places? At least one of them was preparing the food I ate, but I had suffered no ill effects. Should the government take any action against them? I knew they were persecuted by Nero in the aftermath of the great fire. That was twenty years ago and Nero's tortures were so brutal that people began to sympathize with the victims. Since then they had been ignored.

We have persecuted other religions, if they threatened public order. Tiberius drove the cult of Isis out of Rome perhaps fifty years ago. According to Livy, a couple of thousand people were killed when the cult of Dionysus first appeared in Rome, over two hundred years ago. We Romans ask of a new religion not what do they *believe* but what do they *do*? Do they pose any threat to the community? Christians don't seem to *do* much of anything, certainly nothing that endangers the rest of us. They have a distorted point of view that turns the world upside down, but does that threaten anyone else?

. . .

When I returned to my room Naomi was waiting outside the door, pulling a wrap over her shoulders against the chill of evening.

"My lord, your mother wants to speak with you. *Now.*"

I was taken aback by the stress she put on the word but too anxious about Aurora to object to it. "Can't it wait until morning?"

"*Now,* my lord. That was her very word and her emphasis."

Naomi walked in front of me, as befit the servant leading the master. In spite of her age and all she had endured in her life, she walked with a confident step. She was a sturdy woman, though not large, and her dark hair was showing a few streaks of gray. As we crossed the garden she seemed in no hurry, contrary to her stress on the word "now." She paused as we came to the *piscina.*

"My lord, may I say something about your mother?"

"By all means. I've been concerned about her lately. She seems so confused."

"I know, my lord. I've urged her to talk with you about the problem, but she refuses."

"'Problem'? What is the problem?"

"A few months ago, my lord, while she was bathing, your mother found a lump in one of her breasts. The Greeks call it a *karkinos*. Any woman knows it is a death sentence."

My heart sank and my shoulders sagged. Tacitus had once told me that his mother found a lump in her breast. She died two years later. "What is it?"

"We don't know, my lord. But, whatever it is, the lump will grow and spread to other parts of her body."

I had trouble drawing a breath. "Are you telling me that my mother is dying?"

"Yes, my lord. No one knows how long it will take. It could be a few months or it could be several years. But she is dying. She's afraid, terribly afraid. She knows she was unkind to Aurora's mother and she worries that now some god has afflicted her with the same disease that killed Monica."

"She thinks this is some kind of divine vengeance?"

"Yes, my lord. She frets about it constantly. The worry is consuming her as much as the disease. It has left her unable to focus on other things. That's why she forgets names and mixes things up. It's also why she wants to see you married as soon as possible. She feels it's her biggest duty to you, since your father and uncle are both dead."

"But one lump? Why does that mean she's going to die?"

Naomi held her hands up, as though surrendering to fate. "Women know this, my lord. We've seen it happen to our mothers and our sisters—even our daughters. Every time we bathe, we have a moment of dread. Is that a lump? No one knows what it is, but there's nothing anyone can do about it."

"I don't believe that. We need to get a doctor in here—"

"My lord, no doctor has ever found a cure."

I sat down on a bench beside the *piscina*, looking up at Naomi as though she might yet offer me some hope. What I really wanted was for her to hold me and let me cry. "There must be something I can do. I can't just let her die."

Naomi sat down beside me and put a hand on my leg. I did not object. "All you can do, my lord, is go on caring for her as you always have and make her comfortable when the time comes."

Tacitus said his mother suffered greatly at the end. He wished she had killed herself, as some women have done, but she was afraid to leave Tacitus' disabled brother with no one to care for him. If my mother was in pain, that might be a time for Democrites' opiates.

"Why didn't she tell me herself?"

"She doesn't want you to know, my lord. You must not say anything to her about this."

"Why? Did you promise you wouldn't say anything to me?"

Naomi looked offended. "No, my lord. If I had promised that, I wouldn't have said anything to you. Now, she's waiting to talk with you."

I wasn't aware of walking the rest of the way across the garden. *My mother is dying*, I kept thinking. Not long ago I had reminded myself that there were three people in the world I could not bear to lose. Now Tacitus had abandoned me, my mother was dying, and Aurora was blind and had rejected me.

Naomi opened the door to my mother's room and stood aside to let me enter. She did not follow me. My mother, reclining on her couch, gestured for me to take the chair across from her. I leaned over and kissed her on the cheek before I sat down.

"Good evening, Gaius," she began.

"Good evening, Mother. You're looking well."

She looked at me in a way that told me I should not have said that.

"What do you want to talk about?" I asked before she could hatch any suspicions about what I had said.

"It's not an easy subject to broach, but we must." She shifted on her couch. "Livilla has told her mother that she does not want to marry you. I assume she has told you."

"Yes. She talked to me two days ago. Did she tell her mother why she decided this?" I was curious to hear what she said, if she didn't tell the truth.

"She said she realized that you live too dangerous a life. You've been injured several times recently and only barely escaped death in Naples last month. She doesn't want to be a widow by the time she's twenty."

"I see," I said, trying to suppress my relief. "I'm surprised you're only just now finding out about this. News of that sort usually travels much faster."

"Well, just as some travelers can claim priority on our roads, some news is more important than others. The news which Pompeia received from Spain yesterday took precedence."

"From Spain? Isn't that where her older daughter—"

"Yes. Her older daughter's husband is dead."

"By the gods! What happened?" We weren't at war with anyone in Spain. Government service there was essentially a matter of collecting taxes, building roads, and settling court cases. It shouldn't be any more dangerous than walking across the Forum.

"Liburnius slipped in their bath, hit his head, and fell into the water and drowned."

"It must have been a serious injury, if he didn't revive when he hit the water."

"I'm told the wound was quite severe. There was a good deal of blood."

"Wasn't there anyone with him in the bath?"

"From what I understand, the servant who usually attends him had gone to the *latrina* for a moment."

"That's tragic." And very odd, I thought, that a man would receive such a hard blow merely from a fall in a bath, but I was probably over-dramatizing the event. I couldn't imagine what, in a bath, would cut him so badly. Then I chided myself. I've seen too many murders. By the time a report gets from Spain to Rome, a pinprick can become an open vein. "I guess it's just as well we're not planning a wedding now. We would have to postpone it to allow Pompeia's family a proper period of mourning."

"They already have mourning wreaths up on their door. Poor Livia is due home with her husband's ashes in a few days. The messenger who brought the news said she was not far behind him."

"Please give my condolences to Livilla and Pompeia. I'm sure they don't want to see me right now."

"No, they don't, and that is something we'll have to talk about at another time. I'm too tired for such a difficult discussion right now."

Was that a clue to the effects of her disease? How could she not tell me about something so devastating? "I'll let you rest then." I stood up. "Please tell Pompeia that I'll do anything I can to settle Liburnius' estate, or whatever else needs to be done."

"Sit down. What you're going to do is get married." She said it without rancor but with absolute determination. "Before the end of the year."

"But, Mother—"

"What? Do you have some objection to getting married?"

My mother is dying, I heard myself thinking. *How can I deny her anything?*

"No, Mother. But whom do you expect me to marry on such short notice?"

"Naomi and I are working on a list. We'll let you know when we've settled on someone." She shifted her weight again, as though she couldn't get comfortable. "Now, dear, I'm very tired. Please ask Naomi to come in."

Poets are allowed to lie. Who said that? Virgil must have been lying. Like Gaius said, he had no idea what happened between Aeneas and Dido. They probably weren't even real people. As Gaius said, the whole story might have been invented to explain why Rome and Carthage hate one another. What Dido said about her crime was probably put in just to make the meter come out right. The whole story has nothing real in it.

What is real is the touch of Gaius' hand on my breasts, between my legs—it feels so much better than when I do it—and that wonderful feeling when he's poised over me and I can see the desire in his eyes, feel it in his husky breathing. Why should I be denied that just because my father sold me into slavery? Why should Gaius have to spend his life married to a woman he doesn't love?

That's what is so unusual about Gaius. Funny that I couldn't "see" it until I couldn't see. He is capable of actually loving a woman. Ovid wrote all about "the art of love," but what he meant was "the art of seduction."

For him it's all a game that the man wins when he beds the woman. Gaius cares about me, but he knows he has a duty to marry, if not Livilla then some other high-born girl.

I was foolish to say what I did in that cave. I was frightened. I hope Gaius can forgive me. If he won't, that would be reason to kill myself.

I spent a long night moving from my bed to the garden. When I looked in on Aurora once, she seemed to be sleeping, which I could not do. The next morning I left the business of dealing with my clients at the *salutatio* to Demetrius so I could sit with Aurora. I told him that I would not see anyone, no matter how dire their story. "Just give them some money and tell them to come back tomorrow. I'm not going anywhere today, so I won't need them."

"But, my lord, you promised Lucius Bibulus you would help him in his suit."

"I will, but not today."

Entering the room where Aurora had spent the night, I dismissed the two women who had stayed with her. We had positioned her in one corner of the room, with cushions around her so that she had to remain sitting up. She opened her eyes when she heard my voice.

"Good morning…Gaius."

A wave of joy swept over me, made all the keener by the buffeting I had endured the previous day. But what if this was just another aberration caused by the blow to her head? I knelt before her. "I was afraid I would never hear you call me that again. Are you feeling better?"

"Somewhat. I want to apologize for my outburst yesterday. I was frightened and didn't know what I was saying. Can you forgive me?"

"It's forgotten. Don't give it another thought."

"And I'm sorry I threw away the Tyche ring. It meant so much to both of us."

I slipped the leather strap with the ring on it over my head and placed it on her. She clasped the ring and her face lit up. "You found it!"

"I wouldn't have left there without it." I placed my hand over hers and sat beside her.

"Is it day now?" she asked.

"Yes, almost the second hour."

We sat without talking for a while. The bruise on her forehead was still purple and ugly. When I touched it, she winced.

Finally the noise from the atrium subsided. "My clients are gone. Let's go for a walk. The doctor said you should be up and moving around."

Staying under the shade of the colonnade that surrounded the garden, I slipped her arm through mine and started toward the back of the house.

"Gaius," she whispered, trying to pull away, "everyone will see us."

"Let them." I clamped my arm close to my side so she couldn't slip away from me. During a restless night I had decided that I didn't care who in my household saw me showing affection to her. I obviously couldn't conceal how I felt as well as I thought I could.

"You're going to hear from your mother," Aurora cautioned me.

"I will deal with her when I have to. You don't need to worry about that."

"At least you don't have to worry about Livilla."

"Let's not talk about all that." How would I ever tell her that I would soon be engaged again and that I felt a stronger obligation than ever to go through with the marriage? "All you have to do is concentrate on getting well."

"Or learning how to live with being blind."

"Don't talk like that. The doctor says you could wake up tomorrow with your sight restored."

"Or I could never see your sweet face again. I'll accept it, if I must. What good does it do to grieve over something that can't be changed?"

"We don't know that it can't be. The doctor didn't say any such thing." Not like with a *karkinos*.

She leaned closer to me. "I'll be all right, Gaius, whatever happens, as long as I know you're with me."

"That's one thing that will not change. I promise you that."

Aurora sighed deeply. "It is odd, not being able to see. It makes me more aware of sounds and smells. I can sense things going on around me that I didn't notice before."

"Don't tell me you're going to become another Teiresias." When he was struck blind by Juno, Teiresias was given prophetic powers—

a different kind of sight—as compensation by Jupiter, since one god cannot undo what another god has done.

"Would you believe me if I told you that I can tell when you're looking at me and when you're not?"

"You should be able to figure that out from listening to where my voice is coming from."

"I can tell, even when you're not speaking."

"Because you know I'm always looking at you."

She blushed. "Gaius, please, don't. I'm serious. Try me."

Three times she was able to tell whether I was looking at her or not. It did seem like more than lucky guessing. She would cock her head, like an animal sniffing the wind or straining to hear some sound that came only to her ear.

"That's uncanny," I said. "Perhaps you can use this newfound ability to explain why Crispina bolted, or where we should be hunting for Popilius."

"There is something odd about this whole business. Since you mentioned hunting, I feel like we've been given a false scent. Sitting in the dark, I can't do much except think and listen. I've been thinking about the things Crispina said. Some of it doesn't ring true."

We had reached the far end of the garden, beside the *exhedra*. Before I could ask her to explain just what she meant, Demetrius came into the garden and rushed up to us. "My lord, there are some people here—"

"I told you I will *not* see anyone this morning," I snapped. "Tell them to come back tomorrow, and I probably won't see them then."

"Now, is that any way to treat a friend?" Tacitus bellowed from the other end of the garden.

XIII

S TAY RIGHT HERE," I told Aurora, placing her hand on one of the columns that line the garden. "You're just a few steps from the *exhedra* on your left. I'll be right back."

I rushed to Tacitus and threw my arms around him, barely able to hold back tears. "Thank the gods!" I cried. "But I thought you were going to Gaul. Your brother—"

"No, my brother is fine. I'll explain. But what about you? You don't look or sound so good." He put an arm around my shoulder and I winced from the pain in my side.

I told him as succinctly as I could about what had happened since the last time I saw him.

"Aurora's blind?" He shook his head when I finished and looked across the garden at her. "That's tragic. You should have gutted the bastard who did it. I would have, without a moment's hesitation."

"How could I, with Aurora begging me not to?"

"Hmm. I see your point. Don't you wonder sometimes what women are thinking? What are you going to do with her now? I mean, a blind slave—"

"How can you even ask that? I'll take care of her as long as she needs me. She may recover her sight. The doctor holds out some hope. But that doesn't make any difference." I looked at Aurora, still standing by the column where I'd left her. Her head was high, but the expression on her face told me that she was afraid, uncertain where she was. "I need to go to her."

Tacitus held me back. "You've coupled with her, haven't you?"

I turned on him, aghast. If he knew, who didn't know? "How did you—"

"It was obvious the last time I saw the two of you together. At least it was obvious to Julia. I wasn't sure, but from the mournful expression on your face now, even I can tell there's something between you two. What does your mother think? Or your bride-to-be?"

"They don't know, I hope." I straightened my shoulders, trying to go back on the offensive. I would have to explain to him later that the phrase "bride-to-be" didn't mean exactly what it had meant when he left. "We can talk about this some other time. Right now, you owe me an explanation."

"And I will very shortly pay that debt—in full, with enough interest to satisfy even the greediest money lender. Do you think we can get enough privacy in the *exhedra*? The morning is quite fine."

"All right. Let me get Aurora."

"And I have to get someone as well." He turned toward the front of the house and gestured. A man and a woman I hadn't noticed stepped out of the shadows. "This is Lucius Nonnius and his wife, Marcella."

The couple he introduced had the air of rural gentry. Their clothing suggested that they were reasonably well off by the standards of their village or small town, but the way they gawked at everything in my garden made it obvious that they were seeing things like this for the first time, things they would like to copy when they returned home.

"Welcome to my house," I said.

"We're very pleased to be here, sir," Nonnius said with a deferential nod.

I glanced at Tacitus for an explanation for their presence.

"They're neighbors of Crispina and Popilius," he said, "and Nonnius is a cousin of Popilius."

"I see. But how—"

"Let's get settled and then we can talk."

We crossed the garden and I took Aurora's hand. She squeezed mine in relief. "Tacitus has brought some visitors," I told her.

"I wish I could say it's nice to *see* you, my lord Tacitus," she said, picking up on my hint about the presence of strangers. "But it is nice to have you here again."

I decided I would just let Nonnius and Marcella wonder who Aurora was. From the way she addressed Tacitus and from my lack of an introduction, they should be able to figure it out for themselves." "Let's go into the *exhedra*."

"Oh, this is exquisite," Marcella cooed as we took our places on the couches, sitting instead of reclining. I expected Aurora to sit beside me on the high couch, but she stood behind me, with one hand on my shoulder—a more appropriate position for a servant. Nonnius and Marcella, as guests, took the middle couch.

"I've never seen such beautiful mosaics," Marcella went on. "And your garden is a work of art as well. I've never seen anything like the statue of that faun."

"You're very kind," I said. "My late uncle is responsible for most of what you see. I haven't made any major changes here since I inherited the house from him a few years ago. The faun, I'm told, was brought back from Corinth by Sulla."

I looked out over the garden, trying to imagine seeing it for the first time. The sun was high enough now that light fell directly on the garden. Melanchthon had recently trimmed the shrubs and the rain of a few days ago had left everything green and fresh. Marcella couldn't stop looking around. Nonnius' frank admiration was focused on Aurora, although he appeared to be looking at me. I couldn't fault the man's taste, even if his manners left something to be desired. I took a quick glimpse at her myself and was shocked. Standing where she was, with the sun behind her, the outline of her body could be seen through her tunic. I shifted my position on the couch and brought her to stand behind my other shoulder. Nonnius then shifted his gaze to me.

"Now, Cornelius Tacitus," I said, "please tell me what's going on. Where have you been?"

"Well, I decided to do what Aurora suggested and try to find Popilius' farm to see if any of his neighbors could tell me anything about him and Crispina."

"Why didn't you just tell me that was what you were going to do, instead of concocting that story about Gaul?" *And making me feel like you were deserting me.*

"Because you would have wanted to go with me, and I wanted to go alone to see if I could apply what I've learned from watching you. And, if it turned out to be a waste of time, I would not have taken you away from your inquiries."

"Did you uncover anything that will help us unravel this mess?"

"I'm afraid I may have just made it even messier."

"What do you mean? You found these neighbors, even a relative. Can't they clarify some things for us?"

"That depends on what you mean by 'clarify.' They say that everything Crispina told us was a lie."

.   .   .

"A…a lie?" I sputtered. "What do you mean, it was all a lie?" Aurora tightened her grip on my shoulder.

"Just what I said," Tacitus replied calmly. "A lie, a deliberate distortion of the truth. I'm sure you know the meaning of the word. I told them what Crispina told us and they said the only truth in it was that Popilius was her second husband. The rest is a fabrication worthy of a Milesian tale."

Aurora leaned in toward me. "My lord, I'm sorry if I've led you astray." Her voice shook. "She seemed truthful to me. And you heard her story, from her own lips."

"Yes, and I believed it. But, like you said, she may have been just trying to throw us off the scent." I patted her hand to reassure her, then turned to Nonnius and Marcella. "Tell me everything."

Nonnius began, but, from the way his wife's jaw was working, I had the feeling she wouldn't be silent for long. Her face resembled a thundercloud just before a downpour. "Well, sir, as Cornelius Tacitus said, she did speak one bit of truth. Her first husband was Fabius, and Popilius was her second husband. But Fabia wasn't her daughter. She was the daughter of Fabius by his first wife. That wife died giving birth to the girl, and Fabius remarried quickly, to give his child a mother."

"So Fabia was her stepdaughter." That explained Clodius' comment that Fabia wasn't his sister and perhaps his comment that she was mean to him.

"Yes, sir."

"What about the boy?" Aurora asked. "Was he Crispina's son?"

"I'll come to that," Nonnius said, looking at Aurora in surprise. "In due time."

"All right, then," I said. "Fabia was Crispina's stepdaughter."

"Yes, sir. She continued to raise the girl after Fabius died."

"But they never got on well," Marcella interjected, having held her tongue as long as she could, I suppose. "That little Fabia was more than a mother could handle by herself. She was beautiful and everybody told her so. Made her think mighty highly of herself. She needed a man's firm hand to keep her in line. That's why Crispina married Popilius."

"I thought she was trying to keep herself from starving," I said.

"*Pssht*," Marcella said, waving her hand. "She wasn't wanting for anything. She had plenty of her own and Fabius left her even more. Popilius moved into her house after they married because it was nicer than his. They combined their properties, just like Crispina planned all along."

"It's true," Tacitus said. "I've seen her farm. It's large enough to provide a comfortable living, and she has a good-sized *familia* to run it."

"So Popilius wasn't a former rejected suitor?"

"No, sir," Marcella said. "He owns the land next to Crispina's. She wanted to grab that and get some help raising Fabia in the bargain."

"But Popilius—and he is my cousin, sir—wasn't without his own plan," Nonnius said. "Pardon my frankness, but, before he married her, he boasted to me that he would plow Crispina until that field dried up. By then, he said, Fabia should be ready."

The plowing image again. "He wanted the girl? Couldn't he have just waited until she was nubile and then asked to marry her instead?"

"He wasn't sure Crispina would have him as a son-in-law. He didn't realize that she wanted his land, too."

"Oh, tell him the truth," Marcella said, jabbing her husband with an elbow. "That's what we're here to do. How long are you going to keep protecting him?"

Nonnius glared at her and lowered his head. When he looked up and caught my eye, I could see that he had decided to confront something unpleasant. "Well—how shall I put this?—my cousin has always been attracted to…well, to very young girls."

I felt a knot forming in my stomach. Although we Romans expect girls to marry young, we do not approve of men taking advantage of them when they're still children. As is true with so many of our less admirable social customs, there's no law against it, but it carries the same opprobrium as attraction to a member of one's own sex—one of those things that just "shouldn't be done." I noticed that Tacitus' head was down. Whatever his proclivities, at least I know he has never consorted with a child.

"Didn't Crispina know that about him?" I asked.

"No, sir. Popilius kept his secret well. He always went somewhere else to…indulge himself."

"Mostly to Ostia," Marcella said. "You can find anything in that place. It's like the very bottom of a sewer."

"I doubt you'll find many as pretty as little Fabia anywhere," Nonnius said. "Popilius felt he'd arrived in the Elysian Fields. Because Crispina got along so poorly with the child, she was quite happy to leave her in Popilius' care. For her part, I think little Fabia was happy to have a parent who cared about her, no matter how."

"How old was she when Popilius married Crispina?"

"She was seven," Marcella said, "but as flirty as a girl twice that age. She would sit in Popilius' lap and kiss him." She shuddered.

"She was an affectionate child," Nonnius said. "She couldn't have known how Popilius felt about her."

"She was a little tease," his wife snapped, shifting away from him on the couch. "She knew exactly what she was doing."

I needed to intervene before they came to blows, something I suspected they did regularly. "Crispina claimed that Popilius refused to let Fabia get married."

"That much is true, sir," Nonnius said. "He wasn't going to let another man have her. He told me he'd fallen in love with her, even after she became nubile. That's when he usually started looking somewhere else. But Fabia stayed small. Never did look her age. No breasts or hips to speak of."

That description certainly fit the body we had found tied to Tabellius' wheel.

"Popilius said he would never want anyone else," Nonnius continued. "They hid what they were doing from Crispina, but, when Fabia realized she was pregnant, she boasted to Crispina about it, since Crispina hadn't been able to bear a child."

"Wait!" Aurora said. "What about the boy? She told me he was her son."

"Well, only in a manner of speaking," Marcella said. "Crispina had suspected for some time that she couldn't have a child. She'd never gotten pregnant, even though she'd been married twice, and one of the men, at least, had fathered a child."

Nonnius snorted. "As if you can ever be certain who the father is."

Marcella glared at him, and I suspected she had produced a jug-eared heir who resembled the town butcher more than her husband. She resumed her story. "Crispina begged us to help her, being neighbors and friends, even Popilius' family. Eight years ago, when one of our servant girls found out she was pregnant, Crispina pretended she was, too. When our girl gave birth one night, we told her the child had died. The next morning I went to Crispina's house, bringing a load of supplies—including the baby—to help in her 'delivery.' I sent her servant women out of the room to get things. By the time they returned, Crispina had had an easy delivery. She presented Popilius with a handsome son, and nobody was any the wiser."

"You stole your servant's child?" I didn't know if I was more appalled at what they'd done or at the nonchalance with which she told us about it.

"The father was a free man, sir," Nonnius said, "with a wife and family of his own. He didn't want the child. There were going to be all sorts of legal problems, as I'm sure you understand." He looked at me as though I were in the habit of coupling with female slaves—mine or anyone else's—and producing bastards by them. "This way, everybody was relieved and Crispina had her baby."

I never cease to be amazed at how people can justify any action they decide to take. But what if Aurora were to have a child? Roman law would make him a slave because of his mother.

"It was even best for the boy," Marcella said. "He'll grow up a free man, not the child of a slave, if he gets to grow up. Do you know what Crispina has done with him?"

"She left him here. I thought it uncaring of her to abandon him, but if he's not really her son—"

"She cared enough to leave him in a safe place," Marcella said. "May we see him, sir?"

"I'll get him as soon as we're finished with this conversation. I don't think Clodius needs to hear it."

"No, sir. Certainly not. Would it be possible for us to take him home with us? We've no children of our own, and Clodius has always thought of us as his Aunt Marcella and Uncle Nonnius."

"Wouldn't it be uncomfortable to have him in the same house with the servant woman who is his actual mother? What if people see a resemblance?" My mother often comments on how much I look like her.

"No one has noticed so far," Nonnius said. "We worried about that for a while, but the boy seems to resemble his father more than his mother."

"Let me see if I understand this," Tacitus said. "Crispina made her husband think she was pregnant until you could slip a newborn child into the house?"

"She almost got away with it," Nonnius said. "But Fabia figured it out. She told Crispina she had seen her padding herself and she was going to tell Popilius."

Tacitus shook his head. "Was Popilius so obtuse that he couldn't see Crispina was fooling him? I've read comic plays in which women deceived their husbands like this, but I never found them believable. How could a man be so unaware of what his wife was doing?"

"He wasn't much interested in Crispina, sir. He coupled with her now and then, he said, to keep her from getting suspicious about… what he was doing with Fabia. She made sure she seduced him just as soon as we knew our servant girl was with child. I doubt they ever coupled after that. She might have…you know, with her mouth. He liked that, he told me, because the young girls did it well and it didn't hurt them."

"So little Fabia was blackmailing Crispina?" Tacitus asked, obviously as uncomfortable as I was with this turn in the conversation. "How old was she when this happened?"

"She would have been nine," Marcella said. "She was a conniving little wench. Crispina never could control her after that."

"All the more reason, I suppose, for Crispina to be outraged when she found out about Popilius and Fabia."

"'Outraged' doesn't begin to describe it, sir. Popilius and Fabia had to run for their lives. They came to our place and begged for a horse. They had only one. Popilius said Crispina had come after them with an axe. He was able to knock her out long enough for them to escape. That was less than a month ago. We haven't heard from them since."

"Do you have any idea where Popilius might have gone now?"

"No, sir. I'm sure he's trying to get as far away from Crispina as possible," Nonnius said. "You'll never find him."

"If I did, I wouldn't know it," I said. "I have no idea what he looks like."

"It wouldn't help much if you did," Marcella said. "There's nothing remarkable about his looks, aside from him being a bit stoop-shouldered. You wouldn't notice him in a crowd, unless you heard him speak. His voice is odd. I'm not sure how else to describe it, except to say…it's odd. There's something about the pitch of it. Once you've heard it, you don't forget it."

Aurora gasped.

"What is it?" I asked.

"That's the man, my lord, the man who dropped the pot and the bucket when Marinthus' shed was on fire. He was standing next to me in the line."

"Sounds like a clumsy oaf."

"I thought so at the time, my lord. Now I think he was trying to keep us from putting out the fire."

.   .   .

To give myself a moment to gather my thoughts, I looked up at the ceiling of the *exhedra*, where birds had nested for as long as I could recall. The nests were empty now, another generation of young successfully launched into the world. Or were they? So many perils face us. Some—predators, disease, hunger—we can anticipate and, to some degree, forestall, but others can strike so unexpectedly and with such devastation, like a volcano, or a head struck on a rock, or a madwoman with an axe—or a lump in a woman's breast.

And now this. Popilius had been with us at the *taberna*, standing within reach of Aurora. He must have brought Fabia's head to the shed. That meant he had seen us at the villa and knew where we had taken her body. He must have followed us from there to Marinthus' *taberna*. What an unsettling thought that was. Did he set the fire? He must have. It was the only way he could give his lover and his unborn child something like a funeral.

"Can you swear to me that what you're saying is the truth?" I asked Nonnius. "Popilius' description and all the rest of it—is it the truth?"

He nodded quickly and emphatically. "I'll swear by any god you wish, sir, or by all of them. You would get no different story from me if you tortured me. I've no reason to tell you anything but the truth." His eyes shifted briefly to me, then back over my shoulder to Aurora.

"Did Tacitus tell you Crispina's version of how Fabia died?"

"Yes, sir. It was terrifying, but I don't believe a word of it. Popilius adored that girl. He would never hurt her. Crispina killed her. I've no doubt of it."

I reluctantly made myself envision that horrific scene again, trying to imagine it differently, with Popilius tied to the post, forced to watch as his lover—who was carrying his child—was raped and slaughtered. Could a woman have been guilty of such savagery?

"Fabia was violated, numerous times," I told Nonnius and Marcella. "Who could have done that?"

Marcella groaned. "Crispina had several servants with her when she came to our house. But the poor girl didn't deserve that."

Any more than she deserved to have her head chopped off, I thought.

"Were her servants *that* loyal?" Tacitus asked in disbelief. "I mean, a man can't just…perform on command."

"Did you speak to any of her servants when you were at her house?" I asked Tacitus.

"I spoke to one, who met me at the door and wouldn't let me go any further. He said his master and mistress were away on business and he didn't know when they would return."

I felt like I was being tossed around on a ship, unable to predict which way we would bounce next. Every time I thought I had grabbed on to something solid—a bit of evidence, an explanation—it evaporated before my eyes.

"My lord," Aurora said, "if all of this is true, how does the ROTAS square figure in? Did Popilius really think he was destined to kill a king?"

I was sorry Aurora had brought the square into the discussion, since it apparently had no meaning other than the nonsense Jacob had revealed to me. I couldn't silence her with a glance.

"ROTAS square?" Marcella asked. "What's that?"

Nonnius was more openly nervous. "And who's going to kill a king?"

"It's a piece of gibberish scribbled on the wall of a *taberna* on the Ostian Way. Popilius apparently saw it and interpreted it as applying to himself in some way. Crispina showed us a papyrus on which he had worked out the meaning."

Nonnius shook his head. "He couldn't have."

"Why not?"

"He can't read or write."

I felt like the ship had lurched in another direction, leaving my stomach behind. "And Crispina can?"

"Yes, sir, quite well. She's the best educated person in our district. Her father saw to that. Latin *and* Greek. We're always asking her to read and write things for us."

One more damn lie. Why was I surprised? Jacob's comment that Crispina had been more interested in the square than Popilius had been suddenly made more sense, but I didn't want to go into any more detail about the square with these two.

"But she told us she knew only a few letters," I said, "and she spoke like an illiterate peasant. Unlike you two," I quickly added.

"What can I say, sir?" Nonnius shrugged. "That was part of her deception. She could make you believe almost anything. She made Popilius and her servants believe she was going to have a baby."

"And you know how hard it is," Marcella broke in, "for a woman to keep any secrets from the women in her own house."

"I can only imagine," I said. "What I don't understand is why she would spin this elaborate web of lies."

"She's not in her right mind, sir," Marcella said. "I think when she learned what was going on between Popilius and Fabia—and especial- ly when Fabia taunted her about having a child—she just took leave of her senses. And with Fabia blackmailing her—she's been brooding on that for years, I'm sure. When she came to our house looking for them, she was ranting—quite mad. I was afraid she was going to kill us."

"Did Popilius tell you where they were going?" Tacitus asked.

"He said they would go to Ostia and take the first ship they could get on, no matter where it was going."

"Obviously they didn't make it," Tacitus said. "It's late in the sailing season. They would have had trouble finding a ship. I guess that gave Crispina and her people time to catch up with them."

"But then why were Crispina and the boy on the Ostian Way by themselves, my lord?" Aurora asked. "And on foot?"

"We'll be able to answer that question," I said, "when we under- stand more about her plans." I turned to Nonnius and Marcella. "Do you know if Crispina or Popilius had any connection with a man named Sextus Tabellius? It was his villa where we found Fabia's body."

They looked at one another, then Marcella asked her husband, "Was that the fellow's name, the one whose villa they looked at?"

"That sounds right," Nonnius said. He kept his eyes off Aurora long enough to address me directly. "A few months ago they heard about a place that might be for sale up in this direction. Somebody in our village knew somebody up here. Popilius is always talking about owning property closer to Rome. He has grandiose ideas about himself."

"Like wanting to be a king?" Tacitus asked.

"I said grandiose, sir, not insane. They came up to look at the villa, but for some reason the owner's heirs decided not to sell."

"Popilius seemed especially disappointed," Marcella added.

There was the connection I hadn't been able to find. Crispina could not have happened upon the villa at random. She had to have known about it and known that it was empty. But there were hundreds of other places between her farm and the villa where she could have killed Fabia.

"Since they didn't buy the place," I said, "do you know of any reason why Crispina would have chosen that spot to do what she did?"

"Well, Popilius told me he'd like to divorce Crispina, marry Fabia, and move up to that villa."

"Did he really think Crispina would divorce him that easily?" I asked.

"I don't think he knew her as well as he thought he did. As if any man can *ever* know a woman." Nonnius shot a glance at his wife.

I wondered if the point of contention between them was just Nonnius' suspicions about the paternity of a child or something even more divisive. It was obviously serious and had been festering for a long time. It's awkward to see an unhappy couple yoked together like two oxen that keep nipping at one another instead of pulling as a team. I suppose Martial would find material for an epigram in their bickering, but I just wanted to look away. Is that where my marriage would end up?

Marcella sat rigid, determined to ignore her husband, as she said, "It wasn't so much that she loved him. I think she would have let him go—probably let him have what he thought was his son, too—but not once she found out how he had betrayed her, and under her own roof."

"Would he have been so stupid as to tell her he wanted to leave her and move to the villa with Fabia?" Tacitus asked.

"I doubt *he* would," Marcella said, "but I've no doubt Fabia would have thrown it in Crispina's face. She was that much of an ungrateful stepchild."

.   .   .

Once we were satisfied that Nonnius and Marcella had told us all they could, we brought in little Clodius, who seemed overjoyed to see his "Aunt" Marcella and "Uncle" Nonnius. Hashep and Dakla came along with him, escorted by Phineas.

"They've grown inseparable," Phineas said. "We're just back from a trip to the gardens of Maecenas. I thought, after our lessons, they would enjoy running and playing for a while where they had more room than here in our garden."

"Tell them who you saw," Hashep said to Clodius, nudging him forward.

The boy looked uncomfortable.

"Go on," Hashep said with the authority of an older sister.

Clodius looked from one adult to another and, receiving a nod or two from us, said, "I saw one of my mother's servants."

"Which one?" Nonnius asked.

"Eustasius," the boy said.

"What would he be doing here," Marcella said, "if Crispina has left?"

"Is he one of her more important servants?" I asked.

"One of her most trusted, I believe."

"She didn't have any servants with her when she came to my house." I turned to Clodius. "What was Eustasius doing when you saw him?"

"He was looking at your house."

"Did he see you?"

Clodius shrugged.

"I don't believe he did, my lord," Phineas said. "I noticed Clodius looking at the man, so I observed him, too. If he was spying, he wasn't doing a very good job of it. He was standing at the corner of the house to our north, trying to act as though he was waiting for someone, I think."

"Did you try to speak to him?" I asked Clodius.

"No. I don't like him. He's mean."

XIV

W E SENT NONNIUS and Marcella, along with Clodius, back to Tacitus' house, accompanied by two of the servants who had come with Tacitus. They would spend the night there before heading home. Hashep and Dakla stood at the door waving good-bye long after the party had been absorbed into the crowd on the street.

My attention was drawn to the north. Tacitus, Phineas, and I went to an upper room that had a window that gave a view in that direction. "Do you see the man?" I asked Phineas.

"No, sir. He's gone."

"I want someone watching for him," I told Phineas. "Set up a rotation of three or four people. Give them a description. I want to know where he comes from. That will be where we find Crispina, I suspect. If anyone sees him, come and get me. I'm going back to the garden."

As Tacitus and I settled back in the shade of the *exhedra*, I said, "Nonnius and Marcella are quite the pair."

"Julia is much amused by them," Tacitus said. "When they realized that Julius Agricola is her father, it was all we could do to keep them from falling to their knees in front of her."

I winced. "If Domitian heard about that—"

"I know, I know. But he hasn't or we'd have disappeared by now."

"What do we make of what they've told us?" I asked. "Other than the fact that Crispina has lied to us and to everyone else from the very beginning? She told Aurora one story and Marinthus another, and a third to Justus. Then she fabricated a tale for us."

"Don't forget," Aurora said, coming around to sit beside me, "that she lied to her husband about the son he thought was his."

"Yes," Tacitus said. "I'm surprised she left the boy with you. Clodius was what gave her power over Popilius, in spite of his interest in Fabia."

"By now," I said, "I'm sure, Popilius knows the child isn't his. Fabia will have told him. That's why she left him here. What use would he be to her if Popilius knows he isn't his son?"

"Ga—" Aurora caught herself. "My lord—"

Tacitus reached over and patted her knee. "Call him Gaius, my dear. We'll keep it among ourselves."

Aurora blushed. She has a way of looking to one side when she blushes. I don't know whether to call it charming or endearing. Regardless of the term, it melts my heart. "Thank you, my lord… Gaius, please don't talk so callously about a child. He's not just a pawn, a bargaining chip."

I squeezed her hand. "I'm sorry if it sounded like I was dismissing him that way. I'm glad he's safe and we've been able to reunite him with people who care about him. What puzzles me, though, is why Popilius and Fabia didn't make their escape while they could. They must have reached Ostia before Crispina and her servants got there. Did they just wait?"

"Perhaps there was no vessel ready to leave," Tacitus said. "Even an overnight delay would have given Crispina time to catch up with them. Their farm is only about six miles south of Ostia."

"I wonder," Aurora said, "if Popilius was trying to figure a way to take the boy away from Crispina."

"Would he have taken that great a risk just for the sake of a boy who wasn't his?"

"The poor child has no one who really cares for him," Aurora said. "But at least now we understand why Crispina decided to do this horrible business at that villa. She knew Popilius and Fabia wanted to be there together, and she couldn't abide the thought. She turned Popilius' dream into a nightmare that will haunt him as long as he lives."

"This reminds me of Ovid's story of Callisto. After Jupiter raped her, she couldn't stand to be in places that she had loved before, because of what had happened there."

"I think you're right," Tacitus said. "Crispina had visited the place before, when they were trying to buy it, and must have seen that accursed wheel. Someone might even have told her what it was used for."

"I'm surprised his sons or someone at the villa hadn't removed it," I said, "or at least stored it out of sight. It's not a strong selling point."

"It might serve as a reminder to his other servants," Tacitus said.

"Or as an incitement to rise up against their master," Aurora said bitterly.

My eyes met hers. It's a strange feeling to look into someone's eyes and know that all she sees is darkness.

"So," Tacitus said, "where are we now?"

"Right back where we were when we left Marinthus' *taberna*," I said. "We don't know any more now than we did then. The only difference is that we've brought Regulus into the whole business, when apparently there was no need to."

"Do you think we need to investigate any further?" Tacitus asked. "Are we dealing with anything more than a madwoman who's intent on taking vengeance on her husband—a modern Medea? You don't think there's any real danger to Domitian, do you?"

"Medea killed King Creon, my lord," Aurora pointed out.

"Well, one can carry mythological analogies too far," Tacitus said with a bit of annoyance in his voice.

"You brought it up, my lord," Aurora said.

"That's enough, you two," I said. "We do need to carry our investigation to a conclusion. If Crispina did in fact murder Fabia, with the connivance of some of her servants, they all need to be brought to justice."

"Where do you propose we begin?" Tacitus asked.

"This whole business started at Sextus Tabellius' villa. I want to go back out there and take another look at it. Given what we know now, we might find something we overlooked when we were there before. I'll hire the horses this afternoon so we can be ready to go at the first hour tomorrow. That will give us the entire day to examine the house and the grounds."

"We should take Segetius and Rufinus with us," Aurora said. "They told us what the whipping post and the wheel were for. Tabellius may have had other nasty little secrets that wouldn't be obvious to us."

I turned to her in surprise "'Us'? Surely you aren't suggesting that you'll go."

"Don't you think it's possible that someone who's part of this mystery might be at the villa?" Aurora asked. "Maybe even Popilius. He can't go back to his home, and that villa holds special meaning for him. Or he might be at Marinthus' *taberna*."

"True, but—"

"You heard what Marcella said about Popilius' voice. It's the only thing that distinguishes him from a hundred other men. I've heard it. You haven't."

"But, Aurora, how do you think you can ride a horse? You're... you're—"

"Yes, I'm blind, Gaius." She waved her hand in front of her face. "Make sure you hire a strong horse so I can ride behind you. You didn't seem to object to that arrangement on our way out to Martial's farm."

Tacitus didn't have to hide his smile from her. I was glad she couldn't see my look of annoyance.

"I'm sorry, Gaius," she said. "I don't have to see your face to know you think I'm being presumptuous. I do think I could be of use to you, but I will abide by your decision."

"You've made some convincing arguments," I had to admit. "I can't think of any reason why you shouldn't go with us." And I certainly couldn't object to another opportunity to have her clinging tightly to me for a couple of hours, except that we wouldn't be able to go any farther than that.

"Well, if we're going tomorrow, I need to get home," Tacitus said. "Julia isn't always happy about the time I spend away from her. She's a bit jealous of you, Gaius Pliny."

When Aurora wasn't around, I would have to ask him just who was dancing to a woman's tune. We were walking toward the front of the house when Demetrius met us. "My lord, there is a messenger here to see you."

"A messenger from whom?"

"He says he was sent by a man named Titus Lentulus. Do you know such a person?" One of Demetrius' responsibilities is to know everyone I know so he can decide who gets into my house and who is turned away. It wasn't surprising that Demetrius didn't know Lentulus. He was the owner of the villa next to Tabellius'.

"Yes. I met him recently. Let me talk to the man."

We entered the atrium and found Lentulus' messenger standing by the *impluvium*. "You have something for me?" I said.

The man bowed. "My lord, Titus Lentulus sends you greetings.

You asked him to inform you if he saw anything unusual at the villa of Sextus Tabellius. This morning we noticed signs that someone might be in the house."

"Signs? What kind of signs?"

"There was smoke, my lord."

"Did Lentulus send someone to investigate?"

"No, my lord. He said, after what happened to that girl in the garden, he didn't want any of his people to go near the place. He decided to post men to keep watch and send me to inform you."

"All right. Thank you. Demetrius will see that you have something to eat."

As the messenger followed my steward out of the atrium, I turned to Tacitus. "I don't think we can wait until tomorrow to go out there."

"But if we leave now, we won't have more than an hour or two of daylight left when we get there."

"If we wait until tomorrow, whoever is there could be gone. And it might be Popilius."

"Or it might be a gang of bandits who've found a convenient hideout."

Tacitus always looks on the bright side of things. His comment rattled me more than I wanted to show. "We won't know unless we go there, will we?"

.   .   .

While Tacitus went home to let Julia know what he was doing, I rounded up a party of servants to accompany me out to Tabellius' villa. They had to be freedmen so they could carry weapons. Segetius surprised me when he volunteered to go—almost insisted.

"You've been most kind to me and Rufinus, sir. I'd like to do something to repay you. I do know the place inside and out."

Although I still wasn't entirely comfortable with the man, he had shown no reason for me to distrust him, and the stripes on his back ought to earn him some credibility. "All right," I said.

With that settled, I sent one man to cancel my order for horses from Saturius' stable. Because of its location we would have to ride those horses all the way around Rome or walk them through the streets before we actually started for Ostia. Since Caesar's day, only animals being ridden or pulling vehicles on government business, or delivering supplies to a building site, have been allowed in the streets of the city during daylight hours. I sent another servant to a stable on the west side of town to hire horses. Along with him I sent two servants to go ahead and get us rooms at Marinthus' *taberna*.

As I sent people scrambling in different directions, my mother and Naomi came into the atrium. "Gaius," my mother called, "what's the meaning of all this confusion?"

"I have to make a short trip. I'll be back tomorrow."

"You're leaving at this time of day?"

"I'm just going a short distance down the Ostian Way."

"Does this have anything to do with that strange woman with the little boy who was here…yesterday? Or was that…last month? No, it was yesterday. And there was a boy, wasn't there?"

I could see that she was just guessing. Naomi seemed as concerned about her as I was. When the doctor came back to look at Aurora's eyes, I would ask him about my mother's increasing befuddlement. Could it all be caused just by her concern over the *karkinos*? "That's right, Mother. She was here two days ago, with a little boy. We've sent him home with his aunt and uncle. So that's all taken care of. You don't have to worry about it."

Anxiety still clouded her face. "But what about the woman? Is she still here?"

"No, Mother, she's not. I'm trying to find her. And her husband."

"Why?"

"I think they're in trouble and I want to help them." I hoped I wouldn't have to give her any more of an explanation. There wasn't time, and I didn't want to upset her with any gruesome details.

"That's very good of you, Gaius," Mother said. "Just be careful."

By the time my small entourage had packed a bit of food and left the house most people were heading for the baths. We picked a route that kept us on streets away from the largest *thermae*, so we made satisfactory progress to the south side of the city. My servants had procured enough horses, but Aurora wasn't satisfied until she had inspected them with her hands, massaging and kneading. I could have sworn the animals were enjoying it. The thought ran through my mind that someday, if we ever got to be alone again, I might have to pretend to be her horse.

"This one has a lump of some kind in his neck," she told the stable owner.

"I assure you there's nothing wrong with that animal," the man said, stiffening his own neck.

"I guess you can't see it," Aurora said, "but I can feel it. Put your hand right here." She took the man's hand and laid it on the spot that concerned her. The horse neighed and shook its head.

The man's expression changed at once. "I'll have to look at that. Let me get you another horse."

Once the horses satisfied Aurora, we were on our way.

Tacitus had been right. We wouldn't have much time before dark today. We could find out if the person or persons at the villa were relevant to our inquiry. If not, we would have all day tomorrow to explore the place. And I meant to go into the woods around the property, to see if Popilius had left any traces of where he had been hiding when we were there before.

As we rode, staying twenty paces or so ahead of my servants, Tacitus, Aurora, and I mulled over what we had learned from Nonnius and Marcella.

"What I don't understand," Aurora said, "is why Crispina didn't go ahead and kill Popilius at the villa. If she could decapitate Fabia, she must have had Popilius restrained in some way so he couldn't stop her. As enraged as she was, why not finish the job?"

"I think she wanted him to suffer more," I said, "by living with the memory of what he saw."

"Medea didn't kill Jason," Tacitus pointed out. "He was the one she was angry at, but she left him alive after she killed his children and everyone else he cared about. It was the cruelest punishment she could have inflicted on him. Killing him—or killing Popilius—would have been a kindness."

"I don't think Crispina has a kind bone in her body," Aurora said. "How could she feel so little for Clodius that she could just walk away and leave him? Even though he wasn't her own child, she had raised him as though he was for eight years. He believed she was his mother. I saw that when I was with them at the *taberna*. Animals will sometimes adopt young that aren't their own. Aren't we better than animals?"

"Animals will also sometimes kill young that aren't their own," I said. "At least she didn't do that to the boy. But what I don't understand is why Popilius and Fabia waited around in Ostia. Even at the end of the sailing season, they could have found a boat going a short distance up the coast, or over to Sardinia or Corsica. Far enough away to save them from Crispina's axe."

"It must have something to do with Clodius," Tacitus said. "That's the only reason he would have taken the risk."

"Even if he knew Clodius wasn't his son?" Aurora objected.

"We don't know if Fabia had told him what she knew," Tacitus said. "Even if she had, Popilius could have felt paternal affection for the boy. He'd considered him his son for eight years, and it wasn't Clodius who'd deceived him. Or perhaps he was humane enough not to want to leave him in the hands of a madwoman."

I sensed Gaius shaking his head, even if I couldn't see the gesture. And I agreed. Nothing I'd heard about Popilius made me think him capable of such a noble gesture. I'd be quicker to attribute baser motives to him. A man with an unnatural interest in one child might well have a similar interest in another, regardless of the gender. As the two thugs in the cave yesterday had demonstrated, to some men gender is irrelevant.

I tried to imagine myself being touched by an older man in ways that Gaius had touched me. Or doing the things to an older man that Nonnius and Marcella said Popilius liked for young girls to do to him. He might not have killed Fabia, but he deserved to be punished for what he had done to her and to others. A shiver ran through me.

There was still daylight left when we reached Marinthus' *taberna*. His son, Theodorus, greeted us in the absence of his father, who, we were informed, was in Ostia buying supplies. Since Marinthus had earlier expressed doubt about Theodorus' competence to do anything, I guess he faced a dilemma: leave the young man in charge of the *taberna* or send him to do business in Ostia. Marinthus must have decided Theodorus could do less damage here.

"I'm delighted to see you again, sirs, and you, Aurora," he said.

"Good afternoon, Theodorus," Aurora said.

Theodorus' upturned face showed his uncertainty. "Is there something wrong with Aurora, sir?" He touched his forehead at the spot where Aurora's bruise still showed.

"She was struck on the head and temporarily blinded. Now, are there rooms reserved for our entire party?"

"Yes, sir. Will you and Aurora want the same rooms you had last time?"

I didn't like the way he smirked when he said that. From the increased tightness of Aurora's grip around my waist, I knew that she could hear his expression as well as I could see it. "Yes, those rooms were nice."

"Will you need *both* of them?"

I resisted the urge to kick the man in his smug face. From where I was sitting it would be so easy, and I was wearing a heavier pair of sandals—a pair of soldier's *caliga*—for tramping around in the woods. But I had to keep up the pretense, so I contented myself with gritting my teeth and saying, "Yes. *Both* of them. We'll be back shortly and would like some dinner."

"Everything will be ready for you and the lady, sir."

As we rode away from the *taberna* Aurora said quietly in my ear, "He might as well have told us he was the one who took the knife. He knew I didn't spend the night in that room."

"Knowing you weren't in the room doesn't prove he went in there. If *he* knew, I suppose someone else could have known."

"Wonderful. This may turn out to be the worst-kept secret in Rome." Her chin dug into my back.

I put one of my hands over hers. "I wouldn't really mind if it did."

We turned onto the side road that led to Tabellius' villa. As we passed Lentulus' house and the ruins of Tabellius' place came into view, I brought my horse to a halt. I could see several men—Lentulus' servants, I assumed—on guard.

"Has anyone come in or left?" I asked the closest one.

"No, my lord, but there's still smoke." A thin wisp of smoke was rising from the front of the house, through the *compluvium* apparently.

I turned to my own party. "Let's dismount and approach on foot. We can be quieter that way." I designated one of my men to stay with Aurora and the horses while the rest of us made our way to the house.

"I want to go with you, my lord," Aurora insisted.

"No." This time I would not be persuaded. "If we find a man in the house, we'll need you to tell us if he was Popilius, since you're the only one who's heard his peculiar speech. If we run into a confrontation, though, you become a liability."

"It looks like the smoke is coming from the atrium," Tacitus said.

I turned to Segetius. "Are there any entrances we don't know about?"

"There's a spot at the rear where animals kept digging under the wall to get into the garden. A man can slip under there. It's covered by some bushes and a shed."

"You take that. The rest of you, spread out and approach the house from different directions. Whoever's in there, I don't want them to get away, but I want them alive."

As Tacitus and I came up to the bashed-in front door we heard an eerie keening spilling out from inside the house. The hair on the back of my neck stood up.

"That's not a woman, is it?" Tacitus said.

"No, I believe it's a man, but I'm not entirely sure." I tightened my grip on my sword.

"Either way, it's the ghastliest noise I've ever heard."

"Almost otherworldly." I put my head in the door. "Hello? Who's here? We don't mean to hurt you. We just want to talk."

"Go away!" a voice—definitely a man's—shouted. "Go away! I'm going to do it. It's the only way. You can't stop me. Nobody can."

We entered the atrium and were confronted with a man standing on the side opposite the door. The empty *impluvium* lay between us. His dirty tunic had a bloody spot below his stomach. In a brazier in front of him a fire was burning, with a poker sticking out of it. He held a knife in his shaking right hand.

"I don't care if I live or die," he said. "It would be better to die if it let me stop seeing that awful sight."

I had to assume he was Popilius.

"Has he already wounded himself?" Tacitus asked.

"I don't think so. He wouldn't still be standing."

"I can't get the blood off," Popilius muttered, like crazy old men with bulging eyes do as they stumble around the streets of Rome. "Have to cut it off. Burn it off. The only way."

I thought he was referring to the blood on his tunic until he lifted it and placed the knife on his genitals, which were also covered in blood.

"By the gods! He's going to castrate himself," I cried. I started to run around the *impluvium*.

"Stop!" the man cried. "Don't take another step. I'll do it. I really will."

I didn't feel that his threat was serious. He could cut off any body part he wanted. In an abstract sense, I didn't care. But, if this was Popilius, I needed him alive and able to answer questions—if he still retained enough sanity to do that. A man who was threatening to cut off his own genitals was clearly not in his right mind. The fact that he hadn't done it yet made me suspect he didn't really have the nerve to carry out the job, but would he if he were provoked?

I stopped and lowered my sword. "I won't come any closer. My name is Gaius Pliny—"

"I know who you are. You took Fabia's body off that accursed wheel. For that I thank you."

"So you are Clodius Popilius?"

"Yes, I am the wretch who answers to that name—or what's left of him."

Behind Popilius I saw Segetius approaching from the back of the house, moving from column to column in the peristyle garden like a hunter sneaking up on an unsuspecting prey, from tree to tree. I had to keep Popilius talking for another moment or two.

"Why did you take her head away from here?"

"I didn't want somebody to identify her and start looking for me. That was all of her I could carry."

"Weren't you afraid somebody would see you walking around carrying a head?" Tacitus asked.

"I found a bag."

"Where did you go?"

"I hid out in the woods. I didn't know what to do or where to go. But when I saw you and your men taking her body away, I decided to follow you."

"So you reunited her head with her body and then set fire to the shed."

"Yes. It was the closest I could come to giving her a proper funeral. But then someone discovered the fire and tried to put it out."

"You got into the line passing buckets and—"

"And did whatever else I could to—"

Segetius lunged at Popilius and wrapped his arms around the poor man, pinning his feeble limbs to his sides and forcing the knife down.

I rushed over and yanked the knife out of his hand. He was trembling violently, but his grip—induced by fear or panic—was surprisingly tenacious.

"Get him something to eat," I ordered as Aurora and my other servants came into the atrium. "Set him down over here." Segetius and I moved him into a shady spot. His body was so rigid we had to force him to sit down. "You're going to be all right," I assured him.

He shook his head and sobbed. "How can I be all right? She's dead. Ravaged and murdered right before my eyes."

There was a raspy quality to his voice that I'd never heard before. I could understand what Nonnius and Marcella had meant about recognizing him by that characteristic.

"We're trying to find the woman who did it," Tacitus said, with a kindness in his voice that I wasn't accustomed to hearing except when he was talking to his wife. "We need your help."

Popilius' eyes grew wider with fear. "Oh, no! If she ever got near me again, she would do worse to me than she did to Fabia."

"We won't let her harm you," I assured him. "Now, have a little something to eat and we'll talk."

When he had eaten a few bites of bread and cheese and drunk a little wine, the trembling in his body began to abate and his shoulders slumped. Aurora sat on a bench opposite him, feeding him, but we sent the rest of the servants away.

I can't see Popilius, but he's sitting within arm's reach of me. I can hear his raspy breathing. Gaius expects me to give him something to eat. What I want to do is shove this bread down his throat and choke him to death.

Before he left, Segetius said, "Sirs, you ought to see something in the rear garden."

He led Tacitus and me to the spot where Fabia had been murdered. The wheel on which she died had been smashed into bits. The axe used to decapitate her was lodged in the post where Popilius had been tied.

"I guess that's one reason he came back here," Tacitus said.

"He did something many of us wanted to do, sir." Segetius kicked at the splintered pieces of wood.

"Thank you for showing us this," I said. "Now we need to talk to Popilius."

We dismissed Segetius, and Tacitus and I pulled a marble bench over close to Popilius. Aurora sat next to me.

"I know it will be painful for you," I said, "but I have to know what happened when Fabia was killed, and what Crispina is up to—if you know." I wondered if his version of the story would bear any resemblance to what we had heard first from Aurora, then from Crispina, and finally from Nonnius and Marcella. Sometimes historians say that they have found various accounts of an incident in their sources but cannot sift the true from the false. They simply record all of them and let their readers select whichever they find most convincing. I did not have that luxury.

Popilius took one more swallow of wine and wiped his mouth. "I'm surprised to see that fellow in your service."

I looked over my shoulder at the departing servants. "Which one?"

"The one that grabbed me."

"Oh, Segetius isn't exactly in my service. He's a freedman from this house."

"I've seen him before," Popilius said.

"Where?"

"At the *taberna* where you took Fabia."

"You were at the fire, weren't you?" Aurora said.

"Yes, missy, standing right next to you."

I drew his attention back to me. "I understand your reason for wanting to hamper the people who were putting out the fire—"

"But this was before the fire. I was hiding in the woods behind the place. That fellow, that Segetius, he was talking with another fellow."

I couldn't imagine whom Segetius would have known there and would have been talking to. "Did you recognize the other man?"

"Not at first, but when we were lining up to put out the fire I heard someone call him Theodorus."

Tacitus and I looked at one another in consternation. What would Segetius have been talking about with Marinthus' son?

"Could you hear what they were saying?" Tacitus asked.

"Only a few words. I think I heard something about a king."

"A king? Could they have been saying Regulus?"

"Yes, sir, that might very well have been it. Does that mean anything?"

XV

IN MY RAGE I pulled Tacitus into the second garden, where Fabia had been killed, and shoved him up against the wall. His head hit harder than I intended.

"Does it mean anything?" I said through gritted teeth. "Does it mean anything? It means we've been tricked, just like some rustic who falls off a turnip wagon and buys a 'lifetime pass' to the Circus Maximus on his first day in the city. Segetius has played us for fools. And *you* said his appearance was a mere coincidence. I told you from the first time I saw him that he was trailing us."

"Calm down," Tacitus said. "We don't know what they were talking about. There are lots of words that sound like *reg*—"

"Name two that Segetius and Theodorus might have been using in their conversation."

Without saying anything, Tacitus gripped my wrists and pulled my hands off his tunic.

I stepped back from him but continued my onslaught, waving my finger in his face. "I told you, as soon as I heard Segetius had worked in the house of a client of Regulus', that his presence could not be a coincidence. But then you fell for that whole sob story about being beaten—"

"You can't deny those marks on his back," Tacitus was quick to point out. "Whatever he's doing now, he was brutally whipped."

"But how would he and Theodorus know one another?"

Tacitus' impatience began to show in the edge in his voice. "That's no great stretch. Tabellius' villa isn't all that far from here. Given how long both men have lived around here, they could have met. Maybe they were just renewing an old acquaintance. Maybe they'd done business together." With both hands he made a calming gesture toward me. "I know, that sounds as unlikely to me as it does to you."

"If they were old friends, why were they sneaking around in the woods? Why didn't they sit down in the *taberna* and have a drink? That's what old friends would do. Two men who were plotting something or exchanging information would meet out in the woods, where they didn't expect to be seen or overheard."

"Gaius Pliny, I will concede everything you've said and whatever else you're planning to say. Upbraiding me and demonstrating your superior wisdom serves no purpose right now. We need to talk to Popilius some more."

I took a deep breath and rubbed my hands over my face. "Yes, of course. But we need to keep Segetius well out of hearing range."

When we returned to the atrium I was relieved Segetius was nowhere to be seen. Aurora was sitting across from Popilius, now encouraging him to eat more. She slid over to make room for me to sit beside her. Tacitus found a stool and pulled it up next to our bench.

"Clodius Popilius, do you think you could tell us what happened?" I asked.

"I'm not sure you would believe me. How can anyone believe something so horrible? I saw it, and I don't believe it."

"Let's start the story earlier. You were coupling with your stepdaughter, weren't you? Even when she was quite young. You're attracted to young girls, I've been told."

"So you've talked to Nonnius. Well, I can't blame him for telling you. Yoked to that cow Marcella for all these years, he's always been jealous of me. Yes, I adored Fabia. Even after she became nubile, she always seemed so young. And, in my defense, I can remind you that she wasn't actually my stepdaughter. She was the daughter of Crispina's first husband by yet another woman. She wasn't related to either one of us."

"Technically you may be right," I admitted, "but she was a child being raised in Crispina's house, so she had the status of a stepdaughter to you."

"Granted, sir. But she was no closer to Crispina than if they were strangers. She had never gotten on well with Crispina—"

"Do you know why not?" Tacitus asked.

"She blamed Crispina for her father's death. Said she drove poor old Fabius to drink and gamble. After living with the woman for a few years, I could believe her."

"So when Fabia became pregnant, she threw it in Crispina's face."

Popilius nodded slowly. "The girl was not judicious about that. She didn't know what anger Crispina was capable of. The woman went into a rage. She was practically foaming at the mouth. We had to run for our lives."

"You got to Ostia," I said. "Why did you stop there?"

"We couldn't find a ship leaving that day, nor anyone to ferry us across the Tiber. I knew if we continued to flee on horseback, Crispina's men would catch us. It seemed the better choice to hide out in Ostia and hope for a ship the next day. But they caught us. Smashed down the door of the room we had rented and dragged us out. Nobody lifted a hand to help us. They'd told the innkeeper that I had kidnapped Fabia."

"And they took you to this villa."

"Yes. Crispina had it all planned. She knew how much I wanted to buy this house, so she was going to make it the most hateful place on earth for me."

"She waited at Marinthus' *taberna* until everything was ready?"

Popilius took another swallow of wine. "I guess she didn't want Clodius to see what she was doing. After we were tied up and gagged, one of the men went to get her and the boy. Where is he? Did she—"

I shook my head. "She left him at my house in Rome. He's with Nonnius and Marcella now."

"Well, that's fair enough. Even if he's not my son, I do love him and want him to come to no harm. His Aunt Marcella—that's what he calls her—dotes on him."

"I think he'll be well cared for."

"Good. Now I suppose you want me to tell you what she did to Fabia."

"I think we can spare you that. From my examination of the body, I have a sufficient idea of what happened."

"Did you see the stab wounds in her belly?"

"Yes. Three of them. Those were to kill her baby—your baby—weren't they?"

Popilius began to weep. "I couldn't do anything to stop her. And then she…picked up that axe."

"Yes, we know. You don't have to say any more."

"But you don't know the worst."

Could there be anything worse?

"She took the gag out of Fabia's mouth, just so I could hear her scream. Then, after she beheaded her, she picked up her head and brought it over to me, tied to that post like I was. She rubbed it against my groin—"

Aurora groaned as if in pain, putting her hands over her face, and I held out my hand to Popilius. "We really don't need to hear the rest or see any more." That explained the blood on his tunic. If he'd been hiding in the woods for several days, he wouldn't have had a chance to bathe. As crazed as he was, perhaps he hadn't wanted to wash off the blood. It was all he had left of Fabia.

"Then she dropped the head at my feet and left. It took me several hours to work my way out of the ropes and get away." He slumped back against the wall.

"How does the ROTAS square fit into all of this?" Tacitus asked. "Was anyone planning to kill a king?"

"The thought never entered my mind," Popilius said. "We saw it on the wall at Marinthus', and Crispina showed me the thing on a piece of papyrus just before she left the villa. I can't read, so I had no idea what it meant. She said it was proof that I was plotting against the emperor and if I ever came anywhere near her again, she would inform on me and see that I ended up in the arena."

"You've already suffered worse than many people do in the arena," Tacitus said.

"At least they get to die at the end," Popilius said.

I rubbed my chin. "By showing us the square and how she interpreted it, Crispina threw all suspicion off herself and gave herself time to escape. Do you have any idea where she might have gone?"

"No, sir, I don't."

"One of her servants has been spotted in Rome, near my house. Could she be in Rome?"

"Why would she be there, sir?"

"That's the question I have to answer when we get back to the city."

"What do you plan to do now?" Aurora asked Popilius.

"I hadn't given it any thought beyond this, young lady. I didn't care if I died."

"But you had a hot poker ready," I reminded him. "Wasn't that to cauterize the wound?"

Popilius lowered his head, as if in shame. "I'm afraid to die, but I can't stand the thought of living when I can't get that dreadful image out of my head." He put his hands over his eyes. "And I was the one that did it to her, as sure as if the axe was in my hands."

"You can't think that way," Aurora said. "Crispina is a madwoman. She has deceived all of us." She turned to me, as though she could see me. "My lord, is there anything we can do to help Popilius?"

I had been asking myself the same question, but it seemed impertinent of her to pose it first. "We'll take you back to Marinthus' and let you get a bath. I'm sure we can find you some clean clothes. One of the boats that passes by should be able to take you to Ostia. From there I think you'd be wise to get as far away from here as possible."

"But, sir, this is all I have in the world." He grabbed his tunic and I was afraid he was going to lift it again. "The knife isn't even mine. I found it in the kitchen here."

"I'll give you some money to travel on, enough to get to…Massilia, let's say." Even though I found the man reprehensible—a coward who preyed on children—I felt that, by giving his name to Regulus, I had exposed Popilius to potential danger of which he was unaware. The least I could do would be to spirit him away to relative safety. Having him far from Rome might also protect me in case Domitian, alerted by Regulus, began making inquiries.

"A man could certainly do worse than Massilia," Tacitus put in. "I'll give you a letter of introduction to a friend of mine there. He's actually a cousin of my wife."

Popilius' tears began to flow again. "Sirs, I believe you could be gods in disguise." He fell to his knees, with his face on the ground, as though he would worship us.

"Get up," I told him, grabbing the back of his filthy tunic and immediately regretting my action. "We're no more gods than you are. I do think it is wise to get you away from Rome, though, in case word of your alleged plot has come to the ears of Domitian or someone close to him."

Someone like Regulus, to whom I had revealed everything. For all I knew, he had gone straight to Domitian and the Praetorians were scouring the streets of Rome right now for a man named Clodius Popilius.

"When you write that letter of introduction," I said to Tacitus, "it might be a good opportunity to have Popilius adopt a new name."

"How would you feel about that?" Tacitus asked Popilius, who was still on his knees in front of us.

"I am ready for Popilius to die," the wretch said.

.   .   .

We took our little troop back to Marinthus' *taberna*. While Popilius got himself cleaned up, I called Segetius into a corner of the main room and invited him to sit down with Tacitus and me. During the ride back from the villa, I had come up with an idea that solved two problems at once.

"You say you want to do something to repay my kindness to you," I began.

"Yes, sir, I am most eager to do so." Segetius' head bobbed up and down.

"I need someone to accompany Popilius to Massilia."

"Uh, but—"

"You'll have to leave right away, this afternoon, to be able to catch a ship in Ostia tomorrow morning, if one is available. Our first thought was to put you on a boat if one passed by here, but we've hired a *raeda* from Justus, across the way. He'll drive you there. It's the fastest and surest means."

"But, sir, if I sail to Massilia now, I won't be able to get a return ship. The sailing season ends in a few days. I'll be stuck there until spring."

Which was precisely my intention. "That will be inconvenient for you, I know, but I'll give you money to hold you over and Tacitus is going to write a letter to a friend of his there, who will supply you with whatever you need."

"Sir, I—"

"Is there anything that prevents you from going?" Tacitus asked. "Do you have pressing business in Rome?"

Segetius rocked from side to side, like a man presented with a dilemma, neither side of which appealed to him. "No, sir, of course not.

Rufinus will wonder what's become of me, though. We've been friends since we were boys. We've always stood by one another. You may have noticed he's a bit simple."

"We'll take care of him," I said, "and let him know of your assignment. And please think of it in those terms. The only way Popilius' safety can be insured is to get him as far away from here as possible. And I'd like to send a guard with him."

"But, sir, what if that crazy bitch comes after him? You saw what she can do—what she *will* do."

"I'm convinced she has done all the harm she intends to Popilius. Her purpose was to leave him on the edge of madness. By now she must know that we are aware of what she did and that she needs to get far away from Rome. I don't suppose we'll ever catch her, but we will try. I just want to get Popilius out of her reach." I placed a fistful of coins on the table, mostly *denarii*. "Now, see what kind of supplies you can purchase. You may need to wait until you reach Ostia to buy a change of clothes and other essentials."

Segetius scraped up the pile of money unhappily.

Tacitus handed him a sealed letter. "This will introduce you and Popilius—although his name isn't going to be Popilius anymore—to my wife's cousin, Julius Fortunatus. His house is on the northeast side of the city. I've asked him to give you whatever you need and promised that I will repay it."

"You're most generous, sir."

"Oh, here comes Popilius now," I said, like an actor introducing another character in a Greek play, as he entered the *taberna*, fresh from the baths. "I guess we can call him that until he walks out this door and gets in the *raeda*. Then he becomes Clodius Rufinus."

"We thought it would be easier for you to call him that, so you don't give him away," Tacitus said.

"Yes, sir. I'll do my best."

"Now, we need for you to leave us alone with Popilius for a moment."

Segetius left and Popilius took a seat at the table. After explaining what we were doing for him, I leaned over the table and lowered my voice. "I find you one of the vilest men I've ever met. There's a part of me that wants to finish what you couldn't do at Tabellius' villa, then slit your throat and dump your body in the Tiber." I leaned back as

Popilius slumped in his chair. "But, sadly, you haven't done anything that's against our law. You've just violated every law of decency that I know of."

We signaled for Segetius to rejoin us and explained all that we were doing so that both men understood what was expected of them.

"When you return in the spring," I promised Segetius, "there will be a handsome sum waiting for you, but you'll need to bring a letter from Julius Fortunatus assuring us that Popilius is well and telling Tacitus how much he owes."

I hoped that gave Segetius the incentive to carry out this task and not just kill Popilius and dump him into the Tiber for the relatively small amount of money he would be carrying. I really did feel some sympathy for Popilius and wanted to give him a chance to escape the horror of his life here and start over. One day, perhaps, he might wake up in the morning and think of something other than Fabia on that wheel. Tacitus' letter, which I had helped write, explained Popilius' real character.

I was also happy to have Segetius out of my way for several months. Regulus, like a bloated spider at the center of his web, would wonder why there was no vibration—no information—coming from that part of the web where Segetius was supposed to be.

As we watched the *raeda* start for Ostia, Tacitus said, "That takes care of a couple of problems."

"But we still have to be wary of Theodorus and probably Rufinus when I get home. A man who appears to be simple may not be."

"You're right. They say the *princeps* Claudius preserved his life by pretending to be a simpleton when others of Augustus' male relatives were being eliminated on all sides."

·   ·   ·

Sometimes when traveling one is surprised at the quality of a meal in an inn. On this night I was surprised at how bad Marinthus' cooking was—the meat overdone and the pastry little more than raw dough. I suppose he thought it all averaged out.

When we were ready to retire I asked him for the keys to the two rooms at the top of the stairs.

"You want the keys, sir?"

"That's what I said. I am concerned about Aurora's safety because of her blindness."

"Well, sir, I can understand that, I suppose. Let me get them."

With the door locked behind us, Aurora put her arms around my neck. "Oh, Gaius, I never dreamed we'd have another night together this soon."

I kissed her bruised forehead and ran my fingers through her hair. "Darling, I can't believe I'm saying this, but I don't want to make love to you tonight."

She leaned back from me, still in my embrace. "What? Why—"

"I feel like I would be taking advantage of you, and I don't want to do that."

She smiled wickedly. "Good. That will give *me* a chance to take advantage of *you*."

"What on earth do you mean?"

"Please close the shutters and douse the lamps."

I did as she told me.

"There's still some light in here, isn't there? Enough for you to see me?"

"Yes, it's dim, but there is light."

"And your eyes are at their best in dim light. Do you have your weapon with you?"

I handed her the short legionary sword that I have taken to carrying under my tunic. She cut a strip off the bedding and blindfolded me.

"What…what are you doing?"

"Most of the time, dear Gaius, when people make love, they are aroused by what they see." She gave the blindfold a final tug. "But what about what you feel and hear and…taste?"

In complete darkness she removed my tunic and I unfastened the brooch on her shoulder—clumsily because I couldn't see it—and let her tunic fall to the floor. At first I was frustrated because I longed to luxuriate in the beauty of her body, but then her mouth and hands began to work their way over me. I responded in the same way and we fell onto the bed.

She was right. Not being able to see her body made me more aware of places like the backs of her knees, the delicate bones in her hands, the space between her breasts. Experiencing her body this way was totally unlike being able to see her. Touching her without seeing her gave a new mystery—a new allurement—to places I thought I was becoming familiar with. When we finally lay in one another's arms, panting, I didn't even remove the blindfold.

"By the way, Gaius," she said, placing a hand over my pounding heart, "I do check for lumps in my breasts. Regularly."

"I didn't mean…" I pulled the blindfold off. "It's just that I love you so much—"

"It's all right." She kissed me lightly. "I know you're worried about your mother. Rest assured that I do pay attention to it, although it feels a lot better when you do it…and you're much more…thorough." She moaned as I cupped one of her breasts in my hand and kissed it.

.   .   .

The next morning we were home by the third hour, saying farewell to Tacitus as we passed the Aventine Hill. As soon as we entered my house, Demetrius approached me with a piece of papyrus in his hand. Phineas hovered behind him, eager to say something but deferring to his superior.

"This was delivered yesterday evening, my lord," Demetrius said as he handed me the note.

"It's from Nonnius," I told Aurora as I broke the seal and opened the message. "He says Crispina's farm and all of her servants except her steward have been sold, for a considerable sum. Her steward collected the money and says he's going to meet Crispina, but he wouldn't say where."

"She'll be able to get away then, my lord," Aurora said, mindful of her fellow servants. "She can go anywhere she pleases."

"I just hope Massilia isn't on her itinerary."

"At this time of year she's more likely to travel overland, my lord, and that means going north—across the Alps and the Rhine."

Since she couldn't see me, I put a hand on her shoulder. "Have you planned such a trip?"

"Every slave has, my lord."

"Well." What else could I say but "well"? When I looked at Demetrius and Phineas, they both took a sudden interest in the floor.

"Do you remember anything she said to you while you were at the *taberna* about where she was from or her family? Anything that might give us a clue as to where to find her?"

"No, I'm sorry, my lord, I don't. And if I did, I'm not sure we could believe it."

"That's true." I motioned for Phineas to step forward. "Do you have some news?"

"Yes, my lord. As you instructed me, I've kept watch on the men who are watching our house. I followed one of them yesterday."

"Where did he go?"

"He was headed toward the temple of Minerva Medica, my lord, but I lost sight of him in the crowd. I'm not tall enough to see over people, and he was short as well."

"There are several *insulae* in that area. Crispina must be staying in one. I'll follow him next time."

.   .   .

We found my mother and Naomi sitting in the garden, enjoying a spot of sun on a cool day. Aurora hung back as I greeted them.

"Did Demetrius deliver the message that came for you last night?" Mother asked. I was struck that her tone was merely inquisitive, not accusatory.

"Yes, he did." I held up the document.

"Was it anything important?"

"I'm not sure yet."

"That's certainly an ambiguous answer. Anyway, did you have a successful trip?"

"We learned some useful things, I think," I said, "and got a couple of problems out of the way."

"That sounds like the very definition of success." She looked around and beyond me. "And are you feeling any better, Aurora dear? Any change in your blindness?"

Aurora was so surprised to hear my mother addressing her in such a pleasant tone and by her right name that it took her a moment to reply. "No…no, my lady. No change. But I feel fine. Thank you." She looked and sounded like someone who expected a surprise or a trick to be played on her at any moment.

Mother actually smiled. "I'm glad to hear it, dear. Now, Naomi, will you share your news, please?"

"I'm not sure it's news, my lady," Naomi said. "It's actually rather old."

"Get to the point, Naomi," Mother said.

"Yes, my lady. It seems that Phineas says he has found something that will interest both of you, my lord. He's in the library. With your permission, my lady, I'll walk with them."

"By all means," my mother said.

Guiding Aurora by the elbow, I led her back into the atrium and toward the library. As soon as we were out of Mother's sight, Aurora turned to Naomi and, before I could, asked, "Why is she being so kind to me?"

"That's why I wanted to walk with you, and with you, my lord. Because of her illness she regrets the way she has treated Aurora and the animosity she harbored for Monica. She wants to atone."

"'Atone'? That sounds like one of your words. Don't you Jews have a whole day for atoning?" I had heard something about it a few years ago when I served in Syria, where many Jews settled after the destruction of Jerusalem.

"Yes, my lord, each year in the fall. It's called *Yom Kippur*. It occurred recently. Lady Plinia went to the synagogue with us. I explained the meaning of it to her."

One of my greatest fears is that Naomi might persuade my mother to become a Jew, if that's even possible. My mother has always been susceptible to religious hysteria—even more so than most women—and the eruption of Vesuvius frightened her to the depths of her being.

I stopped walking and, still holding Aurora's arm, turned to face Naomi. "Don't think for a moment that she's going to join your cult and give all her money to your…synagogue, isn't it? I know she's already given some gifts to the place, but I can take control of her money if I have reason to believe she's not in her right mind."

Naomi did not cower; she is a courageous woman who has been toughened by all she has survived—the loss of her husband and a child, the destruction of her homeland, and her enslavement. "My lord, you misunderstand me entirely. When your mother asks me questions, I answer them honestly. That's my responsibility as her servant and her friend—to help her find comfort in her time of need. I have never suggested that she might become a Jew."

"Is it possible for her to do so?" It seemed such an alien concept—

my mother, the Jew. I could more easily imagine her running off to join some tribe in Germany or painting herself blue and screeching like the Picts north of Britain.

"Yes, my lord. There is a ritual. It involves a bath—a *mikvah*—but I've never even hinted—"

"See that you don't." Almost jerking Aurora off balance, I resumed walking to the library, mulling over the words in my mind. *Yom Kippur? Mikvah?* Why do so many Hebrew words sound like the person speaking them is choking on something? At least "synagogue" was a word they'd borrowed from the Greeks, for some reason.

.   .   .

Mine is one of the largest personal libraries in Rome. As we entered I inhaled and felt the sense of contentment that comes over me at the sight and aroma of papyrus and ink. Phineas got up from the table where he was working and greeted us.

"Your mother says you have something to show us," I said.

"Yes, my lord."

He picked up a scroll that I recognized as one of the 160 volumes of unpublished notes that my uncle compiled over the course of his life. The scrolls are written on the front *and* back in a minute hand, so the amount of material in them is the equivalent of well over 300 scrolls. But there is no order or system to them. The material was jotted down as my uncle and his scribes came across it. My uncle read voraciously. He had a scribe read to him as he traveled in a litter, while he was soaking in his bath, and while he was dining. Phineas is in charge of several scribes who are copying his notes and arranging the material on new scrolls by categories and writing in a larger hand, so they will be of more use to me.

"There's a passage here, my lord, that suggests applying ice to a head injury, especially if there is any swelling. Your uncle cites an example of a soldier who was temporarily blind after a blow to the forehead until this treatment was used."

"Ice?" I had heard of ice being applied to reduce a swelling but never to reverse blindness. How could the swelling be connected with the blindness?

"Yes, my lord. Your uncle was serving on the Rhine at the time. One of the German auxiliaries suggested the treatment."

"Well, the Germans would certainly know about ice. They spend half their lives living in the stuff. I'll send someone to Servilius Pudens' house to fetch Democrites and we'll see what he thinks."

"While we're waiting, my lord," Phineas said, "may I discuss this square with you?"

"Certainly." I turned to Aurora. "Why don't you sit over here?"

"I'd like to go back and lie down, my lord."

I was disappointed because I was eager to see what Phineas might have divined about the puzzle. "All right. I'll take you."

"I'd like to go by myself, my lord."

"How—"

"I counted the number of steps we took coming here and the turns. I don't want to always have to be led around."

"Very well, if that's what you want."

She bumped against a table as she made her way to the door. I took a step toward her, but she held up a hand.

"I'll be all right, my lord. Please don't try to help me."

Once she was through the door, she turned toward the garden, guiding herself by keeping one hand on the wall. As stealthily as I could, I followed her. As she came to the last turn before entering the garden, she stopped and turned around. "Gaius," she said in a whisper, "stop following me. I have to do this on my own."

I matched her whisper. "I'm sorry. It's just that—"

She put a finger on my mouth. "Don't say any more. You never know who's listening."

After that all I could do was hold my breath and watch as she made her way around the peristyle. Another servant woman offered to help her, but Aurora shook her head and kept moving forward. I felt like a father seeing his child take her first steps. If she succeeded, it would mean she could manage without me. I almost hoped she would run into something and fall so I could rush to her rescue.

Seven, eight, nine. There should be a corner here. Yes, here it is. I've got to do this by myself. I know Gaius is standing back there watching me, just waiting to come help. But, if I'm going to spend the rest of my life in the dark, I've got to be able to get around by myself. I don't want someone

leading me everywhere. I've seen blind people on the streets. They've figured it out.

Two, three, four. The first column should be…yes, here it is. It's not hard from here. Five more columns.

Once Aurora had reached the room next to mine, I returned to the library. All Phineas could tell me was that he couldn't tell me anything about the ROTAS square.

"I've rearranged the letters in every pattern I can imagine, my lord, but nothing makes sense. And AREPO? I've consulted your uncle's lists of Umbrian, Oscan, and Etruscan words, but they contain nothing even remotely similar."

"Have you noticed the relationship between the *A*s, the *O*s, and the *T*s?"

"What relationship, my lord?"

"Each *T* is flanked by an *A* and an *O*. And, when you draw a line connecting the *T*s, you get a square within the square. That's not true of any other letter in the puzzle."

"Do you think that means anything, my lord?"

"I'm not sure, but don't spend any more time on it for now." I pushed the ROTAS papyri aside and picked up my uncle's scroll. Apparently Phineas wasn't aware of the Christian connotations of the square. "Let's take another look at this ice business."

Democrites arrived in less than an hour. When Phineas showed him the passage, his brow furrowed. "I doubt something that simple will help, sir. I have prepared an ointment to put on the girl's eyes and was just waiting for a convenient time to apply it." From the leather bag he was carrying he took a small clay jar with a stopper in it, sealed with wax.

"Meaning no disrespect to your skills, Democrites, but my uncle says he saw this work. I want to try it." It seemed to me pointless to put something on Aurora's eyes. She went blind when she struck her head.

Democrites obviously disagreed with me but could do no more than purse his lips tightly. "Very well, sir. There might not be much ice available in Rome at this time of year, though. What was brought down from the mountains in the spring has been pretty well used up,

I imagine. Only the largest merchants will have stored enough to last this long."

I don't keep ice in my house. In the first place, it's expensive just to haul it down from the mountains or to purchase it from someone who's done the hauling. Even with the best packing, so much of it melts along the way. To keep it from melting while it's stored requires a deep shaft of some sort, and lots of straw and blankets for packing.

People who use a lot of ice are, in my opinion, pretentious and just want to display their wealth. All the proof I need is that Regulus is very fond of using ice at his dinner parties, as was Nero. He used to boil water to remove the impurities and then put ice in it to make it drinkable. Since ice is just frozen, impure water, I'm not sure what he hoped to accomplish beyond showing that he could do it.

"A merchant we deal with keeps a supply," I said. "I'll send someone now."

I had no idea how much might be needed, so I asked Phineas to tell Demetrius to send two servants with some money, a large basket, and instructions to fill it.

As Phineas left the library, Democrites said, "While we're waiting, sir, may I try my ointment?"

"Let's go see the patient."

My mother and Naomi were with Aurora, who was sitting on the bed. When Democrites and I entered the room, they stepped back and remained standing in the doorway.

I put a hand on Aurora's shoulder. "The doctor wants to put an ointment on your eyes. Is that all right with you? Or would you rather wait for the ice to arrive?"

"I see no reason not to use the ointment, my lord. We shouldn't ignore the advice of such an eminent physician, should we?"

Her comment seemed to mollify Democrites, who gave me a look that said, *At least someone around here has some sense.* He opened his jar and set about smearing a vile-smelling concoction over her eyes. With that step completed, he wrapped a bandage around her head.

"It has a bit of an…aroma to it," my mother said from behind us.

"That's often the nature of medicines," Democrites said in a tone that one uses to dismiss the ignorant. "Are you comfortable, my dear?" he asked Aurora.

"It stings," Aurora replied anxiously.

"That's to be expected. It's part of how the medicine works."

Within moments Aurora had her hands to her face. "Ow! By the gods! It burns!"

Democrites pulled her hands away from the bandage. "Give it a few minutes."

"Gaius…Pliny, my lord, it hurts!" Aurora cried, thrashing around on the bench.

Democrites, a small, slender Greek, held her arms down with difficulty. "Will you help me, sir? The ointment needs a few moments to take effect."

I couldn't stand to see Aurora in pain, but I know that sometimes discomfort is part of a treatment. Setting a broken leg hurts as much as breaking the bone. The pain in my rib made it difficult for me to move and before I could get a grip on her, my mother grabbed Democrites' shoulders and flung him aside. I had to step back to avoid being knocked down.

"You fools! The girl is in pain." She tore the bandage off Aurora's face, revealing her red, puffy eyelids. "Oh, dear gods!" My mother took the pitcher of water on the table beside the bed and began washing Aurora's face.

Aurora broke into tears and clung to my mother, who sat down on the bed beside her.

"There, there, child. It will be all right." Mother turned to Democrites. "I don't believe we have any further need of your services."

Democrites stuffed his belongings into his bag. "I'm sorry, my lord, my lady. This is a new formula I made up especially for this patient. I don't understand why this has happened."

I was sorry to see him go. My uncle thought very highly of him, and I didn't want to insult my friend Pudens by rudely dismissing his family physician. I had wanted to ask him about the *karkinos* in my mother's breast, but, if the man couldn't make a simple ointment without doing more harm than good, I didn't see what he could tell me about her illness.

"You need to leave, too," Mother said. I didn't move, so she repeated the order more firmly, then called, "Naomi, get in here."

.   .   .

I had no choice but to step out of their way. At first I took up a position near the door, where I could at least hear what was going on. The two older women made soothing sounds and Aurora gradually stopped sobbing. My mother came out and waved her hands to shoo me away, as though I was some stray dog hanging around, hoping for a bone.

Not knowing quite what to do with myself, I sat down beside the *piscina* and began tossing small pebbles from the pathway into the water. It's hard to believe that Aurora and I swam and played in that water when we were children, the way Hashep and Dakla do now. Swimming in these pools is not something Roman children normally do. The first time we did it was when Aurora had been in the house only a few days. We were playing with small boats in the *piscina* when one floated beyond our reach. With the utter innocence of a seven-year-old, Aurora simply removed her gown and jumped in to get it. Demetrius ran over to the pool in horror. I knew Aurora was going to be in trouble, so I shed my tunic and jumped in with her.

Even after she could speak enough Latin, I never did explain to her that we weren't supposed to swim here, and no one dared to tell me that I couldn't until my mother demanded that we stop when we were nine.

"My lord? My lord?" I was called back from happier, simpler times by one of the servants who'd been sent to get ice. They had returned with an empty basket.

"Was the ice all gone?" I asked.

"You didn't send enough money, my lord."

When I heard the price that Callicles was demanding, I sputtered, "It's just frozen water, not gold."

My mother stepped outside Aurora's room and closed the door. "Why are you even hesitating, Gaius? If you won't pay it, I will. And I'll tell Aurora what you thought she's worth."

"Of course I'll pay it. I'm just surprised at what it costs."

"Callicles says it's the very last of his supply, my lord. He won't have any more until next month."

"All right. Tell Demetrius to give you the money."

When the servants returned the second time, the basket they carried was full of ice packed in blankets and straw. I took it to Aurora's door and gave it to my mother, but she wouldn't let me in the room.

"She needs to rest," she told me, putting her hand to my chest to push me back. "We'll let you know if there's any change."

"But what about the redness and swelling in her eyelids?"

"That's already much improved."

At least I could be thankful for that, and even more for the change in my mother's attitude toward Aurora.

"You just find something to do to keep yourself busy," Mother said, "and out of our way."

The only place I knew I might find something to distract me was the library. I was examining Phineas' progress on my uncle's scrolls when Demetrius entered the room.

"My lord, there are two men at the rear gate. They're…they're Praetorians."

XVI

DEMETRIUS HAD LET the two Praetorians come inside the back gate. They were standing next to the *exhedra*. Even though they weren't wearing their uniforms, their military demeanor couldn't be missed. One was a bit older and heavier, a centurion most likely. The other was taller, with a menacing scowl that looked permanent.

"Are you Gaius Pliny, sir?" the older man asked.

"Yes."

"We'd like for you to accompany us, sir."

"Where?" A knot began forming in my stomach. "Why?"

"You'll have all your questions answered soon enough, sir," the centurion said, "but not by us." He nodded and the taller man checked for weapons by patting my clothing. He stopped when he felt the Tyche ring.

"What's this?" he asked, pulling it out where he could see it.

"It's a family heirloom. An amulet of sorts, I guess you'd say." I knew immediately that was a bad choice of words. The soldier's grip tightened on the ring as he pulled me toward him.

"Are you a wizard, sir? Do you work spells?"

"No, of course not. Here, look at it. It's just a silly old ring. I've had it since I was a child."

"Any hidden compartments in it?" the centurion asked, turning the ring this way and that.

"No, nothing of the sort. Perhaps you should check my signet ring, too." I held out my hand, hoping that would distract them from the Tyche ring, and it worked. The taller soldier tried in vain to twist and turn my signet and nodded that he was satisfied.

"All right, let's go," the centurion said.

"What is this all about?" I asked again, tucking the Tyche ring back under my tunic.

"We were just told to come get you, sir," he said. "We were ordered to come to your back gate, and out of uniform, to spare you any embarrassment. Think of this as an invitation."

I knew it was no such thing. "If it were a true invitation, I could politely decline, but this sounds like an offer I can't refuse. If I do, I'll be arrested. Correct?"

"Yes, sir," the centurion said as politely as if he were offering me a drink. "You and everyone in your house. Now, we need to go."

Demetrius handed me a cloak as we left the house, but I had to wrap it around me as we walked in silence. We made our way down the Esquiline, past the Iseum, and behind the Temple of the Deified Claudius. The only positive thing I could glean from their route was that I was being taken to Domitian's house on the Palatine Hill, not to the Praetorian Camp. People who are taken to the Praetorian Camp do not return. Anyone who crossed our path, though, stepped aside and averted their eyes. The lack of uniforms didn't fool anyone. Who couldn't detect the outline of the swords under their cloaks?

When the Palatine loomed before us, they led me to a door at the base of the hill that I couldn't recall ever noticing before. A prearranged knock caused the door to be opened and we stepped inside. I never saw the person who opened the door and closed and locked it behind us—the most ominous sound I had heard since the eruption of Vesuvius.

We walked down a long, dimly lit passageway bare of decoration—even of plaster—forty paces by my count, then up a set of stairs, emerging into the construction site that would someday be Domitian's imperial residence. Scaffolding, piles of stone, and a crane stood ready for the next day's work as Rome's uncrowned king continued to push everyone else off the Palatine. When we were past them, we went down a few steps to the more finished part of the building on the western side of the hill and into an unadorned room—no bigger than the average room in my house—where Domitian sat, fanning himself with a piece of papyrus.

The *princeps*, now in his early thirties, was by no means a handsome man. His upper lip protruded a bit over the lower, and his chin was short. He wore his brown hair combed from the top of his head toward the front and cut short, a fashion that hadn't caught on yet, as styles do when set by popular rulers. His eyes turned down at the outer edges, giving him a perpetually doleful expression.

"Gaius Pliny, please sit down." He motioned to another chair, set opposite his, with a small table between them. Along with a lampstand and a small chest, they comprised all the furniture in the room.

"Are you sure you don't want me to stand, Caesar? Isn't that what prisoners usually do when they're brought before you?" Domitian expects to be addressed as "lord," but because of some interactions we've had in the past, I refuse to exalt him as a slave does his master. He knows he can't demand that I do it. When you've seen a man wet himself in fear, he loses his ability to impress you. The occasional "Caesar"—a name his family has stolen—was all the respect I would give him.

"Yes," Domitian said. "Prisoners stand, unless they're on their knees groveling for mercy and betraying members of their family to save their own miserable lives. But you, Gaius Pliny, you're not a prisoner. You're a guest." He was working hard to keep his tone affable. "An unhappy guest, I know. Please, sit down and let's discuss a few things."

I sat down, with one Praetorian standing behind me and the other off to my right. Guest or prisoner, I wasn't going to be allowed to make any sudden movement toward the *princeps*.

"What can you tell me about this?" Domitian handed me a copy of the ROTAS square with the interpretation of the AREPO line written below it.

"Did Regulus give you this?" I hadn't given Regulus a copy of the square, but he could have reproduced it easily enough, once he'd seen it. Or he may have realized that Jacob had kept the copy I'd shown him.

"How I got it is irrelevant. What matters is its meaning."

I handed the papyrus back to him. "It has no meaning."

"You seemed to think it did when you asked for a secretive meeting with Regulus, away from all eyes and ears."

Apparently not *all* eyes and ears. "I had been misled about the meaning of the thing. My own scribe, Phineas, has racked his brain over it and cannot fathom it."

"Perhaps if I racked his body—"

I hated myself for even mentioning Phineas. "You'd learn nothing more. The thing is nonsense." And also a Christian symbol, but this didn't seem the best time to bring that up.

"*Ad Regis Excidium Popilius Optatus* doesn't sound like nonsense to me. Who is Popilius and who has chosen him to kill me?"

"Are you a king, Caesar?"

"We both know the answer to that, Gaius Pliny. Let's not quibble."

As succinctly as possible, I told him the tale of Popilius and Crispina and the murder of Fabia. From the arching of his eyebrows and the rapidity of his breathing, he seemed to be experiencing that catharsis—that purging of emotion—which Aristotle says is the purpose of drama.

"A story worthy of an old-fashioned Greek playwright," Domitian said when I finished and he slumped back in his chair. "Where are these people now?"

"I don't know where Crispina is, and that worries me. But Popilius is dead."

"How do you know that for certain?"

"He killed himself. I saw him do it." That wasn't a complete lie. Popilius had said he was ready to die and agreed to the change of his name.

Domitian raised an eyebrow and looked at me, with his head turned to one side, almost like he was flirting with me. "You saw him kill himself and you didn't try to stop him? That doesn't sound like you."

"It happened too quickly. There was nothing I could do."

"I want to believe you, Gaius Pliny. I really do. I could sleep more easily if I knew that one person who wanted to kill me was dead. In my position I am caught by the greatest of ironies." He shifted his weight in his chair and leaned back. "The only absolute proof of a plot against a ruler is the success of the plot. Remember that when someone finally does kill me."

"Caesar, I don't know what you expect from me tonight. I am not involved in any plot against you and I know of none, no matter what Regulus may have told you. Have you considered what *his* motives might be in bringing such a story to you?"

Domitian rubbed a hand over his eyes and down his face. "What makes Regulus useful to me, Gaius Pliny, is that I know exactly what motivates him."

"His greed?"

"Even more basic than that. It's simple self-interest. Everything he does, he does because he sees it as being to his advantage. He doesn't work with me because he admires me. He assists me because it is in his own self-interest to do so. As long as I remember that, Regulus is a useful tool."

"Most people are motivated by self-interest," I said.

"True, true. But you, Gaius Pliny, you're entirely different." Domitian leaned forward as though he wanted to examine a peculiar object more closely. "You don't seem to be motivated by self-interest at all. It is definitely *not* in your interest to be a friend of Agricola and Tacitus, and yet you are. It would be in your own interest to make a friend of Regulus, and yet you oppose him at every opportunity."

"I'd sooner couple with a disease-ridden whore in the shadows of the Temple of Saturn than ally myself with Regulus."

"Yes, that's you—a man of *principle*." He almost spat out the last word. "Men like you make my life so difficult, even if you're not actually plotting against me. Fortunately, you're few in number, but I'd like to rid Rome of every last one of you. You, Gaius Pliny, present a particular problem for me. I know that if I kill you—or even send you into exile—Agricola and his men will sweep up the Palatine like a band of avenging Furies. So I have to stop short of that."

He barely nodded and the Praetorian behind me grabbed me and lifted me up from the chair, as though I were as light as a child, pinning my arms behind my back. The other one hit me hard in the stomach, again, and then again. When I bent over, he landed a solid blow on my jaw and a backhand to the side of my face. Domitian raised his hand and they dropped me back into the chair, resuming their positions behind and beside me, as impassive as statues.

Domitian studied me for a moment, like a sculptor regarding his work, trying to decide whether to chisel off another piece here and there. "As frustrating as it is for me, Gaius Pliny, it is in my own best interests *not* to harm you any more than that. I'm not sure if Agricola's protection extends to your entire household, but I know it embraces you and your mother."

My breathing grew more rapid at the implied threat to the rest of my *familia*.

"So," Domitian continued, "I must find some way to damage your reputation, to discredit you. Since you are a man of *principle*, that matters more to you than your money or your physical well-being, I think. Therefore, at the next meeting of the Senate, when I read a list of special grants that I'm making, I will announce that I've allowed you a reduction in the minimum age at which you may hold the quaestorship. I know that's still two years away for you, but it will mark you as my man even now."

I groaned, and not just from the pain in my jaw and belly and my broken rib. A man has to be twenty-five to hold the office of quaestor, the first step on the *cursus honorum*, the succession of offices which leads to a consulship. To be granted a privilege of this sort—without even asking for it—would signal that I was Domitian's property. He was claiming me, as surely as a dog marks his territory by lifting his leg.

"You don't sound impressed," Domitian continued with an ugly smile. "Let me add this. When you do stand for office, I'll support your nomination. Yours will be the first name on my list. In fact, if there weren't such a disparity in your ages, I'd nominate you and Regulus to be colleagues in the consulship."

Now I knew what it felt like to be pissed on. Each year a certain number of men are nominated for each office in the state. The *princeps* supports particular ones on the list, asking the Senate to look with favor on those friends of his, who are thus assured of election. The Senate then makes their own "free" choices from the remaining names. This is supposed to give the appearance of a republic in action. Such a distinction as Domitian proposed would be the end of my credibility in the eyes of my friends. But, if I publicly declined the honor, I would be declaring war on Domitian.

"How do you think Agricola and Tacitus will feel about you when you become one of my men?" Domitian laughed as though he had just told a riotously funny joke. Because of the pounding my stomach had taken, I vomited into my lap and on the floor.

"I'll take that as an expression of gratitude," Domitian said.

The Praetorians escorted me—dragged me, to be more accurate—back to the rear gate of my house, where they punched me a few more times and kicked me when I slumped to the ground. I tried, with little success, to protect my rib. I regurgitated a lot more than I remembered eating.

When my pounding on the bottom of the door was finally heard, one of my younger servant women opened it, took one look, and screamed. Then she closed the door and ran screaming for Demetrius. I couldn't entirely fault her; I wouldn't want my servants dragging into the house every vomit-soaked derelict with his face bashed in who happened to fall at my door.

After all the fuss and flap had settled and I had convinced my mother that I wasn't going to die ("You won't as long as we don't call Democrites" was her final word) and we weren't going to be arrested, I was allowed to clean myself up and go to bed.

.   .   .

As soon as I awoke the next morning, I hobbled next door to Aurora's room. If I could keep my voice normal and not groan too much, I hoped she wouldn't know what had happened to me. I didn't want to worry her. At least she couldn't see that I still couldn't quite stand up straight.

But as soon as I walked into the room, she cried, "Gaius! What happened to your face?"

"You…can see me?" I dropped to my knees beside her bed. "You can see—"

"Oh, I wanted it to be a surprise for you, just like it was to me."

"What happened? How—"

She took my hands in hers. "I'm not sure."

"Was it the ice?"

"Your mother and Naomi did help me keep ice on my forehead until late in the night, but the swelling was going down and they finally went to bed. They said we'd resume the treatment in the morning. Then the strangest thing happened after that. At least I think it happened."

"You think it happened? What do you mean?"

"I'm not sure it wasn't a dream. Sometime during the night, Jacob came to see me."

"Jacob? You mean Nestor? Regulus' servant?"

"Yes. How many Jacobs do you know?"

Of course it had to be that Jacob. I just couldn't fathom how he could have gotten into my house. I knew Demetrius would not have answered a knock on my door at that time. "He came in the middle of the night? How did he get in?"

"I don't know."

"Demetrius must have forgotten to bar the back gate in all the confusion after they brought me in. But how would Jacob know that? Tell me, from the beginning, what happened."

"I woke up when I heard a man calling my name."

"Didn't you scream?"

"No, I recognized Jacob's voice. I was puzzled, but I knew I had no reason to be afraid."

"What did he say?"

"He said to keep my eyes closed. I didn't see the point in that, because I was blind, but I did as he said."

"And you're sure it was Jacob?"

"Absolutely. When you can't see people, you become very aware of their voices."

"Why did he come to see you?"

"He said his god had sent him to heal me."

Still on my knees, I leaned back, in shock. "To…to heal you? What did he do?"

"I heard him spit several times—"

"You heard him, but you couldn't see him?"

"Remember, dear Gaius, I was blind. And I kept my eyes closed, like he told me to."

"So he spat several times?"

"Yes. Then he put something wet on my eyelids, and he said something in a language I didn't understand. Then he kissed my forehead and left."

"Had he 'healed' you? Could you see?"

"When he left, I got up and opened the door." There was a catch in her voice. "I could see, Gaius! I could see!"

"But the ice could have restored your sight, even before Jacob got here."

"It could have." She shrugged. "This room is so dark. I was asleep when he came in, and he closed the door behind him. *And* I had my eyes closed. There were several reasons I couldn't see anything. Take your pick."

"When you opened the door to your room, did you see Jacob in the garden?"

"No. The garden was empty. I walked over to the rear gate."

"That had to be how he got in and out. Did you bar it?"

"No." She paused. "I know you won't want to hear this. The gate was barred."

"That can't be."

"I saw it."

"Then how did he get in and out?"

"I can't explain it, Gaius, not any of it. I was so overwhelmed that I sat on the bench by your uncle's bust and looked at the stars for a while. I'd been so afraid I would never see them again."

"I wish you had wakened me."

"I did think about coming into your room, but I decided I wanted to surprise you this morning. I was going to pretend to still be blind, but when I saw your face I couldn't help but say something."

None of this made any sense. As unlikely as it was that putting ice on Aurora's forehead would enable her to see again, that technique had the cogency of an Aristotelian syllogism compared to spitting on her eyes. At least Jacob's "treatment" hadn't done the damage that Democrites' had. I looked more closely. Could it have taken care of that problem, too? Aurora's eyelids weren't the least bit red or swollen.

"There has to be a logical explanation," I insisted. "I wonder if the ice had restored your sight. While you were sleeping, you had a dream about Jacob. That wouldn't be unusual. He's someone you know and respect, although I would prefer to think you dream about me."

"More than you know," Aurora said. "And this seemed too real to be a dream. I felt his touch on my eyelids." She took my hand and guided one of my fingers over her eyelids. "Just like that."

"If the rear gate was barred from the inside, how could anyone have gotten in or out of the house? It's just not possible, unless we resort to fables about gods popping up wherever they damn well please."

"It's hard to explain, isn't it?" she said, touching her eyes and then reaching out to me. "We'll just have to ask Jacob. All I know is that I can see again. But this isn't what I wanted to see. What happened to you?"

I cringed when she touched my jaw. "It's nothing, really."

"Nothing? But your face is swollen. Here, put this on it." She reached into the basket on the floor beside her bed and pulled out a small chunk of ice, wrapping it in a piece of cloth. "It's all that's left, but maybe it will help. Hold it to the side of your face."

"Maybe we can ask Jacob to spit on me."

Aurora laughed. "Now, tell me what happened."

Placing the ice to my face, I sat down on the bed beside her, took her hand, and told her about my conversation with Domitian.

"Do you think you're going to be arrested?" she asked when I finished. Her grip on my hand got tighter.

"No, but I think I'm going to be ruined if he makes me look like one of his supporters."

"Are Tacitus and Agricola in any danger?"

"I'm not sure. I need to talk to Tacitus, but I don't feel like going to his house this morning. I'll have to send someone to ask him to come over here. I can't risk writing any of this down."

"I'll go," Aurora said immediately.

"You've just recovered. I don't want you running around the city."

She put a hand on my leg. "I'm fine. And you can trust me to tell Tacitus what happened. You won't have to write it down and he won't have to come over here. Besides, I want to get out to find out if I notice things differently after being unable to see. Will my eyes be better since, for several days, I had no eyes?"

I knew that what she said made sense, and she had been navigating the streets of Rome by herself since she was twelve, often in disguise. But I wanted her here with me. To feel her hand resting on my leg was restoring my spirits faster than any doctor's nostrum could ever do.

"I'll send a couple of men with you."

She shook her head. "I'll be fine. You know I can take care of myself in the streets."

"All right. Here, at least take this." I removed the Tyche ring on its leather strap from around my neck and placed it over her head. "Not that it did me much good last night."

She clutched the ring and kissed me softly on my aching cheek. "You're still alive, aren't you? And you're not in a cell somewhere in the bowels of the Praetorian Camp. I'd call that very good luck indeed."

.   .   .

Of course I wasn't going to let Aurora go out on the streets of Rome by herself, not with Crispina's servants keeping an eye on my house for some reason. The previous day I had sent two of my servants—taller than Phineas—to follow Crispina's man when he left his post. They tracked him to an *insula* but saw no sign of Crispina. I probably needed a wider net of spies to find her, but I was not going to involve Regulus any further.

When Aurora left, I sent two of my servants to follow her without her knowledge. Walking to Tacitus' house, delivering a message, and returning to my house shouldn't take Aurora more than two hours, even at a leisurely pace. Given the time when she left, I expected her to return well before noon. I spent the morning dealing with a few of my clients whom I'd been passing off to Demetrius for several days and then listening to Hashep and Dakla do their lessons with Phineas.

I could not understand how a man like Popilius could have desired Fabia when she was Hashep's age, the way a man desires a woman. Hashep was truly a beautiful girl, nearly ten, but she was still a child. Popilius would have wanted Aurora, I assumed, when she was still my playmate. It weighed on me that, thanks to my generosity, Popilius was going to a place where no one knew his proclivity. Tacitus' letter had warned Julius Fortunatus, but was that enough? Had I turned a predator loose, sent a fox into a house of unsuspecting baby chicks? On the other hand, did I have the right to appoint myself his judge and executioner? By warning Fortunatus in Massilia about him, I consoled myself, I had done all I could.

Philosophers tell us that we should not wish evil on other people, lest the very thing we wish for them be inflicted on us in order to achieve some kind of balance in the universe. The Stoics say we should regard everything that happens with indifference, *apatheia*, because we cannot change anything. But I would not regret hearing that the ship carrying Popilius and Segetius had gone down, with everyone on board except them surviving. Or perhaps the ship had run into a storm and the crew had drawn lots and thrown someone overboard to satisfy the angry gods. I suppose that sort of thing happens only in stories, though, stories like Arion and the dolphin. I always enjoyed that one when I was a child. I wondered if Hashep and Dakla knew it.

·   ·   ·

When the short shadows in my garden indicated it was midday and Aurora hadn't gotten back, I began to worry, pacing—albeit slowly, because of my beating by the Praetorians—around the peristyle. I told myself I would wait another half hour and then go out to look for her. She was probably just taking her time, savoring her ability to see and move about on her own again. I was relieved a few moments later when I heard Tacitus greeting Demetrius. He must have returned with Aurora, I thought. But when he came into the garden, he was accompanied only by the two men I had sent to follow her.

"Where's Aurora?" I asked.

"Good day to you, too, Gaius Pliny. How should I know where Aurora is? She's your…servant. And isn't she blind?"

"Her sight returned overnight. She was supposed to go to your house to tell you that and deliver some other news."

Tacitus clapped me on the shoulder. "Well, that's wonderful, but she hasn't been at my house. The only servants of yours that I've seen are these two."

I turned on my servants. "What happened? Where is Aurora?"

"My lord, we were following her until she went around a corner, just a few blocks from here. By the time we got there, she was nowhere to be seen."

"Why didn't you come back here and tell me?"

"We thought we should try to find her, my lord. We looked for her all the way to Cornelius Tacitus' house, but there was no sign of her."

I lashed out and struck the man across the face. "You fool! If anything happens to her, you will pay more dearly than you can possibly imagine. Both of you!"

"Gaius Pliny," Tacitus said, "it won't help to lose your temper. You don't know that anything dire has befallen her. She's very resourceful. From what you've told me, she's always been able to take care of herself on the streets."

"She's alone, and she may not be entirely recovered. We have to find her!"

"Of course, you're right. Let's go. And, on the way, you can tell me what happened to you." He lifted my chin like a parent examining a child's injury.

Accompanied by the servants Tacitus had brought—a couple of whom had seen Aurora before—and a few of my men, we set out on the most logical route to Tacitus' house.

"Look down every alley," I told them. "Stick your head into every *taberna*. Ask if anyone has seen her. Lift the covers on the sewers. Look behind piles of trash. Don't miss any place where she might be… hidden." I couldn't let myself imagine her lying dead or injured somewhere.

By the time we reached Tacitus' house I had given him a quick account of my interview with Domitian, but we had found no trace of Aurora. His servants assured us that they had not seen any sign of her, either before or after Tacitus left.

"Is there some favorite spot of hers along the way where she might have stopped?" Tacitus asked.

"She wouldn't have stopped anywhere until she had delivered the message at your house," I snapped.

"You don't have to bite my head off, my friend," Tacitus said. "I'm just as concerned about her as you are. But the fact is, she never got here."

"That means something happened to her on her way *to* your house. Let's go back along a different route. Perhaps she went through the Forum."

Putting an arm around my shoulder and pulling me into a corner of his atrium, Tacitus lowered his voice. "Gaius, I don't mean to be an alarmist, but you said Domitian told you that, in his view, Agricola's promise of protection covers only you and your mother. Likewise, I doubt if anyone in my household, beyond myself and Julia, is safe."

He was expressing my worst fear. "But why would Domitian take Aurora? She's just one servant out of more than a hundred in my house."

"You said Regulus made it clear he knew of your relationship with her, when you were out at Martial's farm."

I knew that had to be the answer, as unhappy as I was to hear it. "Yes, he must have a spy at Marinthus' *taberna*. My money would be on Marinthus' son, Theodorus."

"Well, whatever Regulus knows, Domitian knows."

I leaned against the wall, feeling the hope drain out of me. If Domitian had taken Aurora, what chance did we have of finding her? "Are we just supposed to give up?" I asked.

"No. We don't know what happened, and we'll keep looking. I'm just telling you to be prepared for the worst."

Heading back toward my house, we searched as diligently as we could, but—even if she hadn't been snatched by Domitian's thugs—what hope did we have of finding one woman in a city of over a million people, with streets and buildings that spread out in chaotic fashion for almost two miles in any direction from the Forum?

"Something has happened to her," I told Tacitus as we started up the Esquiline. "Something dreadful."

"Maybe her blindness returned," he said. "I hate to think of her wandering these streets, unable to see."

"Somebody could take advantage of her." I felt my panic rising. On the streets of Rome a helpless woman—especially one whose dress marked her as coming from a noble house—would be set upon like a deer falling prey to a pack of wolves. I didn't want to carry that analogy any further because I had seen what the wolves leave behind.

When we arrived back at my house it was late afternoon. I rushed into the garden, hoping to find Aurora calmly sitting there, wondering where I had been. But my mother was the one who asked that question.

"You've missed taking a bath," she said, "and we're preparing dinner. Oh, and there's someone waiting to see you." She pointed to the back of the garden. "It's a messenger from Livilla."

Tacitus and I exchanged a puzzled glance. Why would Livilla be sending me a message? She would be my sister-in-law, it seemed, instead of my wife, but I could think of no reason for her to be communicating with me this soon after the end of our engagement.

The messenger was sitting beside my uncle's bust. He stood when I approached him. "My lord, my lady Livilla sent me to give you this."

He handed me a piece of rolled-up papyrus. Instead of being sealed with wax, it had the leather strap bearing the Tyche ring tied around it. My stomach felt like one of the Praetorians had punched me again.

"This came from Livilla, daughter of Pompeia Celerina?"

"Yes, my lord."

I didn't understand. Aurora might have sent me a message tied up with the Tyche ring in order to guarantee its authenticity, but how had the thing come into Livilla's possession?

"I don't like the look of this," Tacitus said as I untied the strap and opened the note. "Aurora would never have willingly parted with that ring."

The message bore no sender's name and was addressed to Livilla.

> *Come with this messenger if you want to see the dawn of a new era in your life. Do not bring anyone else with you.*

Below that was written: AREPO—*Aurora Remotura Ex Plinii Orbe.*

"'Aurora will be removed from Pliny's world'? It has to be from Crispina," I said. "She's the one who's obsessed with this AREPO nonsense."

"But why would she threaten Aurora, after Aurora was so kind to her?"

"Because she's mad. She doesn't need a reason." I turned to the messenger. "How long ago did your mistress receive this note?"

"Less than an hour, my lord. She sent me to you right away and I came straight here without stopping. She said it was urgent."

"Where is she?"

"She went with the messenger, my lord. He said he had a *raeda* waiting outside the walls."

"Do you know where they went? Did Livilla know?"

"No, my lord. She said you would know."

"And yet she went with him? Why?"

"She said she had to do something to protect Aurora until you could get there, my lord."

"Get there?" Tacitus said. "How can we get there when we don't know where 'there' is?"

"She's been taken to Tabellius' villa," I said. "That's the only thing that makes any sense."

"Do you think Crispina would risk going back to that place?"

"She's obsessed with it. We have to get out there."

"But if you're wrong, Gaius, it will mean Aurora's life."

I put the Tyche ring around my neck. "That's why I can't be wrong."

Where am I? What's going on? By the gods, am I blind again? No, there's something over my head. A gag in my mouth. Hands and feet are tied.

I must be in a wagon, and it's moving. Something over me. Don't panic. I can't think straight if I panic. What happened? How long have I been unconscious?

Think! Think! Let's see. I was on my way to…to Tacitus' house. I had not gotten far from Gaius' house at all. He sent two men to follow me, just as I thought he would. I was proud of the way I eluded them. Suddenly a woman stepped out of an alley and took hold of my arm. It was Crispina. For an instant I was too shocked to do or say anything. That gave her time to pull me into the alley. Two men grabbed me. One put his hand over my mouth. He was holding a cloth, so I couldn't bite him.

The cloth must have been soaked in something that put me to sleep. I don't remember being hit, but I know I've been unconscious. Probably better to be still, not let them know I'm awake. Work on getting my hands free. That could give me an advantage, whatever's going to happen.

XVII

ROUNDING UP the first half dozen of my male servants I could find, Tacitus and I forced our way through the bath-going throngs in the streets until we got to the livery stable outside the gate on the Ostian Way.

"I need horses," I told the owner, catching my breath. "All you have. Right now."

"This late in the day I have only two, sir," the man said.

I slapped money on the table in front of him. "Give them to me."

"It'll take a few moments to get them ready."

I slapped more money on the table. "I don't have time. Get them now."

"Yes, sir."

While the owner scrambled to bring the horses to us, I told my servants to find whatever transportation they could and follow us as soon as possible. One of the men had been with us when we went out to Tabellius' house before. "He knows the way," I told the others.

As I might have suspected, the two horses we got were the only two left because they were broken-down nags. No amount of urging on our part could get them to move faster than a trot, as though we were out riding for pleasure.

Giving up my effort to coax any more speed out of my mount, I said, "I don't understand what she's doing. It makes no sense."

"I agree," Tacitus said. "Right now she's not at all rational. I think she actually has feelings for you, and you know how women are when their feelings take over."

"Feelings? For me? What—"

Tacitus turned partway to face me. "I'm talking about Livilla. Aren't you?"

"No. The only feeling Livilla could have for me is contempt."

"You underestimate her, Gaius Pliny. She's a high-minded young woman. She knows what the loss of Aurora would mean to you, so she's trying to prevent it."

"But she could get herself killed."

"I don't think that matters to her as much as insuring your happiness. Or perhaps she knows she's not going to be happy without you, so it's a sacrifice she's willing to make. That's the way a Roman wife would think."

I fell silent as Tacitus' words made me see Livilla in an entirely new light. What sort of bravery lurked beneath that shy exterior? Contrary to what Domitian believed, apparently there was at least one other person in Rome whose actions were based on some motive other than self-interest.

When we reached Marinthus' *taberna* a group of men were gathered in front, next to a small wagon, talking earnestly. Theodorus was in the center of the group. I intended to ride on past them, but one of them raised a hand and called my name.

I stopped long enough to ask, "How do you know me? I have no time to talk to you."

He approached my horse. "But, sir, I'm Eustasius, one of Crispina's men. I know you because I've been watching your house for several days. I helped kidnap your servant woman, Aurora."

My immediate instinct was to pull out my sword and run him through, but he was honest enough to admit who he was. He might be of some help to us. "Get up behind me!" I ordered him. He took my hand and I pulled him up onto my horse.

"They're at Tabellius' villa," Eustasius said. "But I gather you already know that."

"Tell me everything *you* know," I said as I kicked the nag back into motion. "Tell me fast and I might let you live. Start with when Crispina left my house."

"Well, sir, she stayed in Rome. She was waiting for her steward to bring her the money she expected to get from selling her farm."

"So she planned to sell it all along."

"Yes, sir. She was going to leave Italy. She knew she couldn't go back to her farm after…everything that's happened."

"After what she did to Fabia, you mean. What *you* helped her do to Fabia."

"Yes, sir. To my everlasting shame. I hope I can make up for that to some small degree."

"You can't give her back her life, or the life of her child."

"Her…child? What are you talking about, sir? We didn't kill any child. No one could make me do that, no matter what they threatened me with."

"Fabia was pregnant. Didn't Crispina bother to mention that?"

"By the gods, sir, no." He fell silent. When he spoke again, his voice was subdued. "So that's why she stabbed her."

"Yes, three times."

"We did even worse than we knew. I've thought about little else since then." Eustasius' voice carried what sounded like genuine remorse, but over the last few days I'd learned not to trust anyone.

"Why did she stay within sight of my house, where I might have seen her?"

"She wanted to keep an eye on that girl of yours, Aurora. That was all she could talk about."

The hairs on the back of my neck stood up. "Why did she care about her?"

"She said we could kidnap her and get a big ransom."

"Why did she think I would pay a big ransom for a slave?"

"She thought Aurora was more than just a slave to you, sir. She had seen the way you looked at one another."

"A look doesn't mean—"

"This pretense is getting tiresome, Gaius Pliny," Tacitus said. "The fact that we're here proves she's right."

I wouldn't argue with him in front of another person's servant. "How did you capture her? She would have put up a fight."

"Crispina had bought a potion. We put it on a cloth and clamped it over the girl's mouth."

I had heard of such sleep-inducing drugs, usually drawn from the poppy plant. I didn't know how fast they could work. "What has she done to her?" I demanded.

"Nothing yet, but she's going to."

"I won't pay a ransom if anything happens to her."

"She's not after a ransom, sir. That was just a trick to get us to go along with her. She knew we were all sickened by what she made us do to Fabia."

"How did she 'make' you rape a woman?" Tacitus asked.

"When one of your friends has a sword at his throat, sir, you'll do most anything to save his life. Besides, Fabia hadn't ever done anything to endear herself to any of us."

"That defense would never stand up in court," Tacitus said. "Being obnoxious isn't against the law."

"If she doesn't want ransom," I said, "what does she want now?"

His hesitation told me as much as his words when he finally said, "She plans to kill her, sir, just like she did poor Fabia. She says the only part of Aurora you'll get back will be her head."

I kicked my horse's sides again. The beast whinnied in protest. Another kick produced slightly more speed. "So she's taken Aurora to that second garden in Tabellius's villa."

"Yes, sir."

"And why did she send that message to Livilla?"

"She wants the lady Livilla to see it. She thinks Aurora came between you and the lady, just like Fabia came between her and Popilius. She believes the lady will be glad to see Aurora dead. Maybe even pay her something."

"The woman is mad," Tacitus said. "Absolutely mad."

"That's what we finally realized," Eustasius said. "Me and the others that were helping her. We tried to talk her out of hurting anybody else—said we wanted no more part in it—but she killed one of us. We had no idea she had a knife on her until she stabbed him. Two others and me managed to get away."

"She couldn't chase all three of you, eh?" Tacitus said.

"No, sir, and I was the fastest runner. I heard one other scream before I got into the wagon and out of her reach entirely. I never looked back."

So much for loyalty to friends, I thought. "Does she have anyone with her now?"

"As far as I know, only the man who drove the *raeda* and her steward."

"Will they fight for her?" Tacitus asked.

"The driver, probably, but not her steward. He'd need a spine to be able to fight."

.   .   .

We pulled up within sight of Tabellius' villa. As Eustasius started to slip off the horse, I slammed my elbow into his face. He groaned once and fell to the ground.

Tacitus jumped off his horse. "Gaius Pliny, what—"

"It's far less than he deserves." I dismounted and tied my horse to a tree. "And I don't trust him at all. Remember what little Clodius said: 'I don't like him. He's mean.'"

"He could be an ally," Tacitus said. "We could outnumber them."

"How do we know he's not still in league with Crispina? Except for the part about watching my house, his whole story could be a lie. We've been lied to and duped from the first day of this…this misadventure. I don't want to go in there with someone behind me that I don't trust. Or someone who would desert us at the first sign of trouble. Help me gag him and tie him up." I cut pieces off the blanket I'd been riding on and handed them to Tacitus. "Hurry up!"

With Eustasius trussed up, we made a cautious approach to the villa. The *raeda* with its team of horses was tied up in front of the crumbling house.

"Segetius showed me a way to get under the rear wall," I whispered to Tacitus. "Since I'm smaller, I'll take that. You enter the front door. Neither of us is to do anything until we've seen the other one in place."

Segetius had told me about, but not actually showed me, the spot that animals had created under the wall. Fortunately, it was easy to find. I lay on my back and wriggled under it, emerging behind the concealment of some bushes and a shed. When I had righted myself and peeked around the corner of the shed, I nearly gasped out loud.

Aurora, stripped naked and gagged, was tied to the whipping post.

Crispina stood in front of Aurora, axe in hand. I'd expected her to look mad—frenetic, twitching, hair disheveled—but she appeared as calm and composed as a Vestal Virgin, almost majestic. What I hadn't realized when I saw her in my house was that she was a fair-sized woman, hardened from working on a farm. She had somehow made herself seem frail, beaten-down, when I was talking to her earlier. All part of her act, like Odysseus disguising himself in the swineherd's hut. He had a goddess's help then; I wondered what demon was aiding Crispina—one inside her, I suspected.

Between the post and the front part of the house stood one of Crispina's men, with a sword. Tacitus would have to deal with him. Off to one side sat a wizened man with a wooden chest in front of him and a look of panic on his face. His primary purpose in life at the moment seemed to be making himself as small as possible.

That must be the steward, I thought. *He won't put up a fight. At least Eustasius was right about that.*

The most amazing sight, though, was Livilla standing on the other side of Aurora, looking smaller and more vulnerable than ever against Crispina.

"Please, don't hurt her," Livilla pleaded.

"But she's going to take your beloved Gaius Pliny away from you," Crispina said, in a voice that revealed the madness concealed by her calm demeanor. "When we were together at Marinthus' *taberna*, she kept talking about how sad it made her to think of Pliny marrying you."

Aurora shook her head and I could hear her trying to say something through the gag.

"That may be the way she feels," Livilla said, "but she's not the reason I ended my engagement to Gaius. I just decided that I don't love him and don't want to marry him."

From the widening of her eyes, I knew that Aurora had seen me, so I signaled to her to make no sign. Noting the top of Tacitus' head in his hiding place on the other side of the garden, I ducked back a bit.

Crispina lowered the axe. "Now, child, I saw you come out of his library in tears a few nights ago."

"But that's when I told him I wasn't going to marry him. It has nothing to do with her." She jerked a thumb toward Aurora. It was interesting to see how well the woman who was almost my wife could lie.

"But it's obvious," Crispina said, "how much Pliny loves Aurora. And she was in there with him when you arrived. I saw it all. I just wish I could strap the whore to the wheel, like she deserves, but that self-righteous prig Pliny must have destroyed it."

"Actually, Popilius did that," I said, stepping out from concealment with my sword drawn.

"You!" Crispina cried. "Oh, but this makes it all the better."

She drew the axe back and swung at Aurora with all her might.

I couldn't believe what I saw as I ran screaming across the garden. Livilla lunged at Crispina and, even as small as she was, hit the larger woman hard enough to knock her off balance. Aurora managed to turn her head just enough to escape the blow. The axe lodged in the post with a horrendous *thunk*. If it had hit Aurora, it would have split her face in half.

Crispina cursed in frustration as she tried to pull the axe out of the wood. Before she could loosen it, I tackled her and threw her to the ground. As I tried to get control of her, she swung her arms and thrashed her feet. Livilla tried to grab her feet but got kicked in the stomach. I finally hit Crispina on the jaw, stunning her enough that I could get her turned over and clasp her hands behind her back.

"Find something to tie her up with!" I cried.

I heard the sounds of a struggle and the clanging of sword on sword from the front of the garden, then a groan. When I could spare a glance, I saw Tacitus standing over Crispina's servant, wiping his blade on the man's tunic. The whimpering noise I was hearing emanated from Crispina's steward, cringing in his corner.

"Here," Livilla said, "use this." She handed me a piece of rope.

By the time I got Crispina's hands tied, Livilla had untied the ropes that bound Aurora's feet to the post. I could never have imagined her being this fearless. I took out my blade and cut the ropes holding Aurora's hands. The axe had cut through some of her hair on its way into the post and nicked her ear. I pulled the gag out of her mouth and she collapsed into my arms in tears and loud sobs. The blood from the cut on her ear stained the shoulder of my tunic.

Livilla found Aurora's tunic, which had been cut off her, and handed it to me. I wrapped it around Aurora as best I could.

"Thank you," I said to Livilla over Aurora's shoulder. "I don't know what else to say."

She shook her head. "It's all right. You don't have to say anything."

Crispina moaned and rolled over onto her back. I handed Livilla my sword. "Hold this on her. Don't let her move."

Wriggling over to the post like a turtle trying to right itself, Crispina worked her way to a standing position. "You see which one of you he's holding, don't you?" she said to Livilla. "For him it will always be Aurora."

"Gaius said for you not to move," Livilla said. "Be still."

"How are you going to stop me? You don't have the courage, you sniveling little—"

"That's enough!" I said, one arm still around Aurora.

With both hands Livilla held my sword out in front of her, as though she didn't want the thing too close to her own body.

"I don't understand why you did this," I told Crispina. "What did you think you would gain by killing Aurora?"

"I would gain the satisfaction of knowing that another husband-stealing slut had gotten what she deserved."

"But Aurora isn't Fabia." I wasn't sure that fact was at all clear in Crispina's mind. In her rage she had somehow blended the two women into one.

"Even when you were with me in the *taberna*," Aurora said, "when I thought I was helping you, you already had your plan worked out to kill Fabia, didn't you?"

"Of course, you naïve little do-gooder. My men found them in Ostia, waiting for a ship. I knew if they got even a glimpse of me, they would panic, so I waited at the *taberna* until everything was ready. But I had to listen to your constant whining about Pliny, Pliny, Pliny."

Aurora turned to me. "I don't think I mentioned your name more than twice, my lord."

"It was the *way* you said it," Crispina cut in. "You know what I'm talking about, don't you?" she shot at Livilla.

"And so you came to my house," I said, "to—"

"I came to your house because I needed a safe place to leave Clodius. Once my property was sold, I planned to get as far away from Italy as I could. I had no time for a little traveling companion. I saw Nonnius and Marcella come to your house, so I guess you know the boy isn't really my son."

"Yes, but he's with them now. I think he'll be all right."

"I hope so. He is a sweet lad."

"Once you had dropped off Clodius, why didn't you just leave Rome?" Aurora asked.

"My property hadn't sold yet, and while I was in your house I saw the two of you together and I thought, 'She's no different than Fabia. She deserves what Fabia got.' I rented rooms near your house and waited for my opportunity."

I drew Aurora closer to me, still unnerved by how close I had come to losing her.

"One thing doesn't seem to fit in this mad scheme at all," I said. "Why did you concoct the story about Popilius being chosen to kill…a king?" I couldn't bring myself to use Domitian's name. Who knew who might be listening?

"It gave me something to frighten him with. Popilius is a craven coward. That's why he likes little girls. They're no threat to him."

My eyebrows shot up. "You knew?"

"Of course I knew."

"So you used little Fabia like bait."

"When Popilius came to see me, to pay his respects after Fabius' death, I made sure she was there, as prettied up as a little girl could be. He wanted to hug her—to console her—and I told her it was all right. She ended up sitting in his lap."

"So he wasn't really marrying you—"

"No, he just wanted Fabia."

"But you must have wanted something."

"His land. And after we got married I had him sign it over to me. Of course, he didn't know what he was signing because he couldn't read. I told him it was a will and he made his mark, with my steward as witness." She jerked her head back toward the man huddled over the chest.

"But, if you wanted him to take up with Fabia," Tacitus asked from behind us, where he was still holding his sword on the steward, "why did you get so angry when it happened?"

"He was supposed to lose interest when she started her monthlies. That's how it was with any other girls he had. And then she saw me padding myself, pretending that I was going to have Popilius' child. She stayed small, childlike. She got the upper hand on me. No one had ever done that before."

"And then she got pregnant."

"Yes, and she threw that up to me. She had taken Popilius away from me, right in my own house. I had no choice but to kill her."

"Why didn't you just kill Popilius too?" Tacitus asked.

"I wanted him to suffer, to live in fear for as long as he lived. I've never seen a man so terrified by even the thought of pain."

That would explain why he couldn't bring himself to carry out his own castration, I thought.

"The very idea that he might be arrested and tortured for conspiring to kill Domitian"—Crispina laughed—"I knew he would never get another decent night's sleep. It's hard to sleep when you're always looking over your shoulder."

"But there never was any plot—"

"Don't be ridiculous." Crispina spat the words out. "Did you really think—Gaius Pliny, how could you be so stupid?"

I couldn't explain to her how people in my rank of Roman society have to be sensitive to the slightest hint of a threat to the *princeps*. If he gets wind of even the suspicion of a plot, it could endanger all of us.

I looked at Aurora. She had been right when she said she felt we were being deliberately thrown off the scent. I had made a mistake that would haunt me, I was sure, when I had gone to Regulus to enlist his help.

"Where is Popilius, by the way?" Crispina asked, trying to sound casual.

"You don't really expect me to tell you, do you?"

She tugged at the rope binding her hands, causing Livilla to tighten her grip on my sword. "What could I do to him now?"

"If you don't know where he is, I don't have to worry about that."

Crispina shifted her weight to her other foot. "So, what are you going to do, Gaius Pliny?" she said with a sneer. "You can't arrest me. You have no authority. There are no witnesses to anything I *might* have done."

"That's where you're wrong. Your man Eustasius is tied up out front. He's so remorseful about what you did to Fabia and what you made him do that he will testify against you, I'm sure, especially if he's promised a pardon."

"The little bastard ran too fast," Crispina said with a demented chuckle. "I got the other two, but Eustasius just ran too fast and got to the wagon." She heaved a great sigh. "So I guess it will be the arena for me, eh?"

"I'll make every effort to be sure you end up there," I said. "I don't go to the games, but I will make an exception on the day they drag you—"

"I'll save you the trouble," Crispina said. Pushing herself away from the post with surprising force, she threw herself onto the sword Livilla was holding. Livilla closed her eyes and turned her head at the impact.

Grinning at me, Crispina gasped, "You insufferable…prig." Then she slumped against Livilla, falling to the ground with the smaller woman under her and impaling herself on the sword all the way up to the hilt.

XVIII

THE AFTERMATH of a battle could not have been much more grisly than the scene in the garden, with a corpse, the steward crying, Livilla screaming, and Crispina groaning out her life as blood gushed from the wound in her stomach. Even after we got Livilla out from under Crispina, she would not stop screaming, and I could understand why. Crispina had bled profusely over her. Livilla kept tearing at her gown, as though it were on fire. "Get it off me, Gaius! Get it off me!"

With Tacitus standing guard over the steward and watching over Crispina's death throes, I set Aurora on a bench, shivering and wrapped in her torn gown, and tried to think of some way to calm Livilla. I had to get her into another garment without exposing her. The only person in the garden whose clothes weren't bloodstained was Crispina's steward.

"You," I said, "take off your tunic."

"What—"

"You heard him. Do it!" The point of Tacitus' sword under the man's chin secured his immediate compliance.

I took the tunic and slipped it over Livilla's head, hoping she didn't notice the wet spot near the bottom. "Now, my dear," I said, "unpin your shoulder brooch and, as I let this tunic down, you drop yours."

She fumbled with the brooch but got it loose and we managed to get her clothed in a relatively clean, blood-free garment.

I tossed Livilla's garment to the steward. "You can put that on or not. Suit yourself."

The man slipped the gown over his head, with the bloodstains turned to the back.

I embraced Livilla, looking over the top of her head at Aurora, who nodded and smiled faintly.

"How do we sort this out?" Tacitus asked. "We've got two more dead men out there somewhere."

"Let's start by getting Eustasius in here," I said.

Tacitus pulled my sword out of Crispina's chest. Her body jerked and settled as the sword came out. Tacitus leaned over and spoke to her corpse. "Nero's last line was better, when he threw himself on a sword that someone was holding. He said, 'Alas, how great an artist is dying.' I guess he had more time to prepare it, though."

He handed the sword to Aurora to guard the steward. She pointed the blade at the man. "It's ready when you are," she told him. He held up his hands and drew back, flattening himself against the wall. He would have gone through it or under it if he could have.

Tacitus returned from the front of the house at a trot. "Eustasius is gone."

"Gone? I know I tied him—"

"Those pieces of cloth were too flimsy, I guess. He's gone and so is one of our horses."

"I wonder how much he might have seen or heard before he left." I looked around, not expecting to see anyone but deeply concerned about someone seeing us. "Well, we'll deal with that problem after we clean up here."

"We won't have to worry about the two men Crispina killed. The wolves are already fighting over them. That must have given Eustasius some incentive."

I took my sword from Aurora and stood over Crispina's steward, with the bloody weapon waving in his face. "What's your name?"

"I'm Macarios, sir," he said, his voice shaking.

"What was your role in this business?"

"I had none, sir. None at all. My lady Crispina told me to handle the sale of her property while she was away. I had *no* idea what she was doing. She told me to meet her here with the *raeda*. I just arrived this morning."

"So you took no part in the murder of Fabia or the kidnapping of this woman?" I pointed to Aurora, leaving a trail of drops of blood.

"No, sir. I swear by all the gods that I did not."

"He's telling the truth," Aurora said, "at least part of it. He was here when they brought me in. He did not kidnap me and did not do me any harm."

"Well, Macarios," I said, "today you are indeed as blessed as your name suggests because I believe her. We still have to decide what to do with you, though."

"Aurora," Livilla broke in, "why don't you come with me? I don't want to witness any more of this. Let's see if we can find some clothes." The two women headed for the front of the house, arm-in-arm, the way my mother and Naomi support each other.

I turned back to Macarios, who whimpered like a beaten dog and drew his head down between his shoulders.

"Stop sniveling, man," Tacitus said.

"You don't appear to have harmed anyone," I said. "Are you a slave or a freedman?"

"Freedman, sir. I have my manumission right here." He held up a bag whose contents jingled and crinkled—coins and documents. "I brought everything I valued with me because I knew I wasn't going back to Crispina's house."

"That does simplify things, doesn't it?" Tacitus said.

I could see that he was thinking the same way I was. "Yes. He can go wherever he likes. How much money is in that chest?"

Macarios fished a key out of his bag, opened the chest, and turned it so Tacitus and I could see the contents.

"Impressive," I said, running my hand through the pile of coins, most of them silver but with a healthy sprinkling of gold. "How much did you skim off for yourself?" I pointed to his bag.

He tried to look offended. "Sir, I—"

"We're not going to make you give it back," Tacitus said.

"No." I nodded in agreement. "Working for Crispina must not have been easy. I'm sure you deserve something. Take what you have and get out of here."

Macarios scrambled to his feet.

"There's a horse out front," I said. "He won't be any faster than walking, but you won't get as tired. We'll give him to you in exchange for the *raeda* and your life. Does that seem fair?"

Macarios' eyes widened. "Oh, more than fair, sir. Most generous."

"Our advice," Tacitus said, "would be to get as far away from here as you can. I hear Sicily is nice this time of year."

"That's too close, sir. I have family on Cyprus."

"Even better," Tacitus said. "And don't come back."

As Macarios picked up his bag and turned toward the front of the house, Aurora and Livilla walked back into the garden, each wearing a serviceable, if less than fashionable, gown. Livilla carried Macarios' tunic over her arm.

"You may have this back," she said, tossing the garment to him. "Thank you for the use of it, even if it was a little damp in one spot."

"Thank you, my lady. My apologies," Macarios said, bowing and scraping like the subject of an eastern despot. "And thank you, my lords." He ran for the front of the house, shedding Livilla's blood-soaked gown along the way.

I wish I could stop shaking so I could take in all that's happened today. When those men tied me to that post and cut off my tunic, I was sure I was going to die. Crispina, standing there, brandishing that axe—I couldn't understand why she didn't go ahead and kill me. What was she waiting for? And then, in walked Livilla.

That little girl was so poised, so apparently unafraid. For a moment I believed she was behind it all, that she wanted to see me dead. And then she started pleading with Crispina, trying to persuade her not to kill me. I wasn't the reason she had ended her engagement to Gaius, she said. And the way she threw herself at Crispina! She saved my life.

Now she talks to me like a sister, puts her arm through mine. When we were out of Gaius' sight we held one another and had a good cry. How will I ever repay her?

"That takes care of the living," I said. "What do we do with these two?" I waved my sword from Crispina to her servant.

I was surprised to hear Livilla say, "Leave them for the rats. This place is full of them."

"We can't do that. People at the *taberna* saw us coming out here.

Eustasius may have said something to them. If anybody finds two corpses in this place, they'll make serious trouble for us."

"Is there a well we could dump them down?" Aurora asked.

"That would still leave the possibility that somebody would find them and connect them to us. We've got to get them out of here and dispose of them completely."

"Perhaps Lentulus, next door, would help us," Tacitus said, "if we promise to help him persuade Tabellius' sons to sell this place to him."

Livilla shuddered. "I can't believe anyone would want to own this house of horrors."

"He wants to tear it down and enlarge his vineyards," I said.

Livilla rubbed her hands together. "Then let's do whatever it takes to make that happen."

While Tacitus stayed with the women—who sat and talked like the best of friends—I walked over to Lentulus' house. His jaw dropped and his eyes bulged as I took him aside and explained the situation in Tabellius' villa and offered my help in exchange for his. I would even give him some money so he could make an extremely generous offer to Tabellius' sons. We agreed that he would get some large pieces of cloth and some sewing implements and accompany me back to Tabellius'.

"It certainly is a right bloody mess," he said when we entered the rear garden.

"What are you going to do with that?" Livilla asked, nodding at what we were carrying.

"We're going to sew these two up in shrouds so no one can see who they are," I said. "We'll take them over to Lentulus' house, and he will see that the bodies are burned, along with anything else that might connect us to this place."

"My servants are already building a pyre," Lentulus said.

"That sounds like a reasonable plan," Livilla said.

"I'm glad it meets your approval," I said. Somehow this newfound confidence of hers made me uncomfortable.

Tacitus, Lentulus, and I wrapped the bodies in the cloth and began trying to sew up the edges. That proved harder than it looks when I see my servants sewing.

Livilla pushed me aside and took the needle from me. "We'll be here all night if we wait for you men to do this." Aurora joined her and they made quick work of the task while Tacitus and I scared away the rats that were being drawn by the smell of blood. Lentulus returned to his villa to oversee preparations for the pyre.

"Let's get them into the *raeda*," I said, "and haul them over to Lentulus' place."

In short order we had the two bodies, the two women's discarded clothing, and the money chest loaded. I drove while the others made themselves as comfortable as they could in the back, considering their traveling companions.

.   .   .

After delivering our "cargo," we stopped at Marinthus' *taberna* to get supper and to allow darkness to fall by the time we got back to Rome. That way we could drive the *raeda* on the city's streets. The money chest was too heavy to carry. Only three of my servants had managed to find horses and get out here. I was glad for at least that much of an escort, considering the large sum of money now in our possession.

Livilla took Aurora behind the counter to clean the blood from her ear and fashion a bandage for it. When they returned to our table, Tacitus and I had placed an order and were beginning to discuss in low voices what we should do next.

"What do you plan to do with the money?" Tacitus asked. "If you admit that you have it, you'll have to explain how you got it."

"Only the three of us know where it is or what happened to its previous owner," I said.

"Don't forget Macarios," Livilla reminded me.

"I think Macarios considers himself fortunate to have his life and whatever sum he escaped with. We won't hear from him again."

"He would have no claim on the money in any case," Tacitus pointed out.

"Exactly. The money in that chest, like its owner, is going to simply disappear." I poured us some wine. "When I get home, I'll count it, just to have a record of what I'm starting with. Then I'll invest it and send the interest each year to Nonnius and Marcella for the upkeep of young Clodius. When he reaches maturity, I'll turn the principal over to him."

We fell silent as Theodorus, exuding all the charm of the gods' gift, brought the food to our table. "Is all well with you, sir?"

"Yes," I said. "Why shouldn't it be?"

"It struck me as curious that you two came through here earlier, by yourselves, riding two horses, and now you're driving a *raeda*, wearing bloodstained tunics, and accompanied by two ladies. Two lovely ladies, if I may say so."

"We made a trade, ran into a little trouble, and picked up some passengers," Tacitus said.

"I see."

"But we're *not* accompanied by Eustasius, are we? I think you know more about that than we do."

"Sir? I don't know what you're talking about."

I grabbed his tunic and pulled his face down close to mine. Other conversations in the room came to a halt. "I'm talking about you being an informer for Marcus Aquilius Regulus."

Theodorus lowered his voice and put a snarl into it. "I am no man's informer."

"Then how did Regulus know about…certain things that happened the last time I was here?"

He pulled away from my grasp and straightened his tunic. "You had servants with you then. Servants from noble houses, I'm told, are a garrulous bunch."

"But you were overheard having a conversation in the dark with Segetius, who is one of Regulus' informers," Tacitus said.

"And I'll bet you know something about a knife with a dolphin emblem on the handle," Aurora put in.

"Sir," Theodorus said, "may I be so bold as to buy you some better wine and join you for a few moments? There are several things you obviously don't understand."

I wanted to tell him that I hadn't understood much of what I had been involved in for the last few days. If he could clear any of it up, I was willing to listen.

Theodorus went behind the counter and returned with a jug of wine. Taking a seat at our table, he broke the seal and poured each of us some. We each added water to suit our tastes from the pitcher on the table.

"I'll begin with an apology," he said, "about the knife. The first time Aurora came here, with Crispina, I was…attracted to her, but she snubbed me." He shrugged. "That's how some women play the game, so I didn't think much of it. But when she came back, with you, and I realized she was a slave, I resented her treatment of me."

"You really *do* think you're the gods' gift, don't you?" Aurora said bitterly.

"Let's just say I've cut a wide swath up and down this road," Theodorus said with a smug smile, "and I've had no complaints."

"What does this have to do with the knife?" I reminded him.

"I saw you two go upstairs and I knew what you were up to. I went up to the room that had been Crispina's because I thought there might be something worth picking up. And I must say, sir, it didn't sound like you were getting any complaints either."

He winked at me like we were fellow warriors in a cause. I gave him my hardest stare in return. Aurora slouched in her chair as though she was trying to disappear under the table. Livilla's face turned to stone.

"Well, anyway," he said, clearing his throat, "I didn't find anything worth taking in the room, but the knife was lying right on the bed. It was beautiful, and…I took it. I confess to that."

"Are you in the habit of stealing things from your father's guests?" Tacitus asked.

"Of course not. In this case I knew she was a slave. It's illegal for her to carry a weapon. She couldn't complain if it went missing. And if her master allowed her to carry a weapon"—he looked straight at me—"he would be just as guilty as she was. I had nothing to lose."

"Why did you stab Fabia's corpse with it?" I asked.

He drew back in amazement. "What? What are you talking about? I did no such thing."

"That's where we found the knife after the fire."

"All I did with it, sir, was sell it to Segetius, out in the woods behind the *taberna*."

"What did he want with it?"

"He said it would make a fine gift for his patron, that Regulus fellow you mentioned."

.   .   .

Livilla did not say another word after Theodorus left our table. I paid our bill and we got into the *raeda*. Tacitus and Livilla rode in the back. I drove, with Aurora standing on the driver's platform beside me.

"There's ice forming back there," she said when she stepped up next to me. "And she has every right to be angry at us."

"There will be a steep price to pay for that, I'm sure," I said. "I hope I'm the only one who has to pay it."

Aurora slipped her arm through mine. "I just hope you don't decide that it's not worth the price."

"Never. Not for a moment." I gave her a quick kiss. "Would you like to drive?"

"I would love to." A smile spread over her face as she took the reins.

As she drove, absorbed in the movement of the horses, I studied her, the woman I loved. Loving her would indeed cost me, but what else could I do? I would have to spend my life married to some woman I barely knew, someone I had yet to meet. Couldn't I claim some bit of happiness for myself?

"What do you think Livilla will do?" Aurora asked.

"She already suspected that I love you. She promised me that she wouldn't tell our mothers the real reason for breaking off the engagement, but that was before she learned about…this. Now I honestly can't predict what she's going to do."

"I haven't heard *any* conversation coming from back there," Aurora said. "That can't be a good sign."

I took the reins back from her when we reached Rome. Driving a team of horses on an open road like the Ostian Way is pleasurable, though it requires some effort. Maneuvering through the narrow city streets at night requires finesse. If we had a problem, I didn't want my servant to be held responsible and me to be blamed for letting a servant—a woman to boot—drive. After a few blocks I regretted my decision—another in a long series of mistakes. Aurora could have handled the horses much more deftly than I did. At a couple of points I sensed her wanting to take the reins from me, pulling to the right or left.

When we dropped Livilla at her house, she said a terse good night to Tacitus but not a word to Aurora or me.

Once Livilla was inside, Tacitus stuck his head out of the *raeda*. "In case you hadn't noticed, there's a storm on the horizon, and it's going to be a bad one. I didn't think someone that young and that sweet could be so angry."

"Did she say anything?" I asked.

"Not one word, the whole trip. I made one comment, and she gave me a look that pinned me to the side of the *raeda*. I didn't dare say anything else."

After letting Tacitus out at his house, we drove the *raeda* to my back gate. It took only a few moments to unload the money chest. Then I sent two servants to take the *raeda* to the livery stable where we had rented horses earlier. "Tell the owner he can have the horses in exchange for the two we rented earlier. He'll know he's getting much the better of the deal. The *raeda* is mine now, I guess. Find out what he'll charge to store it at his stable."

Naomi and Demetrius watched us work, barely suppressing their curiosity. Finally Naomi said, "Forgive me, my lord, but you left here on foot and now you come back bloodstained, in a *raeda*, carrying loot like pirates returning from a raid. That gown Aurora is wearing isn't one of ours. What happened?"

"All I will say is that it's a complicated story and the less you know, the better for you."

·   ·   ·

The next day, near midday, my mother called me to her room. She seemed to be in better spirits, but I couldn't ask her how she was feeling because I wasn't supposed to know that she was ill. I was surprised and concerned to find Pompeia there. The expression on her face struck me as self-congratulatory.

"Good morning, Mother. Pompeia Celerina, it's a pleasure to see you, as always."

Pompeia barely nodded to me. I guess her excitement over getting her money back in the lawsuit had worn off. What would I have to do for her next to stay in her good graces?

"We've asked you here," Mother said, "to discuss plans for a marriage between our families."

My mouth moved a few times before I was able to say, "Mar…marriage plans? Between our families? But Livilla told me she didn't want to marry me."

"She doesn't," Pompeia said, "and I think I understand why." She glared at me. "But I have another daughter, if you'll recall."

"Yes. Livia. Wasn't she recently widowed?" I felt as though I had glanced at the horizon and noticed a dark cloud moving toward me, the storm that Tacitus had predicted.

"That's correct," Pompeia said. "But this morning Livilla suggested to me that we arrange a marriage between you and Livia. I rushed right over here to talk to Plinia, and she agrees."

"The marriage doesn't have to take place immediately," my mother said. "That wouldn't be proper, but we do want to have an agreement."

I leaned against the wall to keep my knees from buckling.

"I know what you're probably thinking," Pompeia said. "You've heard that Livia has a different personality than Livilla—a bit more assertive, one might say."

"No, I hadn't heard that." *I've heard that she's a shrew.*

"I won't deny that she was a difficult child to raise," Pompeia said, "but I suspect that several years of marriage to a very nice man will have made her more malleable, like a piece of soft metal that can be worked into something beautiful."

So this is how I would be punished for what Livilla heard at the table at Marinthus' yesterday! I wished she had taken out her anger by hitting me or in some other more direct method, not by condemning me to a lifetime of misery.

"Livia will be returning from Spain by the Kalends of November," Mother said. "We want the marriage to take place early in the new year, but we'll discuss that with her when she arrives."

XIX

*I*T HAS BEEN *almost a month since that awful incident out at Tabel-*
lius' villa, but I still dream about it and recall it when I'm awake if I
happen to touch my ear. Lentulus notified us that he has bought the villa
and is in the process of tearing it down—starting in the rear garden—so
all evidence of what happened there will be erased. As Livilla said, it truly
was a house of horrors.

Crispina and her servant, whose name we never knew, were cremated
and their ashes scattered, Lentulus assures us. I can't feel any sympathy for
the man. He raped Fabia before she was killed and would have done the
same to me, if Gaius and Tacitus hadn't arrived. Livilla delayed Crispina,
but she could not have stopped her by herself.

All that remains, like the distant rumble of thunder after a storm has
passed, is the effect this series of events has had on Gaius and me. We are
closer than we've ever been, but I think Gaius' confidence in himself has
been shaken. He feels he should not have been so easily taken in by Crispina
and that he missed seeing some obvious clues. I've reminded him that I was
misled, too, and I contributed to his confusion. Without my realizing it,
Crispina made me one of her accomplices at the same time that she had me
marked as another victim.

What matters, I keep telling Gaius, is that she did not get away with
murder—neither Fabia's nor mine. And he did recognize that Segetius was
one of Regulus' spies, no matter how much Tacitus and I tried to dismiss
his appearance as a coincidence.

But there are so many other clouds on the horizon—his mother's situa-
tion, her insistence that Gaius marry soon, Livilla's anger at our betrayal of

her, Domitian's determination to undermine Gaius' reputation. We have
some anxious days ahead.

On the second day before the Ides of November, I was supervising
Melanchthon in replacing some plants in my garden that weren't doing so well. The slow-witted Rufinus, still missing his lifelong friend
and protector Segetius, had attached himself to Melanchthon, who is
more comfortable talking to his plants than to other people. Taking
advantage of an unseasonably warm day, Hashep and Dakla were playing in one corner of the garden. Listening to them, I was reminded of
Heraclitus' saying that "Man is most nearly himself when he achieves
the seriousness of a child at play."

Aurora was sitting and reading in the sun outside the room next to
mine, which was still hers and, as long as I had any say about it, would
always be hers. Her hair was done up in a bun to conceal the chunk
Crispina's axe had chopped out. The nick on the lobe of her right ear
had healed nicely, although she was still self-conscious about the little
bit that was missing.

We all looked up when Demetrius called, "My lord, the lady Livia."

The widow Livia, my bride-to-be, had come to see me, uninvited
and unannounced. Instead of waiting for Demetrius to summon me,
she followed him into the garden. With servants in tow, Livia didn't
look like a grieving widow. She wore a red stola and a white cloak with
a red tasseled border. Demetrius barely had time to blurt out her name,
but, even without a proper introduction and never having seen her
before, I recognized this younger version of Pompeia Celerina.

"Good morning, Gaius Pliny," she said, without a hint of friendliness or even warmth.

"Good morning, Livia," I replied, "and welcome to my house."

"Soon to be our house, I guess." As she sized up the garden, her
squint and the wrinkling of her nose showed her dissatisfaction.

I wiped my hands on my tunic, anticipating that she would extend
her hand to me or give me a kiss on the cheek, but she made no move
toward me. "I expected our first meeting to be more formal, with our
mothers present."

"What's the point in that? May we talk privately?"

I gestured toward my room. "We can talk in here."

"You," Livia said to Aurora, "stand by the door and make sure no one interrupts us or overhears us. And that includes you."

As soon as the door was closed, Livia plopped down in the only chair and said, "Gaius Pliny, I know that you don't want to marry *me*, any more than I want to marry *you*."

Not only disagreeable and unsmiling, she was as blunt as the hammer between the eyes of a sacrificial animal. I sat down on my bed and tried to be more courteous. "I know this is all happening too soon after the loss of your husband. I'm sorry my mother is putting such pressure on us. And I'm sorry for your great loss. Have you found a suitable place for your husband's ashes?" I wanted to show some concern.

She snorted, not the way people do when they think something is ridiculous but the way a pig snorts. "Funny thing about those ashes. I was carrying the urn when we crossed the Ebro—for safekeeping, you understand—and it slipped right out of my hands. Sank to the bottom of the river before anyone could retrieve it."

"That is…a shame. And such a great loss." It was all I could say to mask my horror. What had my mother and Livilla gotten me into?

"It was no great loss—neither the urn nor its contents. Liburnius left me quite well off. My mother is pushing for this marriage just as hard as yours is. She wants a grandchild, but she's not going to get one from me. If the lack of children is a detriment to your political career, I suppose you can ask Domitian for the three-child privilege."

This conversation was becoming much too intimate and much too political, much too fast. I felt sure Domitian would grant me the *ius trium liberorum*, but I did not want to mark myself any more clearly as his man by asking for it. "Well, I know there are…ways to insure—"

"The only way to guarantee I don't have a child is for you never to touch me." Her voice had a pitch and a volume that made me wonder if any door could grant her the privacy she desired. "My virginity is still intact and I intend to keep it that way. You can keep your damn *mentula* to yourself."

I swallowed hard. "Very well."

I was certainly happy to comply with her stipulation. Ours would not be the only such arrangement in Rome. I almost chuckled to myself. For several years I have pitied Regulus because he and his wife,

Sempronia, have exactly this sort of marriage, and everyone in the city is aware of it, and aware of, shall we say, Sempronia's devotion to Sappho's way of life.

"I know I'm not the beauty that my sister is," Livia said. "Our mother reminded me of that every day while we were growing up. The bitch never would admit it was because I look so much like her. I doubt you have any desire to couple with me. Nor do I with you, meaning no offense. You're a handsome enough man, I suppose."

"You're too kind."

She was oblivious to my sarcasm. "And I don't prefer other women, if that's what you're thinking. I simply find the whole idea of fucking to be as repulsive as the word."

I recoiled at hearing such a vulgarism fall from the lips of an aristocratic woman. Livia forged ahead as though she were quoting Virgil.

"If my mother wants a grandchild, she'll have to rely on somebody fucking Livilla. You and I can keep up the appearance of a marriage, as my late husband and I did, as long as I have my own quarters and my own money and don't have to account to you for what I do with either of them."

"What…what sort of sum—"

She waved her hand dismissively and tilted her head back so that she was talking down to me. "Mentioning a particular amount at this point would be plebeian. We can negotiate that later. As I said, my late husband left me well cared for, so I won't make a heavy demand on you in that regard. If you have a favorite slave girl—or boy, for that matter, as Liburnius did—I don't care. Fuck her all you like."

"Well, I—"

"Oh, don't bother to deny it. All you men have some little bedmate." She looked toward the door as though she could see through it. "Just don't flaunt the arrangement in front of me or my friends. That's what Liburnius did. Rode around in a litter with his filthy catamite. When I sold off some of our slaves after his death, that little cocksucker was the first to go. And I made sure he would be working in the mines. They have some deep mines in Spain. I hope he's dead by the end of the year."

"I imagine he feels the same way."

"*Pssht.* Don't waste your sympathy on him." She bristled and her voice got louder. "The way he pranced around, a ring on every finger, his nails painted—all nineteen of them. I wouldn't tolerate such humiliation from my late husband, and I won't tolerate it from my next one either. Is that clear?"

I nodded slowly, still reeling from her verbal assault. "I assure you that you will have no cause of complaint from me."

"If we understand one another, then, I will tell my mother that I consent to this marriage. I hope you'll tell your mother the same."

"I think the conditions you've set forth make everything…quite clear. Of course, we should wait to announce the marriage until after you've observed the proper period of mourning."

"If you think so. It doesn't matter to me." She heaved her bulk up from the chair and opened the door before I could do it for her.

As she left, she paused long enough to look Aurora over like a prospective buyer, even putting a pudgy finger under her chin, raising her head and turning it from side to side. When she noticed the bit missing from Aurora's ear, she rubbed the lobe between her fingers and said, "What happened? Did Gaius bite it off in the throes of passion?"

Aurora turned crimson and gave me a wide-eyed look.

"Not at all. I can explain," I started to say.

"No matter," Livia said. "You have excellent taste, Gaius. Just remember what I said. Oh, by the way, Mother and Livilla and I are leaving tomorrow for our estate at Narnia. We'll be there until after the new year, in case you need to contact me."

I came to the door, blowing out a long breath. Tacitus had been right about how profoundly angry Livilla was. I was watching my punishment gather up her servants and waddle toward the front of the house.

"What did she mean about your good taste?" Aurora asked, touching her earlobe, a habit she has developed since that awful day at Tabellius' villa.

"'Excellent taste,'" I corrected her. "She said 'excellent,' and she's right." I held Aurora's hand for a moment as I recounted my conversation with Livia. Due to the penetrating quality of Livia's voice, she had heard more of it than Livia intended.

When I finished, Aurora looked at me in surprise. "And you find that acceptable, Gaius? I thought you had more self-respect than that."

"I find anything acceptable that allows us to be together, my love."

CAST OF CHARACTERS

Unless otherwise indicated, numbers in parentheses refer to Pliny's letters (e. g., 7.16 means book 7, letter 16). Unless otherwise indicated, all dates are A.D.

HISTORICAL PERSONS

Aeneas Survivor of Troy, mythical founder of Rome, and son of Venus. According to Virgil, he did consider staying with Queen Dido in Carthage until Jupiter sent Mercury to kick-start him back on the journey to Italy.

Calestrius Tiro In a letter to Calpurnia's grandfather, Pliny calls Calestrius "one of my dearest friends" (7.16). In another letter he says he loves him "like a brother" (7.23). He refers to him, or writes to him, in several letters (1.12; 6.1; 6.22; 7.32; 9.5).

Democrites Greek physician living in Rome in the mid- to late first century A.D. Pliny the Elder mentions his healing of a young woman (*Nat. Hist.* 24.28). He was a client of one of Pliny the Younger's friends, Servilius Pudens.

Dido cf. Aeneas.

Domitian *Princeps* (emperor) 81–96. The portion of Tacitus' *Histories* that told of his reign is lost. His reputation was tarnished by Tacitus' *Agricola* and Suetonius' biography, as well as by references in Pliny's *Panegyricus*, a lengthy speech in praise of the *princeps* Trajan that makes Trajan look better by making Domitian, his predecessor, look bad. In his letters Pliny also criticizes Domitian every chance he gets. Pliny may have been embarrassed by the fact that his political career advanced smoothly in the last years of Domitian's reign, while friends of his were being arrested or driven into exile.

Erotion Child mentioned in three of Martial's epigrams (5.34; 5.37; 10.61). She died six days before her sixth birthday. Entrusting her to the spirits of his parents, Martial buried her on his farm near Nomentum, which Pliny had given him. Years later, when he sold the farm, he required the purchaser to tend to her grave. There has been much speculation about whether she was his daughter by a slave woman. I argued that she was in my article, "Martial's Daughter," in *Classical World* 78 (1984), 21–24. She figures prominently in my e-book, *The Flute Player*.

Martial Marcus Valerius Martialis, epigrammatist active in the reign of Domitian. His witty poems made him the darling of Roman society. Pliny mentions him in a couple of letters and gave him some traveling money when Martial left Rome to return to his native Spain. Informing a friend of Martial's death, Pliny says his poems might not be immortal, "but he wrote them as if they would be" (3.21).

Plinia Pliny's mother, and sister of the elder Pliny. She is mentioned in only three of Pliny's letters (4.19; 6.16; 6.20). We are uncertain when she died.

Pompeia Celerina The mother of Pliny's first or second wife. She is referred to in several letters (1.4; 1.18; 3.19; 6.10; 9.13) and had a villa at Narnia (cf. in Glossary below). Pliny mentions staying in one of her houses as though it was his own and how well her servants treated him. His relationship with her seems cordial, despite the rocky start I have posited in this book. Her daughter, Pliny's wife, seems to have died about the time Domitian was assassinated, in 96 A.D. He mentions his grief at her death (*Ep.* 9.13).

Regulus Marcus Aquilius Regulus, orator and notorious *delator*, or informer. He earned a fortune informing on people during Nero's reign. Vespasian and Titus were too honest to listen to him, but he regained the *princeps'* ear when Domitian took power. Pliny opposed him in court a number of times and, in his letters, makes no secret of his loathing of the man.

Servilius Pudens Acquaintance of Pliny's who was appointed as his assistant when Pliny was governor of Bithynia. Pliny mentions his arrival in the province in a letter to Trajan (10.25). A Pudens is mentioned in 2 Timothy 4:21 as a companion of Paul, and there is a tradition in the church that a senator of that name was converted by Peter. Scholars generally agree that there is little likelihood 2 Timothy was written by Paul. Regardless of who wrote the letter, the appearance of the name is intriguing, although Pudens is not a rare name in first-century Rome. Martial mentions a Pudens and his marriage to a woman named Claudia (4.13; 11.53). 2 Timothy 4:21 also mentions a Claudia. Cue the "Twilight Zone" theme.

Tacitus Historian of the Roman Empire from the death of Augustus to the end of the first century A.D. His *Annals* cover the period up to the end of Nero's reign (68), though portions are lost. His *Histories* covered from 68 to 96, but everything after 70 is lost. He also wrote works on oratory, on Germany, and a biography of his father-in-law, Julius Agricola. Tacitus' family name (*nomen*) was Cornelius, but we don't know his first name (*praenomen*). Some manuscripts say Publius. He and Pliny exchanged letters and critiqued one another's work. He was a few years older than Pliny and probably outlived Pliny by a few years.

Voconius Romanus Friend of Pliny's in northern Italy. Pliny writes several letters to him (1.5; 2.1; 6.15; 6.33; 8.8; 9.7; 9.28) and recommends him for appointments (2.13), even asking Trajan to promote Voconius to senatorial rank (10.4).

FICTITIOUS PERSONS

Aurora Pliny's servant and lover. She first appeared in *The Blood of Caesar* and has become an increasingly important character in succeeding stories.

Clodius Supposititious son of Popilius.

Crispina Wife of Popilius. It is a Roman woman's name, though not common. It would be derived from the man's name, Crispus, which isn't common either but does occur in Acts 18:7.

Demetrius Pliny's steward, overseer of his household in Rome. Father of two daughters, Hashep and Dakla.

Fabia Stepdaughter of Crispina. Daughter of her first husband, Fabius Albinus.

Jacob (aka Nestor) Steward in Regulus' household.

Lentulus Titus Lentulus, owner of a country villa next door to the one where a horrendous crime takes place.

Livilla Pliny's fiancée. For the purposes of this story, she is the younger of two sisters and so would be known as Livia Minor or Livia Secunda, or Livilla ("Little Livia"). All daughters were given the feminine form of their father's family name. We do not know the names of Pliny's two (or three) wives, except the last, Calpurnia.

Lorcis Common-law wife of Martial and mother of Erotion, also an acquaintance of Aurora. The main character in my e-book, *The Flute Player*.

Marcella and **Nonnius** Neighbors and relatives of Popilius. Aunt and uncle to Clodius.

Marinthus Owner of a *taberna* on the Ostian Road.

Melanchthon Pliny's gardener (see *topiarius* in the Glossary). The name is Greek for "black earth." In the early modern period, when educated people took on Greek or Latin forms for their names, Philip Schwarzfeld, an associate of Martin Luther, renamed himself Melanchthon, since his inelegant German name means "black earth." I hope readers will pardon my little joke.

Naomi Faithful servant of Pliny's mother and mother of Phineas, Pliny's scribe. She and her son were taken captive in the fall of Jerusalem.

Phineas Pliny's chief scribe, a young man of Pliny's age and master of the complex system of shorthand known as Tironian notation.

Popilius Second husband of Crispina and lover of Crispina's stepdaughter Fabia.

Segetius Freedman of Tabellius, along with the slow-witted Rufinus.

Tabellius Sextus Tabellius, owner (deceased) of the villa where Pliny discovers a horrific crime has been committed.

Theodorus Son of Marinthus and admirer of Aurora.

GLOSSARY OF TERMS

Also see glossaries in Death in the Ashes *and previous books in this series.*

auloi Sometimes translated flutes, but actually a reed instrument more like a clarinet or oboe. They consisted of two pipes, usually with a strap to hold them around the player's mouth. Plutarch says the lower pipe carried the melody, just as a husband's voice should dominate in a marriage.

Baths of Titus Built near the Flavian Amphitheatre (the Colosseum), on top of the ruins of part of Nero's Golden House. They were soon torn down and replaced by the larger Baths of Trajan. Pliny's entry into these baths figures in the second book in this series, *The Blood of Caesar*.

caliga Heavy sandals/boots worn by Roman soldiers. The mad emperor Caligula got his nickname "Little Boots" from the pair he wore with the miniature soldier's uniform his mother made for him.

Centumviral Court Like us, the Romans had civil and criminal courts. The Centumviral Court dealt primarily with inheritance cases, although, according to the *Oxford Classical Dictionary*, "its competence was evidently considerably wider." Though the title would indicate a membership of 100, the actual number was 180, usually divided into four panels that could hear cases simultaneously or, occasionally, as a full body. Pliny's letters mention several appearances before this court.

clientela The group of people supported by a wealthy Roman. The root of the word, *cli-*, means reclining or leaning on, as in *triclinium*, three people reclining on a couch. An upper-class Roman tried to support as large a *clientela* as he could, in order to impress others. His clients came to his house each morning and followed him around as he conducted his business in the early part of the day. He recognized their birthdays, invited them to dinner, and helped them in financial emergencies. They were a visible measure of a man's wealth and status. In the absence of a government welfare system, this arrangement provided for a redistribution of some money to the lower classes.

cochlearia A spoon with a long, pointed handle, similar to an ice pick. The Romans had no forks, but they could spear bites of food with the handle of this utensil.

cursus honorum The "course of honors." When a Roman aristocrat reached his mid-twenties he was ready to embark on a political career. The first office on the ladder was quaestor (finance), then aedile (public works), followed by praetor (judicial), and hopefully culminating in a consulship when a man was in his forties.

familia In addition to relatives by blood or marriage, a *familia* consisted of the slaves and freedmen/women in a household like Pliny's. A wealthy man with several homes could have a *familia urbana* in his house in Rome and a *familia rustica* in a country estate.

hipposandals A type of horseshoes. There is some evidence that the Romans used iron or wooden shoes nailed into the hoof of a horse, but the most common way of protecting the animals' hooves and providing better traction was the *hipposandal*. It consisted of a piece of iron or leather that covered the bottom of the hoof and was tied through loops in front and back with a piece of leather. Very few survive today.

ius trium liberorum When Augustus established the principate, he needed men to hold the numerous offices necessary to keep the bureaucracy running and he wanted to encourage members of the aristocracy to have larger families. He set up a requirement that only men who had three children could hold higher offices, inherit property, and exercise certain other rights. But birth rates among the aristocracy were so low that Augustus and later emperors had to grant this exemption, the "right/privilege of three children," to have a large enough pool of office holders. The emperor Trajan granted this privilege to Pliny (10.2) and Pliny asked him to extend it to the biographer Suetonius (10.94).

lararium A niche, usually in the atrium of a house, where the family's household gods were kept.

Maenads Devotees of the god Dionysus/Bacchus. In their rituals they drank a great deal of wine, danced to wild music, and ran through the woods chasing small animals, which they killed and devoured. Paintings and sculptures show them with their hair loose and their heads thrown back. See cover photo of *Death in the Ashes* for a sculpted Maenad head.

mentula A Latin vulgarism for the penis, the *membrum virile*, as the prudish lexicons define it. The Latin language assigns grammatical gender to every noun, regardless of what it describes. Words ending in *a* are typically feminine, those ending in *us*, typically masculine. But this is a rule much honored in the breach. The word for farmer, *agricola*, is masculine, as is *poeta*. Thus one would say *agricola bonus* (the good farmer) or *poeta bonus* (the good poet). The grammatical gender of *mentula* is feminine, even though the thing it describes is definitely not, so one would say *mentula magna* (the big, well, you know). One word for the female genitalia (*cunnus*) is masculine.

Milesian tale Fanciful stories originating in the second century B.C. in the work of Aristides, who set his books in the Ionian city of Miletus. They often featured abandoned children who grow up to be recognized and reunited with their families, or lovers captured and separated by pirates, only to be reunited after an improbable series of adventures. They were typically racy. Petronius' *Satyricon* and Apuleius' *The Golden Ass* are generally recognized as based on Milesian tales.

Minerva Medica A temple in ancient Rome dedicated to Minerva the Healer, mentioned by Cicero. Its exact location is uncertain. The ruin that is now sometimes identified by that name is from late antiquity.

Narnia The appearance of this word in a novel set in ancient Rome may surprise readers, but C. S. Lewis was well versed in classical literature, so he knew that Narnia was a small town northeast of Rome. Martial mentions it in one of his poems (7.93) and refers to the "twin peaks," a feature which figures significantly in *The Lion, the Witch, and the Wardrobe*. Pliny says his mother-in-law had a villa there (*Ep.* 1.4), which even had baths. Pliny the Elder, Tacitus, and Livy also refer to the town.

nomen A Roman man's tripartite name, such as Gaius Plinius Secundus (the elder Pliny) contained his first name (*praenomen*), his family name (*nomen*), and the name by which he was distinguished from other members of his family (*cognomen*). In the case of an adoptee like the younger Pliny, part of the biological father's name would be added, hence Gaius Plinius Caecilius Secundus.

omphalos Greek for "navel." A stone at Delphi was thought to mark the navel or center of the world. (It would probably be classified as an "outie.") By the second century B.C. the Jews, familiar with Greek traditions, had developed a legend that the Ark of the Covenant sat on a stone that marked the center of the world. Today there is an *omphalos* in the Church of the Holy Sepulcher in Jerusalem.

piscina A fishpond. Many aristocratic Roman houses had shallow pools in their gardens. Often they were used for raising fish for the dinner table.

Praetorian Guard Augustus established this elite unit to serve as an imperial bodyguard and a police force for Rome. Roman law prohibited housing armed soldiers within the city, so Augustus kept the Guard scattered at various places around Rome. Tiberius built the Praetorian Camp just outside the walls of the city. The unit's commander, the Praetorian Prefect, came to have enormous power, especially if an emperor was weak. When the Praetorians proclaimed Claudius emperor after the assassination of Caligula, Tacitus says the secret was out: the army made the emperor.

ROTAS/SATOR square One of the most puzzling pieces of graffiti from the ancient world. One example has been found in Pompeii. Sometimes called "the perfect palindrome," it consists of five words arranged so that they are the same whether read left to right, right to left, top to bottom, bottom to top, or in ox-plowing fashion (*boustrophedon*), left to right on one line and right to left on the next, and so on, or up one column and down the next.

```
R   O   T   A   S
O   P   E   R   A
T   E   N   E   T
A   R   E   P   O
S   A   T   O   R
```

Since the word AREPO is not Latin or Greek, no one is certain what it means. Some scholars have claimed Mithraic origins for the square; others have put a wide variety of interpretations on it. The letters can be rearranged to read:

```
                P
                A
        A       T       O
                E
                R
P   A   T   E   R   N   O   S   T   E   R
                O
                S
        A       T       O
                E
                R
```

The extra *As* and *Os* are taken to be Alpha and Omega. In the square form, all of the *As* and *Os* appear on either side of a *T*, the Greek letter *Tau*, which was the actual shape of Jesus' cross. Some scholars dismiss this solution, arguing it is unlikely that Christians would have devised something so complicated, in Latin, before A.D. 79, or that Christians were present in Pompeii before the eruption of Vesuvius. But the church in Rome was active by the reign of Claudius (41–54), and Paul was under house arrest there by 64. Acts 28:13–14 says that Paul, on his last journey to Rome, "came to Puteoli. There we found brethren, and were invited to stay with them for seven days." If the church existed in one spot on the Bay of Naples by that time, some scholars maintain, why not in Pompeii?

Sibylline Books Collection of oracles, usually capable of ambiguous interpretations. When Constantine was attacking Rome in 312, one of the competing emperors, Maxentius, who held the city, read an oracle from the Sibylline Books that said, "Today an enemy of Rome will die." He took that to apply to Constantine and so left the safety of the city's walls and engaged Constantine's forces at the Milvian Bridge. It turns out that Maxentius was the enemy of Rome.

topiarius A gardener, particularly one adept in cutting images or designs into shrubbery. The word "topiary" today refers to the same practice. Pliny says in one letter that his *topiarius* had trimmed his shrubbery in the shape of Pliny's name.

vestibulum Also called the *fauces*, or "jaws." The entry to a large Roman house, usually recessed a few feet from the street. If the house had a second story, it would cover the *vestibulum*, making a kind of stoop or front porch.

ABOUT THE AUTHOR

ALBERT A. BELL, JR. is a college history professor and novelist who lives in Michigan. He and his wife have four adult children and a grandson. In addition to his Roman mysteries, Bell has written contemporary mysteries for children and adults, as well as nonfiction. Visit him at www.albertbell.com and www.pliny-mysteries.com, and also on Facebook.

More Traditional Mysteries from Perseverance Press
For the New Golden Age

K.K. Beck
Tipping the Valet (forthcoming)
ISBN 978-1-56474-563-7

Albert A. Bell, Jr.
PLINY THE YOUNGER SERIES
Death in the Ashes
ISBN 978-1-56474-532-3

The Eyes of Aurora
ISBN 978-1-56474-549-1

Taffy Cannon
ROXANNE PRESCOTT SERIES
Guns and Roses
Agatha and Macavity awards nominee, Best Novel
ISBN 978-1-880284-34-6

Blood Matters
ISBN 978-1-880284-86-5

Open Season on Lawyers
ISBN 978-1-880284-51-3

Paradise Lost
ISBN 978-1-880284-80-3

Laura Crum
GAIL MCCARTHY SERIES
Moonblind
ISBN 978-1-880284-90-2

Chasing Cans
ISBN 978-1-880284-94-0

Going, Gone
ISBN 978-1-880284-98-8

Barnstorming
ISBN 978-1-56474-508-8

Jeanne M. Dams
HILDA JOHANSSON SERIES
Crimson Snow
ISBN 978-1-880284-79-7

Indigo Christmas
ISBN 978-1-880284-95-7

Murder in Burnt Orange
ISBN 978-1-56474-503-3

Janet Dawson
JERI HOWARD SERIES
Bit Player
Golden Nugget Award nominee
ISBN 978-1-56474-494-4

Cold Trail (forthcoming)
ISBN 978-1-56474-555-2

What You Wish For
ISBN 978-1-56474-518-7

Death Rides the Zephyr
ISBN 978-1-56474-530-9

Kathy Lynn Emerson
LADY APPLETON SERIES
Face Down Below the Banqueting House
ISBN 978-1-880284-71-1

Face Down Beside St. Anne's Well
ISBN 978-1-880284-82-7

Face Down O'er the Border
ISBN 978-1-880284-91-9

Elaine Flinn
MOLLY DOYLE SERIES
Deadly Vintage
ISBN 978-1-880284-87-2

Sara Hoskinson Frommer
JOAN SPENCER SERIES
Her Brother's Keeper
ISBN 978-1-56474-525-5

Hal Glatzer
KATY GREEN SERIES
Too Dead To Swing
ISBN 978-1-880284-53-7

A Fugue in Hell's Kitchen
ISBN 978-1-880284-70-4

The Last Full Measure
ISBN 978-1-880284-84-1

Margaret Grace
MINIATURE SERIES
Mix-up in Miniature
ISBN 978-1-56474-510-1

Madness in Miniature
ISBN 978-1-56474-543-9

Manhattan in Miniature (forthcoming)
ISBN 978-1-56474-562-0

Tony Hays
Shakespeare No More (forthcoming)
ISBN 978-1-56474-566-8

Wendy Hornsby
MAGGIE MACGOWEN SERIES
In the Guise of Mercy
ISBN 978-1-56474-482-1

The Paramour's Daughter
ISBN 978-1-56474-496-8

The Hanging
ISBN 978-1-56474-526-2

The Color of Light
ISBN 978-1-56474-542-2

Diana Killian
POETIC DEATH SERIES
Docketful of Poesy
ISBN 978-1-880284-97-1

Janet LaPierre
PORT SILVA SERIES
Baby Mine
ISBN 978-1-880284-32-2

Keepers
Shamus Award nominee, Best Paperback Original
ISBN 978-1-880284-44-5

Death Duties
ISBN 978-1-880284-74-2

Family Business
ISBN 978-1-880284-85-8

Run a Crooked Mile
ISBN 978-1-880284-88-9

Hailey Lind
ART LOVER'S SERIES
Arsenic and Old Paint
ISBN 978-1-56474-490-6

Lev Raphael
NICK HOFFMAN SERIES
Tropic of Murder
ISBN 978-1-880284-68-1

Hot Rocks
ISBN 978-1-880284-83-4

Lora Roberts
BRIDGET MONTROSE SERIES
Another Fine Mess
ISBN 978-1-880284-54-4

SHERLOCK HOLMES SERIES
The Affair of the Incognito Tenant
ISBN 978-1-880284-67-4

Rebecca Rothenberg
BOTANICAL SERIES
The Tumbleweed Murders
(completed by Taffy Cannon)
ISBN 978-1-880284-43-8

Sheila Simonson
LATOUCHE COUNTY SERIES
Buffalo Bill's Defunct
WILLA Award, Best Softcover Fiction
ISBN 978-1-880284-96-4

An Old Chaos
ISBN 978-1-880284-99-5

Beyond Confusion
ISBN 978-1-56474-519-4

Shelley Singer
JAKE SAMSON & ROSIE VICENTE SERIES
Royal Flush
ISBN 978-1-880284-33-9

Lea Wait
SHADOWS ANTIQUES SERIES
Shadows of a Down East Summer
ISBN 978-1-56474-497-5

Shadows on a Cape Cod Wedding
ISBN 1-978-56474-531-6

Shadows on a Maine Christmas
ISBN 978-1-56474-531-6

Eric Wright
JOE BARLEY SERIES
The Kidnapping of Rosie Dawn
Barry Award, Best Paperback Original. Edgar,
Ellis, and Anthony awards nominee
ISBN 978-1-880284-40-7

Nancy Means Wright
MARY WOLLSTONECRAFT SERIES
Midnight Fires
ISBN 978-1-56474-488-3

The Nightmare
ISBN 978-1-56474-509-5

REFERENCE/MYSTERY WRITING

Kathy Lynn Emerson
How To Write Killer Historical Mysteries:
The Art and Adventure of Sleuthing
Through the Past
Agatha Award, Best Nonfiction. Anthony and
Macavity awards nominee
ISBN 978-1-880284-92-6

Carolyn Wheat
How To Write Killer Fiction:
The Funhouse of Mystery & the Roller
Coaster of Suspense
ISBN 978-1-880284-62-9

Available from your local bookstore
or from Perseverance Press/John Daniel & Company
(800) 662–8351 or www.danielpublishing.com/perseverance